SWEET AS HONEY

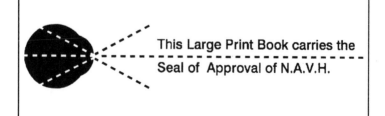

This Large Print Book carries the
Seal of Approval of N.A.V.H.

Sweet As Honey

Jennifer Beckstrand

KENNEBEC LARGE PRINT
A part of Gale, Cengage Learning

GALE
CENGAGE Learning·

Farmington Hills, Mich • San Francisco • New York • Waterville, Maine
Meriden, Conn • Mason, Ohio • Chicago

GALE
CENGAGE Learning

LIBRARY OF CONGRESS CATALOGING-IN-PUBLICATION DATA

Names: Beckstrand, Jennifer, author.
Title: Sweet as honey / by Jennifer Beckstrand.
Description: Large print edition. | Waterville, Maine : Kennebec Large Print, 2016.
 | Series: The Honeybee sisters | Series: Kennebec Large Print superior collection
Identifiers: LCCN 2016034877| ISBN 9781410494818 (softcover) | ISBN 1410494810
 (softover)
Subjects: LCSH: Sisters—Fiction. | Beekeepers—Fiction. | Amish women—Fiction. |
 Large type books. | GSAFD: Love stories. | Christian fiction.
Classification: LCC PS3602.E3323 S94 2016 | DDC 813/.6—dc23
LC record available at https://lccn.loc.gov/2016034877

Published in 2016 by arrangement with Zebra Books, an imprint of
Kensington Publishing Corp.

Printed in Mexico
2 3 4 5 6 7 20 19 18 17 16

SWEET AS HONEY

CHAPTER ONE

Dan Kanagy stopped his open-air buggy in the middle of the deserted road and turned on his flashlight. Shining it along the roadside, he squinted into the darkness.

There it was. The sign that marked the turnoff to the lane he was looking for, a big, white board decorated with flowers in every variety of paint color imaginable. In bold, black letters it read: **BEWARE THE HONEYBEES**.

Dan had never been able to figure out if that warning referred to the large number of hives that dotted the Christners' farm or if it referred to the Christners themselves. The community had nicknamed them the Honeybee Sisters a dozen years ago. The three Honeybee *schwesters* were pretty enough and smart enough to be intimidating, and they lived with their aunt, who was said to be slightly odd. At least that's what Dan had been told. He'd never met the aunt, the *aendi*, but he knew the Honeybee *schwesters* well. He'd gone to primary school with all three of them.

The youngest, Rose, had seemed so delicate that Dan had feared she'd break if he looked at her the wrong way. Poppy Christner had punched him in the mouth on more than one occasion, and the eldest, Lily, was too wonderful for words, and entirely too wonderful for a plain, ordinary boy like Dan Kanagy.

Beware the Honeybees indeed.

Holding the reins with one hand and the flashlight in the other, Dan turned his horse, Clyde, down the long lane. It was a good thing he had his flashlight. At two o'clock in the morning under a new moon in late May, the darkness was profound. Clyde's hooves clip-clopped over a small wooden bridge just wide enough for a buggy or a car to pass over. The light of his flashlight reflected off a pond of still water meandering under the bridge. Maybe *pond* was too generous. It looked more the size of a puddle.

Across the bridge, the lane curved to the right. A variety of tall and short bushes lined the lane to his right, some thick with leaves, others abloom with flowers. To his left, he could just make out a row of beehives, standing guard over the farm.

The line of bushes came to an abrupt stop as he got to the end of the lane. To his left, a small barn loomed above him. A house stood to his right fronted by a lawn full of dandelions and a wide flower bed bursting with blooms. Even by the light of his flashlight, they looked wonderful-*gute.* The bees probably thought they were wonderful-*gute* too.

Dan jumped out of his buggy and tiptoed up the path of flagstones that led to the house, not sure why he tried to be quiet. He was about to awaken the whole house. It couldn't be helped, but he still felt bad about interrupting their sleep like this.

He walked up the porch steps, tapped lightly on the door, and listened. Nothing.

If he wanted anyone to wake up, he'd have to give up trying to be subtle. He rapped his knuckles five times against the sturdy wooden door. Holding his breath, he listened for signs of movement from within. After a few seconds, a faint light appeared behind the front window curtains. The door slowly creaked open, and Dan found himself nose to nose with the barrel of a shotgun.

He should have paid more heed to that sign.

CHAPTER TWO

Dan's heart pounded like a two-deep team of horses as, still gripping his flashlight, he slowly lifted his hands above his head. Lord willing, he had a long life ahead of him and hadn't quite figured out how he wanted to die, but getting shot in the head was not it.

The woman on the other end of the shotgun wore a neck-to-toe white nightgown and a seriously ferocious scowl on her lips. She had fashioned her salt-and-pepper hair into a braid that rested on her shoulder like a strange pet. Dan couldn't begin to guess why he noticed her hair at a time like this, but it seemed to be tinged a light shade of blue. Lovely and odd at the same time.

This must be the *aendi*.

Dan had been warned she was strange, but a shotgun to the face was not quite what he had expected. He hoped "strange" didn't mean "crazy wild woman apt to shoot unsuspecting boys who came to her house."

The three Honeybee *schwesters,* all clad in baby-blue flannel nightgowns and matching braids, flanked their aunt on both sides. Lily, with that cute upturned nose and bright, intelligent eyes, held the lantern and frowned in Dan's direction. Poppy folded her arms and scowled at him while Rose looked so terrified, Dan nearly felt compelled to gather her in his arms for a brotherly hug.

"Ha! We finally caught you," said the aunt.

Lily drew her brows together. "It appears more like he turned himself in."

The aunt motioned in his direction with the barrel of the gun. "What do you want? Come to confess?"

He certainly hoped her trigger finger wasn't sweaty. "I mean no harm. I've come with a message for Lily."

The aunt, Poppy, and Rose turned to Lily with wide eyes.

The shotgun seemed to droop slightly. "You must be Aunt Honeybee . . . I mean Lily's *aendi.*"

"My name's Bitsy. But you can call me Hyacinth, if you like."

A laugh escaped Lily's mouth before she pursed her lips together and resumed her determined frown.

Bitsy glanced sideways at Lily with a smile

11

dancing in her eyes if not on her face. She lowered the shotgun halfway. "Don't you like Hyacinth, Lily? It's very British."

"Hyacinth is awful fancy and takes too long to say. We like you as plain, sensible Aendi Bitsy."

Bitsy scrunched her lips to one side of her face. "The curse of an Amish woman, always having to be plain and sensible."

Dan lowered his hands slowly and carefully. "My name is Daniel Kanagy. We've never met, but your nieces and I went to school together. I've been away in Pennsylvania for two years, so maybe they don't recognize me. I got back yesterday morning."

"Did you forget where you live?" Bitsy asked.

Dan glanced at Lily. "You remember me, don't you? I called you Amtrak in school." Amtrak because she used to have these really cute braces that looked like railroad tracks across her teeth.

Bitsy scowled and raised an eyebrow and the shotgun. She looked at Lily. "Is he the one who . . . ?"

"*Jah,*" Lily mumbled, lowering her eyes. "He's the one."

Is he the one who what? The one who they were planning on murdering tonight?

12

Bitsy's expression was not neighborly. "Do you want me to shoot him?"

Dan pasted a smile on his face as if he were in on the joke. The Amish were pacifists. Bitsy was teasing him.

Probably.

Lily sighed, reached out, and nudged the barrel of the shotgun so it pointed to the floor. "*Nae*, Aendi B. Don't shoot him. We've both grown up since then."

Grown up since when? Had he missed something important? And why in the world had he offered to be the one to fetch Lily Christner? Aunt Bitsy would never have pointed a gun at Dat.

Well, most likely not.

Bitsy rested the gun at her side and leaned on it like a cane. "So, what do you want at two in the morning, Daniel Kanagy? If you're here to try your chances with one of the girls, you'll have to come at normal hours like the rest of the boys."

In the excitement and sheer terror of having a gun pointed at him, Dan had almost forgotten what he'd come for. "It's about my *mammi*."

Lily gasped and put a hand to her mouth. "Is she okay?"

"She's taken a turn for the worse. It won't be long now, maybe before morning. She really wants to see you before she goes."

"Why didn't you say so in the first place?" Bitsy scolded.

"Well, because . . ." he stammered, "there was a shotgun pointed at my face."

Bitsy harrumphed. "There was no need to panic about it."

Dan nodded, trying to be agreeable. He and Bitsy obviously didn't see eye to eye about that. "I'm here to take Lily to Mammi's house if she wants to go. The whole family is gathered to say good-bye."

Lily handed the lantern to Poppy. "Of course I want to go. Give me a few minutes to get dressed."

She disappeared up the stairs while the other three continued to stare at him. Did he look that frightening? He only had a day's growth of whiskers on his chin.

Rose finally broke the uncomfortable silence. "Why don't you come in and sit at the table while you wait?"

Bitsy nodded almost imperceptibly, propped her gun against the wall, and stepped back so Dan could enter.

He stepped into the house as if it might explode — as if someone might start shooting at him if his boots were muddy.

The main floor of the house looked to be mostly one big room. An ample kitchen with a large butcher-block island stood to his left, a sitting room with a fireplace, two sofas, and two overstuffed chairs to his right. A heavy wooden table, large enough to seat a dozen comfortably, sat right in front of him.

The honey-colored wood floor had seen some use. It shone like it had just been polished, but scuff marks and scratches marred the entire surface. And had someone taken a swing at one of the floorboards with an ax?

Dan pulled a chair from the table and sat, never taking his eyes from Bitsy's face. He wanted to be ready in case she pulled a knife on him.

Rose took a coffeepot from the cupboard. "I'll make you a cup of *kaffee.*"

"*Jah,* okay, *denki,*" he said. Even though he'd already had two cups before coming, he instinctively knew it would be best to agree with everything and not give Bitsy an excuse to pull out a peashooter.

Bitsy and Poppy folded their arms and stood over him, like two giant maples guarding the forest. "Hold out your hands," Bitsy said.

Dan tried to act as if he saw nothing amiss with this request. "I . . . I . . . what did you say?"

"Do you have any bee stings?"

Dan held his arms out straight while Bitsy and Poppy examined them. He pushed his short sleeves above his shoulders, just in case they wanted to be thorough.

Bitsy nodded. "You have the muscles of a hard worker."

A grin pulled at his lips as he lifted his trousers legs. Might as well let them inspect up to his knees and be satisfied. Satisfied with what, he hadn't a clue.

This night was getting stranger and stranger by the minute.

Poppy turned her face away when he exposed his legs, but Bitsy chuckled and took a good look. "You have a sense of humor, Daniel. I'll give you that."

He gave her a self-deprecating smile.

She gave him a self-satisfied one. "You're clean, but I still need to know where you were last Monday evening?"

Rose brought a steaming mug of *kaffee* and a slice of some sort of cake to the table. "Bee Sting Cake," she said, setting the plate in front of him. "Lily made it."

The two-layered cake was golden brown with what must have been a whole tree of slivered almonds on top. It looked irresistible. The Honeybee Schwesters were well-known for their baking skills.

"We shouldn't accuse him, Aunt Bitsy,"

Rose said. "He's a guest in our home."

"I got back from Pennsylvania yesterday," Dan said. "I've been there for almost two years."

Poppy frowned and slid her arm around Bitsy's waist. "He didn't do it, B."

Bitsy slumped her shoulders. "I know. But it would be very convenient if he were that easy to catch."

Bitsy and Poppy each slid a chair from the table and sat down. Rose sidled into the chair farthest from Dan. He drank a sip of *kaffee* and took a bite of cake. It melted in his mouth and almost made up for all of the uncomfortable staring.

Almost. Three pairs of eyes bored into his skull. He supposed it was only to be expected. He was a relative stranger sitting in their kitchen in the middle of the night trying not to drown in the *kaffee* Rose had graciously brewed for him.

Rose spoke as if she hoped no one heard her. She'd been timid like that in school. "We're sorry for unjustly accusing you. Aren't we, Aendi Bitsy?"

"Unjustly accusing me of what?" Dan asked, guessing that the apology had something to do with the inspection of his arms.

Bitsy squared her shoulders. "You're right, Rosie. I shouldn't have been so hostile. He's

17

still out of my good graces, but I'm sorry for thinking he could be low enough to hurt our bees."

Why was he out of Bitsy's good graces? They'd only just met.

Poppy glanced at Dan. "Last Monday night, someone tipped over one of our hives."

"Are the bees okay?" Dan said.

Bitsy pressed her lips into a hard line. "We think so. One of the supers is cracked and we lost some brood, but the queen is alive and the bees are still foraging."

"We figure whoever did it must have gotten stung at least a dozen times before he could get away," Poppy said.

Bitsy raised an eyebrow. "Be on the lookout for someone with an unusual amount of bee stings."

What was an unusual amount of bee stings? Dan hoped he'd know it when he saw it. He took another bite of cake, which was turning out to be the best thing about the whole evening. "Do you have a dog? A dog would warn you if someone trespassed onto your property."

Bitsy propped her elbow on the table and rested her chin in her hand. "We have a cat."

Was that a tattoo on her wrist? It looked like a picture of the honeybee, but Dan averted his eyes before he got a good look. He didn't want to gawk.

An Amish woman with a tattoo. Had that ever been done before? And he couldn't be sure, but he thought maybe she had three holes in each ear where earrings might go. Who was this woman, and had the bishop ever gotten a good look at her earlobes?

It made his head hurt thinking about trying to figure out Bitsy Honeybee.

A large, puffy ball of brilliant white fur brushed up against Dan's leg. After all he'd been through tonight, his nerves were a little tight. He nearly jumped out of his skin.

Bitsy rolled her eyes at the ball of fur that turned out to be a fat kitty. "She's not much of a security system. Doesn't make a peep at trespassers and wouldn't attack a robber even if he had a slice of bacon wrapped around his neck."

Dan tried to imagine a place where robbers wore bacon as scarves.

Bitsy picked up the cat and went nose to nose with her as if she were scolding a young child. "Some watch-cat you are, Farrah Fawcett. You're supposed to protect the family from danger."

The cat seemed a little put out with Bitsy's lecture. Her tiny pink nose looked as if she had pressed it against a window and squished it flat. Her eyes glowed bright mustard yellow and her mouth curved in a perpetual frown. Bitsy nuzzled the cat's head against her chin before handing her off to Rose who cooed and cradled the cat in her lap.

Dan's lips twitched into a grin. Bitsy had named her cat after a bathroom fixture? "I suppose the shotgun works if the cat doesn't."

Bitsy waved her hand in the direction of the shotgun propped against the wall. "It's not loaded. I don't believe in guns."

She could have fooled him.

Dan's heart did a little flip when he heard Lily coming down the stairs. For years he'd had a crush on Lily Christner, even if she had completely ignored him since eighth grade. Right before he had left for Pennsylvania, Lily had started going to Dan's *mammi*'s house to read to her. Lily's kindness and Mammi's letters only served to keep her fresh on his mind for two whole years.

Of course, nothing could ever come of his infatuation. Paul Glick was the twenty-foot-high brick wall that stood in his way. And Dan had never been good at climbing walls.

20

CHAPTER THREE

While she pinned her hair into a tight bun, Lily seriously considered sneaking down the stairs and out the back door and driving herself to Dan's *mammi*'s house. The thought of being within a mile of Dan Kanagy sent her into a panic. The thought of being in the same buggy made her ill. What would Paul say? He hated the very sight of any member of the Kanagy family. Even the thought that Lily read to Erda Kanagy three days a week made Paul break out in hives.

She growled in frustration. Hitching up the horse and buggy at two in the morning wasn't practical, and Dan had gone to all this trouble to fetch her. She would ride into town in his buggy, but that didn't mean she had to talk to him. Or look at him. Or fret about him.

Unfortunately, she would have to hear him if he chose to speak. If he called her "Amtrak" one more time, she thought she might burst into tears.

She quickly slipped out of her nightgown and into her dress. She chose the blue dress because Erda liked blue, even if she couldn't see it anymore. Lily felt a hitch in her throat. Was Erda really going to God tonight? And how would Lily fill the hole in her heart when Erda left her?

Lily had already taken her contacts out, so she slid on her old pair of thick glasses. Her eyesight was terrible, and before she got contacts, Dan had teased her persistently about her glasses. She had to give him credit for creativity. He never called her something unoriginal like "Four Eyes." Instead he called her "Coke Bottle" or "Scuba Diver" or his most hurtful favorite, "Frog Eyes."

She'd spent a lot of afternoons after school watering her pillow because of Dan Kanagy. It had been eight years since then but the memories still stung like a hive of bees.

She quickly slipped on her crisp white *kapp* and then her shoes. Even with dread growing in her chest like mold, this was no time to stall. She would feel terrible if Erda passed away before she could say good-bye.

She clomped down the stairs as if she were going to her own funeral and chastised herself for acting so childish. The most important thing was to see Erda before she went to Heaven. Erda was ninety-five years old, eager, and ready to go. They'd been expecting it for several weeks, but now that her death was so close, Lily felt heartbroken. Despite her unfortunate grandson, Erda had become one of Lily's most cherished friends.

When she walked into the kitchen, Dan stood so fast that his chair almost tipped over. His hand shot out and grabbed it before it went down, then he self-consciously shoved his hands into his pockets. "Ready?"

"*Jah,*" she said, grabbing her black sweater from the hook by the door. The first day of summer was almost four weeks away, and the nights were chilly yet.

To her surprise, he sort of yanked the sweater from her hands and helped her into it. "I've got a blanket in the buggy if you get cold."

"*Jah.* Okay."

Aunt Bitsy reached out and pinched Lily's earlobes between her thumbs and index fingers, which was her way of saying "I love you." Aunt B had a thing for ears. "Make sure Erda knows we're thinking of her." Her expression looked stern, like a good librarian, but Lily knew her well enough to recognize the tender emotions in her eyes.

Dan opened the door for her and then offered a hand to help her into his two-seater, open-air buggy. Lily groaned inwardly. She would be forced into very close proximity to Dan Kanagy. How would she stand it?

He sat next to her and snatched a blanket from behind them. "Do you want this? It's pretty cold."

Keeping with her resolve not to talk to him, she shook her head.

Even in the dark, she could see his grin. "Are you sure? It was a gift from an *Englisch* friend. It's got a print of a strange creature on it. His name is SpongeBob SquarePants."

Dan shined his flashlight on the blanket. It was covered with images of a yellow square with eyeballs and buck teeth. Lily had never seen anything so strange. Dan chuckled. "Weird, huh? I knew you'd like it."

Meaning, he thought she was weird. He seemed intent on mocking her with every breath he took.

She folded her arms to ward off the chill. It really was cold, but she wouldn't give him the satisfaction of wrapping his weird blanket around the weird girl sitting next to him. "You don't seem very concerned about your *mammi*," she said, knowing it wasn't a very nice thing to say but hoping to deflect his attention from her strange and ugly self.

He immediately stiffened, and she felt bad that her chiding had hit home. She never dreamed she'd be able to make a dent to his exterior. "I'm sorry if I gave you that impression. My *mammi* is blind and arthritic and in constant pain. She misses my *dawdi* something awful and has been wanting to follow him home ever since he died twelve years ago."

"*Jah,* she has."

Dan stuffed the weird blanket between them, laid the glowing flashlight on top of the blanket, and turned the horse around so they were headed down the lane. "I'm not happy to see her go, but she's happy to be going. I rejoice at a life lived in Jesus. I'm sorry if I offended you."

"I'm not offended," Lily stuttered.

You think I'm weird and ugly. I'm not offended at all.

She fell silent and pretended to be interested in the scenery to her right, even though it was too dark to see much of anything. Hopefully he'd get the hint that she didn't want to talk.

Nae. He didn't take the hint. "While I worked in Pennsylvania, I got a letter from

25

my *mammi* every week. My *schwester* would write it down for her and send it to me." He actually leaned closer and nudged her with his shoulder. "Mammi is very fond of you. Every letter included at least a paragraph about sweet Lily Christner."

Lily's face got warm. No doubt Dan would use something from his *mammi*'s letters to poke fun at her. "I didn't do all that much."

Without warning, Dan pulled on the reins and stopped, actually stopped the buggy on the small bridge that spanned their even smaller pond. He turned his whole body toward her and pinned her with a look that, even in the dim light of the flashlight, could have melted butter. "*Nae,* Lily. You brought so much joy to my *mammi*'s last years. You are not just some girl who read to an old lady. You changed her life. Our whole family is very grateful." His gaze intensified. "You need to understand how we feel."

Lily nodded because her tongue had tied itself into a very tricky knot. How could she resist such surprising sincerity? She didn't deserve it, but she could see Dan believed it.

Smiling sadly, he jiggled the reins and turned his gaze to the road up ahead. "Besides family, you're the only one she wants to see before she goes. That should tell you something."

Lily cleared her throat. She couldn't have anyone thinking better of her than she actually was. "I enjoyed reading with your *mammi* as much as she did. Sometimes I felt almost selfish I took so much pleasure in it."

"You still made a sacrifice, and I am in awe of your kindness."

"It broke my heart when Erda told me she couldn't see well enough to read anymore. I knew how much she loved books, so I suggested we read together. I can't consider it a sacrifice. Erda is like the *mammi* I never had." Lily bit her tongue. Hopefully Dan hadn't noticed that little slip. Lily's own *mammi* lived not ten minutes from here. She should never have implied anything bad about her *mammi*. "Erda shared recipes and wisdom with me, and I brought books and honey."

He didn't say anything immediately, as if he were mulling over what she had said, probably thinking what a wicked girl she was for saying that about her *mammi*. Well, he hadn't exactly been the best example of Christian charity either. He wasn't one to judge. "I just . . . just know that I think

27

you're an angel, and I want to be more like you."

In the dimness, the light of his eyes could have burned a hole through that weird blanket of his. Lily caught her breath and held it, as an unfamiliar shiver traveled up her spine.

He'd caught her unprepared for whatever it was he was doing with her senses. She hadn't expected out of the ordinary. Dan's intense gaze seemed a country mile from ordinary.

Dan's lips curled into a tenuous smile as he cleared his throat and snapped his gaze back to the road. "Almost there."

Erda lived by herself in a tiny home right in the heart of their little town. In the last few months, one of her family members had stayed with her around the clock because she had refused to be moved from her own house. Lily smiled at the thought of petite and determined Erda Kanagy refusing to budge from that chunky lavender armchair she liked so much. Her family had re-arranged their lives so Erda could be comfortable. No matter what Paul Glick thought of Daniel's family, they had treated their *mammi* with exceptional grace.

Dan turned the corner, and Erda's house came into sight. Four bright kerosene lanterns hung from the eaves of her porch, making the small cottage seem like the center of the universe. Lily counted no less than seven buggies parked on the road in front.

Her heart tripped all over itself. She shouldn't be here. She wasn't family. What would they think of Lily Christner barging in on such a solemn, intimate occasion? Was it too late to ask Dan to turn around and take her back?

Dan parked behind the last buggy on the street. Before she even knew what he was doing, he jumped down, slid his hands around her waist, and lifted her to the ground.

That was totally unnecessary, but nice all the same.

"Okay," he said. "Let's go."

She glanced toward the house with her hands clenched to hide her trembling. "I . . . maybe I should wait outside after all." Her voice sounded weak and uncertain, just like she felt.

Dan gently cupped his hand over her elbow. "It's going to be okay, Amtrak. Don't you worry for one minute that you don't belong here. Every member of the family is eager to have you come. They know how happy you made our *mammi.*"

The warmth and sincerity behind his low, musical voice snaked its way into her veins. She forgot her anxiety and remembered how to breathe.

Her lips curled into a half smile. "*Denki.* I am grateful for your kindness."

He smiled back. She'd never seen any expression so reassuring.

It wasn't until they walked into the house and she stood at Erda's bedside that she realized he'd called her "Amtrak." She hadn't even flinched, because when he'd said it just now, she could have sworn there was some affection behind it.

Chapter Four

The sweat trickled down Lily's neck, tickling her skin and leaving her with the almost overpowering urge to scratch, even though it was nearly impossible to scratch when dressed for beekeeping. She bit her bottom lip and ignored the tickle. No beekeeper could afford to be itchy.

A traditional veiled helmet sat on her head with the drawstring pulled tight around the collar of her short-sleeved jacket. She wore a smooth white sweatshirt beneath the jacket and canvas gloves with cuffs that went almost to her elbows. Her jeans legs were stuffed into her boots, and she wore a pair of long socks for good measure. Her outfit provided good protection from stings, but oh, *sis yuscht,* it sure was hot. And today was only June first.

Dressed similarly, Aunt B and Lily's sisters inspected the ten hives on the east side of their farm. A row of half a dozen basswood trees and a barbed-wire fence formed a border between the hives and the wide country road that ran to the east of their farm. The small pond provided a water source for the bees, and the plentiful trees and flowers they'd spent years cultivating supplied pollen and nectar for their hives.

"B?" Poppy said, sending a puff of smoke into the hive with her smoker. "I think this hive is getting ready to swarm."

Aunt B nodded. "Let's split it. I have three extra supers in the honey house."

Lily stepped away from the hive and picked up the sturdy notebook she'd laid on the grass a few feet from where they were working. After peeling off her glove, she made a few notes about Poppy's hive with date and time.

She dropped the notebook and put her glove back on. "The nectar flow has been extra *gute* this spring." Good nectar meant plentiful honey. It would be a good year.

She blew a strand of hair from her eyes. Every couple of years, Aunt B would take Lily and her sisters to Walmart to buy a new pair of beekeeping jeans, which weren't any different from regular jeans, except that the Christners only wore them for beekeeping. The bishop approved as long as the worldly trousers were never worn for other activities. Their farm and apiary were far enough from town that few neighbors wandered onto the property to discover them so outrageously dressed.

Ten hives stood here near the basswood trees. Ten were located next to their field of clover, and ten more sat on the edge of the small orchard of apple and cherry trees they had planted ten years ago when Aunt Bitsy realized they would need some extra money to pay for Lily's braces.

Few Amish people got braces. They were too expensive, as was the mere thought of a dentist. But Aunt B insisted that her girls have *gute* teeth. When Lily's teeth had grown in like a clump of toadstools in the wet grass, Aunt Bitsy set out to find ways to supplement their meager insurance money to pay for braces.

Thus the beehive idea had been born. They'd planted trees and bushes, flowers and herbs. It was strictly forbidden to pluck a dandelion from the lawn and a mortal sin to spray any chemical within a mile of the hives. Aunt B adamantly protected her bees. She had once chased a giant raccoon away from the hives with a frying pan and a turkey baster. She said the sprained ankle was a small price to pay. Farrah Fawcett got a good scolding that day for not being a better raccoon cat.

Proceeds from the honey had kept their farm going, provided money to put away for weddings, and paid for contacts for Lily and a set of braces for each of the girls.

Lily had hated wearing braces and headgear, especially since boys like Dan Kanagy wouldn't leave her alone, but she was glad that now her teeth weren't crammed into her mouth like swimmers at the pool on a hot summer's day. She knew it was pure vanity, but she liked having a nice smile that she didn't have to be ashamed of.

Jah, Paul would say she was as vain as a peacock.

She pumped more smoke into her hive and pried up a frame with her hive tool. Good nectar flow. This super was almost full.

Rose put the cover back on her hive.

"You're so much faster than the rest of us, Rosie," Poppy said.

"She has a calming influence on the bees, same as she does with people and animals," Aunt B said.

"The bees are my friends," Rose said, a shy smile forming on her lips.

Even though they were sisters, Rose, Poppy, and Lily were nothing alike. Lily felt like a plain, hardy dandelion, while Rose was like a rare pink-petaled flower that only bloomed in the moonlight. Poppy fit her nickname perfectly. In the garden, Priscilla — though no one called her that — would have been a bright orange poppy demanding to be noticed. Beautiful, showy, and irresistible. Lily didn't mind that both her sisters surpassed her in every way. She loved them better than her own heart.

"How is Dan doing since his *mammi*'s passing, Lily?" Rose asked.

Why did her heart seem to swoosh to her toes and back again at the mention of his name? She hated the sight of Dan Kanagy, even if he had been exceptionally sweet to his *mammi* right before she died. "Dan? How should I know?"

Rose's voice sounded as small as a mouse. "I'm sorry. I didn't mean to upset you."

Had she sounded upset? "You didn't upset me. Dan and I aren't exactly friends. He treated me badly in school."

Rose moved on to the next beehive. "Maybe he's sorry for all those times he teased you."

"You talked yesterday after the funeral," Poppy said. "What did he say?"

Oh, well, it . . . hadn't been anything. Except it had been very thoughtful of him to seek her out and ask how she was holding up and could he do anything for her? *He* had lost his *mammi.* She had to be holding up better than he was. "He asked how I was doing."

Rose checked the fuel in her smoker. "And how is he doing?"

"I . . . uh, didn't ask."

"Why not?"

"He just . . . Well, he didn't seem to want to talk about himself." Lily groaned inwardly. After the funeral, her mind had been full of thoughts of Erda, and then Dan had looked at her in that strange way that made her spine sort of go tingly. She hadn't been thinking straight. She should have at least expressed her sympathy to him. "He asked how you *schwesters* were doing and Aunt B."

Rose glanced in Lily's direction. "That was thoughtful of him."

"Did he say anything mean to you?" Poppy asked, as if she were looking for a fight. She always stood ready to defend her sisters against stupid boys who called them names.

"*Nae,* very nice. He didn't make fun of my freckles or call me Amtrak."

"I used to punch him when he called you Amtrak," Poppy said, narrowing her eyes. "That one always made you cry."

36

Except for that one time at Erda's house.

Aunt B raised her eyes to the sky. "Lord, I'm getting a little impatient down here waiting for permission to use the shotgun on that boy."

"I think you'll be waiting a long time for that permission, Aunt B." Lily smiled to herself. Aunt B liked to talk to *Gotte* right out loud whenever the Spirit moved her.

Poppy shielded her eyes and looked up at the sky. "I better get changed and get to market before the produce is picked over."

"Go," Aunt B said. "We'll finish up. Will you check and make sure Farrah Fawcett hasn't wandered off?"

Lily smiled. Farrah Fawcett had to be the laziest cat in the world. She seldom wandered more than ten feet from her window seat.

They heard the sound of a horse clip-clopping across their little wooden bridge and turned to see Dan Kanagy in his open-air buggy. He smiled when he caught sight of them and waved enthusiastically.

"What's he doing here?" Poppy complained, propping her gloved hands on her hips.

Lily felt almost as hostile as Poppy sounded. What *was* he doing here? And so early in the morning? He'd never hidden his dislike before. Surely he was as eager to avoid her as she was to avoid him.

"Hello, Lily," he called.

Umm, okay. That actually sounded like he was happy to see her.

Poppy and Rose eyed her curiously.

Well, she wasn't happy to see him. Whatever he wanted, he could turn that buggy around and head back to town. She had no use for boys who called her names and carried Spongey-Man blankets in their buggies, no matter how handsome they were. He was too far away to actually explain all this to him. She'd have to let him get closer.

He prodded his horse out of sight behind the leafy hedge of flowering bushes that ran along the lane. Time seemed to stand still as Lily tracked his progress by listening to the faint sound of his buggy wheels crunching over the dirt and gravel and occasionally catching a glimpse of him through the gaps in the bushes.

When he got to the end of the lane, he parked his buggy near Poppy's perennial flower bed, jumped to the ground, and made a beeline for Lily as if he hadn't a care in the world. As if he weren't about to meet with a swarm of testy bees.

"He's trampling my dandelions," Aunt B

muttered. "I should have brought my shotgun."

Rose moved so that the hive stood between her and Dan. Men in general made her skittish.

Much as she disliked him, Lily couldn't let him walk into an ambush.

"Stop right there," Lily called, hoping the irritation was evident in her voice. His stupid grin faded as he halted dead in his tracks fifteen yards from the hives. "You're going to get stung if you come any closer."

His grin returned as he took two tentative steps backward. "I . . . I, uh, brought you a gift," he said, holding up the package he carried in his hand.

Didn't he know anything? "Well, you can't give it to me right now, not while we're working the hives. You'll have to go."

He raised an eyebrow and motioned toward the house. "I can wait over there until you finish. I don't mind."

"Just leave it on the porch and go."

He took another step backward. "It's okay, Coke Bottle. I'll wait."

Giving an angry huff, Poppy marched right up to him, veil, helmet, boots, and all. Dan looked mildly surprised but didn't back away.

"How dare you?" Poppy yelled. "How

39

dare you?" She laid her gloved hand on his shoulder and shoved him. As a general rule, she didn't slug boys anymore, but she wasn't above a good shove. Being tall and solidly built, Dan didn't budge, even though Poppy most likely pushed with all her might.

Poppy huffed out her disgust, turned on her heels, and headed for the house. Dan simply stared after her with a slightly confused, slightly amused look on his face. He turned back to Lily and grinned, as if he hadn't just called her an offensive name. She wasn't even wearing her glasses today.

Rose clutched her smoker as if it were a lifeline. "I'm sorry about your *mammi.* How . . . are you?"

Dan nodded and there was a gentle kindness in his eyes when he looked at Rose. Lily was impressed. He was sincerely trying not to scare her. "*Denki* for asking. I am doing well. Mammi is one of *Gotte*'s angels now, and I'm sure she thinks she's better off."

"I'm glad," Rose said. She suddenly seemed to remember she was talking to a boy and fell silent.

"I'm glad too," Lily said, trying to deflect Dan's gaze from Rose. There was only so much attention Rose could bear.

Dan took the hint. He held out the gift, as

40

if reminding Lily he had it. "I'll go sit on the porch and wait."

"I'm going to be a very long time." She could stall until he gave up and left.

"I don't mind." He said it so cheerfully, she almost believed him. He turned around and sauntered toward the house.

"Might as well pull some weeds in the flower beds while you're waiting," Aunt B called.

He turned back, his eyes bright with enthusiasm. "You bet. Happy to help."

"But leave the dandelions, do you hear me? Don't you think about pulling up my dandelions. And watch where you step yet."

Dan flashed Aunt B a mischievous smile. "Okay. I'll only pull the dandelions." He turned and tromped away, a certain spring to his step that told Lily he was grinning from ear to ear.

Aunt B gave him an impressive glare, but his back was turned so its power was lost on him. "That boy is just begging for a *hinnerdale* full of buckshot."

Lily stifled a giggle. "He's teasing you, Aunt B."

"Of course he's teasing. But dandelions are serious business. He shouldn't tease about my dandelions."

"Lily," Rose whispered, as if Dan would

be able to hear them from a hundred yards away. "You really shouldn't be so rude. He brought you a present."

Lily frowned. "He called me Coke Bottle."

"I'm sorry," Rose said. "He shouldn't say that to you." She sounded as if she were about to cry.

The last thing Lily wanted was for Rose to feel worse about it than she did. "It's okay. It really doesn't hurt as bad as it used to. And maybe when I get to the house, I'll tell Dan Kanagy to go jump in the lake."

Of course, she'd never actually do that. Such boldness was Poppy's talent, not hers. Lily tended to swallow hurt and not fight back. She only felt worse when she fought back, as if she really had deserved all the unkindness in the first place.

It took another half hour to finish inspecting the hives. Poppy had changed clothes and left for town in the buggy. Lily had watched out of the corner of her eye as Dan had vigorously weeded the flower bed and then moved on to the climbing roses at the side of the house. His diligence impressed her. He didn't have to weed, and he certainly didn't have to do it so enthusiastically.

Apparently, he wouldn't give up and go home. Stalling would only delay the inevitable and keep her from other chores she had to get to today. With Aunt Bitsy and Rose, she tromped across the lawn toward the house, removing her veil and her gloves as she went. She was painfully aware of what a sight she must be to someone like Dan Kanagy in her jeans and boots.

For sure and certain, Paul Glick wouldn't like seeing Lily in pants. He didn't even like it when she wore her canary-yellow dress. He said the color hurt his eyes and drew unnecessary attention when she should be seeking to go unnoticed. A humble girl should not wear a peacock dress.

Paul often lectured her on how to be a proper Amish girl, reminding her that since her *aendi* practically ignored the *Ordnung,* Lily's behavior must be beyond reproach. She hated it when Paul talked about her aunt that way, but she always bit her tongue. In eighth grade, Paul had been the only boy who hadn't teased her about her *hesslich* glasses or her homely face. She had always been very grateful to him.

Paul didn't come to their farm often because he hated bees and all other creepy, crawly creatures. Lord willing, he would never see her in her bee suit and never be the wiser, because she wasn't about to try to tend to the hives in a dress. Bees had a way of crawling into very unusual places, underneath stockings, up skirts, into underwear.

Tenaciously sweeping dirt from the flagstones, Dan glanced at Lily as she followed Aunt B and Rose into the house. Would he make a fuss about her jeans like Paul would have?

Jah.

She paused and turned to him. "I need to change my clothes. You really don't have to wait."

His grin seemed to be a permanent part of his face. "I don't mind waiting, Daddy Long Legs."

Daddy Long Legs? She was only five feet six inches tall. Really? Daddy Long Legs?

Had he forgotten her name?

Nae. It was just another insult to add to his list. A backhanded way of saying he disapproved of the jeans.

Her face burned hot as she ducked into the house. She didn't care if he disapproved or not. She knew she was unappealing. She knew she was awkward and gawky and homely. He didn't have to keep reminding her. Dan Kanagy could go jump in the lake and live with the smelly fish where he belonged. And no, she'd never tell him to his face. He could figure it out for himself.

Lily stomped into the house and seriously considered not coming out for the rest of the day. Let him sweep and weed and grin until he got the hint that she never wanted to lay eyes on him again.

By the time she climbed the stairs to the room she shared with her sisters, she had changed her mind. She should be ashamed of herself for wishing he would go jump in the lake. What an unkind thought to have so early in the morning.

She sighed, knowing it was best to get rid of him soon. If he hung around all day, she'd be miserable, and there was no doubt in her mind that he'd hang around all day. He had already proven himself the persistent type.

If only he weren't also the very rude type.

She put on her yellow dress, just to annoy him, removed the scarf from around her hair, and donned her *kapp,* determined to get rid of Dan Kanagy in thirty seconds flat.

Take the present and dash back into the house before he had time to think of another cruel nickname.

Rose and Aunt B were in the back room putting their veils and gloves away when Lily came down the stairs. "I'll be back soon," she called. In thirty seconds, to be precise.

Rose leaned her head out of the back-room doorway. "Give him one of those cookies you made."

Aunt B chimed in her two cents. "Don't give him a cookie. Boys are like stray cats. If you feed them, they'll keep showing up on your porch."

Lily cracked a smile. She agreed with Aunt B. No feeding Dan Kanagy.

Dan sat on the bottom porch step and had to sort of unfold himself to stand up. With his grin firmly in place, he gazed at her, his eyes dancing in amusement. Probably thinking of how funny she looked in yellow. Like a baby chicken. "*Ach du lieva.* You look so pretty, Amtrak."

Lily felt her face get warm. Only Dan could put *you look so pretty* and *Amtrak* together in the same sentence. Should she be insulted or flattered? She cleared her throat. It would take too much time to decide, and her precious thirty seconds were ticking away.

"I've got chores I need to get to," she said.

Dan seemed to snap to attention. He scrambled up the porch steps and handed her a gift wrapped in brown paper and tied with a piece of twine. She fingered the tight knot. It would take more than thirty seconds to loosen it. She'd have to go back in the house and open it after he left. *"Denki,"* she said, stepping back and grabbing the door handle, a definite signal that she was finished with him. "It's very kind of you."

He didn't take the hint. "Here," he said, fishing in his pocket. "I've got a pocket-knife."

He retrieved his knife and quickly slit the twine. Even though she resisted, the excitement in his eyes was contagious. Maybe she could spare an extra fifteen seconds to open it.

She pulled back the paper to reveal a hardbound book with a beautiful illustration of a boy and his two dogs on the cover. Her heart swelled inside her chest, and she lost complete track of time.

He tilted his head so he could meet her eyes. "Do you like it?"

"Oh my," was all she could think to say.

"My *mammi* said it's one of your favorite books. After all you did for her, I wanted to get you something special."

Lily felt about ten degrees warmer than she had a minute ago. "Dan, this is too much. I already told you that reading to your *mammi* was my pleasure. It's so expensive."

He winked at her. "Worth every penny to see your eyes light up like that."

She lowered her gaze self-consciously. Did her eyes really light up? Did he never stop teasing?

"I bought one for me too," he said. "I've never read it."

Her mouth fell open in mock horror. "You've never read *Where the Red Fern Grows*? That's a tragedy."

"I didn't read much growing up. But since I've been home, I'm starting to get interested. I think it will help me feel closer to my *mammi,* reading all the books she loved so much."

Lily curled the corners of her lips. "We read *Where the Red Fern Grows* together several times."

Dan shuffled his feet. "I thought maybe I could read it, and we could talk about it. Together. You and me." His grin drooped, and he suddenly looked uncertain.

The request caught her off guard. She didn't like Dan Kanagy, but she never could resist a good book. Besides, he seemed so eager. She would never forgive herself if she single-handedly killed Dan's budding interest in reading.

"I suppose that would be all right."

He bloomed into a smile as bright as a whole lawn full of dandelions. "That would be wonderful-*gute.* You've always had such a kind heart."

What would Paul think of her reading with the enemy?

Maybe he'd never find out — like the jeans thing.

It was only one book.

Lily lovingly clutched the book to her chest. "*Denki* for bringing this to me. It was very thoughtful." How much time had passed? More than thirty seconds. "I should probably go away now."

Go away? She didn't need to go away. He did. What kind of strange thing was that to say?

He took a step back and thumbed his suspenders, looking slightly crestfallen. "*Jah.* Of course. You have plenty to do without me around to bother you." He pointed to the pile of weeds he'd pulled from Poppy's flower bed. "Where should I put these?"

"I'll take care of them later."

His lips twisted playfully. "Why should you, when I'm here to help?"

Still clutching her book, she tilted her head and gave him a half smile. "This way," she said.

Dan scooped up the generous pile of weeds and followed her north past the birdbath and three-acre vegetable garden.

Poppy had planted cantaloupes, peppers, and cucumbers, and raspberries bordered the entire north side.

"That's quite a garden," Dan said, pausing to admire the meticulous row of caged tomato plants. "Not a weed in sight. How do you sisters do it all by yourselves?"

She felt a little ruffled by the look of admiration in his eyes. She certainly didn't deserve any such thing. "As you can see by your armful of weeds, we don't always keep up."

"I found a few measly weeds in that huge bed of flowers. I'd say you're wonderful-*gute* at keeping up."

She turned her face and pretended to inspect the raspberries so she wouldn't have to try to make sense of that look in his eyes. She just wanted him to go away. "Poppy is in charge of the gardens and beds yet. We help her weed, but their beauty is all her doing."

"She's got the muscles for it," Dan said, grinning as if Poppy hadn't assaulted him earlier.

Lily should probably apologize that Poppy shoved him, but he'd deserved it and Lily was grateful that her sister always stood up for her.

He didn't seem to expect an apology.

"Poppy used to go after me on a regular basis in school. I was never sure why."

Lily worked hard to keep the disbelief from her face. He was never sure why Poppy slugged him at recess? Were boys really that thick?

"She warned me to stay away from you. I guess she was being protective. She probably saw how much I liked to hover around you."

Hover around her and call her cruel, cutting names that left invisible scars.

She led him to the barbed-wire fence that separated the Johnsons' pasture from their property and pointed over the fence. "The Johnsons gave us permission to throw all our weeds over here. It's their old horse pasture, but they don't keep horses anymore."

Dan quickly dispatched with the weeds and brushed the dirt from his hands. Resting one hand on the fence, he did a quick survey of his surroundings. "Are those your apple trees?" he asked, pointing to the small orchard north of the barn.

"*Jah.* We planted them when we started with our first hives. We wanted our bees to have plenty of forage."

"Will you show me?"

He acted as if he were really interested in

51

apple trees and beehives. Paul was never interested. He'd never set foot in their orchard. Was Dan pretending to care? And why was he pretending to care if he *was* pretending to care? A girl could get quite confused trying to figure some people out.

He raised an eyebrow and concern made a shadow across his face. "Unless you don't have time. I don't want to make a pest of myself."

She *didn't* have time. He *was* making a pest of himself. But a certain vulnerability in his eyes thawed her resistance.

"Okay," she said. "I don't mind."

He held out his hand. "Do you want me to carry *Where the Red Fern Grows*? We could pretend I'm carrying your books from school."

"It's not heavy." She didn't quite know what to do with his disarming sincerity. One minute he made fun of her and called her names, the next he offered to carry her book.

They strolled along the fence line until it turned a corner north, opening to the space where the orchard began. Ducking low, Dan stepped between two rows of apple trees, his expression like a little kid. "My *onkel* Menno has apple trees. We played in his orchard as children, throwing dirt clods at each other and making hideouts out of fallen tree limbs. How many acres do you have?"

"Fifty. Counting the field we rent out."

"Fifty?" he said, as if it were the best news he'd ever heard. He *was* a little kid. Who besides Lily and her sisters got excited about fifty acres? "Plenty of room for the bees."

"Jah," she said, letting her lips curl into a smile. He had surprised her again. "I am impressed that you noticed."

"It makes sense. You've got blooming bushes and trees. Lots of flowers and lots of dandelions. Food for the bees. How many hives do you have?"

Lily pointed to the orchard hives visible through the trees and started walking toward them. "Ten in the orchard, ten by the clover field, and the ten you see when you come over the bridge. We also have twenty hives at Chidester's sunflower farm. He pays us a fee to pollinate his sunflowers."

"Genius," he said under his breath as if he were in awe of pollination.

"Another farmer grows clover on our acreage to the west. Aunt B won't let him cut it until it blossoms and the bees get a feast."

Lily stopped about ten feet from the

orchard hives. The trees were no longer blossoming, but the hives buzzed with activity as the foragers flew in and out, searching farther afield for their nectar. Rose had painted pictures of bright, friendly flowers of different varieties on each hive. On the one closest to them, she had painted a vine covered with tiny midnight-blue blossoms.

"The hives are in full sun most of the day, except in the morning. They do better in full sun."

"The painting is wonderful-*gute*," Dan said.

"Rose loves to paint. She likes the solitude, and Aunt B says the different designs help the bees recognize which hive is theirs."

"I didn't know that."

Patches of morning sun filtered through the trees, speckling the beehives with purified light. "I love how beautiful the hives look when they catch the light."

"Really pretty," Dan said.

She glanced at him and quickly looked away. He wasn't looking at the hives. Surely her face turned as purple as a plum.

He cleared his throat as if he had a buggy lodged in there. "Can we go closer? I'm not afraid of getting stung."

"This is close enough. You might upset the bees."

"They hold grudges against boys who trample dandelions?"

She giggled, actually giggled, at Dan Kanagy, the mean boy who called her Amtrak. "Bees are very gentle creatures, but that brown shirt of yours makes you look like a bear. You'll make them nervous if you get too close."

He rubbed his hand down the side of his face. "I'll have to remember that. No brown. What about green? Are they afraid of frogs?"

"Not that I know of."

"I'll have to buy a green shirt. I don't own one."

"White is fine," Lily said, laughing in spite of herself. "As long as you don't stand in the path of their entrance, you can stand right next to the hive and they won't bother you. But if you want to work the hives, you have to wear a bee suit. At least a veil."

"I really like your bee suit," he said, again with the sincerity she couldn't account for.

She didn't know how to reply, so she reached up and plucked a leaf from the nearest tree and twirled it in her fingers. Of course he didn't like her bee suit. He'd compared her to a spider.

Dan stared at her for a few uncomfortable seconds while she adamantly twirled her leaf and looked anywhere but at him. "I should probably get going," he said. "*Denki* for showing me your farm." Flashing a sheepish grin, he reached out and took the book from her hand. "Can I carry your book home from school?"

She pretended to think about it. "I don't know. How do I know you won't drop it in a puddle?"

"I promise to get you and the book safely home. It's the least I can do."

"The least you can do?"

"For agreeing to discuss this book with me."

Oh, that. Lily didn't mind so much anymore. She almost looked forward to it. Almost. And Paul never had to know.

They ambled out of the orchard, past the barn, and up the flagstones to the front porch. Almost reluctantly, Dan handed her the book. "I'll be going now."

"*Denki* for weeding the flowers."

"Lord willing, Poppy will be satisfied with what I did in her flower bed. If not, she can slug me if it makes her feel better."

Lily hated to be the one to break the news that slugging Dan always made Poppy feel better.

"*Ach!* I almost forgot," she said. "Wait one second." She ducked into the house and grabbed two cookies from the cooling rack.

She returned to the porch and handed them to Dan. "Have a cookie."

"Denki." He took them from her and bounded down the steps. "I'll see you soon."

Only after he turned his buggy around and drove down the lane did Lily remember Aunt B's warning. Would Dan keep showing up on her porch if she fed him? Like a stray cat?

For sure and certain Dan wasn't going to show up all that often.

Maybe stray cats weren't fond of cookies.

CHAPTER FIVE

Paul sat on his front porch step with his arms resting on his knees and his fingers laced together as if he'd been there ever so long.

Lily pulled in front of his house and tied the reins. With canvas bag in hand, she jumped out of her buggy and ambled up his sidewalk. She could tell he was irritated. He gave off an unmistakable aura of annoyance, not unlike how a baby gave off the unpleasant stink of a dirty diaper.

"You're late," he said. "Of all the stuff, Lily. I told you to be here at eleven fifteen."

"Your letter said eleven forty-five."

She shouldn't argue with him. Paul hated to admit when he was wrong. His insecurity came from being raised in a home where his *dat* always had to be right. Paul had grown up fighting for every shred of justification he could get.

His lips formed into that pouty, petulant

frown he got when he thought Lily was trying to be smarter than he was. "I think I should know what my letter said. Of all the stuff, Lily, you need to stop making excuses for yourself. It wonders me if you had your nose in a book and lost track of time."

Lily was tempted to pull the letter out of her apron pocket and show him the numbers he'd written clear as day, but Paul would be humiliated that he'd been wrong. It wasn't worth winning the argument, especially when it meant so much to his manly pride.

"I apologize for making you wait. I know how busy you are." That must have been the reason he'd sent her a letter instead of coming to the farm in person. Things were busy at the store. It surely wasn't that he couldn't be bothered to take the half-hour buggy ride to see his girlfriend. A letter mailed in the morning usually got to Lily by the next day. Paul used the post office as an easy and convenient way to communicate with her.

Paul seldom came to the farm. He was afraid of bees, and even though he never said it, Lily knew he felt uncomfortable around Aunt Bitsy. She wasn't a typical Amish woman and anything out of the ordinary made Paul uneasy.

His expression softened. "I forgive you. At least you remembered to wear your glasses."

Lily nudged the cumbersome glasses over the bridge of her nose self-consciously. Paul's *dat* liked Lily better in glasses than contacts. He thought the contacts were worldly and vain. Whenever she went to Paul's house, she put on her glasses to appease the Glicks.

She secretly rejoiced that it would be impossible to pop the braces back into her mouth. Paul's *dat* probably liked those better too — braces or a mouthful of unruly teeth. That or no teeth at all.

Lily pursed her lips. Vain or not, she liked being able to chew her food.

Paul shrugged himself off the porch step. He stood a couple of inches taller than Lily with curly, brown hair and dark, well-defined eyebrows. He was of a stocky build, solid as a tree at the shoulders but a little soft around the belly.

Aunt B said he was chubby. Not that Lily would have expected anything different from Aunt B. Whenever a boy came calling, Aunt B would find seventeen things wrong with him before he even climbed out of his buggy. It was her way of protecting her girls, and for as mother-bearish as she could be at times, they loved her dearly for watching out for them.

"That one's too big for his britches," Aunt B had said of Paul. "And his britches are already pretty big."

Even Rosie had giggled at that remark, though she felt so guilty about it afterward that she made a cake and asked Lily to give it to Paul and apologize.

Lily smiled at the memory. Paul might have been a little "big for his britches," but who didn't struggle with pride? Lily was proud of her teeth. Paul was proud of his humility.

She forgave him for all of it. In school when the boys teased her, Paul had been her friend. He'd encouraged her to ignore Dan Kanagy. Those Kanagys were a bad lot, and Dan was the worst of them, Paul had said. He'd never stood up to Dan when he teased Lily — that was Poppy's job — but sometimes Paul would whisk Lily to the far end of the playground so she wouldn't hear Dan's insults. Paul had been a true friend. Lily had been trying to show her gratitude ever since.

"Let's go get some supper at the restaurant," Paul said, stepping off his porch and taking a few steps in the direction of the center of town. "We can discuss business while we eat."

Lily groaned inwardly. She hadn't brought enough money. Paul's family owned a large and prosperous market and Amish restaurant in the center of Bienenstock. Lots of tourists shopped at the market, which stocked everything from jams and quilts to Amish butter and chiming clocks. The restaurant was adjacent to the market and equally as popular. Paul and Lily ate there often, except that Paul ate for free and they made Lily pay. Today, she didn't have the money.

Besides, she was eager to avoid Raymond Glick's scrutiny. When Lily went to the restaurant, Paul's *dat* liked to glare at her while she ate.

"Let's talk business here," she said. "I have to get home soon."

"I need to eat, Lily. If you'd been here on time, I wouldn't be starving, but now I've got to have something to eat or my blood sugar will crash."

Paul often mentioned his blood sugar. He'd never actually told Lily what it meant except that it always seemed to be an emergency when he was hungry.

Lily slumped her shoulders. Nothing mattered at the moment but Paul's health. She could always order a roll and a glass of water. They only charged her a dollar for a roll. A dollop of jelly cost twenty-five cents. Extra butter was complimentary. "Okay. I'm sorry I was late."

Paul smiled and gave her arm an affectionate pat. "I've already forgiven you, Lily. Don't dwell on it."

The family restaurant was one block up and three blocks over. They usually left Lily's buggy at Paul's house and walked.

Paul took off quickly down the sidewalk. "Come on before my blood sugar acts up yet." He got ten feet ahead of her before he noticed she lagged behind. "*Cum,* Lily. I'll starve to death before we get there."

She picked up her pace and tried to think of something to get Paul's mind off food. "Did you buy that fishing pole you had your eye on?"

He laughed as if Lily wasn't in on the joke. "It's called a fly rod. Nobody calls what I got a fishing pole. Dat hired a driver to take us to Green Bay. Four hundred dollars. It's a beauty."

Four hundred dollars? Business must be wonderful-*gute.*

His smile faded slightly. "We'll have to wait until the season winds down to try it out. Things at the store are busier than ever."

"I'm glad," Lily said.

"It means I might have enough money to buy the piece of ground right next to my *dat*'s house. I can build my own house soon."

Lily pretended not to understand what it meant if Paul built his own house. He had been dropping subtle hints about settling down and what they would do when they were married ever since they'd turned eighteen. It got harder and harder to avoid the conversation she knew Paul wanted to have.

She supposed it was inevitable, her and Paul. After all, they had been friends since eighth grade, and she owed him a great debt of gratitude. She simply wasn't ready to marry yet. Her family needed her. The beehives needed her. The books needed her.

"Since business is so *gute,* I hope you'll buy our honey again this year," Lily said.

Paul scrunched his lips into a frown. "I already promised, Lily. No matter how bad things get for us, we will always buy your honey. Only for you, because you and I are so close."

She let out a breath she didn't know she was holding. Paul had always been a faithful friend. He wouldn't let her down. Her family needed that money from honey sales, and Paul's family had always been so kind to buy every bit Lily's hives produced, in good years and bad. *"Denki,"* she said.

A shadow seemed to pass across his features. "But I have some bad news. We're not going to be able to pay you as much as we did last year. Dat is saving up for a new freezer and we have to cut back. We can only pay you a dollar a pint."

"A dollar a pint? But that's almost fifty cents less than last year."

"I'm really sorry, Lily. That's the best I can do. The good news is that we will probably be able to sell most of it."

The good news didn't cheer Lily at all. She had figured their income from the price they got last year. She did some quick numbers in her head. If they got a good amount of honey in the first extraction, it would probably be enough to fill the liquid propane tank for another couple of months.

What would Aunt B say? She'd always had such confidence in Lily's ability to manage the family's finances — confidence that Lily feared was misplaced. Aunt B might change her mind about letting Lily do the books from now on. It seemed they were getting deeper in the hole when Lily should have made them rich by now, or at least comfortable enough not to have to always be squeezing every penny.

No roll for her today. Maybe she could get by with a pat of butter.

They turned at the corner where the Yutzy family ran a small fruit and vegetable stand. This early in the season, they sold doughnuts and produce from out of town. Hannah Yutzy, her sister Mary, and their brother James were frying a fresh batch of doughnuts on their portable propane stove.

"Lily!" Hannah shrieked.

"Lily!" Mary repeated.

Hannah was a tall, mousy brunette who only knew how to speak at two volumes — loud and ear-piercing. Mary, short and compact, was as enthusiastic as Hannah and even more giggly.

Paul shoved his hands into his pockets, turned his back, and sauntered a few feet away as if he had no interest in the conversation or the Yutzy girls. Their small fruit and vegetable business competed with his family's market. He tended to be protective where his family's profits were concerned.

Lily stepped inside their little enclosure and gave both Hannah and Mary a hug. James looked up from his pot of doughnuts and grinned. Lily smiled back. Was he blushing?

"Ach du lieva, Lily," Hannah exclaimed. "I haven't seen you for ages. *Ages."*

66

The sisters' enthusiasm always made Lily smile. "I missed you at the gathering at Miller's."

Mary nodded. "On account of we was in Mexico getting my *mamm*'s goiter cut out."

Hannah propped her hands on Lily's shoulders. "I love that green dress. It makes your eyes so bright."

She turned Lily toward Mary. "Don't you think, Mary?"

"*Jah.* Bright and green, like a Granny Smith apple. I haven't seen you wear your glasses for ages. Just ages. Are your contacts broken?"

Lily glanced at Paul who wasn't paying the least bit of attention. "I like to wear my glasses sometimes."

Hannah sighed loudly. "It doesn't matter. You're so pretty, with or without."

Lily fixed her eyes in the direction opposite of Paul, not even daring a look his way. He disliked such talk. "How is your *mamm* since the surgery?"

Mary flicked her wrist in Lily's direction. "She's fine. She sits in her easy chair and orders me and Hannah around all day. She's happiest when she's bossing other people."

Lily raised an eyebrow at Hannah. "And how is Max?"

The sisters exploded into a fit of giggles

that made Lily want to join in.

"Don't even ask," Hannah said, obviously eager to tell. "Diana Bieler told me that her cousin saw him kissing an *Englisch* girl. I forgave him, and we were back together for a week when I caught him kissing Diana at Walmart." Hannah didn't seem too broken up about it. She almost couldn't talk through the giggling.

Mary leaned her head closer and lowered her voice so that no one outside of a three-hundred-foot radius would have been able to hear it. "Hannah told Max that her lips would never touch his again, on account of she didn't want Diana Bieler's germs." The giggling intensified. "You should have seen his face."

"And here's the part where you come in, Lily."

"Me?"

"*Jah,*" Mary said. "Diana gave Max her cold sore and he told Hannah that he'd been stung by one of the Honeybee Schwesters' bees."

Lily widened her eyes. "He blamed my bees?"

Mary nodded, her eyes bright with amusement. "Of all things."

So much mirth floated around that Lily couldn't help but join in. "That's it. Max is never getting one of my honey cookies ever again."

Hannah nodded. "That'll show him. He loves your honey cookies."

Mary grabbed Lily's hand. "We're having a quilting frolic two weeks from next Monday."

"*Nae*, Mary," said Hannah. "Three weeks from last Monday."

"Same thing," Mary insisted. "Two weeks from next Monday. You're invited, Lily. I know it's laundry day, but will you come?"

"Can I bring my sisters?"

Hannah nodded. "And your aunt Bitsy. She makes the tiniest stitches I've ever seen. I don't care what Eva Schrock says. Bitsy is as *gute* as any Amish *frau*."

Hannah had meant it to be a compliment, but the significance behind her words pricked Lily's heart. Many people in the community saw Aunt B as an outsider. They were suspicious of her colorful hair and temporary tattoos and her fondness for having conversations with *Gotte* in public places. Aunt B had lived in the *Englisch* world for twenty years before coming back to the church. All those years immersed in wickedness made the gossips in the district nervous.

Lily swallowed the lump in her throat and

nodded, making sure her lips curled cheerfully. Hannah meant no offense. "We all love to quilt, except for Poppy. She doesn't have the patience for it."

"Then we'll see you on the twentieth. Noon at our house."

Paul cleared his throat as if he were trying to start a gas-powered engine. His blood sugar must be acting up again. He tapped his hand on the counter. "Let's go, Lily."

She glanced at him and smiled at the Yutzy sisters. "I'll see you later." Lily bent her head to the side to make eye contact with James, who was faithfully frying doughnuts. "Nice to see you again."

James raised his eyes to her face and quickly let them drop. "You too," he mumbled.

Mary grinned. "He thinks you're pretty," she whispered loud enough for both Paul and James to hear. With his back to them, James slumped his shoulders and seemed to shrink about four inches.

Paul frowned. "Come on, Lily."

"Wait!" Hannah retrieved two glazed doughnuts from the tray and handed them to Lily. "Take these. They're a new recipe."

"I don't have enough money —"

Hannah giggled as if Max had been kissing *Englisch* girls again. "I'm not selling.

I'm giving. We love you like family, Lily, and family doesn't pay."

Lily gave Hannah a quick peck on the cheek. "Are you sure?" She suspected that Hannah and Mary loved a lot of people like family. She didn't want them to go broke feeding all their surrogate siblings.

Mary snatched two napkins from the counter and stuffed them into Lily's apron pocket. "Max blamed you for his little lip problem. It's the least we can do to make it up to you."

"We don't need them," Paul said. "We're going for supper at the restaurant."

"How nice," Mary said, clapping her hands together. "Your *mamm*'s rolls melt in my mouth."

Paul might not have wanted to accept doughnuts from the competition, but Lily was definitely taking them. They were better than the glass of water and the pat of butter waiting for her at the restaurant. If Paul didn't want one, she could eat them both. She smiled to herself. *Would* eat them both.

Hannah brushed her hands down her apron. "You can eat dessert first."

"Denki," Lily said. "We will see you at the frolic."

"Bring a thimble," Mary said.

71

Lily took a bite of one of the doughnuts as she and Paul walked away. Pleasantly warm and deliciously sweet. "Mmm," she sighed.

Paul eyed her resentfully. "How can you learn to be humble if people like James Yutzy think you're pretty? He shouldn't be looking, and you shouldn't encourage him."

Lily felt herself blush. "James is only sixteen. It's kind of cute. I'm flattered."

The frown turned into a scowl. "Of all the stuff, Lily. Flattery is the seed of vanity, and you, of all girls, have to fight the temptation, especially considering what you used to look like."

The bite of doughnut nearly stuck in her throat.

What she used to look like.

She had been a *hesslich*, ugly teenager. Paul had looked past the glasses and the pimples and seen her heart. Now that her teeth were straight and her skin was smooth, she understood why he constantly admonished her about humility. Mary's compliment had sent warmth tingling all the way to her toes. Why had she have let such talk tempt her?

Paul looked on the heart, just like *Gotte* did. She'd never deserve someone so deeply good.

She lost her appetite for those doughnuts. "You're right. I shouldn't have let them tempt me. I'm still so weak yet."

"I forgive you, Lily. It's not your fault that your aunt pushed you to get the braces and then the contacts."

"The contacts are better for my eyesight," she said, immediately regretting it. It sounded like she was trying to justify her sin.

"I hoped the glasses might help, but people see right past them."

Lily heard someone call behind her. "Well, if it isn't Coke Bottle!"

She turned and nearly groaned out loud. The last thing she needed was an encounter with Dan Kanagy while out with Paul Glick. And why wouldn't he quit teasing her about her glasses? Paul liked them. Dan turned them into a joke.

Paul stiffened beside her as if someone had rammed a pole down the length of his spine. There was probably no one Paul hated more than Dan. His dislike stemmed from the fact that Dan had been so mean to Lily in school. It pleased her that Paul was ever the loyal friend.

Dan's smile was as wide as Shawano Lake as he jogged to catch up to them. He carried a plastic shopping bag in one hand, which he held out to show her. His grin dimmed briefly as he gave Paul a furtive glance, but it came back with full force within seconds. "This is perfect timing. I just bought this for you."

Her heart fluttered. She felt torn between being charmed that Dan the Mean Boy had bought her yet another gift and sheer panic that Paul would find out about the whole reading-together thing.

"Hullo, Dan," Paul said, his tone a taut wire of resentment.

"*Gute maiya,* Paul," Dan said, without even looking at him. He kept grinning at Lily. "That dress brings out the green in your eyes. They're so pretty, like looking into a lake."

Paul took a step closer to Lily so his sleeve touched hers. "Lily doesn't care to be called 'pretty.' "

Well, she *shouldn't* care to be called pretty.

Ach. She attempted to ignore the thrill of pleasure that traveled up her spine. Pure vanity; that's what it was.

"It's too bad she is pretty then," Dan said cheerfully, but almost daring Paul to contradict him. "She's going to hear it a lot." He gave up on the subject of Lily's appearance and jiggled his plastic bag. "Can I show you the gift I bought you?"

Lily glanced down at the half-eaten doughnut in one hand and the untouched doughnut in the other. Whatever the gift, she wouldn't be able to hold it.

She hadn't thought it possible to hold her breath and speak at the same time. "Do you want one?" she said. It was rude to hog all the doughnuts for herself.

Every time she thought Dan's smile was as wide as it could go, he surprised her. "Sure," he said, taking half her lunch.

Well, she *had* offered it to him.

She reached into her apron pocket and pulled out a napkin while he made a third of the doughnut disappear in one bite. "Must be one of Yutzy's," he said.

She nodded.

"They make the best doughnuts."

"My *mamm* makes the best rolls," Paul muttered.

"*Jah.* Her rolls are wonderful-*gute,*" Dan said, with a look of good-natured forbearance. He finished off the doughnut just like that and wiped the sticky glaze from his hands. Having dispensed with the doughnut, he reached in the bag and retrieved a boxed set of books. He held it up for her to see. "*Little House on the Prairie.* Nine-book set."

"Oh," Lily said, a bit *ferhoodled.* He'd

bought them for her? They couldn't have been cheap.

"Edith at the book shop says the first one takes place in Wisconsin."

"It does," she said, almost reverently. The *Little House on the Prairie* books had been some of her best childhood friends, especially after her parents died.

"I know they're for children, but I thought maybe you'd like them. Edith says I can return them if you don't."

Lily didn't know what to say. Dan was practically a stranger to her. Why would he do this? "It's . . . it's too much, Dan. I can't accept this."

He suddenly seemed uncertain, young, like a little boy who had drawn a picture for the teacher he had a secret crush on. "Have you read them? I really wanted to get something you'd like."

Even though profoundly aware of Paul standing beside her, disapproving and stiff, as if rigor mortis had set in, Lily couldn't let Dan believe for one minute that she didn't appreciate such a beautiful gift. "I . . . I love them."

The uncertainty fled from his face, and his smile could have lit up a dark room.

She handed Paul her half doughnut, ignoring the hard line of indignation on his lips and the glint of utter surprise in his eyes. She took the box from Dan and read the titles. *"By the Shores of Silver Lake* is my favorite."

Dan traced his finger down the space between two of the books. Were his hands trembling? What did he have to be nervous about? "Mammi had a set of these on her bookshelf. Aunt Rebecca took them back to Wautoma with her."

Paul was a barely controlled eruption. He firmly, petulantly, slipped the box from Lily's hands and handed it back to Dan. "She already said she can't accept it. Don't make her uncomfortable by insisting."

Embarrassed by Paul's rudeness, Lily nearly reached out and snatched the books back. Paul despised Dan, but there was no reason to talk to him like that. Instead, she assumed a posture of humility and lowered her eyes. Paul probably saw her courteous conversation with Dan as a slap in the face.

She couldn't lift her eyes to look at him, but Dan's voice sounded like a flat glass of soda. "I see I shouldn't have interrupted." He slipped the books back into his bag. Lily closed her lips on a plaintive sigh.

Why should she regret the books? She'd already read them.

"I'm taking her to lunch at my restaurant,"

Paul said, the boast apparent in his tone.

"I hope you have a nice time," Dan said, as if he were talking about a trip to the hospital for appendix removal.

Lily raised her head and dared a look at Dan. She saw a tinge of sadness in his eyes, but thank goodness, he didn't seem angry with her.

He lifted his eyebrows as if he were attempting more cheerfulness than he felt. "Maybe I'll see you both tomorrow at the gathering?"

"We're busy," Paul said. "Aren't we, Lily?"

She knew what he expected. He expected her to turn up her nose at Dan Kanagy and send him packing with one scowl. But she couldn't be that rude when Dan was being so nice. "I think I'm busy," she said, her voice barely above a whisper. She showed him a polite smile to temper her words.

The lines around his frown relaxed slightly. "Maybe we'll see you some other time."

"*Jah.* Maybe."

He turned and marched back the way he had come, and she said a little prayer of gratitude that he hadn't mentioned that they had an arrangement to discuss *Where the Red Fern Grows.* Paul would have erupted again.

Guilt lodged in her throat like a dry doughnut hole. She shouldn't keep such a secret from her boyfriend. But why should she unduly upset the boyfriend when there was nothing for him to be upset about?

She didn't notice the silence between them until she turned to see Paul looking at her as if he had a sour stomach. "He likes you," he said, as if everything Dan Kanagy had done were her fault.

"I read to his *mammi* before she died. He's grateful, that's all. Maybe he's sorry for how he used to treat me."

"*Used to* treat you? He called you 'Coke Bottle.' "

Lily shrugged. It hadn't hurt so bad. "I know, but he was nice after that."

Paul looked at her as if she'd said something completely idiotic. "Nice? Lily, Dan Kanagy isn't nice. He's called you all sorts of bad names. He's a cheat and a liar. You can't defend that."

She should have just let it die. It was never a good idea to correct Paul. Dan may have teased her mercilessly, but he couldn't have been kinder to his *mamm*i. He'd weeded Poppy's flowers. He'd braved the bees to bring Lily a book. She deeply doubted he was a liar or a cheat even if his *dat* was. "Dan didn't cheat your *dat.*"

"His whole family was in on it. You don't know anything, Lily."

Paul had told her the story so many times, she had it memorized. Instead of seeking to forgive, Paul wore the Kanagys' insult like a badge of honor.

She fingered the strings of her *kapp* and tried to be more sympathetic. Paul's family had been wounded deeply. "I'm sorry. I'm not questioning that it happened."

"John Kanagy bought thirty acres from us with the strict agreement that we would buy it back in two years. He needed it for two years, he said. We agreed that he was only renting it from us. But when the time came to get the land back, John demanded five times what we had sold it for. We couldn't afford to buy it back. We nearly lost everything because of that land."

Jah, she'd heard the story. Dan figured nowhere in it. But she wasn't going to argue with him anymore.

"I was only twelve," Paul said. "But Dat trusted my judgment. Every time I saw Dan at school he'd tell me, 'Don't worry. We'll help you out. We'll make it right.' I believed him. My *dat* believed him. If we had known how dishonest the Kanagys were, we never would have sold that property." He slid an arm around her shoulder and nudged her in the direction of the restaurant. He ran touched her, so she knew he was seriou "Don't be deceived because he's handsome Lily. He is a wolf in sheep's clothing. Don't forget all those names he called you." Paul looked away and chewed on his thumbnail. "He called you even worse names behind your back."

Lily's throat suddenly felt raw. "He did?"

Paul kept his eyes turned away. "He said you were ugly as a dog and that you belonged with the pigs instead of with the other girls at school."

Lily felt as if she'd been slapped as the pain of school came rushing back, making her head spin and her stomach lurch. The surrounding air became moist and oppressively hot, and she couldn't catch a breath.

Paul nodded smugly. "Dan Kanagy is rotten to the bone. You'd be wise to stay far away from him and burn any books he gives you."

"I will," Lily said, determined to go home and at least consider burning *Where the Red Fern Grows*.

Paul bent his mouth into a thoughtful scowl. "He wants something from you. I wouldn't be surprised if he and his shifty *fater* try to buy your property right out from under you."

ught of Dan's enthusiasm at see-
rm. Was he interested in their
A seed of doubt grew. "They can't
We own our farm free and clear."
on't be caught off guard if they try, and
n't believe any of his promises." Paul
seemed to have forgotten how hungry he
was. He slowed his pace as they got closer
to the restaurant. "I'm worried for you, Lily.
Dan is only interested because you're not
ugly anymore. Don't be tempted by all his
talk of green eyes. He's found your weak-
ness. Don't let him feed your vanity."

Even though his words stung, she knew
she deserved the lecture. She felt so grateful
for a friend like Paul. He would never dream
of feeding her vanity.

CHAPTER SIX

Dan blew into his house like a tornado, itching to give the door a good, hard shove and rattle all the windows. He didn't. With his knuckles white around the doorknob, he shut the door as gently as if a baby were sleeping just inside.

He had to do something with his hands or his blood would boil over. Steam was probably coming out of his ears.

He stormed into the kitchen. A stack of dirty dishes sat in the sink. Perfect. He would have smiled if he hadn't been in such a terrible mood. He could take out his frustration on the dinner plates. After emptying the sink and plugging the drain, he filled the sink with steaming hot water and about three tablespoons of soap. Bubbles. He wanted lots of annoying bubbles.

Even though as a Christian he should love everyone, Dan had never been able to stomach Paul Glick. Paul was the boy who always thought he was right. Always *had* to be right — the kind who dug in his heels harder when someone proved him wrong or questioned his pompous intelligence.

Dan scrubbed his rag across the plates with a vengeance. Pompous intelligence and unbearable arrogance.

He who is angry with his brother is in danger of hellfire, or something like that. He took a deep breath to calm his racing pulse. It didn't help.

In eighth grade when Dan had started taking an interest in Lily Christner, Paul had too. At recess, Paul would drag Lily to the far corner of the playground and they'd sit and talk while the rest of the boys played baseball or Kick the Can. Dan had never been able to understand what Lily saw in Paul, but from eighth grade on, they were fast friends.

For his own sanity, he'd tried to keep clear of Lily Christner. It had been plain as day that she and Paul were destined to marry, and Dan hadn't really wanted to make a fool of himself chasing after another boy's fianceé. He had hoped that two years in Pennsylvania would dull his interest, but Mammi wrote so often of Lily and their time spent reading together, he couldn't quite achieve indifference.

And now he had returned, and Lily was as beautiful as ever, and he couldn't stand the way Paul treated her — as if she were someone he had to beat down to make himself bigger, someone small and insignificant who shouldn't be allowed to make her own decisions or spread her wings and fly. And Paul had succeeded in convincing Lily it was true. Dan saw it plain as midday that she honestly believed she didn't deserve any better than Paul Glick.

Not that Dan was a great catch or anything like that. Lily deserved better than him too. She deserved the best man in Wisconsin. She was certainly the best girl.

Dan growled and dumped another stack of dishes into the sink. If he'd stayed away from Lily after Mammi's funeral like he'd promised himself he would, his feelings for her wouldn't have resurfaced and he wouldn't be standing here pushing plates around the sink, up to his elbows in bubbles.

"Have a bad day?"

He snapped his head around. Mamm stood in the doorway holding a recipe and a bottle of cooking oil. "What makes you think I had a bad day?"

"You clean when you're angry."

"I clean when I'm not angry too."

"It's true," Mamm said. "I trained you

85

well. You're one of my best helpers. But from the way plates have been clattering around in here, it sounds like you're a hairbreadth away from hurling a few at the wall."

"You probably wouldn't like that."

"Probably not."

Dan pulled a bowl from the water and washed it as if it were a fragile crystal figurine. He smirked at Mamm. "Is that better?"

Mamm cocked an eyebrow. "Wonderful-*gute*. Did you buy the chocolate chips yet?"

If there'd been any other store in town that sold chocolate chips, he wouldn't have had to patronize the Glick Family Amish Market. The thought of contributing any money to Paul Glick's prosperous future made him ill. In addition to the little trip to the store, he'd spent way too much on books Lily would never read and had been cut down to size by a big-headed, self-righteous fool. The trip into town had been very productive.

Whosoever shall say to his brother, thou fool, shall be in danger of the council. Dan didn't know exactly what "the council" was, but he might be willing to risk it if it allowed him to stay mad at Paul forever.

His anger distracted him from the depressing thought that pretty Lily Christner would be miserable married to Paul Glick. All those bright sparks of joy and beauty would be snuffed out within a year. Dan clenched his teeth. He couldn't stand to think about it. Better to be angry.

He pressed too hard and one of Mamm's dinner plates cracked in his hand. He shoved it back under the water so Mamm wouldn't see.

"Well, did you?"

"Did I what?" Dan said, trying to remember what his *mamm* had just asked him.

"Get chocolate chips."

"Jah." He slumped his shoulders. "I left them in the buggy."

Mamm curled one side of her mouth. "At least they made it home."

Dan pulled his hands out of the water. They were covered in bubbles. "I'll get them."

"I'll go," Mamm said with a wink. "I want you to finish those dishes. But don't break any more of them." She turned as if to go outside and then turned back. "But first, tell me what you're so upset about."

He didn't want Mamm to know what a fool he was being over a girl who already had somebody else. "It's nothing. I'm already over it."

"What's her name?"

"What?"

"Nothing is as frustrating as a girl."

"I can't believe you'd admit that, Mamm, since you're a girl."

Mamm bloomed into one of her teasing smiles. "I'm not saying we're not worth it."

Worth it? Lily Christner was definitely worth it. With her hair the color of dark amber honey and her eyes all kinds of green and blue, she stole his breath every time she looked his way. Lily was kindness and radiance and light all wrapped up in a cute, irresistible package. He couldn't help but smile when he was around her. Her joy was infectious. Paul hadn't killed it yet.

Dan loved everything about Lily, but that didn't mean he should keep making a fool of himself, not when she and Paul were probably engaged already. It was unfortunate that Dan had been the one they sent to fetch Lily when Mammi had died. That encounter with Lily had been his downfall. She was too wonderful not to hope for.

He couldn't remember exactly how it had happened, but ever since he was eleven or twelve he'd had a crush on her. He didn't mind that she could beat him and every other boy reciting times tables or spelling words like *chrysanthemum*. He admired her sharp mind and abundance of freckles.

Not to mention how she had always treated the little kids. They'd flock around her at recess, and she would tell them stories and recite poems. Recite poems! He had barely been able to memorize his address.

The day before he'd left for Pennsylvania, he'd gone to Mammi's house to say goodbye. He'd walked in the front door and heard Lily in the next room reading a book to his *mammi*. He'd stood in the hallway for nearly fifteen minutes captivated by Lily's voice. She had been reading a story about sheep and buttons, and Mammi had chuckled and sighed every few sentences. Standing in the entryway of his *mammi*'s house, he nearly burst with longing. He could have sat all day and listened to Lily read the dictionary.

Dan rinsed the last plate while Mamm stared at him, waiting for him to spill the beans about some mystery girl. What could he tell her? He'd rather be the only witness to his total failure with Lily Christner.

"It's not so much the girl," he finally said. "It's the boy she's engaged to."

Mamm winced. "No wonder you're frustrated."

"I know what you're going to tell me. I

should forget her and move on."

"Easy to say. Hard to do." Mamm laid her recipe and oil on the table. "If we send you to Ohio, my cousin Owen could find you a wife."

"That trick didn't work out so well in Pennsylvania."

Smiling, Mamm folded her arms and dared Dan to contradict her. "It wasn't a trick. We sent you to Onkel Titus and Aendi Barbara's to learn how to care for cattle. Your finding a bride would have been a wonderful-*gute* bonus."

Dan shook his head and stifled a grin. Aunt Barbara had introduced him to a new girl almost every week. She had insisted he write to his *mamm* regularly and give her updates on his love life. No doubt they had conspired to find him a wife.

Mamm came close, got on her tiptoes, and laid a loud kiss on his cheek. "I'm sorry about the girl with the fiancé. It hurts to like someone who doesn't like you back."

Jah. It hurt something wonderful. An ache deep in his chest that throbbed whenever he saw Lily Christner.

"And there's nothing I can do about it," he said.

Mamm tilted her head to one side. "She's engaged?"

"Maybe not. She has this longtime boy-friend, but they might not be engaged yet."

She pressed her lips together as if deciding whether to say anything. "It would be better to forget her, Daniel."

"I know, but I can't. I don't want to — at least not until she's married to that . . . other boy."

Mamm huffed out a breath. "I can't believe I'm encouraging this, but make yourself available but not annoying. Give her a chance to get to know you. If she still chooses the other boy then she doesn't deserve you."

"I don't deserve her."

"She already has a boyfriend, so no one must suspect that you're trying to court her. Be her friend. Make friends with her sisters and aunt. Be yourself. Any girl in the world will fall in love with you if you just be your own wonderful self."

"Her sisters and aunt?"

Mamm smiled sheepishly and shrugged. "I see it plain as the wart on Dawdi David's nose. You couldn't take your eyes off her when she came to Mammi's."

"You think I'm *deerich*, foolish."

"She is a sweet girl. We all love her for how considerate she was to your *mammi*.

91

But Paul Glick has his hooks in her but good."

Something raw and fierce flared inside his chest. He stepped away from the plates. "You should see the way he treats her, Mamm, as if she was his property instead of his girlfriend."

Mamm shook her head. "I'd ask why she lets him do that, but I already know the answer. A girl starts to believe she doesn't deserve any better. It's the way with Martha Glick, Paul's *mater.* Since the day they married, Paul's *dat* wore her down until she doesn't even know she's a daughter of Christ anymore."

"But why would Lily be friends with Paul in the first place?"

"Lily has a kind heart. Maybe Paul needed a friend. Maybe Lily needed a friend."

Dan frowned. "Lily has plenty of friends. Everybody likes Lily."

"Maybe she wanted a boy to pay attention to her."

He threw up his hands. "I paid attention to her. I did a lot of stupid things to try to get her to notice me."

Mamm's lips twitched. "Maybe she thought you were stupid."

Dan chuckled in spite of himself. "I'm sure she did." To keep his frustrated hands busy, he picked up a dish towel and started drying. Carefully. "I don't want to be stupid now."

Mamm sighed, a gruff, it's-a-lost-cause sigh from deep in her throat. "Mostly, it would be better if you just let her alone. I'd rather not see you hurt."

Dan bowed his head. "I'd rather not see me hurt either, but it will hurt worse if I don't try."

Mamm gave him a firm pat on the arm. "Then give it a try. And try not to break anything."

CHAPTER SEVEN

Lily unhitched Queenie from the buggy and made a beeline for the house. She was famished. A doughnut and half of the roll Paul didn't want hadn't even made a dent in her hunger. She deeply regretted giving a doughnut to Dan, mostly because she thought she might die of malnutrition, but partly because he had said such ugly things about her in school. He hadn't deserved that doughnut.

Upon thinking of Dan, a lump of coal settled in the pit of her stomach and her feet felt as heavy as if she were wading through a meadow of honey. She'd never make it to lifesaving food if her feet were stuck fast.

The smell of something substantial and delicious wafted from the house, giving her the determination to make it up the porch steps. She practically threw open the door and stumbled into the kitchen. Home.

Nothing felt as good as home.

With spoon in hand, Aunt B stood at the stove stirring something in a large sauce pot. Poppy kneaded dough at the island. Nothing soothed a bad day like Poppy's homemade honey wheat bread. Rose stood next to Poppy, cutting out heart-shaped sugar cookies, no doubt to give to one of the neighbors. Rose was thoughtful like that. It was said that people in town scheduled unnecessary surgeries just so they'd get a plate of Rose Christner's treats. Aunt Bitsy had taught them how to cook, and all three of the Honeybee Sisters enjoyed making goodies in the kitchen, especially if they could be together.

Aunt B turned when she heard the door open and gave Lily an affectionate lift of her eyebrows, which said "I love you" better than any words could convey.

Lily took one look at Aunt B and forgot why she'd been so depressed. She giggled under her breath. Gawdy gold earrings hung from Aunt B's ears. They were so long, they brushed against her shoulders when she turned her head and tinkled softly with every movement. They looked oddly out of place next to her plain white *kapp* and drab gray dress, and they were altogether out of place in an Amish home, but Aunt B loved

95

her earrings. She'd amassed quite a collection when she'd lived as an *Englischer,* and she'd told her girls that she couldn't bear to throw them away.

"I like your earrings, Aunt B," Lily said. If they made Aunt B happy, they made Lily happy.

Aunt B fingered the post attached to her earlobe. "I wore these to my first Van Halen concert, 1986."

Even though earrings would in no way meet with the bishop's approval, Aunt B pulled them out occasionally and wore them around the house. They brought her so much pleasure, and neither Lily nor her sisters would ever dream of tattling.

On bad days, she wore three earrings in each ear and sang strange *Englisch* songs that Lily had become familiar with.

"I'm starving. Is there anything to eat?"

"Dinner's not for two hours yet," Poppy said.

Lily was so desperate, she considered pinching off a glob of Poppy's bread dough and stuffing it into her mouth. Instead, she went to the fridge, examined the shelves of sparse leftovers, and pulled out a dish of peas from last night's supper. Beggars couldn't be choosers. After grabbing a spoon from the drawer, she sat at the table with her snack and shoveled cold peas into her mouth.

Rose giggled and handed Lily a scoop of cookie dough. "You can have as much as you want."

Aunt B pressed her lips together as if she were ready to scold someone but didn't have anyone to scold. "Did he take you to the restaurant again?"

Lily nodded and trained her eyes on her glob of cookie dough. She wouldn't be so ungrateful as to roll her eyes behind Paul's back. "He shared half his roll."

Aunt B turned back to her steaming pot. "That boy," she muttered.

Lily didn't want Aunt B to think badly of Paul. He was her future husband, probably, and she wanted her *aendi* to be wildly enthusiastic about the boy she married. Even though it was hard to come by, Aunt B's approval meant everything to Lily. "It's not really his fault. His family can't afford to feed me every time we go to the restaurant, and I didn't bring enough money to pay for my own meal."

"Don't worry, Lily," Rose said, placing the last of her cookies on the pan. "Aunt Bitsy wouldn't approve of Paul even if he were one of the blessed apostles."

"That's right," said Aunt Bitsy without

turning around. "Nobody is good enough for my girls."

Lily's mouth curved upward. That thought made her feel strangely better. Aunt B was cranky about boys in general; the three boys who had hung around Poppy last winter, the delivery boy who'd tried to flirt with Rose, and the bishop's son who acted interested in all three of them. Paul was no exception.

"Your meeting with Paul went wonderful-long," Poppy said with an air of nonchalance. "Did he want to do some kissing afterward?"

Aunt B puckered her lips into what passed for a stern look. "Nobody is allowed to do any kissing in this house."

Poppy's eyes sparkled mischievously. "That's okay, B. They weren't in our house."

With her earrings tinkling merrily, Aunt B half growled, half laughed and swatted Poppy on the bottom with a spatula. "I'm watching you closest of all, Priscilla. Absolutely no kissing."

Poppy squeaked, giggled, and went back to her bread dough. "No need to watch me. Boys are stupid. I'd have to scrub my lips off."

"I wouldn't dare kiss a boy," Rose said, glancing doubtfully at her sisters. "I'd have to have a conversation with him first, and the thought of talking to a boy scares me to death."

"Who says you'd have to have a conversation first?" Poppy replied, pumping her eyebrows up and down.

Rose drew in a breath in amused shock. Lily laughed at the look on Aunt B's face.

Aunt B smothered a smile and jabbed her spatula in the air toward Poppy. "I'm watching you the closest."

Poppy ignored Aunt B and leaned toward Lily with her hands pressed against the countertop. "So, *were* you kissing?"

Lily swallowed hard. Kissing Paul sounded like eating a spoonful of shortening. Why would she want to?

She knit her brows together. Would she have to talk herself into the idea?

She forced a smile and tried to put the thought of Paul's lips out of her mind. "Paul and I have never kissed."

Aunt B turned her face to the ceiling. "*Denki,* Lord. I was beginning to think You hadn't heard my prayer this morning."

Lily giggled. "You prayed that I wouldn't kiss Paul today?"

Aunt Bitsy curled one side of her mouth. "I prayed that He would keep you from the Valley of the Shadow of Death. Same thing."

Kissing Paul wouldn't be as bad as a walk through the Valley of the Shadow of Death. Would it? All the same, she was grateful to Aunt B for the prayer. It couldn't have hurt.

"After we ate, Paul wanted to show me some of the new products they're carrying at the market. They're buying a new freezer, so he showed me where it will go. The bishop has approved it." Many Amish businesses used electricity and phones. Glick's market was nearly as modern as the Walmart in Shawano.

She didn't mention that Paul had also taken her back to his house to show her where he was going to build a house. He already had a floor plan mapped out and wanted to show her where everything in the house would be.

If she mentioned the property, the conversation would inevitably turn to why Paul wanted to build a house and if Lily planned on getting married this fall. They were questions she didn't want to answer. Questions she didn't even have the answers to.

Aunt B threw a pinch of salt into her pot and looked up. "I almost forgot. I wish I could forget. That other boy brought something for you."

Lily's chest tightened. "What other boy?"

"That one boy who steps on dandelions

and calls you names."

Oh. That boy.

Aunt B searched briefly, as if she couldn't remember where she'd put it, then found it under one of the pillows on the window seat. "He begged me to be sure to give it to you."

The tightening in the chest joined a sinking feeling in her stomach as she recognized the box. The entire nine-book *Little House on the Prairie* set. He was mocking her — mocking the ugly girl because her boyfriend had dared to stand up to him.

She bit down on her tongue to keep the tears from pooling in her eyes. Who cared what Dan Kanagy thought?

"He seemed upset. He probably stepped on my dandelions and didn't want me to know . . ." Aunt B paused midsentence and studied Lily's face.

Lifting her gaze, Rose gasped. She immediately rushed to Lily's side. Poppy weaved around the island and put an arm around Lily as if she thought she might faint.

"What's wrong, little sister?" Aunt Bitsy said, pulling up a chair and reaching out for Lily's hand. "Little sister" was what Aunt Bitsy called her when things were really bad.

Lily obviously wasn't very good at hiding

her distress.

She huffed out a breath, embarrassed that she let the name-calling upset her. "Dan said something horrible." Even though she'd heard it for the first time today, Dan had said the ugly words years ago. They had both been fourteen years old. It was plenty long to hold a grudge.

Poppy squeezed her shoulder. "I knew I should have shoved him harder the other day."

"Oh dear," Rose murmured, oozing compassion as she sat next to Aunt B at the table.

Lily couldn't resist all that sympathy. She burst into tears and buried her face in Aunt B's neck.

Aunt B rubbed Lily's earlobe between her thumb and forefinger. "There, there. Sticks and stones may break my bones, but a shotgun would really do the trick on that boy."

Lily laughed in spite of herself.

"I'm serious," Aunt B said.

She wasn't really, but she'd made Lily smile.

"I should have followed my instincts that first night and refused to let him in the house," Aunt B said.

"Did you see him in town today?" Poppy

asked. Lily could see the wheels turning in her head — probably resolving to accompany Lily wherever she went to protect her from stupid boys.

Lily's nose started running. Rose handed her a tissue. "He wasn't mean today. Paul told me that when we were in school Dan said I was ugly as a dog and that I belonged with the pigs instead of the other students."

Poppy squeezed Lily's shoulder so hard, her fingers felt like a pair of carpenter clamps. "B, if you won't use the shotgun, I just might."

Rose reached across the table and took Lily's hand. "You know that isn't true. You're as pretty as a garden of gladiolas."

"And too good for a boy like Dan Kanagy," Poppy said. Lily could already see her plotting revenge. How she loved her sisters!

The lines around Aunt B's mouth deepened. "Why would Paul tell you that?"

"He's my friend."

Another line appeared between Aunt B's eyebrows, as deep as if someone had taken a plow to her face. "A true friend would never hurt you like that."

"Paul didn't say it. Dan did."

"But there was no reason for Paul to repeat it, especially when it happened years ago and hurt your feelings. You didn't need to know."

"But, B," Poppy said, "it's not Paul's fault."

Aunt B shook her head. "It *is* Paul's fault. The only reason Lily is crying is because of what Paul told her."

Taken aback by Aunt B's reaction, Lily sort of tripped over her own tongue. "But if someone said something bad about you, wouldn't you want to know?"

Aunt B folded her arms. "*Nae.* It would only upset me, and then I'd have one more person on my long list of people I need to forgive. Cruel words are always better left unsaid and unrepeated."

Lily opened her mouth to argue but promptly closed it and studied the *Little House on the Prairie* books Aunt B had set on the table. Not only did Paul have a good memory about something that happened years ago, but he had seemed quite eager to share the bad news with Lily.

It was plain he didn't want Lily to have anything to do with Dan or his books, but could his contempt for Dan be more important to him than Lily's feelings? The thought sliced right through her heart.

She shook her head. How could she even entertain the idea that Paul deliberately wanted to hurt her? He would never do that. Aunt B simply didn't understand. Paul thought Lily was being too friendly with Dan — she'd given him one of her precious doughnuts, hadn't she? — and Paul simply wanted to remind her of the kind of boy Dan really was. He didn't want her to make a fool of herself with someone who thought she was as ugly as a dog.

"Paul never liked Dan," Lily finally murmured.

Aunt B slapped the table. "Well, I don't like either of them. One's too big for his britches, and one's too small for his mouth."

Lily almost smiled. Aunt B had never met a boy she liked.

Fire seemed to spew from Poppy's mouth. "I hope he comes to the gathering tomorrow night. I've half a mind to give him a knuckle sandwich."

Lily held up her hand. "No one is giving anyone a knuckle sandwich."

Poppy frowned. "It's just an expression."

Aunt B sighed as if she felt it was her duty rather than her desire to correct Poppy. "A good Amish girl has taken a vow of nonviolence and does not talk about giving someone a knuckle sandwich, even if he deserves a mouthful of your fist."

"I used to punch Dan Kanagy almost

every day in school," Poppy said.

"Every day?" Aunt B said.

"Every day that he made Lily cry. He never fought back, never ran away, and never told Teacher; just stood there and grinned like he thought I was funny."

"He probably did think it was funny that a sixth grader tried to beat up a boy five inches taller than her," Lily said.

"I guess," Poppy said. "He didn't get mad about it. Not like Ben Mast who tattled on me after every recess or Vernon Beiler who gave me a shiner and a fat lip."

Aunt Bitsy's mouth fell open. "That was Vernon? You told me you fell coming home from school."

"B, I never fell coming home from school."

Aunt B shook her head. "I should have known. My visits with the teacher were an almost weekly event."

"I had to defend my sisters, didn't I? Lily from the teasers and Rose from any boy who scared her."

"But you know you can't punch Dan Kanagy now?" Rose said, seeming uncertain and a little afraid that Poppy might say no.

Poppy puckered her lips in frustration and blew an errant wisp of hair out of her eyes. "I know. But I'm going to give him a good talking-to."

Lily wiped the leftover tears from her eyes. "No, you won't. Dan Kanagy doesn't even care."

When Poppy lifted her chin like that, there would be no talking her out of anything. "We'll see how much he cares after I've yelled at him."

Lily loved Poppy for wanting to defend her, but confronting Dan might cause a terrible scene at the gathering, and for what? "Please don't yell at him, Poppy. For my sake. Think of the attention you'll draw. Like Aunt B said, cruel words should never be said or repeated. No one needs to be reminded how ugly I am."

Aunt B looked as if she were an angry bull seeing red. "Ugly? Don't ever say that about yourself, little sister. My girls are the prettiest girls in Wisconsin."

Lily propped her elbow on the table and leaned her chin in her hand, in a casual gesture meant to show Aunt B that she wasn't upset. At least she could pretend. "It doesn't hurt my feelings that Poppy and Rose are beautiful and I'm not."

Rose looked positively stricken. "Lily, you are a hundred times prettier than I am."

"It's not bad to be ugly. Paul says it's hard to be humble if you're pretty."

Aunt B gave a throaty grunt. "That boy."

Poppy snorted. "I'm sure all the out-of-town boys at the Memorial Day auction stared at you because you looked so humble."

"They weren't staring."

Poppy smirked. "Lily, you can't see what's right in front of your face."

"Probably because we have one mirror in this house, and it's the size of a DVD," Aunt B said.

"You'll see," Poppy said. "At the gathering tomorrow night, notice how many boys secretly steal a look at you."

Even amidst her frustration, Lily couldn't suppress a grin. "If they do it secretly, I'll never notice."

Poppy rolled her eyes and gave Lily a nudge. "You know what I mean."

"I'm not going to the gathering anyway," Lily said. "So I won't be able to prove you wrong."

Rose's face brightened. "If you're not going, then I'm not going."

Aunt B seemed to perk up as well. "*Gute* idea. Keep away from the boys. You can all stay home and help me scrub toilets yet."

Poppy caught Lily's eye, and her gaze could have seared a hole through the entire *Little House on the Prairie* collection. Lily knew exactly what Poppy was thinking. Lily had just given Rose an excuse for missing another gathering. How were they ever going to help her overcome her fear of people if she locked herself in the house with nothing but her paintings and recipes for company?

Rose had only been five when their parents died in a car accident, and she had barely spoken a word for over a year after. Two years later, she had witnessed an ugly case of child abuse within the community. She'd been so traumatized that she hadn't trusted men ever since. Because of her sisters and Aunt B, Rose had made more progress this last year than ever before. As long as her sisters were with her, she would agree to go to gatherings and *singeons,* and last week, Lily had seen her actually visiting with a boy after *gmay.*

Rose had even said a few words to Dan Kanagy. Lily stopped to consider how unusual that had been. Why hadn't she noticed the day it happened? When Aunt B or one of her sisters was around to speak for her, Rose seldom said anything, yet she had asked Dan about his *mammi.*

Strange and wonderful-*gute.*

Lily would have to swallow her selfishness and go to the gathering. Rose's happiness was more important than Lily's pride. Paul would disapprove of pride. But he would also disapprove of her attending the gathering when they had both told Dan earlier today that they wouldn't be going.

She took a deep breath. It didn't matter about Paul. It didn't even matter about Dan Kanagy. They *had* to go for Rose's sake. "You know how eager I am to scrub toilets, Aunt B," Lily said. "But Lorene asked Rosie to bring a cake. We don't want to disappoint her."

Rose's lips drooped. "I could send the cake with Poppy."

"Nonsense," Poppy said. "You're going. You have to take your cake, and I have to pick a bone with Dan Kanagy."

Lily shot darts at Poppy with her eyes. "Don't you dare. I'm already embarrassed enough as it is."

Aunt B's eyes seemed to be dancing beneath all that scowling she was doing. "Keep away from the boys. They fall in love with you girls and come over and trample my dandelions. I'd rather they stay home."

A puff of air escaped from between Lily's lips. "Don't worry, Aunt B. Nobody is going to fall in love with 'Coke Bottle.' "

Aunt B shook her finger in Lily's direction, making her rather large earrings tinkle softly. "That's precisely what I'm afraid of."

Rose caught her breath and squealed as if she'd been pinched. "A mouse! Aunt Bitsy, did you see that mouse?"

Lily jumped from her chair as a tiny streak of brown fur raced along the wall and disappeared into the storage room. Rose leaped onto the window seat. Poppy, who prided herself on not being afraid of anything, ran to save her bread even though the mouse hadn't been on the cupboard. Cradling the lump of dough in her arms, she hopped in the air like a bunny rabbit and landed sitting on the counter, sending a puff of flour into the air. Poppy was brave, but even she couldn't stand mice. Sometimes they crawled into the hives in the winter and were killed by the bees. A dead mouse at the bottom of a beehive was never a pleasant sight. It gave Lily the creepy-crawlies.

Aunt B was the only one who didn't panic. She jumped from her chair and snatched the meat cleaver from the block. "Oh, *sis yuscht,* where is that cat?"

Right on cue, Farrah Fawcett strolled into the kitchen as if she hadn't smelled a mouse in the house for years. She sauntered to the window seat, looked up, and eyed Rose indignantly. Rose was perched on Farrah Fawcett's soft, fluffy bed. It was obviously an insult to her dignity.

"Farrah Fawcett," Aunt B scolded. "You have one job in this house, and you are failing miserably." She pointed the meat cleaver in the direction of the storage room. "Go get that mouse."

Farrah Fawcett merely twitched her whiskers and stared up at Rose, waiting for an apology.

Aunt B narrowed her eyes and shook her head. "You are a testament to my failure as a cat trainer."

Rose stepped down from the window seat and gathered Farrah Fawcett in her arms. "You poor little kitty," Rose said in her most sympathetic voice. Farrah Fawcett merely turned her face from any affection and tried to ignore the disgrace of being treated like a baby.

"B, we should set some traps," Poppy said.

Aunt B nodded. "Either that or I'm going to have to get very fast with this meat cleaver, because that cat is no help."

Lily laughed. "Farrah Fawcett might not be useful, but at least she's pretty."

"Useful is much better," Aunt B said.

Lily took a deep breath. Useful was much better. She should be happy with what *Gotte* had allotted to her.

CHAPTER EIGHT

He shouldn't have come. Gatherings were for teenagers, and Lily had said she would be *busy.* There wasn't any reason for him to be here. Mamm liked it when he went to gatherings with Reuben and Leanna so he could watch out for his brother and sister and make sure they didn't get into any trouble, although what trouble they could get into in the deacon's backyard was a mystery to Dan.

He thumbed his suspenders as he ambled around the yard and watched *die youngie* play croquet and volleyball, games he didn't have the enthusiasm for tonight. Not only had Lily not shown up, but neither Luke nor Josiah, his two best friends, were there. He should just go and take the buggy with him. Reuben and Leanna could catch a ride home with one of the neighbors. Dan could go home and do some dishes.

But that probably wouldn't make him feel better.

Suddenly, like the clouds parting after a storm, Lily Christner and her sisters strolled into the backyard. Lily looked like morning sunlight in her pale yellow dress. Dan couldn't take his eyes off her, even though he knew he shouldn't stare into the sun.

Lily with Poppy, in a royal blue dress, walked on either side of Rose as if they were her guardian angels. Dan wouldn't be surprised if Lily were an angel. She was pretty enough. Rose looked young and innocent in light pink. She carried a cake as if afraid she'd drop it, a mixture of anxiety and reservation on her face.

He didn't know quite what came over him, unless it was plain, unbridled happiness, but he lost all sense of restraint. "Hey, Amtrak," he yelled, so loudly that all the dogs in a twenty-mile radius could have heard him. Lots of heads turned as he jogged toward the sisters.

Okay, he didn't jog. He ran. He shouldn't have run. It made him seem pathetically desperate, but in all his elation, he couldn't hold back.

When he got closer, he realized he shouldn't have charged at them with so much enthusiasm. Rose's eyes widened, and she raised the cake in front of her like a shield. Poppy scowled and propped her hands on her hips as if preparing for a fight, and Lily turned pale.

When he saw their reactions, he slowed to a walk and willed his lungs to quit pushing against his rib cage and his mouth to quit smiling so wide. This was no way to sneak up on Lily Christner's heart. He couldn't do anything about the smile. Whenever he saw Lily, his lips naturally spread to their maximum length. She could probably count all his teeth.

"Hi, Lily. I didn't think you were going to come."

She wouldn't look at him. Poppy grunted her disapproval — probably at the way Dan had come running up like a wild man — and stepped between him and Lily. "The only reason I haven't socked you yet is because Lily made me promise I wouldn't and because Aunt Bitsy says godly people do not hit." She stuck out her chin. "But mostly because I promised Lily."

With that, Poppy wrapped her arm around Lily's shoulders and led her away.

Dan tried to scrape his jaw off the ground. All this because he'd made a fool of himself? Or was it because of Paul Glick? Maybe he'd warned Lily to stay away from Dan.

Dan took a deep breath in an effort to keep his blood from boiling over. If Lily took her orders from Paul without fail, Dan was all but finished.

To his surprise, Rose — the girl who never talked to any boy if she could help it — hung back from her sisters and leaned close to him. "It's going to take some time to forgive you," she whispered. "Just give her some time."

Time to forgive him?

She gave him an uncertain half smile and followed her sisters. At least one of the Christners was willing to throw him a bone.

Lily was mad about something. *Nae.* Not mad. Hurt. That was the emotion he had seen in her eyes. As he stood alone in the middle of the deacon's yard, Dan's mind raced through every possible thing he might have done to hurt Lily's feelings.

He ate one of her doughnuts yesterday.

He thumped his palm against his forehead. How could he have been so greedy?

Nae. Wait. She had offered it to him. Should he have said no?

He'd bought her books. She said she couldn't accept them. He'd pushed her to take them. Was she mad about that? He had taken the books to her house without getting her approval. Had Paul been mad about that? Had he taken his anger out on Lily?

Dan tamped down his irritation. He shouldn't jump to conclusions. Even Paul Glick deserved the benefit of the doubt.

He needed to talk to Lily, ached to talk to Lily. He'd get down on his knees and beg for forgiveness for whatever he'd done. He couldn't bear to think he'd lost his chance with her when the chance had just been given to him.

He watched helplessly as the sisters walked to the eats table and deposited their cake before going to the part of the yard farthest from Dan and picking up three croquet mallets.

Poppy was the problem. She wouldn't let Dan get within ten feet of Lily, and she looked especially frightening with a deadly mallet in her hand. He'd have to be tricky.

Mahlon and Moses Zook must have thought Dan looked lonely standing all by himself in the middle of the yard. "Hey, Dan," Moses said. The Zook brothers were sixteen-year-old, redheaded twins. They had both just finished eighth grade when Dan had left for Pennsylvania, and now they were in *rumschpringe.* Dan liked them because they were kind to everybody and never took offense when people did stupid things. Rose Christner seemed to have

117

formed a tentative friendship with Mahlon, who was about as fearsome as a potato.

Dan held out his hand. "Moses, Mahlon, how are you?"

"We haven't seen you for two years," Moses said. "How did you like Pennsylvania?"

"Fine. Lots of tourists. I'm glad to be home."

Moses nudged Dan's shoulder with his fist. "Dat says you went to find a wife."

Dan chuckled even though he felt numb after his encounter with Lily. "My parents wanted me to find a wife. I didn't want to cooperate." He glanced in Lily's direction. "Moses, do you like croquet?"

Lily found it hard to concentrate on croquet when Dan stood there staring at her. He was probably trying to decide what kind of dog she looked most like. A bulldog? A hairless Chihuahua? A mutt?

She couldn't understand why a boy who found her so repulsive always seemed so happy to see her. Maybe he was a naturally cheerful person. Maybe he secretly made fun of her in his head. Whatever the reason, she certainly wished he'd quit staring.

The three sisters played croquet by themselves, while most of *die youngie* played volleyball or sat and listened to music on Benji Schmucker's portable CD player. Benji hadn't been baptized yet, and he took his music everywhere. Lily thought the blaring noise messed up a perfectly good gathering, but many of the younger teenagers enjoyed it.

Poppy hit her ball right at the wicket, only to have it stall in a divot in the grass. She groaned. "Your turn, Lily."

Lily had never been good at croquet, but it was the one game Rose seemed to like, so they played. Of course, if Rose had known they were only playing for her benefit, she never would have agreed to it. She hated to impose on anybody and went out of her way to make sure no one ever knew what she truly wanted. She would have much rather accommodated everyone else.

For Rose's sake, Lily and Poppy both pretended they liked croquet, but Lily did a lot more pretending than Poppy did. Lily had always been clumsy and uncoordinated and would much rather have curled up with a good book than run around the yard chasing balls.

Out of the corner of her eye, Lily saw Mahlon and Moses Zook each pick up a mallet. "Can we play?" Moses said.

Lily glanced at Rose. Rose had talked to

Mahlon at the last gathering. She was probably as comfortable around him as any boy, probably because he was young like a little brother. Rose gave Mahlon a weak smile and nodded.

The boys put their balls down and took their turns. Since Lily, Rose, and Poppy were in the middle of a game, the boys took a few extra turns to catch up. Just as Lily thought she might die of boredom, Moses hit an impressive ball through the wicket, and it came to rest touching Lily's. His eyes darted between Lily and some thick bushes to the side of the deacon's house.

"Sorry, Lily," he said before planting his foot on his ball, hitting it with the mallet, and sending Lily's ball into the bushes. He grinned sheepishly. "No hard feelings, I hope."

"Not at all," Lily said, grinding her teeth together and forcing a smile. "It's all part of the game." Part of the stupidest game on Earth. She dragged her feet to the bushes with half a mind to get lost in the foliage and escape out the other side. Getting on her hands and knees, she tried to find her ball. She couldn't see it anywhere.

She stood and squeezed herself through a gap in the bushes just wide enough to accommodate her and found herself in a small open space surrounded by tall bushes. And Dan Kanagy.

Well, she wasn't really surrounded by Dan Kanagy. It only felt that way because he stood well over six feet tall and had broad shoulders, and she felt small when she thought of all the things he'd said about her. He smiled and held up her croquet ball as if it were a prize. "I found your ball."

Why did her ball have the misfortune of rolling under this particular forest of bushes? And why was Dan Kanagy lurking here? Her face must have been glowing bright red. He'd probably take one look at her and call her "Beethead" or some other equally cruel name.

She reached out and practically snatched her ball from his fingers. *"Denki,"* she said, turning around to squeeze out of this horrible place.

"Wait, Lily," he said. "Please wait."

It wasn't really the words he said but how he said them that made her hesitate. His smug smile had disappeared, and his voice sounded like a mixture of gravel and dejection, as if he were really sorry for something. As if he knew he deserved her disdain and felt bad about it.

With more reluctance than she'd ever done anything besides play croquet, she stopped, pulled her arm back from between the bushes, and took a tiny step toward him. She folded her arms around her waist and squared her shoulders. Poppy wasn't here to protect her. Paul wasn't here to scowl. She'd have to be strong on her own. "What do you want?"

Her look seemed to pain him, as if she'd stuck him with a pin. *"Ach du lieva,"* he said. "It must be really bad."

"What must be really bad?"

He took off his hat and ran his fingers through his golden hair. "Lily, I don't know what I've done, but I want to apologize. You look like you want to kill me."

She frowned. "I would never wish to kill you or anybody. That's a horrible thought."

He held up one hand. "I know. You're right. We were getting along so nicely. You showed me your beehives. I stepped on your dandelions. But now you're upset. Can you please tell me what I've done so I can make amends?"

Lily felt as if the foliage closed in around her. Dan Kanagy didn't deserve an explanation. Dan Kanagy didn't really want an explanation. "I've got to get back to the game." It spoke volumes that she'd rather play croquet than spend another minute with him.

She might as well have stuck him with a hundred pins. "Is this about Paul? I didn't mean to make him mad yesterday. I just really wanted to give you those books. I'll take them back if that will make it better."

The thought of his nasty insults made her ill, but if she'd learned one thing about Dan Kanagy, she knew he was as persistent as a bloodhound. He'd probably camp out all night amongst the bushes until she took pity on him.

Lily sighed in surrender. "Paul told me what you said."

Something came to life behind his eyes, something almost like hope. She couldn't begin to figure this boy out. "What I said when? What did I say?"

She couldn't look at him. It would be humiliating to see the truth of what he said in his eyes. "You said I'm as ugly as a dog and that I should go live with the pigs."

Silence felt like an avalanche between them. When Dan spoke, his voice sounded stiff and hard, as if someone had sucked all the emotion out of his lungs. "When did Paul hear me say this?"

She looked up. He'd wrapped his hand around his opposite arm and gripped it tightly. The muscles of his jaw flexed, and though his face was blank, she could tell he was angry, so angry he seemed like a taut wire about to snap.

Lily lowered her eyes again. "In eighth grade."

"You've been mad since eighth grade?"

"He told me yesterday."

"Paul has an amazing memory," Dan said, with a tinge of bitterness in his voice.

Something shifted on his face and his anger seemed to melt away, leaving an emotion profoundly sad and deeply hopeful at the same time. He reached out as if to touch her, but must have thought better of it. His hand fell to his side. "Lily, I don't know if Paul thought he heard something he didn't or if his memory is playing tricks on him, but I would never in a million years say that about anybody, especially you."

"Are you . . . are you sure?"

"Never in a million years," he whispered. Now he did touch her, gently cupping his hands around her shoulders. For some inexplicable reason she didn't pull away. "Those words must have hurt you something wonderful."

He looked so concerned that if she'd tried to say one word, she would have started crying in relief and humiliation. Even if Paul had told her only yesterday, it had happened — or not happened — eight years ago. Dan must have thought she was incredibly child-ish.

"Lily, you have always been . . . I have always thought of you as . . ." He sounded thick and deep and sincere. He cleared his throat. "Lily, I think you are prettier than a hundred sunsets."

She thought of his favorite nicknames for her. "You do not."

"I would never lie about that."

The way he looked at her made her heart do a little skip. Her heart shouldn't be do-ing little skips. Paul would admonish her for her vanity. Still, it felt nice to hear someone, even Dan Kanagy, give her a compliment.

She banished all vain thoughts from her head and drew her brows together. "So you really didn't say that about me?"

"Lily, I was a stupid boy in eighth grade, but I wasn't mean."

Jah, he had been mean, but maybe she wouldn't scold him for that today. It was enough to know that he hadn't said she looked like a dog. How could Paul have got-ten it so wrong? One look in Dan's eyes told her he wasn't lying. That assurance made her feel a thousand times better.

"I'm sorry I got mad at you for something you didn't say. And I should have forgiven you, even if I thought you had said it."

He shook his head. "Those kinds of things are hard to forgive. I feel bad you thought they were true." He seemed to realize that he still had hold of her shoulders. He dropped his hands and took a step back, coming up against the bushes behind him. "Will you do me a favor? If Paul has any other memories of eighth grade, will you let me know? I should at least get a chance to apologize before you decide to hate me."

Lily bowed her head in embarrassment. "A good Christian would have forgiven you first thing."

He grinned. "Maybe. But if I had said those things, I would have deserved one of Poppy's best shoves. Or a good sock in the mouth yet."

A giggle of relief tripped from her lips. "Poppy thought so too. I told her she wasn't allowed to hurt you."

He swiped a hand across his forehead as if he'd escaped with his life. "Phew. I'm glad you're around to protect me."

He smiled with his whole face, as if there wasn't enough room in his mouth to contain all his happiness. The way he looked at her made her want to blush, as a pleasantly warm sensation trickled down her arms to the tips of her fingers.

Dan Kanagy could be rude and insensitive, but she didn't hate him. She'd come pretty far in three minutes.

She held up her ball. "I should get back to the game."

"It looks to me like you're losing pretty soundly."

Lily's lips twitched involuntarily. "I always do."

Dan peeked between the bushes. "They seem to be doing fine without you. You could forfeit. We could sit here in our little hideout and talk about books. I finished *Where the Red Fern Grows.*"

"I wish I could," Lily said, smiling to soften her refusal. "But Rose is so nervous at gatherings. I should be with her yet."

He didn't seem the least bit offended — a little disappointed maybe — but he grinned as wide as ever so she couldn't be sure. "Of course. You should be with your sister." Before she squeezed back through the bushes, he said, "Could I drive you home?" She stopped as if she'd frozen in place. He tilted his head to look her in the eye. "We could talk about books."

"I . . . I don't know."

And she really didn't. Aunt B usually drove her and her sisters to gatherings, and Paul usually drove them home.

"Paul isn't here," he coaxed.

Did he know how to read minds? "We were going to catch a ride with Hannah Yutzy."

"Why ride home with her, when you can go with me? My buggy is really comfortable, and we can decide if Billy should have cut down that big old tree just so his dogs could catch a raccoon."

It took her half a second to realize he was talking about the book. Her lips twitched teasingly. "Of course he should have. There was no other way."

"I would have climbed up and scared the critter down. No sense killing a perfectly good tree."

She smiled. "I see we have a lot to talk about."

"Then you'll ride home with me?"

"My sisters and I won't all fit in that courting buggy of yours."

"I brought the other buggy. It wouldn't be right to take you without your sisters."

"Okay," she said.

His smile was as blinding as the sunshine. "Okay? You'll let me drive you home?"

"*Jah.* Okay."

He looked like a little boy who'd gotten seven puppies for Christmas.

She laughed. Who knew it was that easy to make a boy happy?

Dan cupped his fingers around her elbow to help steady her as she went back through the gap in the bushes. "Will you be sure Poppy knows I'm not as terrible as she thinks I am? I'd rather she not break my leg in an attempt to protect you."

"Okay," she said, as his touch set off some sort of explosion in her head.

And why did her heart do that wild dance inside her chest? A fifteen-minute buggy ride was nothing to get excited about, and she had only agreed to it because Paul wasn't there to take her. Paul usually drove her and her sisters home, even though he'd made it clear what an imposition it was. But for all his complaining, he never would have let Lily actually find another ride. He wanted other boys to understand that Lily was taken.

Dan didn't seem to care that Lily was taken. Probably because he really wanted to talk about that book.

So, it seemed, did she.

CHAPTER NINE

Poppy insisted on sitting in front next to Dan. Either she didn't believe that Dan had reformed or she wanted to glare at him the entire buggy ride home.

Lily told herself she didn't mind, but a tiny seed of disappointment festered in the pit of her stomach. She should have been the one up front to make talking about books that much easier. If she sat up front, Dan might flash one of those cute smiles that made her toes curl.

Disappointment was silly. He would likely call her some mean nickname or tease her about her glasses. Paul would be annoyed enough when he found out Dan had driven her home.

If he found out. Why would he ever need to find out?

She should be ashamed of herself that she'd started keeping a list of things she hoped Paul would never know. It didn't seem right to be sneaky with the boy most likely to be her future husband.

Dan didn't seem to mind that Poppy studied him like a chicken might study a tick. If his smile had seemed a little forced when Poppy sat in the front seat, he acted cheerful enough and had even offered her the Spongey-Man blanket in case she got chilly.

Dan had a good hand with the reins but didn't seem compelled to push the horse all that fast. They pulled away from the gathering at a leisurely pace. The sun had set below the horizon, but it was still light enough to see the road ahead of them. "There's another blanket on the floor if you get cold back there," he said.

"Denki." Rose tucked the blanket around their legs. "It's a tiny bit chilly yet."

Smiling, Dan quickly glanced back at Rose and Lily. "Everyone loved your cake, Rose. I saw Mahlon and Sol Petersheim playing rock-paper-scissors over the last piece, and Junior Zook asked the deacon's wife if he could lick the plate."

Rose smiled that tentative, shy smile she always used around people she didn't know very well. "You're teasing. Junior wouldn't dream of getting crumbs on his shirt."

Dan shook his head. "Not teasing. That

131

cake tasted wonderful-*gute.*"

"It's Lily's recipe. She thought of putting almond extract in the frosting."

"You said it's a honey cake. I'm assuming there's honey in it," Dan said.

Rose smiled, for real this time. "*Jah.* We use honey in most of our recipes."

"What other desserts do you make with honey?" For being a boy, he seemed unusually eager to talk about recipes. Paul wouldn't have gone near the topic.

"Well," Rose said, nibbling on her fingernail, "we make honey buns and Dutch Babies and honey cookies filled with jam. Poppy's honey-peach cake is the best thing you've ever tasted in July when the peaches are fresh from the tree."

Lily did her best not to gawk at Rose. She'd said more in the first few minutes of their buggy ride than she ever said in a whole trip with Paul. Had this been Dan's doing?

Of course. His seemingly genuine interest in honey recipes was coaxing Rose out of her shell a bit.

Lily could have kissed him.

Well, not really kissed him, because she never, ever wanted to kiss incorrigible Dan Kanagy. Ever. But his kindness certainly made up for a lot of past sins.

To Lily's delight, Rose didn't fall into a timid silence like she often did when she thought she might be doing too much talking. "When the hives really started producing, Aunt Bitsy realized we could make a whole business out of it. We sell beeswax and royal jelly, even a queen once in a while. And of course Poppy's bread and Lily's cookies sell well at auction."

Poppy turned her head and gave Lily a significant look. She had noticed it too. Rose was talking to a boy.

Could have kissed him.

"I think it's fascinating that bees can make so many different things: honey, beeswax, propolis. Did you know honey is good for burns?"

"Jah," Rose said at the same time Poppy spoke. "Of course."

"Some hives get stacked so high with supers, they're hard to manage," Dan said. "I noticed you stack two or three shallow supers on top of a couple of brood boxes. Much easier to work with. And you're smart to have planted trees and flowers that bees love. I understand why Bitsy is protective of her dandelions."

Lily found herself gawking again. In a few sentences, Dan had spouted off more beekeeping facts than Paul had ever learned.

133

Paul didn't even know what a super was. He'd never been interested in their beekeeping operation.

Lily cleared her throat. Why did Paul need to know anything about beekeeping? He was her boyfriend, not her assistant.

"How do you know so much about the hives?" Rose asked, sounding more than mildly impressed.

Poppy folded her arms and smirked in an obvious attempt not to look amazed. "Were you secretly a beekeeper's apprentice in Pennsylvania?"

Dan turned his face toward Lily and grinned sheepishly. "I've been doing some late-night reading."

Rose's eyebrows inched together. "About bees?"

Dan chuckled. "I wanted to get to know . . . you sisters better. I thought if I read some bee books, we could have a more intelligent conversation about them."

Poppy inclined her head in Lily's direction. "Lily is the smart one. You can always have an intelligent conversation with her."

Dan turned and winked at Lily. Actually winked! Her heart became a whole troop of circus tumblers. "I'd love to have hundreds of conversations with Lily."

"But how many bee books have you read?"

Rose asked. She seemed concerned that Dan might not be getting enough sleep.

"The library only has three," Dan said.

Three more books than Paul had read. Lily tried to ignore the warmth that pulsed through her veins. Dan had stayed up late reading bee books for her. He wanted to get to know her.

Well, not just her. All the sisters. And Aunt Bitsy.

It was a very nice thing for such a mean boy to do.

"Why did you go to Pennsylvania?" Rose asked, continuing to impress Lily with her fearlessness.

"My *mamm* and *dat* claimed they sent me to learn how to care for cattle and other livestock. My onkel Titus knows more about caring for cows than most people who go to college. We're expanding our dairy, and Dat wanted me to learn animal husbandry so we don't have to call a veterinarian so often. But they really sent me to Pennsylvania because they wanted me to find a wife."

Lily tensed. She hadn't heard anything about Dan looking for a wife in Pennsylvania. Dan's *mammi* had kept her well informed of Dan's activities while he was away. Dan had been his *mammi*'s faithful letter writer, and Erda had shared Dan's detailed letters with Lily. Erda had always been so proud of her grandson, and Lily hadn't been inclined to tell her how mean Dan had been to her in school.

He hadn't said anything about a girlfriend in his letters — at least, Erda hadn't mentioned a girl — but maybe he'd left that part out. It would make sense that a boy wouldn't be keeping his *mammi* updated about his love life.

Thank goodness Poppy wasn't afraid to ask the rude questions. "And did you fall in love?"

"Not in Pennsylvania." Yet again, Dan briefly turned to look at Lily. He gave her a mischievous smile that shouldn't have been so endearing. "I've always preferred Wisconsin."

Too soon, they came to the dirt road that bordered the east side of their farm. Lily had never enjoyed a buggy ride quite so much as she had this one. They'd talked about Pennsylvania Amish customs, dairy cows, Rose's latest beehive painting, and Poppy's penchant for slugging boys in primary school. He said he loved Aunt B's blue hair, and Lily could tell he meant it. They talked about bees and other critters and told him about the mouse that Farrah Fawcett refused to catch.

He had also made Rose laugh twice, and even Poppy relaxed enough to crack a smile occasionally. Dan could certainly be charming when he wanted to be.

"*Denki* for giving us a ride," Lily said as they approached the turnoff to their lane. "It was very kind of you."

"If you ever need a ride, I'd be happy to take you. That is, if Paul can't do it."

Instead of stopping the buggy so they could get out, Dan turned his horse as if to go down their lane. Lily tapped Dan on the shoulder. "This is where Paul lets us out."

Dan cocked an eyebrow in puzzlement. "Why?"

Poppy snorted softly. She seemed to think that if she did it quietly enough Lily wouldn't be offended. Poppy often snorted when Lily talked about Paul. She thought Paul was a baby for the way he fussed whenever a fly or a bee or any other buzzing insect landed on him.

Lily tried not to be annoyed with her sister. Poppy didn't know Paul the way she did. Poppy hadn't been the painfully awkward girl in eighth grade befriended by Paul. He had sacrificed his recesses to be with Lily, sharing scriptures with her and discussing ways that girls could be *gute* wives and boys could be *gute* husbands. He had assured her that glasses and braces and pimples were nothing to be ashamed of. They helped make her humble, and every boy wanted a humble wife.

"Paul doesn't want bees to fly into his buggy," Poppy said.

"He's terribly afraid of bees," Rose said. She probably sensed Lily's irritation. Dear Rose had always been sensitive to other people's feelings. She sincerely wanted everybody to be happy, healthy, and content.

Poppy smirked. "He's not afraid. He just doesn't want to be bothered."

"Poppy," Lily scolded. "You know that's not true. It's not that long of a walk from here, and it's too hard to turn his buggy around at the end of our lane."

Dan didn't hesitate, even at the thought of having to turn his buggy around. He prodded his horse over the small wooden bridge. "I'll brave the bees if I can spend an extra five minutes with the Honeybee Schwesters. Besides, I can't let you walk home in the dark."

When they got to the house, Dan jumped out, slid the buggy door up, and let Rose and Lily climb out his side. Rose took Lily's hand and squeezed it and then did something so bold Lily wouldn't have expected it in a hundred years. "Would you like to come in?"

Come in? Inviting a boy to come in after a gathering wasn't a casual thing. It meant you might be interested in forming a more serious relationship. It meant he was welcome into the family circle. Lily didn't know how she felt about inviting Dan Kanagy in.

What would Paul think? What would Aunt Bitsy say? She didn't react well when boys came over.

By the light of the lantern hanging on the porch, she saw the slight curl of Dan's lips. Did he want to come in or was she imagining the hopeful restraint behind that half smile? "What do you think, Amtrak?" he said.

And there it was, the little jab to remind her of her ugliness. To remind her that she was Lily Christner and he was Dan Kanagy, the handsome boy who could put her in her place with a single word. She felt the blow as if someone had thrown a rock at her. It was like being back in eighth grade all over again.

She took a deep breath and tried to pretend his words hadn't hurt. "Tonight is not a good night."

It would never be a good night.

His disappointment was palpable, as if

she'd spit in his face and he didn't know how to pretend it hadn't happened. "Oh. Okay." He stuffed his hands in his pockets. "It's late. I should get going."

Lily nodded. Rose glanced at her. Poppy huffed and marched up the flagstones as if Dan had insulted her instead of Lily. Lily grabbed Rose's hand for support, and they marched toward the house.

"We still need to talk about that book," Dan said, almost as an afterthought.

She turned her head in a barely civil acknowledgment. "*Jah.* Okay. Sometime. Good night."

"Good night."

They heard him climb into his buggy. The wheels crunched against the gravel, and it sounded as if he had no problem turning his buggy around. The noise faded as the buggy made its way down the lane.

"Lily," Rose whispered, a hint of urgency in her voice. "I think he likes you."

Lily frowned. Whatever gave her that idea? "He called me Amtrak."

"I know, but I still think he likes you. A lot."

"How can you say that, Rose? After eight years, he still calls me names. And they still hurt."

"Maybe they're not meant to hurt."

"Maybe he's never outgrown the urge to put people down."

"I don't think he's like that. He's really nice, Lily. And really easy to talk to."

Lily lifted her chin obstinately. "Then make him *your* boyfriend. See how long it takes him to start calling you names." The thought of Dan being Rose's boyfriend sunk Lily deeper into dejection.

Rose smiled one of those smiles that made her seem wise beyond her years. "I don't like him that way. He's too energetic for me. I don't think I'd be able to live with all that enthusiasm. Besides, he likes my sister."

Lily growled and quickened her pace, dragging Rose up the porch steps. "He does not."

"You can't be so sure."

"I already have a boyfriend. I'm not one of those flighty girls who moves from boy to boy like bees go from flower to flower."

"You don't have to buzz around the entire meadow. You only need to find the right flower," Rose said. "Maybe it's a dandelion. Everybody overlooks dandelions because they're weeds. People don't even give them a chance."

Lily lifted a teasing eyebrow. "And you're saying Dan is a weed?"

"He can be insensitive, but he's got potential."

"I've got Paul."

"Okay. Paul." Rose sighed. "I'm sorry if I upset you."

Lily wrapped an arm around Rose's shoulder. "You didn't upset me. I know you mean well, but I've already got my own weed." They burst into giggles.

Paul Glick. Lily's very own weed.

She couldn't have been more content.

CHAPTER TEN

Paul's *mamm* walked with a shuffle and a hunched back, as if she were tired of her life. Lily had always felt a little sorry for her. Aunt B said Martha Glick was depressed. The Amish didn't usually talk about such things, but Aunt B had lived amongst the *Englisch* for twenty years. She knew enough to be concerned.

"Are you sure you wouldn't like another cup of *kaffee,* Lily?" Martha asked, holding up the pot.

"*Nae. Denki* just the same," Lily said. Refills of *kaffee* were free at the restaurant, but Lily had already had three cups. Any more and she'd be swimming out the door.

Paul sat next to her, mopping up the last of his gravy with half a biscuit. "The gravy is extra-*gute* today, Mamm."

His *mamm* flashed a rare smile. "I'm glad. Pork and beef drippings."

Paul picked up Lily's unused spoon and

scooped up a generous spoonful of gravy from his plate. "Here, Lily. Try the gravy."

He spooned it into her mouth as if he were feeding a baby. Lily savored the creamy, salty taste. Her stomach growled. Biscuits and gravy would have been so good for supper.

She looked down at her pathetic half-eaten piece of shoofly pie. Day-old pastries were usually half price, but Paul had talked his *mamm* into giving Lily a slice for free. It would have been thrown away otherwise. Too bad she hated shoofly pie.

Paul's *dat,* Raymond, marched into the small restaurant with his thumbs hooked around his suspenders. Raymond Glick was short and slight with not a speck of gray in his long beard. His eyes were like Paul's, dark and wide-set, and he had a little paunch that hung out over the waistband of his trousers. Paul probably weighed fifty pounds more than his *dat.*

Without even acknowledging Lily or Paul, Raymond handed Martha a slip of paper. "Northern Adventures Tours called. They're bringing in a busload for dinner."

Martha jumped as if she'd been poked with a pin. "*Ach du lieva.* I better get to roasting some chickens."

"I already sent Perry to fetch the Zimmerman girls for extra help."

"*Denki,* Raymond," Martha said as she hurried to the kitchen.

Raymond watched after her. "And you know better than to let Mattie Zimmerman bake the rolls."

"*Jah,* Raymond. I'll be sure to do it myself."

Lily had always been a little uncomfortable with the way Paul's *dat* treated his *mamm,* like a piece of furniture, as if she were invisible unless he wanted her for something. It seemed Paul's parents rarely spoke unless Paul's *dat* was giving Martha orders or criticizing the way she did something.

Lily had tried once to talk to Paul about his *mamm,* but Paul had become defensive, so she kept her concerns to herself. She hadn't even shared her apprehension with Aunt Bitsy. In one breath her *aendi* would tell the girls that no one was good enough for them and then warn them to watch how a boy's *fater* treated his m*ater.* She said it was a pretty good sign how the son would treat his own wife. "The apple doesn't fall far from the tree," she'd say, then look up into heaven and ask the Lord to bring her girls someone like Donny Osmond.

Having lived amongst the *Englischers* for

so long, Aunt B was wise in the ways of the world, but Lily just knew Paul would be different than his *fater*. Hadn't he been kind to her when no one else had been? Didn't he buy her honey as a favor to her family? Sometimes the apple fell from the tree, rolled down the hill, was snatched up by a bird, and dropped far afield. Paul's apple was in a whole different county than his *fater*'s.

Paul's *fater* came to their table and stood over them like a good host. Lily squirmed under his observation. She hadn't worn her glasses today. "How were the biscuits?"

"Wonderful-*gute*," Paul said. "And I could have eaten a bowl of gravy."

Raymond nodded. "Lord willing, it will keep the customers coming in." He glanced at Lily. "Lily, we are always glad to see you in our restaurant. Did Paul tell you we are getting a new freezer?"

"*Jah.* I'm sure you need the extra space." The freezer was the reason they couldn't pay more for Lily's honey. She nibbled on her bottom lip. Should she ask for a better price?

It was the battle she had in her head continuously. Care of the family finances was her job, but Aunt B would have been able to manage things so much better. Probably *anybody* else would have been able to manage the finances better. She wasn't as good at numbers as Paul and she felt too much of a sense of loyalty to question the price he paid her for honey.

Ach, if only she didn't feel like such a *dumkoff* all the time.

But Aunt B trusted her. That had to count for something. She'd do her best.

Lily's accounts book sat open on the table. She and Paul had been discussing the prices for different sizes of honey jars. Raymond pointed to the figure she'd written on the paper. "You have small writing. How can you read it without your glasses?"

Lily pressed her lips together. "I have my contacts."

Raymond's mouth barely hinted at a frown. "It's better with your glasses."

"She doesn't wear the contacts often, Dat, but she can read better with them."

Raymond nodded. "I see. When you marry, I suppose you won't need contacts. You'll not be doing as much reading when the babies come."

Lily stiffened in her chair. Raymond thought reading was a worldly waste of time. She couldn't agree with him. Even when — or if — he became her father-in-law, they would never see eye to eye about it. She'd be doing plenty of reading before and after the babies came.

Unless . . .

What would Paul want? It would be wicked to go against her husband if he was dead set against her reading.

That thought troubled her more than she cared to admit. As a wife she must submit to her husband. Paul was so much smarter than she was and more capable of making the right decision. She'd defer to him, of course. But could she give up reading simply because Paul frowned upon it?

Surely he wouldn't make her give up her books. He didn't see reading as a frivolous pursuit like his *fater* did. One time she'd told him the story of *Summer of the Monkeys*, and he seemed truly eager to know if Jay Berry Lee had bought the horse or used the money to pay for his sister's surgery.

She wouldn't dare disagree with Raymond. "Lord willing, I will always meet with *Gotte*'s approval."

Raymond bestowed a smile on her. "You have turned out quite well, Lily. I worried when Paul told me you two had become friends. I knew your aunt Elizabeth as a teenager. She was a wild one. But I should have trusted *Gotte.* You Christner girls have come out okay in spite of it."

Lily sat like stone and listened to Raymond spout his insulting compliments. An invisible weight pressed against her chest and made it impossible to breathe. She was fully aware of what people said about her aunt — that she was an outcast, a fence-jumper who'd only returned to Bienenstock because she wanted money from the church to help raise her nieces. But Aunt B hadn't ever taken one penny from the church. They'd managed just fine on their own.

"Denki," Lily sputtered, because she truly didn't know what else to say. Did the whole community believe Paul was too good for her? Paul was from one of the most prominent families in the community. Not only were they rich by Amish standards, but his *dat* was a minister and Paul's oldest brother had been ordained bishop in one of the districts in Cashton. Lily was a homely, awkward girl who would rather read a book than quilt or sew or can green beans. She wasn't ashamed of her family, but she was fully aware that the community whispered about Aunt B behind her back. What kind of *gute* Amish boy would even consider Lily for a wife?

Paul would.

He didn't care about her appearance, and he seemed perfectly willing to marry Lily even though she had too many faults to count.

Paul's *dat* tapped on the table with his knuckle. "I must make sure they're making plenty of rolls. Martha doesn't make enough and then we're left with unhappy customers."

He tromped quickly into the kitchen as if there were a fire that needed extinguishing. Lily sat quietly, the lump in her throat making it impossible to speak.

Paul narrowed his eyes, obviously sensing something was wrong. She tried to fake a serene expression, as if her face were water on the lake undisturbed by even the slightest of breezes.

She didn't fool him. "Quit worrying, Lily. My *dat* likes you just fine, even when you don't wear your glasses. He thinks it's wonderful-*gute* that you have been able to overcome your upbringing."

"But, Paul, you don't feel that way about Aunt Bitsy, do you?"

Paul studied her face, raised his brows, and cleared his throat. "Me?" he sputtered. "Me?" He took a swig of milk. "*Nae, nae.* Your aunt Bitsy is a very *gute* person."

She had the distinct and disloyal feeling that Paul wasn't telling her the whole truth. "Aunt Bitsy gave up everything to raise us.

150

She taught us how to work and nurtured our faith in *Gotte*. She came back to the church for us." Lily couldn't help the bitterness that tinged her voice. "Isn't that enough for you?"

Paul stuck out his bottom lip slightly when he frowned. "Of all the stuff, Lily. I said she's a *gute* person. You don't have to bite my head off. Even you have to admit that your *aendi* isn't exactly the most pious church member. She talks to *Gotte* out loud. If that doesn't smack of pride, I don't know what does. There's rumors that she wears fancy earrings in her sleep. And her hair is blue."

When Paul talked about Aunt Bitsy like that, Lily usually swallowed her indignation and changed the subject. Paul didn't like confrontation. It made him unhappy. He was never one to pick a fight.

Another reason she didn't deserve him.

Maybe she was hungry or worried about the family finances or fed up with Raymond Glick's harsh judgments, but for Aunt B's sake, she dared to scold him. "I won't listen to talk like that, Paul, not from someone who is supposed to be my friend." And future husband.

His nostrils flared in surprise, and he set his fork down even though he hadn't fin-

151

ished eating. "Of all the stuff, Lily. I'm just telling the truth. You know how I despise pride."

She should have let it drop, smooth things over so Paul wouldn't realize how upset she was. But, *ach du lieva,* even Dan Kanagy, mean Dan Kanagy, liked Aunt B's light blue hair. She slammed her accounts book shut. "Pride? Who is the one at this table who thinks they're better than Aunt B? *Thou shalt not judge.*"

A headache throbbed at the base of her skull. She really shouldn't accuse him of pride. When the dust settled, she'd be apologizing to him for days.

To her surprise, the sullen expression on his face shifted. He must have realized he'd crossed some sort of line. He tried to backpedal, but he didn't do it very well, probably because she'd never seen him backpedal in his life. "Okay, okay. I didn't mean it. Your aunt can color her hair purple for all I care. You don't have to get in such a tizzy about it. Of all the stuff!"

Lily stood up, unsatisfied with Paul's weak apology and her own behavior. *Blessed are the meek.* How could she have forgotten herself like that? She should probably apologize right now and get it over with, but she couldn't bring herself to do it. Let

Paul gloat over her some other day.

She turned on her heel and marched to the door. To her utter amazement, Paul chased after her. He must have seen how serious she was or he never would have left a perfectly good bite of biscuit and a pool of gravy on his plate. "Lily, okay, Lily. You shouldn't be angry. It's a sin."

She stopped before she opened the door and slumped her shoulders. He was right. How could she leave like a pouty child who hadn't gotten her way? They should be able to talk things over like two people in love were supposed to talk. "I'm sorry. I should hold my temper."

"*Jah,* you should."

"But I wish you wouldn't speak badly of my aunt."

"I forgive you, and I hope you'll forgive me for upsetting you." He patted her cheek. "You see. I'm humble enough to admit I upset you."

"*Denki.*"

He laid a hand on her shoulder. "I always want to speak the truth between us, Lily, but I suppose some things are better left unsaid."

"I suppose they are."

He opened the door for her, and they walked outside.

153

"I won't see you Sunday at *gmay*," he said. "My *fater* is preaching in another district, and we are going with him."

"Okay," she said, not really listening. She just wanted to go home and repent. Maybe write Paul a long and earnest letter of apology. Sometimes she wished she could start a day over again.

"You can walk back to your buggy okay, can't you?" Paul said. He no doubt wanted to get back to his gravy.

"*Jah*. You finish eating."

"My blood sugar always does better that way."

Mahlon and Moses Zook passed them on the sidewalk, each holding a half-eaten doughnut in their hands. They'd been to Yutzy's doughnut stand.

"Hello," Mahlon said. "Have you tasted these doughnuts? They're so soft."

"My *mamm*'s rolls are even softer," Paul said.

Moses nodded and grinned. "Your *mamm*'s rolls are my favorite. I eat them with Honeybee Sisters honey."

Mahlon motioned toward the restaurant. "Did you eat?"

Well, one of them had.

"Biscuits and gravy," Paul said. "No one makes them as *gute* as my *mamm*. There's

154

still some left if you go in before the dinner rush."

"We already had supper." Mahlon held up his doughnut. "This is dessert."

Moses took another bite of doughnut. "Did you ever find your croquet ball at the gathering, Lily?" He said it with a grin, knowing perfectly well that she had found Dan Kanagy along with her ball in the bushes.

"*Denki* for being so concerned. I was never going to win that game anyway. It was better I dropped out."

"At least you got a ride home out of it," Moses said.

She could practically see Paul's ears perk up. "What ride?"

Mahlon slapped Moses on the back. "We've got to get to the harness shop if we ever want to get that field sown today."

Moses nodded. He waved his doughnut at Lily as he and his brother marched away toward the harness and tack shop. "We'll see you at *gmay.*"

Paul concentrated on Lily's face as if he were trying to read tiny letters written on her forehead. "You said you weren't going to the gathering."

Actually, Paul hadn't bothered to check with her before he had told Dan she wouldn't be at the gathering. Lily clenched her teeth and did her best to quell the fire that flared to life. Paul didn't deserve her anger. He was only asking a question. Why was she so out of sorts with him? "I, uh . . . I decided to go. Rose wouldn't go unless Poppy and I went with her. You know how nervous she gets."

Paul intensified his gaze. "You've got to stop babying her, Lily. If Rose is ever going to learn to be a good wife, she has to be brave enough to go to gatherings by herself."

Lily nibbled on her bottom lip and reminded herself there was no reason to be mad at Paul. "It makes Rose happy when we come."

"Who drove you home?"

Lily wouldn't have answered that question for a whole set of Carol Ryrie Brink novels. "Paul, I need to go. I'm reading to the children at school and then I have to run to Coblenzes and see how their *dat* is doing. Poppy made them a cake. And then I'm off to the —"

"Lily." Paul narrowed his eyes and scrunched his lips together, the look he gave her when he got ready to scold her for something. "Moses said you got a ride out of it. What did he mean?"

"I . . . Moses sent my croquet ball into

the bushes. I happened upon Dan Kanagy, and he offered to drive me home."

He stuck out his bottom lip so far he could have caught raindrops with it. "You let Dan Kanagy take you home?"

"He took Poppy and Rose too."

"He's a cheat, Lily. He calls you bad names. He said you were *hesslich*, ugly. How could you have agreed to a ride home?"

The word *ugly* felt like a little pinch, on purpose. "You weren't there, and we needed a ride."

"If I had known you would accept a ride from Dan Kanagy, I would have come to the gathering and taken you home myself. He could have hurt your feelings."

"It's okay, Paul. It's sweet that you're worried about me, but he was nothing but nice."

The corners of Paul's mouth seemed to droop all the way to his toes. "Nice? He didn't call you names?"

She lowered her eyes. The buggy ride had been nice up until the last minute. "*Jah*, he did."

"I thought so."

"But he talked to Rose, and Rose talked to him, and he reads beekeeping books."

"So what. Anybody can read a beekeeping book."

Anybody could; not everybody did. Sighing, she wrapped both arms around her accounts book and hugged it to her. "Maybe it's time we forgave him, Paul. He's probably sorry for what he's done."

Paul stuck that lip out again. "Forgive him? You might still be holding a grudge, Lily, but I'm not. I forgave Dan and his family almost before they cheated us. But I haven't forgotten, and you'd be wise not to forget either. If you forget how he hurt you, you're inviting him to hurt you again. That's why I don't forget. I don't want to be tricked, and I don't want him to insult you. A boy like Dan will put you down over and over again."

Lily nibbled on her bottom lip. Dan had used his charm on her in the buggy and then when her guard was down, he'd called her Amtrak. Paul was right. She should forgive, but she shouldn't forget.

"I'm sorry I let Dan take me home," she said, more out of a need to placate Paul than actual regret for doing it. She'd rather he not stew over it.

He took a deep breath as his annoyance came to rest. "From now on, I don't want you to go to gatherings without me." His attempt at a smile came out more like a grimace. "I'm jealous when another boy takes you home."

"I wouldn't want a boy who's never jealous."

He didn't stick his bottom lip out again, but he was definitely pouting. "You wouldn't make me jealous on purpose, would you?"

"Of course not. I wouldn't play with your emotions like that." She glanced at the sky. "I've got to go, Paul. I'm due at the school at one thirty."

He rubbed his hands together as if he were eager to get moving himself. "Okay then. I'll walk you to your buggy."

"No need. Go finish your dinner."

"What kind of a boyfriend would I be if I let you walk by yourself? We don't spend enough time together as it is."

He motioned for her to lead the way, and she tried not to let the shock show on her face. He never walked her back unless he happened to be going that way already.

Paul had willingly left gravy on his plate.

Her riding home with Dan must have shaken his confidence.

It had certainly shaken hers.

CHAPTER ELEVEN

Willing his heart to slow down, Dan tucked the large roll under his arm and tapped on the Christners' door. He obviously didn't have a very strong will, because his pulse kicked into a gallop at the mere feel of Lily's door beneath his knuckles.

He didn't even know if she'd be home. He hoped like crazy she'd be home, but he had really come to see Bitsy. Just like the way to a man's heart was through his stomach, if he wanted Lily to notice him, he'd have to go through Aunt Bitsy.

Bitsy opened the door with a suspicious look on her face and her hand on the shotgun leaning against the wall.

"Hullo, Bitsy," Dan said, smiling and resisting the powerful urge to glance at the gun. It wasn't loaded, was it?

Bitsy wore a cherry-red apron over a bright purple dress with her hair tied up in a blindingly fluorescent pink scarf. The scarf wasn't unusual. Many Amish women wore a scarf instead of a *kapp* when they did chores. The color was a bit outrageous, but Dan liked it — something festive to wear to do ordinary work.

He tried not to gawk at her hair. He could have sworn the salt-and-pepper gray had been tinted blue. Today it was a shade of lime green — light and subtle — but definitely green.

Bitsy sighed and arched one eyebrow. "She must have fed you."

"What?"

"The last time you were here, Lily fed you, didn't she?"

"Uh." He had to stop and think. "*Jah.* She gave me two cookies. I finished them off before I got to the end of your lane. They were delicious."

Her other eyebrow rose to meet the first, and she nodded as if she had the mysteries of the world figured out. "If you feed a stray cat . . ."

A heavenly smell wafted from the kitchen. "I hope I'm not interrupting anything."

"*Ach, nae,*" she said, looking skyward as if she were holding a silent conversation with someone up there. "I've been lounging on the couch eating ice cream and waiting for suitors to show up."

Dan chuckled. "What I meant was, I hope I'm a welcome interruption."

She smirked, but there was good humor in her face. *Ach.* If only he could read the thoughts behind those eyes. "I won't know if you're a welcome interruption until I know why you've come. I don't think you're worth burning the muffins for."

"Please, don't let your muffins burn on my account."

"If you're looking for one of the girls, they're gone. Poppy and Rose are thinning apples, and Lily is in town talking business with Paul."

Dan did his best not to let his smile droop. He should have expected Lily would be with Paul. He couldn't let it bother him. This whole attempt to get Lily's attention was probably futile, and if he got upset about Lily spending time with Paul, he'd be perpetually miserable.

Bitsy must have seen the shadow pass across his face. "So. You're here to see Lily." Her eyebrows inched higher. "You know she's got a boyfriend?"

Dan took a deep breath and let the word *boyfriend* wash over him. Miserable. He'd be eternally miserable if he didn't discipline his feelings. He pulled the paper-covered roll from under his arm. "Actually, I'm here to see you. I brought you something."

Bitsy seemed resigned to the possibility of burned muffins. She propped her hands on her hips and eyed him as if she were trying to count his nose hairs. "You're a smart boy, Dan Kanagy. And persistent. I'll give you that." She stared at him for a few uncomfortable seconds before stepping back from the doorway. "Come in then," she said, "and let's see what you've got to say for yourself."

The Christners' fluffy white cat lazed on the window seat as if she'd been there all day. She probably had.

Leaving him standing just inside the doorway, Bitsy went into the kitchen, slid two chunky oven mitts onto her hands, and opened the oven. She pulled out a tin of golden-brown muffins and set it on the cooking rack next to the stove. "You're off the hook for the muffins," she said.

"They smell delicious."

She peeled off her oven mitts and shook her finger at him as if he were a naughty little boy. "Don't get your hopes up. I don't feed strays."

Was he a stray?

Before he could decide the answer to that question, the tattoo on her wrist diverted his attention. Last week, it was a honeybee, and it had been on her left wrist. This week, it was a purple butterfly on her right wrist. It matched her dress perfectly. He stole a look at her other wrist to see if maybe he'd missed the butterfly last time.

Nope. The honeybee has disappeared.

How had she managed a traveling tattoo?

He laid his bundle on the table and hoped against hope she'd like it. Despite her vivid attire and butterfly tattoo, she seemed like a person who would appreciate a practical gift.

Bitsy turned the muffins out of the tin, righted them on the cooking rack, and wiped her hands on the towel hanging from the fridge handle. "Let's see what you've got," she said, holding out her hand.

He stepped aside and let her unwrap the paper from around the roll of mesh. "Hardware cloth," she said. He might have detected a little lilt in her voice. "What size?"

"Eight mesh. The bees can't fit, but the Varroa mites fall right through. It's the most useful size for a beekeeper." He cleared his throat, trying not to get carried away by his eagerness. "At least that's what it says in the book I got from the library."

Her lips curled so slightly, he wasn't sure he'd actually seen it. "*Jah.* I know all about hardware cloth."

His breathing grew rapid and his stomach

tied itself into a complicated knot. Maybe she liked it. Maybe she would tell Lily what a thoughtful young man he was. Maybe she'd give her blessing to their happy marriage.

Whoa there. He was getting ahead of himself. Far ahead. Five counties ahead. His heart did cartwheels in Minnesota. Bitsy hadn't even thanked him. Maybe she had rolls and rolls of number eight mesh already stored in her shed. Maybe she despised hardware cloth and shot any boy who presumed to bring it onto the property.

But there was something in the twist of her lips and the glint of her eye that told him he might be on the right track, at least with Bitsy. Who knew what kind of a track he was on with Lily? Probably the railroad track, and he was tied to it.

"So tell me, young man, why am I the lucky one to get hardware cloth?" Bitsy folded her arms and looked at him as if she already knew the answer to her own question.

"I hoped it might be something you could use."

"*Jah.* We can use it," she said.

"Lily has agreed to discuss *Where the Red Fern Grows* with me. I thought mesh would be a nice thank-you gift."

Bitsy looked like a cat stalking an unsuspecting mouse. "What else?"

He'd been afraid of this. What if Bitsy grilled him until she forced him to admit that he was in love with Lily and that he'd buy her a whole buggy full of mesh if it would make her like him better? His lungs got tight, and he had to squeeze air out of them to speak. "I . . . I want to get to know your family better."

She looked at him sideways. "What if my *family* doesn't want to get to know you better? What if my *family* has a boyfriend?"

Ach du lieva, she knew! Why had he ever imagined he could pull one over on Aunt Bitsy? He curled his lips in feigned innocence. "I'm hoping this mesh will soften you up?"

"I'm always impressed by a boy who knows his meshes."

Dan snapped his head around as the door opened, and the girl of his dreams entered in a pretty gray dress. Okay, the dress wasn't pretty, but the girl inside sure was. His heart tripped all over itself, and it was all he could do to keep from shouting her name out loud.

He'd made a fool of himself with his eagerness once. He wasn't about to do it again. He leaned his elbow casually against

166

the butcher-block island. It wasn't as tall as he'd anticipated and his torso bent awkwardly in an attempt to strike a natural pose. Yep. He looked like an idiot, but it was too late to unbend himself now without seeming more foolish. "Lily," he said. "What a pleasant surprise."

Surprise? She lived here. How surprised could he be at seeing her in her own home? He mentally pounded his head against the wall.

Lily was the one who looked surprised, as if a visit from the deacon would have been less of an intrusion. "Dan," she said. "What are you doing here?"

Bitsy picked up the mesh roll. "You fed him cookies."

"I thought you might need some hardware cloth," he said, pushing away from the butcher block and unkinking his back.

"Hardware cloth?"

"Number eight mesh," Bitsy said, carrying the roll into a room on the other side of the kitchen wall and coming out empty-handed. "He's been doing some reading."

Lily stared at him briefly before giving him a half smile. "That's very nice of you."

Poppy and Rose marched into the house with cheeks rosy from exertion. Both of them wore scarves covering their heads, and both of them had wisps of hair sticking out in several directions. Poppy had a streak of dirt down her cheek.

Rose gave him a genuine, timid smile. "Dan. I didn't know you were here."

"Lily fed him," Bitsy said.

Lily and Poppy exchanged a puzzled look that Dan knew he wasn't meant to see. "He brought us some hardware cloth," Lily said.

Dan hoped that was enough of an explanation. He didn't want Poppy asking probing questions about why he'd brought it or who he'd come to see or why he was madly in love with another boy's girlfriend.

"That's so nice," Rose said, hooking her elbow around Lily's arm. "Don't you think so, Lily?"

"*Jah,* very nice."

They all fell silent and stared at each other. He should have taken the hint to leave, but Lily had just gotten here. Could he steal another minute to gaze at her?

Rose seemed determined to keep the conversation going. "It was nice of you to come all the way out here."

"I got, uh, really excited about the mesh. I wanted to show it to Bitsy to make sure I bought the right kind."

"Number eight mesh is a very useful size," Lily said.

A glimmer of hope almost stole Dan's breath. If she had wanted to get rid of him, she wouldn't have made an attempt to be encouraging. "I hoped you'd like it. You can use it for screened bottom boards, screened inner covers, moving screens, and screened ventilation ports." He'd memorized the list of uses for number eight mesh on the way over here. Had he left anything out? They'd know if he left anything out. "It keeps wasps and hornets and small animals out."

Lily's smile was amused and warm and sweet all at the same time. "*Jah,* we know all about mesh."

He almost melted into a puddle right there on the kitchen floor. If she looked at him like that when he talked about mesh, what would she do if he started discussing beeswax? All he knew was that he was going to go home and memorize that book.

They were staring at him again as if they were expecting him to do a dance or spout off more interesting facts about bees. If only he'd committed more of that book to memory!

He cleared his throat. "And I hear duct tape is very useful."

"*Jah,*" Lily said, still with that slightly amused, incredibly sweet smile in place. "We use it all the time."

He was grasping at straws, and they were wishing he'd go away. Much as he wanted to be near Lily, he couldn't be a nuisance any longer. "I should go. I just wanted to bring that mesh."

"It's a long ride back," Rose said. "Why don't you stay for dinner?"

Stay for dinner? He'd give one of his molar teeth to stay for dinner. "I should probably get home."

"I don't think we should feed him again," Bitsy said.

Rose nodded at Lily. "What do you think, Lily? Don't you think it's the least we can do for him bringing the mesh?"

Lily's smile faded into uncertainty. "We would be very happy if you stayed for dinner, Dan."

Was she being polite or did she really want him to stay? Did it matter? He smiled with his whole heart. "I'd really like that."

He'd make sure that neither Lily nor Rose regretted inviting him.

Bitsy shook her head in resignation. "Don't say I didn't warn you."

Bitsy was a lost cause. She regretted it already.

Poppy seemed indifferent to the whole thing. She took Rose's hand and led her to the stairs. "We'll wash up."

Lily and Bitsy left Dan trying to find a comfortable way to lean on the island and went to the sink to wash their hands. Lily retrieved a frying pan from below the sink and set it on the stove.

"Can I help?" Dan asked.

The question seemed to catch Lily off guard. "Are you sure?"

"You're feeding me. I want to help."

Her lips twitched upward. "Do you know how to cook? Aunt B won't like it if you ruin dinner."

"I won't like it if you ruin dinner," Bitsy said, not really paying attention to the conversation. She stood on her tiptoes to reach for a bottle of tomatoes on one of the higher shelves.

Dan practically raced to her side to reach the bottle for her.

Bitsy looked him up and down as if noticing him for the first time. "A tall boy is very useful. You have my permission to stick around."

Lily's smile grew in strength as she pulled a knife from the block. "Have you ever chopped anything besides wood?"

"I'm not completely lost in the kitchen," Dan said. "Being the middle of nine children, I do a lot of stuff for my *mamm*."

"Stuff like chopping?"

171

"I almost cut my finger off dicing carrots. Does that count?"

Still smiling, Lily raised her eyebrows and slid the knife back into the block. "Maybe you should stir. We don't want blood in the spaghetti sauce."

Bitsy went from cupboard to cupboard pulling out noodles and spices and pans. "You could quit bothering us and go sit at the table until we need someone tall."

Dan flashed her a playful grin. Bitsy couldn't ruffle his feathers that easily. "I'm more than just a portable ladder. I can chop. I can dice. In an emergency, I can mince."

"Can you boil water?" Bitsy said.

Lily nudged his arm. "It doesn't involve sharp objects."

Dan got all wobbly when she smiled at him like that. He'd do anything to see that smile every day. "I am the Shawano County water-boiling champion. Three years running."

Lily laughed. "I must have missed that in the newspaper."

"I try not to brag about it."

Bitsy shoved a pot in his direction, and he filled it halfway with water before setting it on the stove and lighting the burner.

"Aunt B," Lily said. "He knows how to use a stove."

Bitsy looked heavenward. "Thank you, Lord, that Dan Kanagy hasn't blown up the house yet. It's been my daily prayer."

Dan placed the lid on the pot and turned around. "Okay, water is warming. What is my next assignment?"

Lily reached into the fridge and pulled out a package of hamburger. "Since you've proven yourself *gute* with the stove, you can brown the meat."

"Do you know how to brown meat?" Bitsy asked.

"I am also the Shawano County meat-browning champion. For three years in a row."

Bitsy coughed. Dan wanted to think that it was to hide a laugh. She used her spoon as a pointer. "Go sit at the table, young man, and quit causing trouble."

Dan lit the burner and placed the meat in the frying pan. Lily stood ready with a fork. Their hands brushed when she gave it to him, and a jolt of electricity shot through his body. Oh, *sis yuscht,* she had soft fingers. Like an angel. Or for sure a baby rabbit. He'd never actually touched an angel's fingers before.

He stirred the meat, which wasn't much of a job, but at least they let him help, and he got to stand back-to-back with Lily as she chopped vegetables at the island. The only thing better would have been face-to-face.

He nearly jumped out of his skin when Lily squealed. He dropped his fork and whipped around to look at her. "Did you cut yourself?"

"The mouse!" She grabbed his arm, dragged him around the island, and pulled him up onto the window seat with her.

Mice didn't frighten him, but he was more than willing to be led to the window seat if it got him this close to Lily Christner, especially since they shared the bench with Bitsy's cat. The white ball of fur didn't even stir from her nap as they jumped up beside her.

Bitsy's eyes did a frantic search around the room. "Where is that cat?"

Lily squeaked and pointed at her feet. "She's asleep."

Without hesitation, Bitsy growled and pulled a seriously frightening meat cleaver from the knife block. "Where did the mouse go?"

Lily leaned against Dan and pointed to the corner next to the sink. "Over there, Aunt Bitsy. He's right there."

A tiny brown mouse sniffed the floor in the far corner of the kitchen. Bitsy zeroed her focus on the rodent and tiptoed carefully forward. She wielded a meat cleaver like Moses Zook wielded a croquet mallet. Dan almost felt sorry for that mouse. It was about to lose its head.

Bitsy made a terrible racket as she swung the cleaver and buried its sharp edge half an inch into the floor. Dan almost chuckled. No wonder the floor looked as if someone had used it for a chopping block. The mouse scurried along the baseboard and disappeared around the corner into the next room. Undaunted, Bitsy chased it. Dan heard another bang and a frustrated grunt. She'd missed the mouse and put another dent in the floor.

He probably should have jumped down and helped Bitsy get rid of the mouse, but he was preoccupied sniffing Lily's hair. She smelled like vanilla and apples.

Lily braced her hand on the wall and leaned forward. "Did you get him, Aunt B?" She leaned a little too far and lost her stable footing on the deep, chunky window seat cushion.

She gasped as he shot out his arm and grabbed her around the waist. He pulled her close to him to make sure she regained her balance. Suddenly, he lost the ability to breathe. This was so improper. Very improper. Stunningly improper. He couldn't even begin to tell himself how improper it was for him to be standing on the window seat holding her like this. Still, if he hadn't grabbed her, she would have been flat on her face sprawled on the kitchen floor. He'd done the right thing.

But he should probably let go of her now, even though she smelled so good and she felt so soft and a herd of cattle stomped around inside his chest.

She lifted her face to him and brushed an imaginary strand of hair from her eyes. *"Denki,"* she stuttered. "I wasn't being very careful. I'm really afraid of mice."

Was she blushing? Of course she was blushing. A boy who didn't look much like Paul had his arm all the way around her waist and was holding on for dear life.

He should definitely let go now.

He slid his arm from around her and jumped down from the window seat. She took his offered hand and stepped down herself.

Bitsy tromped back into the kitchen with the meat cleaver but no dead mouse. "I can't tell where he hides," she said, "but there must be a hole in that storage room somewhere."

"I take it Bathroom Faucet doesn't chase

mice," Dan said.

Both Bitsy and Lily looked at him as if he had a sprig of broccoli growing out of his ear. "What did you say?" asked Bitsy.

"The cat," Dan said, pointing to Bathroom Faucet sleeping on the window seat. "You said she wasn't a good watch cat. She doesn't chase mice either?"

Dan didn't think he'd ever seen Bitsy smile, and he definitely hadn't heard her laugh. In that moment, she did both. She laughed so hard Dan feared she might pop a blood vessel in her throat or suffocate from lack of oxygen. Lily laughed too. The sound of her laughter was as infectious as water trickling from a spring.

He had no idea why they were laughing, but the sight of Bitsy so amused struck his funny bone. "What did I say?"

"It's only to be expected," Bitsy said between breaths. "But I get such a kick out of the Amish sometimes."

Including herself? "I'm glad I'm so entertaining."

Her laughter subsided, and Bitsy wiped the meat cleaver on her apron and slid it into the block. "Maybe that cat would be less of a prima donna if I called her Bathroom Faucet."

Dan glanced at Lily. "What is a prima

donna?"

She grinned and shrugged her shoulders.

"A princess. Someone who thinks they're too big for their britches," Bitsy said.

Dan nodded. Someone like Paul Glick.

He clamped his mouth shut for fear of saying that particular thought out loud. Instead, he gazed at Lily, who still seemed to be a bit shaken by the encounter on the window seat. So was he. His palms were sweaty and his breathing irregular like he'd run a footrace.

Was she shocked and disturbed that he had put his arm around her? Because it was one of the most glorious things that had ever happened to him, and he hoped they'd see many more mice before the day ended.

Lily returned his gaze briefly before blushing again and lowering her eyes to the meat-cleavered floor. He couldn't resist reaching out and touching Lily's arm to get her to look at him. He gave her what he hoped passed for a brotherly pat. "Did I call the cat by the wrong name?"

He really liked Lily's smile. If he could bottle it and sell it like honey, he'd be a wealthy man. "Her name is Farrah Fawcett," she said. "After one of Aunt Bitsy's favorite movie stars."

"I've only seen six movies in my entire

life," Dan said.

"Six?" Lily said.

"Was Farrah Fawcett in *Star Wars*? I saw one through six."

Bitsy shook her head. "*Nae,* Farrah Fawcett was not in *Star Wars.* I loved the first three. I mean the ones that came out first but were numbered four, five, and six. I had a crush on Han Solo, but Jar Jar Binks?" She raised her eyes and spoke to the ceiling. "Couldn't you have helped them do better than Jar Jar? He ruined the whole trilogy." Was she talking to *Gotte* or someone on the second floor?

Dan chuckled. He was partial to Yoda.

He really had to stop staring at Lily. With incredible self-control, he drew his eyes from her face, went to the stove, and stirred his hamburger. He would be mortified if it burned. Bitsy would never let him in the house again.

Lily went back to cutting onions while Bitsy measured spaghetti noodles in her fist and dumped them into the boiling water.

"I did a *gute* job on the water, didn't I?" he said.

Bitsy merely grunted. It might kill her to admit that he'd been helpful.

Dan heard sniffling behind him and turned to see tears streaming down Lily's face. He panicked. Without thinking, he slid his arm around her shoulders. "Lily, what's the matter?" Was she upset because of their little incident on the window seat when he had accidentally touched her waist and then accidentally let his arm linger there? He suddenly realized that he was touching her again and snatched his hand off her shoulder. How could he have been so *deerich*? "Is it because of the waist thing?"

She swiped the back of her hand across her face. "What waist thing?"

"Never mind. Why are you crying? If I've done anything to hurt your feelings . . ."

She sniffed back the tears and giggled. "Dan, calm down. I'm cutting onions. They're making my eyes water. You haven't done anything wrong lately."

"Lately? That's not very comforting." He nudged her aside. "Here, let me cut. Onions don't bother me."

"You'll get blood in the spaghetti."

"I promise not to cut myself." He held out his hand, and she reluctantly gave him the knife. It was gratifying that she trusted him at least that far.

She watched him for a few seconds to make sure he wouldn't sever an artery, then pulled out her own cutting board for mushrooms and peppers. *"Denki,"* she said. "I hate cutting onions."

It struck him hard that he never wanted to see her cry again, no matter what the reason. Lily should always be smiling.

Bitsy paused her stirring to go around to the other side of the island and study his face. "You were telling the truth. You really don't cry when you cut onions."

"Tear ducts of steel," he said.

She frowned. "You have two unusual talents, Dan Kanagy."

"Only two?"

She didn't smile. She was probably truly convinced that he had a sum total of two talents. "You're tall, and you can cut onions without tearing up. I still want you out of my kitchen, but at least you're more useful than that cat."

Dan shrugged. "Being tall isn't really a talent. It's more a state of nature."

Bitsy nodded thoughtfully. "I'm sorry to tell you that you only have one talent. Don't bury it under a bushel."

Dan bit his tongue to keep from laughing. Should he be offended that Bitsy thought his only good quality was onion cutting? "How do you think I could best use my onion talent? I could go from house to house and offer to cut onions for people." He could come here every day and cut onions for the Christners. That sounded *wunderbarr.*

Bitsy waved her hand as if she were swatting him away like a fly. "*Ach,* young man, don't tease me. I sincerely hope you develop another talent or two, though right now I don't see anything promising."

Lily smiled at him as if she liked him, as if she enjoyed standing in the kitchen cutting vegetables together. His heart rolled around his chest like a buggy wheel. "He's a good weeder," she said.

Bitsy swiped a towel across the table. "Not that good. And he tramples dandelions as if they were weeds."

"He has lots of friends, and he knows how to care for sick cows." Lily spoke as if she were talking about the weather, but Dan thought he might burst. "And he's generous. He brought me the *Little House on the Prairie* nine-book set. Nine books, Aunt B." She glanced at him and smiled, and he found himself wondering what other books he could get for her.

He hadn't been completely invisible to her. She'd noticed him, and she actually had some nice things to say about him. He could have taken her in his arms and whirled her around the kitchen. Instead he pressed his lips together and tried not to explode into a

182

smile. His lips would probably fly off his face in all his elation. Lily would not like a boy who didn't have lips.

She brushed the peppers from her cutting board into the frying pan. "His smile puts people at ease and makes you feel better, no matter how bad of a day you're having."

"It does?" he said.

"Until you say something that makes me want to run away screaming." She cocked an eyebrow and tempered her words with a grin.

It was true. He always seemed to put his foot in his mouth.

He resolved to never speak again. Just smile. Lily liked his smile. He could have done cartwheels all the way down the lane.

Bitsy folded her arms across her cherry-red apron and scrutinized Dan as if she were buying a horse. "*Nae.* I don't see it."

Lily sighed while a smile played at her lips. "Aunt B, you are impossible."

Dan didn't know why he laughed. It mattered very much what Bitsy thought of him, and apparently, she wasn't impressed. But he could work on Aendi Bitsy, because Lily had given him hope.

She liked his smile. It was at least a place to start.

CHAPTER TWELVE

Paul's voice clanged in her head like a fire alarm.

Forgive but don't forget.

The trouble was, Dan Kanagy had an uncanny ability to make her forget, especially when he sat two feet away from her at the kitchen table smiling as if he were the happiest boy in Wisconsin. His smile practically begged her to smile back. So she did. She liked seeing his smile widen every time she returned his gaze, every time she gave him a sliver of attention.

What was so wrong about forgiving *and* forgetting?

Paul said if she forgot how much Dan had hurt her, he would have the power to hurt her again, worse than before. Maybe so, but it exhausted her to hold back her friendship simply because Dan might call her Amtrak again.

Paul never had to know how she treated

Dan in her own kitchen.

Poppy and Rose sat on one side, and Lily and Dan sat on the other, with Aunt B at the head of the table. Poppy and Rose had made a salad while Dan had watched Lily finish the spaghetti. She hadn't minded him standing so near, teasing her about the way she stirred the sauce, asking for tastes every minute. Dan, despite all his faults, made her smile. He made her laugh.

He made her forget.

Paul need never know.

Bitsy held out her hands. Lily took one and Poppy took the other. Poppy slid her hand into Rose's and Rose reached across the table to grab Dan's. Surprise flickered in his eyes before he curled his lips into that ever-present smile and took Rose's hand. After a moment of hesitation, he reached out and enfolded her hand in his. He had really nice hands. Long, thin fingers and rough palms callused from farmwork.

She felt the heat travel up her neck as she tried to decide if she liked or hated this little tradition of Aunt B's. Holding hands for prayer had never bothered her before. But holding hands with one of her sisters was a far cry from holding hands with a boy like Dan Kanagy. Electricity tingled through her fingers and up her arm. Was this normal?

Would she feel the same thing if she held hands with one of her boy cousins on her *dat*'s side? Would Paul Glick's touch make her skin feel this twinkly? It was all too confusing. She opted to pretend that she didn't have hands.

In spite of her hands, she wondered what Dan would think of their suppertime ritual. They said two prayers before every meal. A holding-hands, out-loud prayer offered by Aunt B and then, because Aunt B wanted them to be devout and proper Amish girls, a silent prayer as well.

Lily focused her attention on Dan out of the corner of her eye to see how he would bear up under the strangeness of it all. He acted unsure for mere seconds, then bowed his head and closed his eyes at the same time Aunt B did.

"Dear Heavenly Father," Aunt B began. "We give thanks for the bees and for each other. And while we're not especially grateful that Dan Kanagy saw fit to drop by right before dinnertime, we are grateful that he brought number eight mesh and that he did not cut off his finger, even though he should have stayed out of my kitchen in the first place. Bless him to learn not to make a pest of himself. And bless that whoever tipped over our beehive will see the error of his ways. Either that or please give him a case of heat rash in a very bad place. Amen." They all raised their heads, but Aunt B growled and lowered hers again. Lily had been expecting this. Aunt B always forgot to bless the food. Everyone at the table bowed their heads again. "And, Heavenly Father, please bless this spaghetti that it won't make us sick. Amen."

Lily immediately opened her eyes to see Dan's reaction to the fact that Aunt B had insulted him in her prayer.

He squeezed her hand, sending the electricity all the way up her shoulder, and smiled that glorious smile of his, as if he were the sunrise on a clear summer's day.

"Sorry," she whispered.

He leaned close and whispered back, "Your aunt Bitsy is really warming up to me."

Lily stifled a giggle and glanced across the table. Poppy gave her one of those "What is going on?" looks, and Rose simply watched them, her eyes glowing with a hundred different secrets.

What were they muddled about? Dan had simply whispered in her ear. She'd simply smiled back.

"Silent grace now," Aunt Bitsy said, bowing her head without waiting to see if anyone followed her.

Lily bowed her head and tried to concentrate on her prayer. At least she had her hands to herself. It was easier to pray with hands. Once they'd said silent grace, they passed the food around the table. Always to the left. Aunt Bitsy was very particular that they always passed to the left.

"You haven't had any more beehives tipped over, have you?" Dan asked as he scooped noodles onto his plate. "I don't like thinking someone is bent on harming you like that."

"Nae," Aunt B said. "No more beehives overturned."

Lily glued her eyes to her plate. No need to tell him about the other thing. She hadn't even told Paul.

Rose turned one shade paler. "Someone is still out there, though."

Dan frowned as if he'd lost his best friend. "Has something else happened?"

Rose's voice sounded small and thin. "He tore our laundry from the line and threw it in the mud yet."

The sight of the soiled pile of dresses had shaken all of them, but poor Rose had been terrified. She had climbed into bed with Lily that night.

The lines around Dan's mouth seemed to

cut into his face. He turned to Lily. "When did this happen?"

"Three nights ago. It might have been a teenager playing a prank."

A look of deep disquiet glowed in his eyes as he gazed at Lily, but when he turned to Rose, he had extinguished it, giving her a reassuring, almost carefree, smile. "*Jah,* it was most likely one of the local boys with nothing to do but play pranks on the Amish. They are harmless. And your *aendi* has a shotgun."

A hint of a smile pulled at Rose's lips. "No one would dare cross Aunt Bitsy and her gun."

Bitsy narrowed her eyes and nodded. "A little buckshot might teach those Shawano boys a lesson."

Lily near jumped out of her skin when Dan found her hand under the table and squeezed it. Her eyes flew to his face. Was he trying to get fresh? *Nae,* his concern was deep and cold, like Lake Michigan in January. She squeezed back and nodded. They could talk later — about Rose and vandals and the inappropriateness of squeezing a girl's hand like that and almost giving her a warm, mushy heart attack.

He cleared his throat and changed the subject right quick. "Do these muffins have honey in them? They're delicious."

Rose perked up even more. "*Jah*. Lily's recipe."

"How much honey do you get every year from your beehives?"

"Lily keeps all those records," Aunt B said. "She can tell you to the pound."

Dan looked at her as if she wore a plate of his favorite doughnuts on her head. "Lily is about the smartest girl I've ever seen."

She knew she shouldn't let flattery make her blush. It didn't matter that she wasn't smarter than anybody. She still felt the warmth on her cheeks.

"The amount of honey depends on the year. Some years we might get a hundred pounds. Our best year we averaged almost two hundred pounds from each hive."

He winked at her. "You were always good at math."

Lily thought of how little they would get for their honey this year. He wouldn't think she was so good at math if she couldn't find a way to make ends meet. "I'm not that smart."

Paul has always told her it didn't matter to him that she wasn't smart. It was harder for smart girls to be humble. He wanted a godly wife, not someone who knew how to divide fractions in her head.

Aunt Bitsy pointed her fork at Lily like she always did when she was about to give her a lecture. She thought that Lily was putting herself down when she said things like that, but in truth, Lily was only being honest. She kept the family's accounts book, but as Paul always reminded her, it wasn't all that hard to add and subtract numbers. A first grader could do it.

Before Aunt B opened her mouth to scold her, Dan protested. "What do you mean you're not that smart? I've heard you read to my *mammi.* You never stumble over words like I would, and your pronunciation is perfect. Not only do you read like a teacher, keeping account books is more than just adding and subtracting. You know stuff like how many pounds of honey the average beehive produces in one year." He twirled some spaghetti around his fork. "Whose idea was it to rent hives to the Chidesters to pollinate their sunflowers?"

"I don't remember," Lily said.

Dan sprouted a self-satisfied smirk. "It was yours. Mr. Chidester told me so."

Poppy propped her elbow on the table and looked at Dan as if seeing him for the first time. "It *was* Lily's idea, but she never wants to take credit for anything."

Lily slumped in her chair to make herself

as small as possible. "It's pride to think you're smart, and pride is a sin."

Dan didn't seem annoyed with her at all, even though she contradicted him. His lips twitched into a silly grin, and he nudged her with his elbow. The spaghetti slipped off his fork. "I would never call you proud. You're using the talents *Gotte* gave you for the good of your family. You're very capable, Lily. Don't let anyone tell you otherwise."

Dan looked around the table, as if he hadn't noticed everybody staring at him. He pulled back his enthusiasm and stuffed a forkful of spaghetti into his mouth. Nobody spoke. Her sisters and Aunt B looked at Dan as if he'd found a cure for cancer. Lily wasn't quite sure what to make of that. Dan had all but given her permission to be proud.

Dan took a swig of water and wiped his mouth. "When do you extract your honey? I read that some beekeepers do it all at once at the end of the year. Others do it in the middle of the season."

"It was an early spring, and the hives are strong. We're extracting next week," Poppy said, eyeing him with something akin to approval on her face. "You wanna help?"

His enthusiasm immediately resurfaced. "You'd let me help?"

192

Lily couldn't help but smile. Pulling honey was hard, sticky work. No one with half a brain wanted to help, unless they didn't know what they were getting into. She found herself hoping Dan wouldn't realize how hard it would be. It might be fun to have him around on extraction day.

"He'll only be in the way," said Aunt B as if she'd already lost the argument.

She had. Both Poppy and Rose were unusually insistent. "Oh, *jah,* Aunt B," Poppy said. "He's coming."

"We could really use his help with the supers," Rose chimed in.

Lily might as well throw in her two cents. "We can always use an extra pair of hands." She sounded eager, like a silly girl hoping a boy would notice her. She wasn't eager, just mildly willing. Dan would be a lot of help. Like a hired hand.

Bitsy shrugged. "We start on Tuesday. I hope you can keep up."

Dan lit up the room with his smile. "I'll be the best apprentice beekeeper you've ever seen. You won't regret it."

"I already do," Aunt B said, but there was amusement in her tone. Not even Aunt B could be callous enough to burst Dan's bubble.

Dan gasped and leaped from his chair.

193

"Bitsy, have you got a piece of paper?"

Aunt Bitsy raised an eyebrow. "In the drawer right there."

Dan found the paper drawer, snapped a sheet from the pile, and pulled a clean glass from the cupboard. He went to the end of the table opposite Aunt B and set the glass upside down.

"What are you doing?" Poppy asked.

Dan carefully slid the paper between the glass and the table. "I caught a bee."

"Wait!" Aunt B yelled. "Before you . . ."

Smiling calmly, Dan lifted the paper and glass with the bee trapped between them and ambled to the door. "I thought we should let it outside. My book says to never kill a bee."

Aunt B expelled a slow breath. "That's right. Never kill a bee. They are the future of the human race." She rested her elbows on the table and cradled her head in her hands. "That was close. I thought you were going to kill it. I'm happy to tell you that you have one additional talent."

Dan chuckled as he opened the door. "I'm really glad to know that. Maybe if we spend enough time together, you'll discover a few more." He walked onto the porch and pulled the sheet of paper from the bottom of the glass. The bee flew out and away.

It was a small thing, but Lily couldn't help but be impressed by the Dan Kanagy she didn't really know at all. Dead bees made Aunt Bitsy very upset.

Dan came back in, shut the door, and sat down at the table. "You probably have bees in your house often."

"It's not unusual," Lily said. "Since there are several hives nearby."

"You have a wonderful-*gute* piece of property here. I know how hard it is to find fertile land at a *gute* price."

Paul's voice intruded into Lily's thoughts. Dan's family had practically stolen Glick's property. She let thoughts of Paul evaporate like dew. *Forgive and forget.*

Aunt Bitsy nodded. "When my sister and her husband died, I bought the land with the insurance money so my girls could live near family and have plenty of room to grow."

"They had insurance?" Dan asked. The Amish did not usually buy any kind of insurance. That part always puzzled people.

Pain flickered in Aunt B's eyes. "I bought a life insurance policy on my sister after Lily was born. She told me that if anything happened to her, she planned to leave the babies in my care. I knew I would need some money to do it properly if it ever came to that."

Dan put down his fork and laced his fingers together. He glanced at Lily uncomfortably. "Is it okay if I ask how your parents died? I mean, if it's not, you can throw me out of the house."

Lily shook her head and looked at him as if he deserved a scolding for thinking she'd be annoyed by that question. "Of course you can ask. They left us with our grandparents while they hired a driver to do some Christmas shopping in Green Bay. The roads were slick. They were killed in a car accident."

The memory still hurt, but the pain wasn't fresh and raw like it had once been. Mamm and Dat were in a better place, and while that knowledge didn't help Poppy much, Lily took a lot of comfort from it.

Dan lowered his voice, as if he feared they'd be offended if he asked his question too loudly. "How old were you?"

"Almost fifteen years ago," Lily said. "I was eight. Poppy was six. Rose was five yet."

He acted as if it had been his own parents who'd been killed. "I'm sorry."

Lily gave Rose and Poppy a half smile. "We still have each other, and we have Aunt B. We never would have survived without Aunt B."

Aunt B wiped some moisture from her eyes and swatted away Lily's praise. "You girls are the ones who saved me. I was miserable until you came along." She took the last bite of her muffin. "Now I'm more miserable."

Everybody laughed, even Rose, who took their parents' death harder than all of them. Even though Aunt Bitsy couldn't bring herself to spoon out compliments, her girls knew how much she loved them. It was the anchor that kept their lives from going adrift.

Dan jumped up almost before they finished eating and started clearing plates from the table. He filled the sink with water and wouldn't budge when Lily tried to scoot him out of the way. "I'm washing," he said, with that mischievous smile of his. "Your hands will get wrinkly if they're in the water for too long, and you need to save them for the bees."

Lily smirked and grabbed a dish towel. She didn't have a witty reply because Dan had completely disarmed her with his offer to wash dishes. To Paul, after-supper cleanup was women's work, and he wouldn't have dreamed of putting his hands into a sink of soapy water.

Lily frowned to herself. She should really

stop comparing her boyfriend to Dan Kanagy.

Poppy put away leftovers while Rose wiped counters and Aunt B swept the floor. They had the cleanup routine down almost like a dance. A dance that Dan had become suddenly, naturally a part of.

He obviously had a lot of experience washing dishes. She could see it in the way he drew the rag along the plates front and back, checking for leftover food, making sure he didn't leave excess bubbles.

He rinsed the first plate with hot water, smiled, and handed it to her to dry. "I hope you can keep up," he said. "I've been known to keep three dryers busy at once."

Lily raised her eyebrows. "You can't go fast enough for me."

Dan raced through the plates and cups and put some elbow grease into the frying pan. He still had time to flick drops of water on the back of her neck when she wasn't looking and smear a handful of bubbles up her arm when she reached for another plate. Did he never stop teasing?

They finished the dishes in record time, each trying to prove to the other how fast they were. Lily almost regretted the last dish. They'd been having such a *gute* time. Maybe she should have dried slower.

Aunt B hung up the broom and dustpan on the special hook on the wall and turned to look at Dan who rinsed the last of the bubbles out of the sink. "Well, Dan Kanagy, it's not that we don't appreciate your help with the dishes, but it's time for you to go away now. You've worn out your welcome."

Lily blushed down to her toes, but to her relief, Dan didn't seem the least bit ruffled by Aunt B's bluntness. He grinned at Lily, dried his hands, and grabbed his hat from the hook by the door.

"I hope you'll let me come back sometime."

"It's unavoidable," Aunt B said.

He chuckled as he opened the door and glanced at Lily. "Then I'll see you later."

The dimming light of sunset offered him enough light to see by. He stepped onto the porch, paused briefly, and caught his breath. Without warning, he turned and pulled the door toward him. Holding it as if it were a shield, he stuck his head back into the house, grabbed Lily's hand, and pulled her outside with him. Lily gasped as he practically yanked her onto the porch.

"I really want to talk to Lily in private for a second," he said, before slamming the door, no doubt leaving Aunt B and her sisters wondering what in the world had come over him.

What craziness was this?

He pulled her toward him so that their faces were mere inches apart, and her heart jumped into her throat. Was he going to kiss her? Why would he ever dream for one minute he had the right to kiss her?

Her gaze involuntarily traveled to his lips. Did she want him to kiss her?

Absolutely not. No matter how many somersaults her heart did or how warm her cheeks felt, Dan was not her boyfriend. Number eight mesh was not a good enough reason to expect a kiss.

"Dan Kanagy," she said, trying halfheartedly to pull her hand out of his. "What do you think . . . ?"

He put a finger to his lips. "Shh." There was no glint of a tease in his eyes or even an I-want-to-kiss-you look she might have expected. His eyes glistened with something deep and troubled.

"I didn't want to alarm Rose," he whispered, his voice sounding even lower and deeper when he made it soft like that. "But you have to see this."

He pointed across the lane to where the barn stood facing the house. Someone had painted black, ugly letters on their red barn door: **YOU WILL BURN IN HELL.**

Lily clapped her hand over her mouth. A wave of nausea attacked her like a charging bull. "Dan, what . . . what does it mean? Who would do such a thing?"

He squeezed her hand tighter. "It's okay. It's going to be okay. It must have happened while we ate dinner. It wasn't there when I arrived."

Lily's skin crawled. Someone had been sneaking around their property while they had been just a few feet away? Terror gripped her, and she grabbed on to Dan's arm like a lifeline.

Dan rubbed his hand up and down her arm. "Lily, I'm going to go have a look around. Can you stay right here and wait for me?"

"Is he . . . is he still here?" The thought that he might be lurking anywhere near made Lily light-headed.

He cupped his hands gently around her arms. "I don't think so, but that's what I want to find out. Are you going to be okay if I leave you? I'll only be a few minutes."

The panic rose in her throat like bile. He was going to leave her alone on the porch? What if the man came back and attacked her?

The concern on his face deepened in the lines around his mouth. "Maybe you should go back in the house and wait for me. It's just that I don't want to frighten Rose if we don't have to."

If she was this panicked, Lily could only imagine how something like this would affect Rose. She took a deep breath and nodded slowly. "I'll wait here for you."

His hand traveled down her arm, and he found her hand again. His touch made her feel safer. "If you see anything or hear anything, call for me and I'll come running, okay?"

"Okay," she said, nearly choking with fear.

He released her hand and bounded quietly down the steps. Clutching the porch railing, she watched him disappear around the side of the barn. The irrational thought that he might have disappeared forever stole her breath away. Was something sinister waiting for him in the orchards?

With her eyes trained into the gathering darkness, she counted to sixty again and again. She flinched when she thought she might have heard rustling to her left but talked herself out of panicking. If she burst into the house trembling and pale, as she surely was, Rose would never sleep in her own bed again.

How many times had she counted to sixty? Where was Dan? She'd never forgive herself if something horrible happened to him.

She nearly jumped out of her skin as she heard something stirring to her left. For certain this time. "Lily?"

She thought she might faint at the sound of Dan's voice. Willing her heart to slow to a gallop, she looked to the bushes that stood between the lane and the house. They rustled again, and Dan squeezed through a gap. She never would have believed that she could welcome the approach of Dan Kanagy, but right now he was the most comforting sight in the world. He seemed to glide over the flagstones and up the porch steps. Relief overcame her, and she finally let out the breath she'd been holding.

He must have seen something in her eyes he didn't like — maybe the glassy stare of someone who would surely faint any minute. He gathered her into his arms and held her tight, as if she might fall to pieces if he let go. In the back of her mind, she knew she shouldn't, but she melted into his embrace and let his warmth seep into her brittle bones.

"You're shaking," he said.

"I was afraid you wouldn't come back."

She heard the smile in his voice. "Your *aendi* Bitsy would have liked that. I trampled some dandelions out there."

Lily giggled in spite of her fright. "I promise I'll never tell."

"I might have to plant a tree to placate her."

His light tone helped Lily regain some of her composure, at least enough to know that she should not be swaddling herself in Dan's arms like this. She nudged away from him.

He seemed reluctant to let go. Maybe he felt as shaken as she did.

"Did you find anything?"

"Whoever it was is gone. There was a half-empty can of spray paint behind the barn, but it's too dark to see footprints."

She shivered involuntarily as ice threaded up her spine. "Who hates us this much?"

The muscles of Dan's jaw tensed as he gazed toward the barn. "I don't know. But right now, they seem to be bent on making mischief but not doing any real harm."

"Our bees might disagree with you."

He gave her a half smile. "I was trying to make you feel better."

She rested her hand on the railing. "I know. *Denki.*"

He brought his hand on top of hers. He really shouldn't do that. "We've got to make sure Rose doesn't find out about this."

"What can we do? She gathers eggs at five thirty."

"Can you keep her in the house the rest of the night?"

She knit her brows together. "*Jah,* we don't usually go out this late."

"I can paint over it before she wakes up. She'll never know."

Lily felt giddy with gratitude. "That is so kind. I don't know what to say."

His smile came back with full force. "Anything for the Honeybee Schwesters."

She frowned. "It could take some time."

He thumbed his suspenders and looked away. "I'd be up late reading about bees anyway."

"Okay," Lily said. "I will go in and distract Rose and tell Poppy and Aunt B what happened." She turned to go into the house and then turned back. "What reason am I going to give them for your strange behavior? You pulled me out of the house as if it were on fire."

He cocked an eyebrow. "You could tell them I had the overwhelming urge to kiss you, and it couldn't wait."

She widened her eyes in mock indignation. "I'm not going to lie to them."

The way he looked at her made her forget how to breathe. "Who said anything about lying?" He took a step closer. Too close. She could smell fresh-cut hay and leather. "If you'd rather be completely truthful with your family, we should do a little kissing right now."

He stood too close. Though she couldn't meet his eye, she was sure he wore that teasing smile on his face. The heat traveled up her face clear to the tips of her ears. At least he wouldn't be able to see her flaming red ears in the dimness.

He didn't back away, not one little bit, as if eager to talk her into it. "Your story would be more believable if we actually kissed."

More believable? None of her family would ever believe Dan Kanagy would kiss her. He'd made it clear that he thought she was homely and unappealing. She *was* homely and unappealing.

Her heart stumbled over itself and fell in the mud. Paul was the only person who would ever consider kissing her, and that was only because he'd have to someday.

She took a giant step back. "I'll . . . I'll think of something to tell my family."

She must have mistaken the look in his eyes for disappointment. Surely he didn't really want to kiss her. He'd only been teasing.

Whatever she saw in his gaze disappeared,

replaced by that irrepressible smile, gentle and accepting. "Do you have paint?"

She nibbled on her bottom lip. "Oh dear. Not a bit of red. Rose's paints are on the workbench in the barn, but if she has red, it's not much."

"Luke Bontrager lives close. I'll see if I can borrow paint from him." He rubbed his hands together. "I'll be back as soon as I can. And try not to worry. That painter, whoever he is, is long gone."

"Okay," she said. She would do her best not to worry. She didn't know if she would succeed.

"And be sure to tell your aunt what I'm up to. I don't want her to see me lurking in the shadows and load her shotgun."

Lily grinned. "She doesn't believe in guns, remember?"

"I don't know if I'm convinced of that."

He stared at her until she had to say something to break the silence. "I . . . I don't know how to thank you. Words don't seem enough."

He winked at her. "Your smile will always be enough."

That grin of his would not make her faint. Even if it killed her.

CHAPTER THIRTEEN

Dan, Luke Bontrager, and Josiah Yoder regarded the barn door by the light of Dan's flashlight.

"Who would do something like this?" Josiah asked.

"I don't know," Dan said. "Somebody out to play a prank."

Luke took off his hat and ran his fingers through his hair. "Somebody who knows there's no man here to protect them."

After he'd left the Honeybee Farm, Dan had gone to Luke's house and then Josiah's to borrow paint. Both of his best friends had insisted on coming back to the farm with him. Looking at the vandal's work, Dan was glad he hadn't been able to talk his friends into staying in bed. Painting the barn door would be a bigger job than he'd anticipated.

Dan glanced at the seven paint cans at his feet containing various shades of leftover paint. Four cans from Luke's house, three from Josiah's. "Unless we match this color exactly, we'll have to paint the entire door. Both panels."

Luke nodded. "And they still might notice."

"Rose will worry herself sick if she suspects," Josiah said.

"We'll just have to do our best in the dark." Dan picked up a can of paint and shook it hard. "Let's test a patch of each of these. Lord willing, this can contains the exact same color on the barn."

Luke smirked. "That would be too easy."

It was harder to tell in the dark, but the first can they opened seemed nowhere near red. It looked more like a lovely shade of pink. Luke shoved Josiah in the shoulder. "Pink? What kind of barn color is that?"

"Hey!" Josiah said. "It's mauve, and my sister's always fiddling with the paint colors. All these are supposed to be red."

Luke grunted. "I've never heard of mauve. Must be one of those girly colors."

Josiah chuckled. "If you lived next door to your sister, you'd know a lot more than what mauve looks like. You'd also know how to burp a baby and change a diaper."

"I can safely promise you that I will never change a diaper," Luke said. "It's bad enough that I now know what mauve is."

"That's why you'll never get a wife," Josiah said.

Luke shoved him again.

Dan squatted next to the remaining six cans. "Do you think you two could concentrate long enough to help me find some red?"

Luke pointed to one of his paint cans. The dried paint on the outside of the can looked red enough. The label even had a picture of a barn on it. "This looks promising."

Dan shook the can and pried it open with a flathead screwdriver. He grabbed one of the smaller paintbrushes, also supplied by Luke, dipped it in the paint, and swiped it over the top of the black spray paint. Luke's cherry-red paint was about ten shades too bright for the country red of the Christners' barn.

"It's closer than mauve," Luke said.

While Josiah and Luke opened the rest of the cans, Dan slipped into Lily's barn and found a small can of black paint. Maybe they could darken the red a little.

They mixed black with the bright red plus another red from one of Luke's cans and came up with something they hoped was pretty close to the barn color. At least it looked that way in the dark. They each picked up a wide paintbrush and started painting. Luke and Josiah each took one end and Dan started in the middle. It would need at least two coats.

Luke made long vertical strokes with his brush. "How did you see this? The Christners' house isn't exactly on the way to your house."

Dan smiled to himself. In spite of how the evening had ended, Lily Christner had smiled at him more than once. And the touch of her hand had felt like a jolt of pure energy. "I brought over some beehive mesh for Bitsy."

"What is beehive mesh?" Josiah said.

Luke narrowed his eyes. "And why did you bring it?"

Dan painted like a madman. "I . . . just, well . . . you know."

Both Josiah and Luke interrupted their painting to stare at him. Surely it was too dark for them to see the light dancing in his eyes.

"In case you didn't notice, Lily Christner has a boyfriend," Luke said.

Josiah drew his brows together in concern. "The same boyfriend she had when you liked her in eighth grade, Dan."

Luke shook his head. "I hate to break the news to you, but you're not good-looking enough to change her mind."

It was always the same way with his friends. Josiah was the thoughtful and serious one. Luke was flippant and realistic. Neither of them wanted him to get hurt.

"Paul Glick thinks he owns her," Josiah said.

Luke scowled. "I hate that guy."

"We're not supposed to hate anybody," Dan said, clenching his jaw.

Luke huffed out a breath in surrender. "I don't hate him. I just can't stand him."

The feeling was mutual.

Josiah dipped his brush in the paint can. "I thought you'd given up on that two years ago. You went to Pennsylvania to find a wife."

"I meant to give up. Even when I came home I was going to leave her alone. But my *mammi* died, and Lily was there and it hurt too much when I thought about not trying."

Josiah glanced at him between paint strokes. "It's going to hurt even worse when she marries Paul."

Dan scrubbed his hand down the side of his face. "I know."

"So why go to all the trouble?" Luke said.

Dan's lips twitched upward. "Because it's

going to feel really, really *gute* if she chooses me."

Josiah lost that stricken look and smiled. Luke laughed out loud before remembering that they were supposed to be quiet. "All you have to do is show her what a *dumkoff* Paul is."

"Nae," Dan said. "I can't get Lily to love me by putting Paul down."

Luke filled his brush with more paint. "Then what are you going to do?"

"I'm sort of sneaking up on her."

Luke smirked. "Were you sneaking around her barn tonight? Is that how you discovered the spray paint?"

Dan raised his eyebrows. "They invited me to dinner."

Luke looked mildly impressed. *"Gute* work."

"I took the sisters home from the gathering Friday. Even Poppy was nice."

"I don't believe that," Luke said. "Poppy would just as soon smack you as look at you."

Dan flashed Luke a smug smile. "You maybe. Not me."

"Ha," Luke said.

Josiah dabbed at the same spot over and over again as if he were concentrating real hard on painting. "Does Rose ever talk about me?"

Luke snorted softly. "Have you and Rose ever had a conversation?"

Josiah lifted his chin. "Three months ago at a gathering I said, 'Your honey cake is delicious,' and she said *'Denki.'* "

Luke rolled his eyes. "You two are pathetic." He motioned toward Josiah with his paintbrush. "Rose doesn't even know you're alive." He tilted his head in Dan's direction. "And Lily has a boyfriend."

"Only a true friend would kick a guy when he's down," Dan said, smiling as if Luke's teasing hadn't made him feel about two inches tall.

Lily had a boyfriend, and there wasn't much Dan could do about it. What a depressing thought.

Josiah dipped his paintbrush in the bucket. "Well, Poppy despises you. So you're in the same boat as the two of us."

Luke looked as if he'd swallowed a bee. "Poppy? Why would I be interested in Poppy? I'm glad she despises me, because I can't stand her."

"I don't think so," Josiah said. "I saw the way you looked at her after *gmay* last week."

Luke swatted at Josiah like a fly. "I was not. She may be pretty, but she's got the temperament of a badger. I want a wife

214

who's soft and feminine. Someone who has never given me a bloody nose. Is that too much to ask?"

"I've always pictured you with someone a little feisty yet," Josiah said.

Luke pinched his lips together. "Nope. Soft, gentle, and sweet. Not Poppy."

"It's not like anyone is going to have you, Luke," Dan said. "You're a grump. Girls don't like grumps."

"Lily does. Just look at Paul," Luke said.

Dan deflated like a balloon. Paul was more than a grump. He was downright cantankerous, and he would ruin Lily in a matter of weeks after they married.

Luke glanced at Dan, and the corners of his mouth drooped. "I'm sorry. I shouldn't have said that."

Dan swallowed the lump in his throat. "It's true. I just don't like it."

Luke growled low and deep. "Oh, *sis yuscht,* I hate Paul Glick."

Josiah shook his head. "You shouldn't say that." He was always the one to chastise Dan and Luke if they strayed too far from the straight and narrow. "Jesus wants us to love everyone."

"Some folks are extra hard to love."

It only took the three of them half an hour to paint the barn door, but with the time it had taken to round up his friends and mix the paint, it must have been almost ten o'clock. Morning was going to come plenty early.

They stepped back and looked at their handiwork by the light of the flashlight. They'd successfully covered the nasty words. Rose would never suspect they'd been there. The color didn't look quite right in the dim light, but Lord willing, it would be close enough.

Luke gathered all the dirty paintbrushes in his empty bucket. "Not too bad for a paint job in the dark."

"As long as Rose is happy, I'm happy," Josiah said.

Luke leaned toward Josiah as if he were spilling a big secret. "She doesn't know you're alive, remember?"

Josiah pressed his lips into a hard line. "She will."

Luke smirked. "As long as you don't scare her off first."

Dan snapped his head around when he heard the front door open. Someone came toward them holding a lantern in her hand. He tried not to let his heart gallop when he saw that it was Lily. She hesitated at the last flagstone, holding her lantern higher as if to make sure the three boys standing in front of her barn were friendly. She wore her gray dress and a black bonnet but had no shoes.

He hoped they hadn't awakened her. "Is everything okay?"

She smiled tentatively and took his question as an invitation to come closer. "I couldn't sleep knowing you were out here slaving away on my barn. I came to see if you needed my help."

"We're all done," Dan said. "It was as easy as pies and cakes."

They stepped aside so Lily could see the new paint. She opened her mouth as if to speak and promptly closed it again. She got closer to the barn door and held the lantern against it. "Uh . . . the color is . . ."

"We mixed four different colors to get it right," Dan said. "What do you think?"

"It's . . ." She let out a long breath. The lantern reflected the warm glow in her eyes when she turned to him. "It's perfect. Perfect. I can't believe the three of you did this for us. We're not even family."

"Anything for Rose," Josiah said. Luke nudged him in the back with his shoulder. "All the Honeybee Schwesters," Josiah added.

Dan stifled a grin.

"I hope you know how grateful I am," Lily said. "For everything." The look she gave

217

him could have melted ice on Shawano Lake. The air grew twenty degrees warmer, like a tropical heat wave.

He wanted to bask in that smile forever, but there was really no reason to hang around now that the barn was done. His mind raced for an excuse to stay.

Luke turned his back on Lily so only Dan could see the look on his face. He smirked and cocked an eyebrow. "I've got to get going."

Dan did his best not to act disappointed that he'd be forced to leave. "Okay. I'll drive you home."

Luke picked up his paint cans and bucket full of paintbrushes. "No need. I'm the Christners' nearest neighbor. I'll walk."

He turned and sauntered down the lane, no doubt with a smug grin plastered on his face.

Josiah had his own way home. He'd ridden his horse over. He picked up his paint cans and set them in Dan's buggy. "I'll fetch these from you tomorrow," he said, nodding as if he were the smartest friend in the world. "We will see you later, Lily. Tell Rose I said hello."

"I don't know if that would be such a good idea," Lily said.

Josiah seemed to wilt. "Oh. Okay."

Lily laid a hand on Josiah's arm. "Rose will wonder where I saw you between suppertime and bedtime. She might grow suspicious yet."

Josiah stood up straighter. "Your reasoning is wise."

She smiled that summery smile again. "I'll be sure to put in a good word for you as soon as an opportunity arises. Anyone who comes in the middle of the night to paint my barn deserves a good word."

Dan could see Josiah trying not to smile too hard as he mounted his horse and waved good-bye.

"That was nice of you," Dan said under his breath.

"Josiah is a *gute* man. I like him very much."

He really liked her smile. It almost made him wish the Amish weren't against photographs. He'd take a thousand pictures of Lily's face.

Standing close together, they watched Josiah disappear down the lane. Being with Lily felt comfortable, like coming home. Like a bowl of warm bread pudding. Like the song of a bird outside his bedroom window or the touch of his *dat*'s strong arm around his shoulders. There were no awkward silences that he felt obliged to fill, no

219

clumsy words he needed to say. He savored every second of nearness to Lily because any moment now she would break the connection and tell him he had to go.

"It's a beautiful night," she said. "I know it's late, but would you like to sit for a minute on the porch?"

Would he? "I don't want to keep you up too late."

"I can't sleep." She gazed at him doubtfully. "But if you need to go, I understand. Cows come early in the morning."

"I wouldn't be able to sleep even if someone hit me over the head with a two-by-four." She had turned him inside out. He might not ever sleep again.

"*Cum* then. Let's sit."

He took the lantern from her, and they sat on the top porch step looking out at the barn, which they couldn't really see in the dark. "You worked everything out with Rose?"

Lily nodded. "I told Aunt Bitsy and Poppy about the barn. They were very grateful that you were painting it."

He wanted to ask her who she thought might be making mischief on their farm, but he didn't want to upset her on such a pleasant evening. When he had offered to paint the barn, he was thinking as much about Lily's feelings as he was about Rose's. The message troubled Dan greatly, but Lily didn't need to know that.

"Are you cold?" he asked when she wrapped her arms around herself.

"A little."

He leaped to his feet and retrieved the SpongeBob blanket from his buggy. A tingle traveled up his arms as he laid the blanket over her shoulders. "You know, we've never talked about that book," he said, sitting down and leaning back on his hands.

"Did you cry at the end?"

He nudged her shoulder with his. "Bawled like a baby."

She beamed like the moon itself. "It takes a strong man to admit that."

Dan tilted his head and gazed at the stars while Lily gave her opinion about *Where the Red Fern Grows.* He could have listened to her rich, lilting voice all night. She laughed at something funny he said. He told her she was clever.

All the while, he fought hard to keep his thoughts on the book and the stars and even the barn door instead of imagining how nice it would be to wrap Lily in his arms and kiss those soft, inviting lips.

Ach du lieva.

He never should have thought about the

221

lips. Once the idea crept into his mind, he found it impossible to think on anything else. As they sat there talking about books and beehives, the urge to kiss her grew so powerful, he gripped the edge of the step to keep from moving any closer.

Lily had a boyfriend. Lily didn't care one whit for boys like Dan Kanagy. Lily was too wonderful to hope for.

Dan practically erupted in an effort to get on his feet and get moving — away from those lips and the cute little dimple that appeared every time she smiled. Lily would not appreciate an uninvited kiss. She'd be appalled if she guessed Dan's thoughts were within a hundred feet of her lips.

"Ach," he said. "I need to go."

He took heart from the fact that she looked disappointed. "*Jah.* I should get to bed before Rose wakes up and realizes I'm missing. *Denki* for painting the barn."

He held up his hand to stop more gratitude. "It was my pleasure, Amtrak."

Smiling almost sadly, she handed him the blanket and said good night. He waited on the steps until he saw her safely into the house. Painting the barn had been his pleasure. But it had also been his profound pain.

It was torture squeezing bits of hope from

every word she spoke, every smile she gave him. Despair and faith warred constantly inside his head. Would she send him crashing to the pavement with an engagement announcement? Had he run out of the time before he'd even started?

He shook his head. She *had* smiled at him. A lot. She had laughed and teased and held on tight when she thought there was danger. Surely she liked him.

He'd grab every shred of hope she offered him. Maybe it would be enough to keep him from falling on his face.

CHAPTER FOURTEEN

Lily dialed the number for the market, feeling almost ashamed for hoping that Paul would not be there.

"Hello, Glick's Amish Market."

Her heart sank at the sound of Paul's voice. It wasn't that she didn't want to talk to Paul, she just didn't want to talk to him today. She'd already wasted precious time hiking to the phone shack. She didn't want to have to spend time explaining herself. "Paul?"

"Lily?"

"I got your note this morning."

"*Gute.* I want you to come and see what I've done at the market. Peter and I rearranged the displays so the Amish-made jams and jellies are right at the front of the store. We're going to put your honey there too."

"It sounds wonderful-*gute,* Paul," Lily said, steeling herself against his reaction.

"But I can't come to the market today."

She heard the frown in his voice. "Why not? I had Perry make sure to deliver the note early so you could rearrange your plans."

"We're pulling honey today, Paul. Poppy and Rose have already started, and I need to get back to help. I called because I didn't want you to wait for me."

"Of all the stuff, Lily. How long will that take?"

"All day for the next three or four days," Lily said.

"Four days?" She could tell the frown deepened without having to see it.

"Sorry, Paul. We have a lot of hives." Lily paused for barely a moment and wondered if Paul even knew how many hives they had. Dan Kanagy knew the number of hives plus where they were located.

She shook her head in an attempt to banish that thought. Paul was her boyfriend. His good qualities greatly outweighed the fact that he didn't know how many hives she had. Lately, it seemed she'd been almost purposefully trying to find fault with him. What was wrong with her?

"Let's hope you don't get too much honey. We'd hate to be stuck with a surplus at the store."

"I don't think there can ever be too much."

Paul sighed loudly. "That's because I promised we'd buy all of it. You know we're taking a risk."

Lily felt a twinge of guilt that Paul would buy all her honey no matter what. It only proved what a good person he was. "You know I'm grateful, Paul. Your family has always been *gute* to us."

"I know. Don't mention it. I just wish you could come to the market today. Can't your sisters take care of the honey?"

Lily didn't want to argue with him, not when he was being so nice about the honey. "Maybe I can come on Saturday."

"Saturday? That's almost a whole week away." She knew he was pouting on the other end of the phone. She just didn't know what she could do about it. "You would think my girlfriend would make more of an effort to see her boyfriend, if I really mean that much to you."

"Paul, you are very special to me."

"It doesn't seem like it," he said. "It sounds like you don't even want to come."

She closed her eyes and took a deep breath. "I'm sorry, Paul. We have to get the honey in." Silence on the other end. "We have extra help today. Maybe we'll finish early enough that I can come over tonight. I can't promise anything, but I'll see."

"Who's helping?"

Oh dear. She shouldn't have said anything. He might be pouting now, but he'd be positively petulant if he ever found out who was helping with the honey. "A boy from town."

Technically true. Miles away from the truth as far as Paul was concerned.

"Don't pay him more than five dollars an hour."

"We won't." Dan had volunteered to help. Dan was irrationally excited to help. He would be offended if they offered him money.

Paul would be offended if he knew she'd allowed Dan onto her property. Lily bit her tongue. One more thing Paul would never have to know. She didn't even feel guilty about that list anymore. Paul was happier not knowing. What could be so bad about that?

"I'll see you on Saturday then," she said.

"Okay, I guess."

Lily hung up the phone and sighed with her whole body. Was it her imagination, or were conversations with Paul becoming more and more taxing? It was so hard finding the right words to keep him happy, measuring her responses so he didn't get offended or think she was arguing with him. Sometimes, she simply wanted to say what she thought without the fear of ruffling Paul's feathers.

She huffed out a sigh and forced her lips into a smile. It would be better when they were married and she had more freedom to speak her mind.

She gingerly made her way down the steep incline to the dirt road. Six families shared the phone shack partially hidden in the trees far enough off the road that a casual pass-erby wouldn't see it. Poppy wanted the family to get their own phone. The bishop prob-ably would have allowed it since they had a honey business. Most Amish businesses in Bienenstock had phones.

Still, Lily had talked it over with Paul, and he hadn't seen the need for it, especially since their business was small and they didn't deal with the public all that much. Paul's family took care of all the sales details, and they could always take the short ride into town if they needed anything else. Still, on days like today when a phone would have saved her nearly half an hour of pre-cious honey time, Lily was tempted to covet one.

She quickened her steps, wishing she

hadn't taken the extra time to call Paul. He would have been furious when she hadn't shown up at the market, so the choice between losing precious honey time and angering Paul hadn't been much of a choice. She'd just have to work extra fast to make up for being gone for half an hour.

She heard a horse and buggy come up behind her. "Daddy Long Legs," Dan Kanagy called. *Ach.* The last thing she needed was Dan's insults. She had dressed in her beekeeping clothes first thing this morning since they were going to be working with the bees on and off all day. He didn't need to remind her how inappropriate he thought her outfit was.

She didn't have the heart to be mad at him, though. He had spent Saturday evening painting her barn just to protect Rose's feelings. He could call her whatever he wanted, and she resolved not to be cross.

She turned to him, and his smile completely disarmed her. He stood in his two-seater courting buggy as the horse pulled it down the road, oozing with enthusiasm and waving as if there might be a chance she hadn't seen him. He stopped his buggy next to her and transferred both reins to one hand. "What pleasant surprises you can find by the side of the road!"

She shooed his flattery away. After the Daddy Long Legs comment, she didn't believe him anyway.

He held out his hand to her. "Would you like a ride? I assume we're going to the same place."

A reluctant smile fought through her wounded feelings, and she held out her hand and let him pull her into the buggy. A ride with Dan would save her a few minutes. Maybe they'd get the orchard hives done today.

Dan couldn't seem to stop smiling as he prodded the horse with a gentle tap of the reins. "Out for a stroll before we do honey?"

"*Nae.* I had to call Paul."

Did his lips droop slightly? "Is he coming to help?"

Lily shook her head. "He wrote me a letter asking me to come to the market today. He didn't know we were doing honey. I had to call and tell him I wouldn't be coming."

His lips twitched, as if he were thinking of something clever to say. "He wrote you a letter? He lives not a half hour away."

Her gaze fell to the floor of the buggy. "He finds it convenient to send letters."

"I see." He prodded the horse to go faster. "I'm sorry I'm late. Bitsy said to be here at six but I had to finish helping Dat and my *bruders* milk the cows."

"Your help is very much appreciated, tardy or not."

"*Gute,* because I wouldn't have missed it, even if Dat had forced me to milk a thousand cows first."

In good conscience, she couldn't let his excitement go unchecked. "Dan," she said, pinning him with a serious look. "I have to tell you something."

His smile faded. "Did I say something wrong?"

Besides the Daddy Long Legs comment? "I know you are excited about helping with the honey today, and while it is gratifying to see full jars of honey lining the shelves of the pantry, you will not have a *gute* time."

He raised an eyebrow. "I won't?"

"Pulling honey is hard work. The supers are heavy, the bees can be uncooperative, and it's hot and uncomfortable because we have to keep the doors to the honey house closed tight or we'll get swarmed with bees. And" — she took a deep breath — "it's likely you'll get stung." She slumped her shoulders. "I should have told you the other night when you volunteered, but I was being selfish. I thought it would be nice to have your help."

His eyes seemed to dance. "Are you saying you thought it might be nice to have me around?"

"Well, *jah.* That's what I said, but I should have warned you first."

Her apology only made him smile wider. "Lily, no matter how cute you look when you try to apologize, there is nothing in the world I'd rather do than be with the Honey-bee Schwesters."

"But you act as if you think it's going to be fun."

"Fun?" He pushed back the brim of his hat and grinned. "Of course it's going to be fun."

"But it will be hard. You understand it won't be pleasant?"

He bounced the reins in his hands. "I wake up at four thirty every morning to milk a hundred cows with my *dat* and *bruders.* I've herded cattle in the heat of a Pennsylvania summer and listened to Onkel Titus tell his hernia story seven times. I can also wash up the dinner dishes in ten minutes flat. I'm not afraid of hard work. Besides, I get to see you in that outfit all day."

She poked her elbow in his ribs. "Don't tease me about my clothes. They're a necessary evil yet."

He turned onto their lane and crossed over the little bridge. "I'm not teasing. I love them. Very practical for beekeeping. I read all about it in my book. You don't want to get stung."

"*Nae,* and neither do you."

He pointed to the floor. "I brought a few appropriate clothes. But I don't have a veil."

"We've got an extra one."

Leaning close and lowering his voice, he said, "I'm eager to see the barn door in the daylight. How does it look?"

Lily nibbled on her bottom lip, but she couldn't keep the corners of her mouth from turning up. "Well . . ." She had known the minute she saw it that night that it wouldn't be anywhere near the right color.

They got to the end of the lane before she had to answer that question. He gasped in horror. "Wha . . . ? Did I do that?"

Lily giggled quietly, just in case Rose was close by. "I'm afraid so."

"How could we have gotten it so wrong?"

"It's hard in the dark."

His eyes grew as round as buggy wheels. "Not that hard."

They stared at the barn door. It had turned out a lovely shade of dark orange. "I think it looks quite good against the red barn," Lily said. "Like a pumpkin resting on a pile of red delicious apples. It makes me think of autumn time."

"What did Rose say?"

"She didn't notice until yesterday. Aunt Bitsy told her that maybe it was something the sun had done to the paint."

"Only the paint on the door?" Dan said.

"Rose is convinced they used cheap paint on the door and it finally started to age."

"She really believes that?"

Lily shook her head. "I don't know. Maybe she's humoring us. But even if she's not quite sure, at least she doesn't suspect what really happened."

He finally drew a breath and chuckled. "All that hard work for orange. I'm coming back and painting it in the daylight this time. You deserve a matching barn door."

Lily tilted her head to the side and examined her door. "I don't know. I kind of like it."

"Now you're just being nice. I must be . . ."

She put her hand on his arm, and he froze in midsentence. "Dan, you went to bed extra late so that my sister could sleep easier. I don't care what color that door is. I'm never going to be able to thank you properly."

He grew serious and put his callused hand over hers. "I already told you. One of your smiles is thanks enough."

She'd never noticed how brown his eyes were. Deep brown like a cup of hot chocolate.

They both jumped at the sound of Aunt Bitsy's voice. "I'm not paying you to sit there all day. The honey isn't going to extract itself." She stood on one of the flagstones between the house and the lane with her veil in one hand and a hive tool in the other. "And kindly take your hand off of Lily's."

Lily thought she might die of embarrassment. How could Aunt B seriously think she and Dan had been holding hands? He wasn't even her boyfriend.

Dan seemed unconcerned. He slid his hand away as if Aunt B would forget it had been there if he moved slowly enough. "I hate to remind you, Bitsy," he said, "but you're paying me as much for sitting in the buggy as you are for doing the honey. Nothing."

Bitsy slipped the veil onto her head. "You volunteered, young man. I'm not about to negotiate a price now."

He jumped from his buggy and gave Lily a hand down. "I wouldn't want you to. It wouldn't be fair to work for money when I'm already being paid in smiles." He cocked an eyebrow. "Right, Lily?"

"Well, if you expect a smile from me," Bitsy said, "you'll be disappointed. I haven't smiled for thirty years yet." She wagged the hive tool at him. "And I don't smile at young men who get sneaky and try to hold hands with one of my girls."

"So you're saying I shouldn't be *sneaky* about it?" Dan winked, actually winked, at Aunt B. He'd get a close look at the barrel of that shotgun for sure and certain.

Lily couldn't be sure under the veil, but it almost looked as if the lines around Aunt B's mouth turned upward and her eyes flashed with a glint of amusement. She shook her head and walked past the both of them, murmuring all the way. "Why did we ever feed him, Lord?"

Lily tried not to let her mouth fall open. She never knew anyone who could tease Aunt B without getting tossed out on his ear. She'd never seen anyone try. She glanced sideways at Dan and curled her lips. *"Cum reu,"* she said, motioning with her head. "Let's go find you a veil."

He nodded eagerly.

"And maybe a muzzle."

He chuckled. "If you think it will help."

"Nothing will help."

Dan's eagerness turned to amazement in a

236

matter of minutes. "I can't believe you four do this all by yourself."

Poppy, who led the horse and small wagon, stopped Queenie on the little path next to the orchard hives. "We're not altogether helpless, Dan Kanagy. And we've never needed a man to tell us how good we are at keeping bees."

"Of course not, but I never knew how amazing you Honeybee Schwesters really are. I mean, I knew, because I know you, but I didn't really know."

"You're not making any sense," Bitsy said. She looked up to the sky. "Lord, if he's going to hold hands with my girl, at least give him half a brain to work with."

Dan truly felt like he only had half a brain standing here with Lily and her beehives. It was as if he'd never even read the books. He had only a vague idea of what Lily and her sisters were going to do, and he had no idea how to help them. Still, he'd rather be lollygagging in the orchard staring at Lily than just about anywhere else in the world — except maybe sitting in his buggy holding her hand.

"But, Aunt B," Lily said, giving him an encouraging smile. "He's going to come in handy when we move the full supers to the honey house."

Dan took a step closer to the hive. "How many boys can say they're going to come in handy?"

Poppy eyed him from behind her veil. "He can probably carry two full buckets of honey at a time."

Dan flexed his arms. "I toss calves and hay bales on a regular basis."

Rose gazed at him in concern. "You toss calves?"

He winked at her. "Not far."

"At least he'll be good for carrying supers and buckets," Bitsy said.

Dan did his best not to stare, but he was trying to decide what that was on Bitsy's neck. She was covered head to toe for beekeeping, but he could see her bare neck beneath her veil. It looked as if a bee were resting on her neck just below her chin, except Dan knew it wasn't a real bee because it hadn't moved. The traveling tattoo was back.

Though Dan wanted to help any way he could, the sisters had their operation well organized. They were perfectly capable of handling heavy supers and angry bees all by themselves.

He knew from his reading that a full super could weigh eighty pounds.

Lily motioned for him to come closer as

she pried the top super open with a hive tool. Dan expected to see bees everywhere, but he didn't see one in the shallow super. Lily pulled one of the frames from the super with a tool that looked like a pair of double pliers. She pointed to the rows of tiny white hexagons that nearly covered the frame. "This frame is full of honey. You can see how the bees have capped each cell for storage. We take it to the honey house, scrape off the caps, and spin the frames. The honey comes right out."

"I'm surprised there aren't more bees on the frame," Dan said. "The pictures show hundreds of bees."

Lily lowered the frame back into the super. "The day before we pull honey, we put an escape board below the supers we're going to take. The bees can get out of the supers full of honey, but they can't get back in. So by morning, the supers are mostly empty of bees. This is where Dan is going to come in handy," Lily said to Bitsy. She turned to Dan. "Do you mind some heavy lifting?"

He felt as if he were going to explode with happiness at the way she looked at him. He so wanted to be useful. "There's nothing I'd like better."

"Can you lift this super and carry it to the

wagon?"

"Of course." Dan grasped the super by the shallow indents on either side and hefted it off the other supers in the stack. "Whoa. This is heavy." He lumbered to the wagon and set the super toward the front. "Okay," he said, glancing at Poppy and then Bitsy. "I don't mean to insult anybody, but how do you manage to lift these into the wagon by yourselves?"

Lily giggled. "Rose and I lift together."

Poppy folded her arms and raised her chin. "I can carry one by myself."

"Now, Poppy," Rose scolded. "Sometimes you can."

One corner of Poppy's mouth twitched upward. "If you must know, I only carry the lighter supers. Bitsy helps me with the heavier ones."

Dan bowed in Poppy's direction. "That in no way diminishes your accomplishments, but I hope you realize how happy I am that I can help and make it a little bit easier for you."

Poppy cracked a smile. "I guess I don't need to break my back when you are willing to break yours for me."

"I'm not going to break my back. I toss cattle, remember?"

Lily smiled so sweetly, she could have

been made of honey. "And we're very glad for your help."

She pried the next super free from the one below it, and Dan picked it up and deposited it in the wagon. Once he removed the super, Lily pulled a thin board off the top super and pressed the lid on the supers that were left. She held up the thin board with a circle cut from the center of it. "This is an escape board or a bee excluder," she said. "Bees can get out of the honey supers, but they can't get back in. We can take the honey without fighting the bees for it."

"It was Lily's idea," Rose said. "She's always coming up with improvements for our hives. The escape boards make collecting honey four times faster. We used to have to brush the bees off before we could take the supers."

Dan gazed at Lily. He already thought so highly of her, her cleverness didn't surprise him at all. "It's pure genius, Lily. Pure genius."

She didn't say anything, but he thought maybe she blushed under her veil. At least she didn't contradict him or try to deflect the compliment to one of her sisters. Paul might regularly tear her down, but hopefully she was starting to see what Dan saw — a smart, delightful girl, capable and talented, not to mention uncommonly kind and stunningly beautiful. There weren't enough *gute* words to describe her.

Bitsy rolled her eyes and propped a gloved hand on her hip. "If you stand there too long, the bees will find their way back to the full supers and we'll have to start all over."

Dan realized he'd been staring dumbly at Lily. "Sorry. I'm awestruck at this whole operation. It's amazing, and you certainly don't need my help."

"*Nae,* we don't," Bitsy said, prying another hive open.

"But I'm glad you let me join you, all the same."

Rose gave Dan a worried half smile. "Aunt Bitsy, how can you say we don't need Dan's help? Look at how much help he's been already."

Bitsy grunted. "It's *gute* to remind the young men that they don't have to swoop in and save us. We can take care of ourselves."

"I would never doubt that," Dan said, smiling at the expression on Bitsy's face, as if she were taking him to task and egging him on at the same time.

"At least you're not one of those arrogant types who thinks a bunch of women don't know anything," she said.

Dan took another super from Lily. She smiled and raised her eyebrows at him as if to reassure him that she truly did want him hanging around. It was the most beautiful sight he'd seen all day. Lily wanted him around, even if he was nothing but a nuisance to Bitsy. As long as Lily smiled at him, he'd be happy to annoy Bitsy.

Bitsy, Poppy, and Lily pried lids off the remaining hives and kept Dan busy toting full supers to the wagon. Rose, the only one not in a bee suit, scraped the thick and waxy amber-colored substance from the edges of the full supers with a hive tool and collected it in a jar. "It's propolis," she said when Dan gave her a questioning look. "We sell it to health food stores. It's got dozens of uses."

After she'd scraped the supers, Rose put a damp towel over each one. "So the bees don't come for it again," she said.

"Is this all the honey you get every year?" Dan asked.

"Nae," Rose said. "Once we've pulled the honey, we bring the supers back so the bees can fill them again. The bees clean the frames for us, and we do one more extraction in the fall."

It took less than an hour to take twenty-three supers from the orchard hives. Dan had stacked the supers on the wagon two

243

deep and the ten escape boards sat propped vertically between two supers.

Poppy led Queenie slowly down the rutted path to the smoother lane in front of the barn. The rest of them followed, peeling off veils and gloves and outer jackets as they walked.

They marched past the barn and its orange door, down the lane, and into the honey house, an ample shed that housed the equipment for extracting and storing honey.

Dan shooed Lily and her sisters away when they tried to help him lug supers into the honey house. Once he'd brought all the supers into the honey house and stacked them four deep against the wall, he clapped his hands together. "What now?"

An extra short wooden table sat in the middle of the room with a shiny metal can sitting on top of it. The can was about the size and shape of a galvanized metal trash can, with a spigot protruding out the side near the bottom. Next to the can sat a large white plastic box also with a spout at the bottom.

Lily grabbed his hand and pulled him forward. He nearly had a heart attack. "This is our honey extractor. We secure the frames in the slots in the extractor and then spin the honey out of the frames. The honey drips to the bottom of the extractor and out this spigot."

Bitsy fit a stainless-steel strainer on top of a white plastic bucket and put it between the extractor and the plastic box so that both spigots would drain into it. "This catches and strains the honey at the same time."

"How do you power the extractor? Or do you spin it by hand?"

"We use a generator to power the extractor and a battery for the uncapping knife." Lily smiled at him as if she were pleased he wanted to learn. Of course he wanted to learn. Honey was a big part of Lily's life. He couldn't know her completely until he knew about this.

Poppy went to the long table and picked up a tool that looked like a long, thin spatula with a power cord attached to its wooden handle. "This is an uncapping knife. It heats up, and makes it easier to scrape the beeswax caps off the frames before we spin them."

Lily pried the first frame from the nearest super and rested it on the wooden bar that ran across the top of the plastic box. She took the uncapper from Poppy and slowly sliced her way up the frame, skimming the beeswax caps off the comb and letting the wax fall into the plastic box. At the bottom of the box, a screen caught the beeswax and let the dripping honey pass through.

"That is about the niftiest thing I've ever seen," Dan said.

Lily answered him with a twinkle in her eye.

Once she uncapped the frame, Lily slid it into the extractor and started uncapping the next frame.

"This is really a two-person job," Bitsy said, as they watched Lily uncap another frame. "But we want you to see how it's done before we multitask."

Dan wasn't even sure what "multitask" meant, but it sounded like they wouldn't be standing here watching Lily and Rose for too much longer.

Lily uncapped the last of the six frames and put it into the extractor. Poppy went outside and started up the gas generator, then Bitsy showed Dan how to turn on the machine. He watched as it spun and slung the honey against the side of the extractor.

"Don't stick your hand in there," Bitsy warned, as if she feared he was regularly so foolish. "You'll lose it."

"Don't worry, Bitsy," he said, stealing a quick look at Lily. "I'll do it when you're not looking."

Bitsy cocked her eyebrow. "Young man, I am not laughing."

Their aunt might not have been pleased, but Lily, Poppy, and Rose smiled as if they were about to burst. At least somebody found him amusing.

They let the extractor spin for ten minutes, and when it stopped, a deep pool of honey sat at the bottom of the extractor.

Bitsy removed the cap that covered the spigot and golden, sweet-smelling honey began to flow from the extractor. The three sisters each pulled two empty frames from the extractor. Lily didn't hesitate. She pulled another full frame from one of the supers, rested it on the wooden bar on the plastic box, and picked up the uncapping knife.

Dan looked at the stack of full supers against the wall and did a few calculations in his head. It would take a full day to extract all this honey.

Bitsy picked up her veil and gloves from the table. "Now, Dan Kanagy," she said. "Do you think you can manage the extracting with Lily? Poppy, Rose, and I are going to the clover field hives and put in bee excluders so those hives will be ready to pull tomorrow."

Dan watched as Lily sliced through the layer of beeswax with her knife. "I'll do my best."

"Don't worry," Lily said, flashing him a reassuring smile. "We'll do it together."

Dan's pulse sped up at the prospect of doing anything together with Lily.

"I know you're not that sharp," Aunt B said, "but Rose was helping with the honey when she was nine. You'll do fine as long as you don't cut your finger with that uncapper knife. I don't want blood in my honey."

Dan gifted Bitsy with his most mischievous grin. "Don't worry. I'll only cut my fingers off when you're not looking."

Bitsy gazed at the ceiling and growled. "Lord, I don't care what You say, this is not what I prayed for. And if this is a joke You're playing on me, You know I've never had a sense of humor."

She tromped out the door with Poppy and Rose close behind.

Rose turned back before she left, her cheeks glowing and her eyes bright. "Have a *gute* time."

For some inexplicable reason, Dan's heart started knocking around in his chest as if he hadn't just spent the entire morning with Lily already.

Willing his pulse to resume a normal

rhythm, he watched as she skimmed the beeswax from the comb. It fell onto the screen inside the plastic box. "What do you do with all that beeswax?"

"We sell it to Colleen Grow in Shawano. She makes candles and such with it. Paul thinks we should make the candles ourselves to bring in more money, but with everything else we have to do, there doesn't seem to be enough time." She glanced at him doubtfully. "Do you think that's a bad decision? I feel like I always get it wrong."

Because of Paul Glick, Lily was starved for confidence. Dan wished he could give some of it back to her. "You're much smarter than I am, so I would never second-guess your decisions. You don't want to wear yourself or your sisters out."

Lily gave him a very nice smile and placed the frame in the extractor. She had tied her hair up in an emerald scarf that brought out the green of her eyes. Finding it impossible to concentrate on anything when he looked into those eyes, he cleared his throat and turned his gaze to the full supers against the wall.

"This will take most of the day," he said, thrilled with the prospect of spending eight hours in this little room with Lily Christner, but a little overanxious to prove himself

249

charming and lovable and worthy. What if he came across as forced or fake from trying too hard? The formidable challenge made his head spin.

A frown cast a cloud over her features. "If you have to go, Rose can help me."

He gave her a look of mock indignation. "And miss all the fun? Absolutely not."

"You won't think it's so fun after a few hours."

He couldn't help himself. He reached out and hooked his index finger around hers. "What could be more fun than spending the day with Lily Christner?"

Dan was overjoyed to see that the color rose to her cheeks as she tried to stifle a smile. Maybe she didn't mind their fingers touching so much.

Maybe she wouldn't mind their lips touching so much.

Dan coughed as if his throat had swelled shut and quickly pulled away from her.

No kissing.

No daydreaming about kissing.

Kissing was surely the farthest thing from Lily's mind, and if he let his daydreams run wild, she'd run screaming for the hills.

CHAPTER FIFTEEN

Giddy. That was the only word she knew to describe how she felt.

Giddy.

Giddy and toasty warm all over.

And she couldn't stop smiling.

"I can't believe we finished before five o'clock," Lily said as she washed the strainer in the small sink in the honey house.

She'd spent the entire day with mean, insensitive Dan Kanagy and had thoroughly enjoyed every minute of it. She had never met a more cheerful soul or a harder worker. He seemed determined to make the most of every second, running, not walking, to fetch frames to scrape, sweeping floors or wiping surfaces while the extractor spun honey. Even with his frantic pace of activity, he told her stories and made her laugh or listened intently as she shared her opinions about Laura Ingalls Wilder and fruit trees.

Should she feel ashamed that she took so

much pleasure in his compliments or the way he looked at her when he told her she was pretty and smart? Paul would say that a boy should never feed a girl's vanity by giving her compliments. Paul might be right, but Dan and Lily had been alone in the honey house and no one else had heard his flattery. Surely there was no harm in it.

They had taken a break at noon when Rose brought them bologna sandwiches on honey wheat bread. They ate under the shade of the basswood trees. Dan seemed excited about everything from the bushes that lined the lane to the acres of clover fields behind the barn. He fit in with the family quite nicely. He didn't seem like an intruder like other people sometimes did.

Dan snapped the lid onto the half-full bucket of honey and smiled. "The best day I ever spent, I think."

Poppy and Rose finished drying out the extractor and hung their towels on a hook by the sink. "A wonderful-*gute* harvest for June," Rose said.

"I feel bad I can't come back tomorrow," Dan said.

Lily felt more than a little disappointed herself. "We can manage."

"Will you stay for dinner?" Rose said, out of the blue.

Lily chastised herself for not thinking of that before Rose did. "*Jah.* It's the least we can do to thank you for all your help."

His look left her knees a little weak. "I've already been amply thanked. But I would love to stay for dinner."

"*Gute,*" Lily said, locking her knees so she wouldn't collapse into a heap. "We are making honey curry chicken in honor of our first extraction day."

Dan smiled at Rose. "I like your hive paintings."

Rose blushed and lowered her head. "They're nothing."

It was the Amish way. Never give a compliment. Always deflect praise. Dan didn't seem to keep with that tradition. "It's no sin to tell you they're beautiful. Even a blind man could see that." Dan handed Lily the clean uncapper. "I still can't believe you do this without help."

Lily saw Poppy stifle a smile, pretending not to be pleased with Dan's utter amazement. He couldn't help but make them all feel as if they truly did something wonderful when they tended to their bees. "You mean without a *man's* help," Poppy said.

Dan curled his lips sheepishly. "*Jah.* That's what I mean. You have to admit my arms came in handy today."

Poppy shook her head. "I don't have to admit anything."

Dan laughed. Insults from Lily's family members didn't seem to faze him. He was too good-natured to take offense. She really liked that about him, because Aunt B considered it her duty to offend every boy who set foot on Honeybee Farm. Poppy was little better.

Even though Poppy protested that she didn't need a man to help her out, Dan insisted on helping them take the empty supers back to the orchard, then took the wagon back to its place and stabled Queenie while the rest of them went back to the house to change.

They emerged from the orchard to see a buggy parked at the end of the lane. Buggies in the community were all similar, black with sliding doors and reflectors. But this buggy looked extra familiar. With a sinking feeling, Lily peeked in the window. Nobody in there. Where was he, and why had he come?

"Whose buggy is that?" Poppy asked.

Lily pushed ahead of her sisters and Aunt B, hurried up the porch steps, and opened the front door. Paul sat on the sofa in the great room, reading the Bible that Aunt B kept on the bookshelf. He looked up, slammed the Bible shut, and rose to his feet, his face a puffy, purple bulb. He looked as if he were about to pop like a pimple.

He opened his mouth to speak and promptly closed it as he took a good look at her. His expression changed from pouty anger to sputtering shock. "What are you wearing?"

Lily looked down at herself. Jeans, a sticky sweatshirt, and a scarf. She could only guess at how much hair had escaped from the scarf and how unkempt she must have appeared.

Poppy, Rose, and Aunt B sidled into the room and stood staring at Paul like a trio of statues. Poppy wore that hostile expression that she used on all the boys. Rose looked positively terrified. Aunt B had a disgusted smirk, probably wishing she had a dog to chase away the strays Lily collected.

"This is my beekeeping outfit, Paul," Lily said, giving her voice a matter-of-fact tone, as if the *Englisch* clothes were common knowledge.

He drew his brows together until they were touching. "Of all the stuff, Lily," he said, as if it were a chore to speak, "I've never seen anything so inappropriate."

She wanted to cry. "It's to protect us from bee stings."

Paul shook his head. "As a member of the fellowship of Christ, I should report you to the bishop. You could get shunned. What would my *dat* say?"

"The bishop approved it," Lily said, wishing her family wasn't here to witness this. How embarrassing to have Paul chastise her in front of everybody. "So we won't get stung."

Aunt B scrunched her lips together and gave Paul the evil eye. "It's bad manners to let yourself in."

Paul eyed Aunt B as if she were a dog who'd pooped on his lawn. "A hundred bees flew into my buggy. I wasn't going to stay out there and get stung." He reached into his pocket and pulled out two one-hundred-dollar bills. "And look what I found in your Bible. Two hundred dollars. You shouldn't leave money lying around like that."

"Well, Paul Glick. It's bad manners to search through other people's stuff."

"I wasn't searching," Paul sputtered. "I was reading the Good Book. Something I suspect you should be doing more of."

"Put it back, young man," Aunt B said.

Lily nearly smiled. It wasn't uncommon for her to find cash while reading. Aunt B stored money on every bookshelf. She didn't trust the banks.

Utterly disgusted that he seemed to be the only person in the room with any sense, Paul shoved both bills back into the Bible.

"Not like that." Aunt B bustled over to the sofa to fix the damage. "Lord," she said, looking at the ceiling, "all I want is a boy who won't steal my money or trample my dandelions. Is that too much to ask?"

Paul's nostrils flared. He found Aunt B's vocal prayers both irreverent and inappropriate. He'd expressed his disapproval to Lily on more than one occasion. "What, what is all this?" he said, waving his hand around to indicate the entire house and everyone in it. "I come here to find money strewn about the house, bees everywhere so I can't even get out of my buggy safely, and all four of you dressed like *Englisch* boys. It's shameful, Lily, and I won't stand for it."

Rose found some courage to speak up, probably because she hated to see Lily upset. "We only wear the jeans when we work with the bees, Paul."

Paul barely gave Rose a glance. "Then maybe you should find another profession."

Lily tried to smooth things over. "No one ever sees us. I'm real sorry about it."

The lines momentarily softened around his mouth. "Go change before anyone else sees you like that."

Lily nodded and took two steps toward the stairs. Her sisters, also dressed in jeans, stayed put, perhaps in silent defiance of Lily's boyfriend.

Paul held up his hand. "Wait. There's something else."

Lily stopped in her tracks.

"Is it true that Dan Kanagy was here today?"

Poppy folded her arms and smiled smugly. "He still is."

Lily felt ill. She should never have kept that secret from her boyfriend. He'd somehow found out about Dan on his own, and he must have been livid if he'd actually made a special trip out here to discover the truth.

She wrung her hands as the guilt and shame overwhelmed her. "He . . . he helped with the honey."

Paul stuck out his bottom lip. "Dan Kanagy is a liar and a cheat. And you always seem to forget how mean he was to you at school. Why would you let him near you, especially knowing how he's treated me?"

Lily didn't have an answer to that. Well, she did have an answer, but Paul wouldn't want to hear it.

He's nice and funny. He's a fast worker, with strong arms and capable hands. And he

258

wanted to help — didn't even care that the work was hard or that it would take all day.

Even while Lily felt guilty for such disloyal thoughts, she also felt a tiny bit justified. Dan had offered his help. Paul never did.

The front door stood open, and Lily heard Dan's quick footsteps on the porch. She wanted to find that mouse of theirs and crawl into his hole.

Dan came into the house, beaming like an extra bright battery-powered flashlight. When he caught sight of Paul, he stopped as if he'd run headlong into a wall, and his smile faded to nothing.

"Oh. Hello, Paul," he said, as if he'd come face-to-face with an *Englischer* holding a camera.

Poppy seemed to come to life. She laid a hand on Dan's back and nudged him a little farther into the room. "We've invited Dan to dinner."

Paul grunted as if all his annoyance were stuck in his throat. "Well . . . Dan . . . that's too bad because I've invited everyone to have dinner with me at the restaurant tonight."

Dan folded his arms across his chest and spread his feet apart slightly as if he were a mountain that would not budge. "That's nice."

The shadow of a scowl traveled across Paul's face before he made a valiant attempt at a smile. "Doesn't that sound nice? A day off from cooking?"

"We can't afford it," Aunt B said, with a tinge of sarcasm in her voice.

Paul coughed violently, nearly choking on his words. "I'm paying for everybody."

Lily had to work hard to keep the surprise from showing on her face. Paul must really be upset. He never offered to pay.

Paul glared at Dan. Dan stared back, his face an unreadable canvas even though Lily could see the tension in his arms and tightness of his jaw. It looked as if Dan and Paul were locked in an intense game of checkers, and it was Dan's move. Would he back down and uninvite himself to dinner? That's what Lily would have done in the face of Paul's anger — anything to appease her boyfriend.

Paul motioned toward the stairs. "Why don't you four go change, and we can get going." He looked down his nose at Dan, which must have been difficult because Dan stood about four inches taller. "Good-bye, Dan. Maybe we'll see you in town sometime."

Dan didn't say a word. Apparently he wasn't going to back down, but he wasn't going to insist on staying either. He was obviously waiting for someone else to make that decision. If Lily wanted him uninvited, she'd have to be the one to do it.

But she didn't have the heart, not even to placate Paul. Dan had saved them hours of work today. She could find the courage to stand up for what she knew to be right. No matter what Paul thought, sending Dan away would be rude. Besides, she sort of liked having him around.

Paul looked at her and smiled one of his threatening smiles — the kind that said, *You better do what I want or I'll pout for three days.*

Lily's gaze turned to Aunt B. Aunt Bitsy laced her fingers together and raised an eyebrow. Lily knew that look. She'd get no help from her *aendi.* She swallowed hard and offered Paul her sweetest smile. "We promised Dan honey curry chicken."

Though his expression didn't change, Dan visibly relaxed. Paul, on the other hand, grew more agitated in a subdued sort of way. "Then you and I can go without your family. They can eat chicken while we get some of my *mamm*'s famous rolls."

Lily felt as if all the wind had gone out of her sails. The perfect solution. If she agreed to eat at the restaurant, she could probably keep Paul's pouting to a minimum, and if she offered to pay for her own meal, he'd probably forgive her for the whole Dan thing.

Paul must have sensed her hesitation, and he was irritated about it. "I'll even pay for dessert. Anything you want."

The trouble was, no matter how disloyal she felt, she didn't want to go to the restaurant. Paul would feel better, but she wouldn't, and her family would think she'd abandoned them. But she could see no other way to make things right with Paul. She would do just about anything to avoid his wrath.

A big, fat, heavy lump of coal settled in the pit of her stomach as she silently surrendered. She glanced at Dan. "Okay, Paul. I'll go change my clothes." It would be better this way. Paul was her best friend, after all. A true friend would try to make him happy.

Paul pursed his lips, as if not expecting anything less. "Hurry up, then. We don't want all the rolls to be gone."

She started up the stairs.

"And put on your glasses," he said. "You know how my *dat* likes them."

Ach, but she wanted to scream. If he wanted her to hurry, she'd best leave her contacts in. It would take too long to get them out.

Lily had never changed her clothes or fixed her *kapp* so quickly. Paul was naturally impatient, and she didn't want to irritate him further by being pokey. Not only that, but she trembled at the thought of Paul being alone with her family and Dan for any length of time. He might say something he'd regret. Aunt B would definitely say something Lily would regret.

She adjusted her *kapp* before bounding down the stairs. Paul sat stiffly at the table while Aunt B, Rose, Poppy, and Dan stood in a line leaning against the butcher-block island staring unapologetically at him, as if he were some bizarre animal at the zoo. It didn't look like any of them had attempted a conversation. Lily breathed a sigh of relief. Things were safer that way.

"I'm ready," she said, making a beeline for the front door. The sooner she got Paul out of the house, the better.

Paul's chair scraped loudly against the floor as he stood and followed her. "I like your glasses."

"Have her home by seven," Aunt B said.

Paul screwed his lips into an argument before he seemed to think better of it and nodded. Maybe he realized he had pushed everyone to the edge of their patience.

In spite of her rudeness of inviting Dan to dinner and then leaving, Dan gave her a genuine smile. She smiled back, feeling a hundred times better knowing that he harbored no ill will.

"Have a nice time," he said. "Eat one of those delicious rolls for me."

His manner was so kind and his expression so handsome, Lily reconsidered going. Wouldn't it be fun to sit next to Dan during dinner and listen to him tease Aunt B? What if he and Poppy got into one of their good-natured arguments? He might even be able to convince Rose to attend the gathering next week. Lily would love to be there to see it.

Paul placed a hand on her shoulder. "She can eat all the rolls she wants. I'm paying."

Lily paused to gaze into Dan's eyes, hoping to communicate an apology to him without saying anything. One side of his mouth curled up, and he winked. Lily lowered her head and tried to think of anything else besides Dan Kanagy's chocolate-brown eyes. Paul would be suspicious if she blushed.

They walked down the steps and across the flagstones while Dan, her sisters, and Aunt B watched from the porch. Lily nearly jumped out of her skin as Paul squealed like a little *buplie,* waved his hands wildly around his head, and ran around the grass as if he were being chased by a rabid dog.

"You're trampling the dandelions," Aunt Bitsy yelled, but Paul was too busy doing his little dance to hear her.

"Paul, what's wrong?" Lily said.

Paul flailed his arms and shook his head so hard his hat fell off. "There's a bee on me. Get it off. Get it off."

Lily grabbed one of his suspenders and pulled him toward her. "Hold still, and let me see."

Breathing heavily, he did as he was told, only flinching once when Lily brushed an imaginary bug off his shoulder.

"It's gone now."

"You know," Poppy called from the porch, "if you hold still and don't make any sudden movements, the bees will usually fly away."

Lily shot her family a warning look. Poppy looked on the verge of hysterical laughter. Rose seemed almost as amused as Poppy. Aunt B had her eyes turned to the sky, but what she particularly wanted to complain to the Lord about remained a mystery. She didn't say a word.

Dan covered his mouth with his hand as if he were casually fingering the whiskers on his face, but Lily suspected he hid a big grin behind it. She couldn't blame him, but she was grateful that he tried to cover it. Surely Paul felt plenty embarrassed yet.

Paul huffed out an angry breath and refused to turn his eyes to the porch. "Let's get out of here."

He didn't say another word until they were safely over the bridge and on the road. "Of all the stuff, Lily. Why do you have to have all those bees?"

CHAPTER SIXTEEN

Lily squeezed the water out of her hair with a towel after her shower. It felt so good to wash off the sticky honey and grime from two days' worth of honey harvesting. They'd spent another full day extracting the honey from the clover field hives. Lily and Rose had spun the honey while Poppy and Aunt B had replaced supers and weeded the garden. They'd do the basswood tree hives tomorrow, and next week they'd start on the hives at the sunflower farm. The job there took more time because they had to load up the supers and transport them three miles to the honey house.

Maybe Dan would be able to help.

Maybe not. At dinner last night, Paul had all but ordered her to banish Dan from their property forever. She hadn't agreed to a banishment, but she had told Paul she would think about it.

She couldn't ask Dan to never come back.

He was so willing to help, so excited to learn about their bees, so eager to get to know her family better. And they still had so many books to talk about. She couldn't hurt his feelings and tell him not to come anymore, even if Dan had no problem hurting *her* feelings, as Paul had reminded her several times last night.

Rose came into the bedroom and sat down on Lily's bed. The three girls shared a room, but they each had their own bed. Lily loved being so close at night without having to sleep in the same bed as her sisters. Poppy kicked something terrible, and Rose liked to cuddle. Lily appreciated her space.

Enticing aromas wafted from the kitchen. Aunt B had made meat loaf for dinner with her famous honey glaze. Lily didn't realize how famished she was until she smelled that smell.

"I think you should put on your yellow dress for dinner," Rose said, intently studying the Log Cabin pattern on the quilt that covered Lily's bed.

"Why?"

"Dan Kanagy's downstairs."

Lily's heart did that involuntary thumping thing again, and she hadn't even been exercising. Dan was here. That wasn't anything extraordinary.

So why was her heart jumping up and down inside her chest?

What would he say to her about last night? She had been pretty rude. Still, he had smiled at her just before she climbed into Paul's buggy. He didn't seem angry, and he wasn't the type to hold a grudge.

"Did he come to help with the honey? He's a little late."

"*Nae.* Last night he told us that as soon as the cows were milked in the afternoon, he would come and help us catch our mouse. That mouse made an appearance last night, and Aunt Bitsy put another dent in the floor with her meat cleaver. Farrah Fawcett didn't so much as twitch a whisker."

Lily laughed. "I hope Aunt B doesn't chop off her own foot someday."

"Dan said he could come tomorrow morning first thing and help us load the supers onto the wagon." Rose studied Lily's face and smiled tentatively. "He's real nice, Lily. He ate three helpings of chicken and helped do dishes. He scrubbed the chicken pan, even. I like him a lot."

"He didn't get mad about my leaving last night."

Rose frowned. "That wasn't your fault. Paul is hard to say no to. Aunt Bitsy says he's high maintenance."

"What does that mean?"

"I'm not sure. Some *Englisch* expression." Rose grabbed Lily's hand. Her eyes sparkled as if she had a secret. "Maybe we can talk Dan into staying for dinner again."

Lily dressed quickly — in her yellow dress — and ran halfway down the stairs before she realized how childish she must look. She slowed her pace to a walk, and entered the kitchen like a mature young woman.

Dan and Aunt B stood at the island intently studying what looked like a pile of odds and ends on the counter.

Dan's smile would have put the sun to shame. "Lily. I've been anxiously waiting for you. I get so forlorn when I don't see you."

Lily rolled her eyes. "Ha ha. Don't tease me, Dan Kanagy."

"I would never," he said, and for a second, he looked so sincere, she believed him, but then the playful glint in his eye gave him away.

"*Ach,* Dan Kanagy. Stop it."

Aunt B didn't even look up. "So first I need to cut this bottle?"

With what looked like great effort, Dan tore his gaze from Lily's face and nodded at

Aunt B. "J*ah*. I will do it for you if you want."

"I don't want you bleeding on my counter when you cut off all your fingers," Aunt B said.

"What are you doing?" Rose asked as she followed Lily down the stairs.

"We're making a mousetrap."

"A humane mousetrap," Dan said. "You can catch the mouse and set it free in the field."

Aunt B smirked. "If I set it free, it will just come back. I'm going to feed it to the cat."

Lily eyed Farrah Fawcett lounging on the window seat. "I don't think Farrah Fawcett could be bothered to eat a mouse, even if she were starving."

Aunt B's smirk drooped. "Farrah Fawcett won't even eat dry cat food." She shook her finger in the cat's direction. "You are a food snob, Farrah Fawcett. The mice know if they come to our house, they'll be perfectly safe to roam the halls and eat our food."

Dan showed Aunt B how to make the mousetrap. She cut the plastic water bottle so that only a small piece held the two ends together. They made four holes and stuck two bamboo skewers through either side, then used string and rubber bands to fashion something that stayed open until a mouse ate the cheese inside and sprung the two sides of the bottle shut.

"Very clever," Lily said.

Aunt B picked it up and studied it from all angles. "What's to keep the mouse from escaping through the slit in the bottle?"

Dan shrugged. "I don't know. The book at the library said it would work."

"I suppose," Aunt B said. "But I won't get my hopes up." She took the mousetrap into the storage room. "I'm putting it on the floor in the corner," she called. "It's the last place I saw him."

It was also the place with the most meat cleaver divots.

Aunt B emerged from the storage room with a bottle of chowchow and a jar of cherry jam. "Much as I hate having to feed you all the time, Dan Kanagy, you did bring a mousetrap, which is more than Farrah Fawcett's done since I got her. You might as well stay for dinner."

Dan beamed. "I'd love to if it's not too much trouble."

"Of course it's too much trouble, but I've invited you, so I won't take it back no matter how much I want to." She grasped the lid of the jam jar, and her face turned red trying to unscrew it. Without asking, Dan took it from her and opened it as easy as you please. He handed the bottle back to her and flashed a wide grin.

"Don't get cocky," Aunt B said.

Dan merely grinned wider and made Lily giggle.

Aunt B narrowed her eyes and poured the chowchow into a bowl. "The meat loaf's almost done. Rose, why don't you go find Poppy while Lily and Dan set the table? I have to go upstairs." She stuttered a little. "Because I have to go up there."

What did she mean by that?

Rose went outside while Bitsy disappeared up the stairs. Lily retrieved five plates and cups from the cupboard. When she turned around, Dan stood right behind her as if he'd meant to get that close. When she jumped a little, he smiled that dazzling smile, held out his hands, and took the plates from her. "You, uh, you smell really good."

She felt warmth travel up her face as she took him by the shoulders and turned him around. "Dial soap," she said, nudging him in the direction of the table. "And don't get fresh."

He chuckled. "I didn't mean to embarrass you." He set the plates on the table. "How did extraction go today? I'm sorry I couldn't be here."

"We got less honey than yesterday, but it took almost two hours longer."

"I can come tomorrow morning and lift supers for you."

He was so willing, and she was so undeserving. The guilt gnawed at her like a mouse on a piece of cheese. Swallowing hard, she decided a quick, straightforward apology would be best. "I'm sorry about going off with Paul last night after we'd invited you to dinner."

He had his back turned to her so she couldn't see his expression. "You don't have to apologize. Those things happen."

She wrung her hands. "I felt like I needed to be with Paul. He was so excited to take me to dinner. I didn't want to disappoint him."

He finally turned around and gave her a half smile. "You did what you thought was best. I trust your judgment."

"Did you like the chicken?"

"Delicious." His smile grew in strength. "Bitsy made two new dents in the floor with the meat cleaver and ordered me out of the house three times. I think I'm starting to make a *gute* impression."

Lily felt her shoulders relax even though she hadn't realized she'd been tensing them.

Dan seemed more disappointed than angry. A little flicker of pleasure leaped in her chest when she thought that Dan's disappointment might have stemmed from the fact that she hadn't been there.

She adored how good-natured he always was.

She caught her breath as something wide and deep opened up inside her.

She didn't adore just that one thing about Dan Kanagy. She adored most everything about him. His joy, his thoughtfulness, his unbridled enthusiasm, and his shameless compliments. She loved the way he teased Aunt B and got under Poppy's skin and inspired Rose to say more than three words at a time.

Did that mean she liked him?

Of course she liked him. Who wouldn't like such an endearing smile?

Well, Paul wouldn't.

She shouldn't like anyone besides Paul in that way, should she? She and Paul weren't engaged yet, but didn't her sense of loyalty demand that her heart be locked away for him and only him? She cleared her throat. These feelings for Dan Kanagy were unexpected and disconcerting, but of course her heart was locked away for Paul. He had been her first and only love.

That didn't mean she couldn't be friends with Dan. Good friends. Close friends.

She took a deep breath. What would Paul think? He told her to forgive but never forget. Was she being foolish to let down her guard?

It was too late. Her guard had fallen from the tower and drowned in the lake. She hoped she wouldn't regret it.

Dan pulled knives, forks, and spoons from the silverware drawer. "Did you eat a roll for me?"

Her head spun with questions. She had to concentrate on his face to make any sense of his words. "What?"

"At Paul's restaurant. You said you'd eat a roll for me."

Ah, yes. The restaurant. "I ate a roll and a chicken pot pie in your honor."

That was all she had eaten. Paul had only offered to pay because he knew she wouldn't be persuaded to come unless he did, but she had known better than to strain his generosity. Chicken pot pie was the cheapest thing on the menu, and he had still been grumpy about having to pay for it.

"What kind of dessert did you pick? Dat says their seven-layer chocolate cake is so rich, it could put you in the hospital."

Lily used the excuse of grabbing a handful of napkins to turn her back on him so he wouldn't be able to see her face. "I didn't have dessert."

"Too full?"

She didn't want to lie, but something told her Dan wouldn't like the real reason she didn't order dessert. She lowered her head and concentrated on straightening the napkins into a nice neat pile. "I just didn't have any."

All movement on his side of the room ceased. She didn't dare look up for fear he'd see the hesitation in her eyes.

"Lily," he said, in a tone he might have used to coax Rose out of her shell. "Why didn't you have any dessert?"

"It doesn't matter."

"It matters very much to me."

Oh, *sis yuscht.* The compassion in his voice made her want to bare her soul. How did he do that?

She couldn't look at him, but she tried to sound flippant as she folded and unfolded the flimsy paper napkins. "It was nothing. I knew Paul would be annoyed if I got dessert. He doesn't like to spend the money."

"But he promised," Dan murmured softly, the incredulity evident in his voice.

Lily looked up, forced a smile, and fanned the air nonchalantly with her paper napkins.

"I know, but he still would have been mad about it. He's funny like that sometimes."

Dan came around the island, took the napkins from her hand, and laid them on the counter. She couldn't read the dark expression in his eyes as he gently grasped her upper arms with his rough, warm fingers. Tugging her a little closer to him, he asked, "How long has it been this bad?"

"How long?" she replied in a barely audible whisper.

"When did it get this bad with Paul?"

Her eyes inexplicably stung with tears. How could a little compassion undo her like that? Blinking quickly, she shoved all that emotion deeper inside herself and forced a smile onto her lips. "It isn't. I mean, it's nothing. We disagree sometimes, that's all. All couples have disagreements."

A spark of fire leapt into his eyes. "Disagreements? Lily, you're afraid to cough without Paul's permission."

With great effort, she lifted her chin and pulled herself away from his grasp. "What do you know about me and Paul?" She wanted to sound strong, indignant. She managed to sound pathetic.

The fire flared in his gaze, and he looked almost angry. She had never seen Dan angry before. "You don't smile when you're with him, he rarely has a kind word for you, and he gives you orders and you obey."

"He gives me orders?"

"He insisted you give those books back. He made you put on your glasses last night."

Her heart shrank to the size of a cold, hard pebble as doubt and embarrassment pressed her into the floor. "That's . . . that's what you do in a relationship. You try to please each other. Paul likes it when I wear glasses. I care for him, so I try to make him happy."

"Does Paul ever try to make you happy?" Dan said, the tension evident beneath his quiet words.

"Of course he does. Paul was kind to me when no one else was."

Dan's agitation grew with every word that came out of Lily's mouth. He scrubbed his fingers through his hair. "Lily, he was nice to you in eighth grade. I don't see it any-more."

How could someone like Dan Kanagy hope to understand what Paul's kindness meant to her? "Well, I guess you won't see what you don't want to see."

"What I don't want to see?" He spread his arms wide. "All I've ever wanted is to see you happy."

What a lie. All Dan Kanagy had wanted to do was put her down, to remind her how small and insignificant she was compared to him. "I've learned to appreciate Paul for who he is, and he likes me the way I am. He doesn't care that I'm not pretty or smart. Other boys aren't so tolerant."

She might as well have insulted his entire family. She could see the muscles of his jaw twitch as he balled his hands into fists. "You act as if you don't think you deserve any better, Amtrak."

Lily recoiled as if he had struck her. That one word spoke volumes. She couldn't breathe properly anymore. *That* was what Dan truly thought of her. To him, she would always be the homely, pathetic fourteen-year-old. The easy target of his cruel wit. The butt of every joke.

She'd let her guard down, and he'd slapped her in the face with that one word.

Oh *sis yuscht,* it stung.

Paul had tried to warn her. He'd cared enough about her feelings to be wary of Dan. She wished she had heeded him. It was amazing how fast the faucet could turn on. Before she could bite back impending tears with sheer determination, they were running down her face.

The lines in Dan's forehead deepened into furrows as he reached out for her, as if he actually wanted to touch the lonely, unappealing eighth grader. "Oh, Lily. I'm sorry."

She folded her arms and turned her face toward the wall. He would not break down her defenses again. "*Nae,* you're not."

Her gaze snapped to the door as Poppy and Rose came tripping into the house like two little girls home from a picnic. Her sisters couldn't see her like this. Rose would make herself sick with worrying, and Poppy would probably challenge Dan to a fistfight.

In an attempt to act as if nothing had upset her, she swiped the tears from her cheeks and snatched the first thing she could reach off the counter: Aunt B's meat cleaver. Holding it in her hand as if she knew exactly what she wanted to do with it, she nodded resolutely at Rose and Poppy and spoke past the lump in her throat. "Start dinner without me. I have to go check on something outside."

She hoped they wouldn't ask her what she needed to check on with a meat cleaver. She had no answer for that. All she knew was that she had to get out of this house, away from Dan Kanagy, and to a safe spot where she could cry her eyes out without being seen. Dan had humiliated her enough for one day.

Dan watched numbly as Lily, head held

high, marched out the door with the meat cleaver in her fist.

The profound ache in Lily's eyes had cut him deeper than any meat cleaver could have. What had he done? He would have rather lost his horse than hurt Lily's feelings, but he had managed to reduce her to tears with a few careless words. He clenched his teeth. How he hated himself right now.

How hard would it have been to keep his stupid mouth shut? He'd let Paul's behavior push him past the point of patient silence, but how could he stand idly by and watch that boy beat Lily down again and again?

With a wide gaze, Rose hooked her elbow with Poppy's, and they eyed Dan as if he'd stolen all their books — the ones with money in them.

"Dan Kanagy," Poppy growled, "if you mess this up, I'll never forgive you."

He had no idea what to say to that. "I'm . . . I'm not trying to."

Rose looked to be on the verge of tears, but she didn't say a word, as if speaking would push her over some imaginary edge. She simply stared at him with those big, sad eyes. Her look stung worse than Poppy's fist.

Yep. He'd really done it up good this time. Much as he deserved Poppy's glares, he couldn't spare another minute here, not even for Rose. He brushed past the sisters to the front door.

"Whatever it is," Poppy said, "you'd better make it right, or you'll not be allowed back in the house."

He'd make it right or pull out his hair trying. He'd never wanted anything so badly in his entire life. He'd never wanted *anyone* so desperately, nor felt so desperately sorry for something he'd said. He deserved everything she threw at him, including the meat cleaver.

He hurt plenty already.

CHAPTER SEVENTEEN

Lily abandoned all her pride and ran like the wind to the weeping willow tree near the pond on the south end of their farm. This was her favorite spot on the farm. She often concealed herself beneath the tree's protective branches to read books or spend a few minutes by herself when afternoon chores were done. In full summer, the tree's branches floated mere inches above the thick grass, creating a canopy that gave her shade as well as privacy. The willow hovered over the pond, sometimes dipping its fingers into the water when the breeze blew just right. It was her own little cottage in the deep woods where she could find solitude and peace without leaving the farm. Dan wouldn't think to look for her here. Maybe he'd give up for good and never come back.

Her breath shook. She'd like that very much.

She sat down with her back against the

tree, laid the meat cleaver on the ground near her feet, and indulged the tears. She'd been so foolish to believe that Dan actually liked her. He'd made it perfectly clear that he didn't. It felt as if she were back in school all over again.

Hey, Amtrak. What time does the train get in?

To Lily's surprise, Farrah Fawcett came padding into her tree sanctuary as if she visited there often. She must have followed Lily out the front door. Without asking permission — Farrah Fawcett never conde-scended to ask permission for anything — the cat crawled onto Lily's lap and made herself comfortable. Lily wrapped her arms around Farrah Fawcett and nuzzled the cat's furry face against her cheek. "You were always a *gute* friend, Farrah Fawcett."

Farrah Fawcett gave Lily that snooty, I-really-couldn't-care-less look, but she gave herself away when she purred softly and let Lily run her hand along her snowy white fur. Even though Farrah Fawcett was a snob, she didn't mind Lily being homely or dumb or wearing glasses as thick as Coke bottles. She didn't even seem to mind the beekeeping outfit that both Dan and Paul had found so outrageous. Best of all, Farrah Fawcett turned up her nose at both boys whenever they came over. She had better judgment than Lily ever would.

"Lily?"

Ach du lieva. It had taken Dan mere minutes to find her clever hiding place. She should have expected it. She wasn't nearly as clever as she wanted to be.

"Go away, Dan."

With a purely miserable look on his face, he parted the stringy branches of the willow like a curtain and stepped into her space. She retaliated by scooting partway around the tree so her back was to him, taking the cat and her cleaver with her.

"Please, Lily. Please can I apologize?"

She refused to look at him, even when she heard his footfalls come closer. "Why are you even here?"

He squatted in front of her and tilted his head sideways so he could meet her eye. She blinked away her tears and studied a blade of grass near her big toe. Why was he so persistent with someone he despised so much?

"You should always let a person apologize," he said.

She buried her fingers in Farrah Fawcett's fur. If she didn't look at him, she could pretend she hadn't been bawling her eyes out. "Why do you care about apologizing?"

Dan picked up the meat cleaver sitting in front of Lily and carefully moved it to the side. "Let's move this out of reach, shall we?" He sat cross-legged directly in front of her, but that didn't mean she had to turn her eyes to him. Besides, she'd be doing him a favor if she didn't force him to look directly at her offensive face.

She'd let him apologize, but she would never trust him again, never let down her guard, never invite him to dinner, no matter how much she enjoyed his company. It was all a show he put on, but for what purpose, she couldn't begin to guess.

"How did you find me?" He should have taken the hint and left her alone.

"I asked Farrah Fawcett to sniff you out."

"You did not."

"*Jah,* I did. That cat might not be a good mouser, but she's a skilled bloodhound. She led me right to you." When Lily didn't return his grin, he cleared his throat and gave her a doubtful look. "I'm really sorry what I said about Paul. I'll do anything to see that smile again."

She twirled a piece of grass between her fingers. "If you left me alone, I'd smile again."

She heard the subtle tease in his voice. "But if I was gone, I wouldn't get to actually see your smile."

"No great loss for you, I'm sure."

A long pause. "You're wrong about that. I think I'd die if I couldn't see your smile again."

Probably because he wouldn't have anyone to insult anymore.

He reached out and smoothed Farrah Fawcett's ears. Farrah Fawcett looked sufficiently put out. Lily could have kissed that snooty cat. Farrah Fawcett knew how to deal with Dan Kanagy. "Your relationship with Paul is none of my business," Dan said. "I crossed over a line I shouldn't have even gone near."

Lily plucked another piece of grass from the lawn. "You might as well come out and say it. You think I'm stupid and *deerich*, foolish, for going out with Paul."

She didn't miss the astonishment in his eyes. "Stupid? Lily, you are the smartest girl I know. You can read a book faster than I can write a letter. You know all sorts of things about farming and bees, and Poppy says you never lose at Scrabble. I don't think you're stupid." He frowned. "If that's what made you cry, then I am doubly sorry. It's not what I meant. I don't want to see Paul hurt you, that's all." She shot darts at him with her eyes, and he cleared his throat yet again. "I'm sorry. You and Paul. None of my business."

She couldn't have this conversation face-to-face with Dan. He looked too handsome by half, and she was in very great danger of getting pulled in by his good looks. She nudged Farrah Fawcett off her lap and stood. Annoyed at losing her comfortable lap, Farrah Fawcett mewed curtly and strutted out from under the tree, probably to return to her comfortable window seat away from all the inconveniences of the great outdoors.

Dan rose to his feet too, as Lily ran her hand along the bark and stepped to the other side of the trunk where she could keep Dan at a distance. "Why do you keep coming to our farm, Dan?" she murmured, not really wanting to know the answer to that question.

He leaned his head around the trunk so she could see his face. Raising his eyebrows doubtfully, he said, "Why do you think, Lily?"

"If you find me so repulsive, why don't you just stay away?" It shouldn't cut her so deeply, but in that moment, she felt ashamed of her looks and ashamed of the vanity that made her care. Why, oh why, couldn't she staunch this flow of tears? It humiliated her enough to admit her ugliness without the tears making her that much more vulnerable.

His face clouded with confusion, and he took two steps around the trunk of the tree as if he couldn't restrain himself. "What gave you the idea that I find you repulsive?"

Her throat constricted, and she could barely force out the humiliating admission. "Amtrak. Coke Bottle. Daddy Long Legs." She hated even saying the insults out loud. "I know how ugly I am. You don't have to keep reminding me. Why can't you leave me alone?"

Dan could have been made of stone. He stood frozen to the ground and stared at her, his dark eyes swirling tempests of shadow. "Oh, *sis yuscht,*" he whispered. "Oh, *sis yuscht,* Lily."

"Paul befriended me when all the other boys made fun of me. When *you* made fun of me. He was the only one who stuck by me. The only one who didn't make cruel jokes about my glasses or braces or pimples or everything else wrong with me. I know you don't care for him, but I thank *Gotte* every day that Paul came into my life."

Turning pale and breathing heavily, Dan scrubbed both hands through his hair. "All these years, and I thought . . ."

290

"You don't have to tell me. I know I am wicked for holding on to this, for not forgiving you as Jesus said, but every time you call me Amtrak or Coke Bottle, it's a knife slicing right through my heart."

He took two steps closer, and the pain in his eyes took Lily's breath away. "Lily, how could you ever think . . . ? I never wanted to . . ."

"I know it's childish, Dan, but your words still sting — just as they're meant to. Why do you want to hurt me over and over again like that?" The tears flowed in rivers now. "It's like I'm back at school again, crying into my pillow every night because Dan Kanagy won't leave me alone. I don't want to be hurt anymore, Dan. Can't you stay away?"

Inconceivably, he reached out as if to pull her into his arms. She stepped away from him. How could he think his touch would be welcome? He studied her face and dropped his hands to his side, aging fifty years before her eyes. He frowned so deeply that the lines around his eyes and mouth looked to be etched there like carvings on a gravestone. His chest heaved in and out as if every breath were his last. He didn't take his eyes off her face, and a storm still raged in his eyes.

She brushed the tears from her face. It was done. He could go now and never come back. They need never plague each other again. That thought made her inexplicably sad, but why would she ever regret Dan Kanagy? "They're waiting dinner for me."

"Lily," he said, his voice deep and silky and completely irresistible. "Will you sit? I want to tell you a story."

"I need to get back."

"Please, Lily? Ten minutes isn't going to ruin your dinner." She'd never seen such a forlorn smile.

She huffed out a small breath and nodded. Why she even gave Dan Kanagy the time of day was a mystery — probably had something to do with that chocolaty satin voice of his.

She sat with her back to the tree but kept her posture ramrod straight so Dan would get the message that she refused to let down her guard again.

He sat next to her, also with his back against the tree but far enough away that there was no risk of any part of his sleeve or arm brushing against hers. He stared at the canopy of branches straight ahead of him. "I remember the first time I saw you. It was the first day of fourth grade, and you and your sisters had just moved into town."

Lily pressed her lips into a tight line. She had been ugly enough to make an impression on him even then.

"You were so cute with that upturned nose and the freckles that dotted your cheeks. Of course, I was ten, so you were still just a girl to me, but I admired what a *gute* reader you were. School never came easy for me."

He seemed nearer to her, although she hadn't noticed any movement on his part. A breeze could have nudged his sleeve against her. "And then seventh grade came. I got more awkward and dumb, and you got cuter and cuter."

Lily felt the warmth travel up her face. Flattery had no power to soften her, for sure and certain.

Dan glanced at her before resuming his study of willow branches. "I used to sit at my desk and stare at the back of your head, wondering what I could do to make you notice me. Recess proved futile. You spent it huddled with your sisters and a gaggle of teenage girls. I couldn't get within ten feet. In eighth grade about harvest time, you showed up at school with those adorable braces and headgear."

Lily snorted. "Adorable?"

"Those braces finally gave me a way to

make you notice me. I thought you would think that my nicknames were clever. I wanted you to know I was alive." He nudged her shoulder with his. "Lily, I was a stupid teenage boy grasping at straws to try to get you to notice me."

Lily drew her brows together. "You expect me to believe that you thought I was cute?"

He nodded earnestly.

"Dan, I had thick glasses, pimples, and a mouth full of braces. You couldn't have possibly."

"I didn't care about all that stuff. The braces gave you an extra shiny smile. The glasses made you look even more intelligent. And who doesn't have pimples at fourteen? You wouldn't think a boy as stupid as I was would notice, but you were nice to everybody. You helped the little kids with their schoolwork. You shepherded Rose around like one of your little chicks. Who wouldn't think that was cute?"

Lily nibbled on her bottom lip and found the courage to meet his eye. "How can this be true? You were so mean."

"Not in my mind. I wanted you to notice me. The nicknames got me noticed. It got a few bruises from Poppy too. I thought I was making progress. You have no idea how jealous I got when Paul befriended you. I never dared even talk to you, and there was Paul, whispering with you during class, monopolizing all your time at recess, getting the smiles I wanted. Being a *dumkoff,* I redoubled my efforts, coming up with stupider and stupider nicknames and being loud and obnoxious. It's a wonder Poppy didn't level me every day."

Lily stared at Dan in disbelief. Could this really be true? She couldn't make heads or tails of it. "You don't think I'm ugly?"

He closed his eyes and winced as if he were in pain. "*Ach,* Lily. You have always been the most beautiful girl I've ever known, and it makes me sick that I made you believe otherwise."

"You're not a stupid teenager anymore, Dan Kanagy. Why do you still call me those cruel names?"

Another wince. "I thought you'd remember those names with the same fondness I did. I didn't realize you never thought of them that way or that they might have hurt you deeply."

She lowered her eyes. *"Jah."*

He growled with all the force of his torrid emotions and pressed his palm against his forehead. "All these years, I've missed out on being with you because of my own stupidity."

She'd truly been on his mind that long? The layer of winter snow around her heart began to melt. Dan, the boy who helped spin honey and painted barn doors, hadn't ever meant to be cruel. She admitted to herself that she'd come to care for him a great deal, and the boy who trampled dandelions wasn't rotten at the core like she feared. The realization felt like ointment on a burn.

His voice shook with longing. "The worst of it is I made you unhappy. I am sick to think how much my careless teasing hurt you."

The intense ache in his gaze made her catch her breath. The rest of the snow melted like a Popsicle in July.

"I would do anything to go back and erase all the stupid things I said to you."

It suddenly became easy as pie to smile. She blinked away all remaining tears. "Dan, everything is going to be all right. I forgive you with all my heart."

He didn't seem to like that answer. "*Nae*, Lily. I want you to take some time to think about it. You can't so easily forgive something like this. Make me suffer. Heaven knows I've made you suffer for years."

"I'm not that kind of person, Dan, and neither are you. Now that I know there was no malice in it, forgiveness is no effort at all."

He studied her face. "I don't deserve it."

What could she say to wipe that frown off his face? "Everything can be put to rights if you smile."

He must have truly been in despair. He couldn't even manage a grimace.

Lily leaned close to him so their sleeves finally touched. "I'm just happy you don't find me repulsive."

"Never," he whispered.

Dan hesitated for a moment before slipping his hand into hers and rubbing his thumb along her knuckles. Her heart thumped and clattered like a band in a parade. She couldn't form a coherent thought, let alone pull her hand away. She would have to let it be until she got her wits about her. They might sit like this forever. With his hand touching hers, she feared she'd never see her wits again.

"I'll be grateful to Paul until the day I die," Dan said.

"You will?"

"He was a friend to you when I wasn't."

With a thick lump in her throat, Lily nodded. Maybe Dan understood better why she had always been so loyal.

"It was my fault you needed a friend.

297

That's *Gotte*'s justice if I've ever heard it."
He looked more stricken than ever. "I've
ruined everything." After what seemed like
an eternity, he stood up and turned away. "I
should go now."

Surely he knew he didn't have to leave,
especially now that everything had changed.
"But aren't you going to stay for dinner?"

He turned sideways, but he didn't really
look at her. "*Nae*. I've got chores to see to."

"Are you sure? Aunt B invited you. She's
probably invited three boys to dinner in her
entire life."

Nothing, it seemed, could pierce through
his dark mood. He shook his head. "*Denki*,
Lily, but tonight I'm not fit for company."

She felt as if he was somehow slipping
away from her, and she couldn't abide the
thought of losing him, not when their
relationship had become brand-new. She
wrapped her fingers around his arm before
he could escape. "We can still be friends,
can't we?"

He seemed to thaw slightly as he gently
placed his hand over hers. His touch proved
as unnerving as ever. "If you want my
friendship, you will always have it."

She followed him out of the leafy canopy
and down the lane, but he didn't pause to
wait for her to catch up to him. "Will we

see you tomorrow?"

He turned and gazed at her, disbelief evident in his expression. "You still want me to come?"

She blew air from between her lips in exasperation. "Dan, I've forgiven you, and that's the end of it."

His lips curved into a weary smile. "You're a better person than I'll ever hope to be, Lily Christner. Better than I'll ever deserve."

She didn't bother to contradict him, not with the more pressing matter at hand. "But you'll come? And it's not because I want to get out of the extra work."

"If you've got a lazy hair on your head, I've yet to see it." He eyed her as if waiting for her to banish him from the farm.

She could be persistent when she had a mind to. "It wonders me if you'll come."

He stroked his hand down the side of his face. "If you still want me, I'll come."

Her face relaxed into what she hoped was an appealing smile. She pointed to the hives near the row of basswood trees. "We'll be there at six."

"So will I," he said, without his ever-present cheerfulness. He turned and walked away. At least he'd agreed to come. She could work on his mood when she next saw him. She didn't immediately follow. Instead, she stood in the lane and watched Dan get his horse from the barn and hitch it to the buggy. Then he turned his buggy around and drove down the lane, giving her a wave and a subdued frown as he passed.

She waved in return, throwing much more enthusiasm into it than she usually did. Dan had to see that she truly held no malice toward him in her heart.

A boulder-size weight had been lifted from her shoulders. She felt happier than she had for weeks.

Dan, it appeared, had never felt worse.

CHAPTER EIGHTEEN

The tall battery-powered lamp was Dan's only companion as he vigorously scrubbed the cement floor on his hands and knees. His knees screamed at him to stop this madness, and his neck and shoulders were stiff with tension. Still, he didn't quit. The soreness took his mind off the ache in his chest, an ache so sharp he could barely breathe.

He'd lost Lily.

And losing the girl he loved had been all his own doing.

That pill was the bitterest he'd ever swallowed.

He scrubbed even harder. He'd already worn out one scrub brush in his attempt to clean the floor of the milking room. This next scrub brush also looked ready to give up the ghost.

"Oh, *sis yuscht,* Dan. What are you doing?"

Dan knew that voice without having to

301

turn around. He didn't even pause with the scrub brush. "I wouldn't expect you to know, Luke Bontrager. You've never cleaned a floor in your life."

"Mopping floors is women's work," Luke replied.

Dan heard two sets of footsteps behind him. "That's why you'll never get a wife," Josiah said.

Dan looked up from his floor to see his best friends eyeing him warily, as if he'd lost his mind and they were here to coax him into the asylum.

Luke raised his eyebrows. "Your *mamm* told us it was serious, but we had no idea it was this bad."

Dan pretended not to know what Luke was talking about. "What's so bad about cleaning up a little? You should try it sometime. The girls wouldn't keep away if you didn't smell so bad."

Luke gestured toward Dan's scrub brush. "You could eat off this floor."

Dan swiped his brush at a particularly stubborn piece of manure. "*Gute.* A dairy should be sanitary."

"Sanitary? With cows walking in and out all day?"

Josiah grabbed three milking stools from their pegs on the far wall, placed them in a circle, and sat down. Luke sat next to him while Josiah motioned toward the other stool. "Do you want to take a break?"

Dan shook his head. "Not really." Talking about it would only make him feel worse than manure. He'd scrubbed enough of it to know.

"*Cum*," Josiah said. "You always try to work yourself to death when you're upset, and we'd rather not bury our best friend at the ripe age of twenty-two."

"I'll be twenty-three in October."

Luke's lips twitched. "*Gute* for you."

Dan huffed out a frustrated breath. Josiah would wait all night if he had to. Luke would try to browbeat him into submission. He might as well get it over with. Dropping the scrub brush into the bucket of steaming soapy water, he rose to his feet and stifled a groan. His knees were stiffer than he expected. Maybe he should take a break from the floor and start on the walls. He managed to hobble to the stool and sit.

Luke smirked. "That's why I never scrub floors. It'll give you bad knees."

"That is nonsense coming from a carpenter," Josiah said. "You've laid plenty of wood floors yet."

"I use knee pads."

Dan propped his elbows on his knees,

laced his fingers together, and stared at Luke and Josiah as weary sadness enveloped him. He shouldn't have stopped scrubbing. At least it kept the pain at bay. "Isn't it past your bedtime?"

Josiah folded his arms and leaned toward Dan with deep concern in his expression. Luke merely looked put out.

"Your *mamm* sent your brother to fetch us," Josiah said. "She told us you came home from Christners', brushed down all three horses, mucked out the stalls, mopped the floor, and did a load of laundry, all without dinner. She got a little worried."

Dan's lips curled slightly. "Only my *mamm* worries about a person working too much."

Luke shook his head. "*Nae.* My *mamm* would worry. She'd think I was coming down with something if I worked that hard."

"What happened at Lily's?" Josiah said.

Dan forced a breath from between his lips as the pain flared like a forest fire. His whole life had been ruined; that's what had happened. "I made a mess of things with Lily, and it's a mess that can't be fixed." The words almost choked him. "I don't deserve her, and Paul Glick does. He's already won."

Luke snapped his head up and raised his voice so he almost yelled. "Whoa, whoa, whoa. Paul Glick doesn't deserve anything over you."

Josiah fingered the whiskers on his chin and studied Dan's face. "It wonders me why you say that. You are the best kind of man. Surely Lily sees that."

"Do you remember in eighth grade when I got interested in Lily?"

Luke cocked an eyebrow. "We remember. It's all we ever heard about." He made his voice high in a pathetic attempt to mimic Dan's eighth grade self. " 'Isn't Lily Christner pretty, Luke? Don't you think Lily's smart? I'm going to faint if Lily talks to me.' "

Dan frowned at Luke. "I don't faint."

Luke snorted. "You would have."

Josiah gave Luke a not-so-subtle sock in the shoulder. "You were saying, Dan?"

Dan propped his chin in his hand. "I spent hours racking my brain for ways to attract her attention. I studied spelling words so she would notice how smart I was at the spelling bee."

"You're not that smart," Luke said.

"Be quiet, Luke," Josiah scolded.

Dan chuckled in spite of himself. Sometimes Luke's sarcasm was just what he needed to keep from falling into the depths of despair. "It's true. I am the stupidest boy in the whole world."

Luke leaned away from Josiah in case Josiah wanted to shove him again. "I wouldn't say that. All I know is that I'm smarter than both of you. It gives me a lot of satisfaction."

Josiah shoved Luke again, even though he had tried to keep his distance. There was good humor in Josiah's exasperation. Josiah was gentle and kind and never lost his temper, even with his sometimes-annoying friends. He didn't have a mean bone in his entire body. "Luke, I never thought I'd say this to one of my best friends, but shut up."

Luke grinned. "It's my job to knock down Dan's pride whenever I can. Pride is a sin, you know."

Josiah draped an arm around Luke's shoulders and softened his tone. "Can't you see his pride's already been knocked down?"

They turned their eyes to Dan.

Luke sighed in resignation. "If he's surrendered to Paul Glick, I'd say he's been knocked down about as far as he can go."

"Tell us what's happened," Josiah said. "And Luke promises not to interrupt."

Dan sat up straight and scrubbed his hands through his hair as a wave of fresh pain came over him. "I wanted Lily to notice me so I started calling her names."

Luke nodded. "Amtrak, Coke Bottle. We

heard them all."

"Luke," Josiah warned.

Luke raised his hands in surrender. "I'm not interrupting, just adding to the story."

Dan pressed his lips together. *Ach,* if only he could take it all back. "I would never have called Rose names. She would have wilted like a flower in the desert. And Poppy would have wanted to beat me up every day. But I thought Lily secretly enjoyed the nicknames. I guess I believed they made her feel special, gave her a clue that I liked her."

"They didn't?" Luke said, with more of a statement in his tone than a question.

Dan massaged his forehead as if to rub the memory clean out of his brain. "They devastated her."

There was a long, heavy pause. Luke and Josiah were both thinking on it. "So you hurt her feelings," Josiah said.

"She told me she used to cry every night because I" — he pounded his chest — "*I* teased her. I brought heartache to the one person in the world I would never purposefully hurt."

"You'd never purposefully hurt anyone," Josiah murmured.

Luke suddenly had it figured out. "Then, knowing you liked her, Paul Glick took advantage of the situation and moved in on

Lily. He's always hated you."

"*Nae,* Luke. Paul Glick was the friend I should have been. No wonder she loves him."

Luke made a face. "Did she say that?"

"Not in so many words," Dan said, feeling worse by the minute. "But she said she thanks *Gotte* every day that Paul came into her life."

"Did you explain to her that you never meant to be cruel?" Josiah said.

Dan nodded. "She says she forgives me."

Josiah swiped his hand down the side of his face. "Of course she does. She's too *gute* of a girl to hold a grudge."

Luke knew how to deliver a knife right to the heart. "But she still loves Paul."

Dan clenched his jaw until he thought his teeth might crack. "She needed him, and the only reason she needed him is because I was mean to her. Why would she ever choose me over him?"

Josiah scooted his stool a few inches closer as if he were ready to get down to business. "Help me understand, Dan. Tell me what Lily said. Is she dead set on Paul?"

"How could she not be?"

"But what did she say about him?"

Nothing could help, but Dan was grateful that Josiah wanted to try. "She's very loyal.

He's got her all tied up in knots over the smallest things, but she doesn't want to see it. She refuses to see it. It makes me want to tear my hair out."

Luke growled deep in his throat. "I really dislike that boy."

Josiah glared at him.

Luke raised his hands in surrender. "I didn't say *hate.*"

"Did she ask you to stop going to her farm?"

"Nae," Dan said. "She told me I could come and trample dandelions anytime I want, and she says she still wants to be friends."

Luke grimaced. "Ouch."

Josiah gave Luke a sideways glance. Dan was impressed. He did it without even rolling his eyes. "So she doesn't hate you, and she still wants to see you, in spite of Paul."

"Maybe," Dan said, barely allowing himself to hope. "Maybe she was just being nice. She's real nice."

"She invited you to come again," Josiah said. "I think she would have told you to stay away if she were finally set on Paul."

Luke nodded. "And she wouldn't have put up with you this long if she hated your guts."

Dan knit his brows together. "I certainly gave her enough opportunity to end our friendship." He curled one side of his mouth. "Come to think of it, she seemed pretty determined that I come by tomorrow."

"Because she likes you, despite how badly you've messed things up."

Dan didn't have Josiah's forbearance. He rolled his eyes. "*Denki,* Luke, for that vote of confidence."

Luke didn't even acknowledge the veiled sarcasm. "And the girls think you're way more handsome than chubby Paul Glick."

"I'm sure Paul has many fine qualities," Josiah said, nudging Luke with his hand. "But you can't give up, Dan. I've seen the way Lily looks at you. There's something there."

Dan's heart swelled. Josiah was never one for insincerity. If he thought Dan still had a chance with Lily, then Dan would take it. She *had* seemed happy when he promised to help with the hives in the morning. Maybe she didn't mind having him around. Maybe her heart could be softened. Maybe she could be persuaded to love him eventually.

Josiah leaned closer and lowered his voice as if he shouldn't even be thinking what he was about to say out loud. "Paul and Lily are not well suited, Dan. Don't you see?

You have to do this for Lily. She can't be bound to Paul Glick for life. She'd be miserable, and she doesn't deserve to be miserable."

Dan squared his shoulders with renewed determination. He loved Lily Christner. He ached for her to love him back, but he would keep trying if for no other reason than to save Lily from an unhappy future. He would give anything to see her happy.

He stood quickly, chastising himself for the searing pain in his knees. Would it have killed him to wear knee pads? "I've got to go to Walmart. Do you guys want to come with me?"

"Now?" Luke asked, as if Dan had lost his mind.

He didn't know if he'd lost his mind, but he'd certainly lost his heart. "It's open twenty-four hours, and I need to pick up a few things for Bitsy. Is anybody with me?"

"I'll come," Luke said. "It wouldn't hurt to pick up some nails."

Dan put his hands on his hips. "And a couple of new scrub brushes for Mamm."

Josiah raised his hand as if volunteering for a dangerous job. "You can count me in. Somebody has to keep you two out of trouble."

Luke pointed to Dan's bucket of water

while Josiah hung up the stools.

"Dump it," Dan said. "I'm done for the night. Who ever heard of a sanitary milking floor?"

Luke dumped Dan's soapy water into the floor drain, and Dan threw his scrub brush away. Lord willing, he would never again be upset enough to wear out two brushes in one night.

The three of them walked out into the dark night toward Luke's buggy. Dan had never been more grateful for his two friends. They always brought just what he needed.

"Dan," Josiah asked. "So, I'm wondering. Does Rose ever talk about me?"

Luke shook his head. "You are pathetic, Josiah. Absolutely pathetic."

CHAPTER NINETEEN

The phone shack seemed to move farther and farther down the road every time Lily needed to make a phone call. She found it an increasing nuisance to call Paul every few days, but it couldn't be helped. If she didn't call him this morning, he'd be worried when she didn't show up at the market. At least she liked to think that Paul would be worried instead of annoyed.

Dan, on the other hand, would be worried sick when he found out about the latest vandalism on the farm. Somebody was definitely trying to send them a message, but Lily had no idea what message they were supposed to get or who would be so depraved as to frighten and bother three orphan girls and their aunt. It didn't make sense.

She reached the phone shack, dialed the number to the market, and asked for Paul when a female voice answered on the other end. Probably Paul's sister, but she didn't take the time to ask. At the moment, she wasn't in the mood for light conversation.

"Hello?"

"Paul, it's Lily."

Silence on the other end. He must have known she was going to cancel on him again.

"Paul, I can't come today."

"Of all the stuff, Lily. This is the second time in a week. Don't you even care about my feelings anymore?"

"I can't come, Paul. One of our buggy wheels is missing."

"You're talking nonsense again, Lily. I wish you'd stop. I hate having to try to guess what you're thinking."

Lily took a deep breath. "Three weeks ago, someone tipped over one of our beehives. Then they tore our laundry off the line and stomped it in the mud. Last night, they managed to take a wheel off our buggy. It can't be driven."

"Who would be so *deerich* as to remove someone's buggy wheel?"

"We don't know, but it's a little frightening to think they're sneaking onto our property to play tricks on us."

She didn't mention the writing on the barn. Only Dan, Poppy, Aunt Bitsy, and Lily knew about that. Rose must never catch wind of it.

Paul grunted. "It's probably some of those high school kids from Shawano."

Lily tried to sound unaffected so Paul wouldn't worry about her. "Probably." She certainly hoped it was something as harmless as a high school prank. But the message on the barn that Dan had painted over hadn't seemed so innocent.

"What about *gmay* tomorrow? You can't miss church on account of a buggy wheel."

Lily sighed. *Gmay* was the least of her problems. "I suppose we'll cross that bridge when we come to it."

Someone in the background said something to Paul. "Lily, look. I have to go. We got in a shipment of cheese that's got to go in the fridges. How soon can you get the wheel back on? I was counting on your visit today. You never seem to have time for me anymore."

"I don't know, Paul. I'm sorry."

She could have heard his pout from the next county. "It doesn't sound like you're trying very hard to come to see me. Can't you think of something?"

Lily slumped her shoulders. She had enough to worry about without the extra burden of Paul's sulking. "I've tried. We

315

were supposed to visit Mammi and Dawdi Kiem this afternoon." She didn't have many options, certainly not ones Paul would like. But if he was that eager to see her . . . "I suppose we could ask a neighbor to drive us over."

Paul's voice sounded like fingernails on a chalkboard. "You were thinking of Dan Kanagy, weren't you?"

"He could bring me to the market. He drove me into town last night to go to the library. I checked out some books." She pursed her lips. After the library Dan had bought her a burnt almond fudge ice-cream cone and taken her up to the Shawano Lake overlook. She had started reading *Caddie Woodlawn* to him as they watched the sun set over the lake. Paul definitely didn't need to know that, even though she and Dan were just friends.

Friends. Her heart thumped at the very word. She and Dan were friends, and strangely enough there was no friend she'd rather spend time with.

"He plans on coming later today to help Aunt B with another mousetrap. The first one didn't work."

"Of all the stuff, Lily. I warned you to keep away from him. He's up to no good."

If what Dan had done on their farm the

last week was "up to no good," then she'd eat her black bonnet for breakfast. Yesterday morning he showed up as promised to help move the supers into the honey house with a smile as irresistible as ever. Not only had he lifted supers, but he had brought a homemade honey extractor made out of a metal garbage can rigged with ball bearings and bicycle rims and powered by an electric drill. Even Aunt B had been impressed.

Lily knew he had his own chores to get to, but he had stayed the whole morning helping with the extraction, which with two extractors, had gone almost twice as fast as the day before. They'd finished the honey by one o'clock.

Warmth traveled up her spine. He had come back later last night and taken her for ice cream. How she loved burnt almond fudge!

"I'll ask Dan," she said, without really thinking.

"Stuff and nonsense, Lily." Paul's voice rose in pitch. "I wouldn't ask a stranger to drive my girlfriend anywhere. I'll take you to your grandparents' house."

She found herself momentarily speechless. She knew how busy they were at the market. "Uh . . . that's nice, Paul, but do you have time? You just got that cheese in."

"Of course I have time. How could you even ask that, Lily? I always have time for the girl I love."

The girl he loved.

She could count on one hand the times he'd told her that he loved her. Less than one hand. Three fingers at the most. His declaration should have made her heart go pitter-patter. Instead, it set her teeth on edge.

Why was he suddenly so accommodating?

The answer crept over her like smoke from a leaky stovepipe. Paul was jealous.

Of Dan Kanagy.

She probably should have said something to reassure him that she remained completely loyal to him, that she didn't think about Dan Kanagy that way, but she couldn't do it. After ice cream and home-made honey extractors and heartfelt apologies, she couldn't pretend that Dan hadn't pricked her interest — as a friend, of course — but the fact that she got all shivery and twitchy when she was around him would make Paul very unhappy.

The guilt just about knocked her over.

Dan's *dat* had nearly ruined Paul's family financially. Was she being disloyal or forgiving? Lily couldn't blame Paul for having trouble letting go of the past. Forgiveness didn't come easily for anyone, and poor Paul tended to hold things tight.

She'd been silent too long. Could Paul hear her doubt over the phone?

"I'll pick you up at one," he said.

"Okay. *Denki,* Paul. It will be nice to see you."

"And wear your glasses."

He hung up, and Lily slowly let out a breath. If she truly cared about Paul, she'd wear her glasses because it made him happy. Wasn't that her most important job as a girlfriend, to make her future husband happy?

She thought of Dan and that worried look in his eye and didn't feel so sure anymore. *Does Paul ever try to make you happy?*

She lifted her chin. Of course he did. He had offered to drive her into town. If that wasn't true love, she didn't know what was.

Lily's grandparents lived not far from the little cottage where Dan's *mammi* had spent her last years in a small house with almost two acres of land. Dawdi grew pumpkins and tomatoes, and Mammi kept an herb garden. Mammi used fresh herbs in all her recipes during the summer and dried herbs for use when the snows fell. Aunt B had clearly learned her cooking skills from

Mammi Sarah. When Mammi Sarah cooked, even oatmeal tasted good and broccoli was a treat. She experimented with exotic flavors and spices, and no one left hungry when they went to Mammi's for dinner.

Since Dawdi had no sons and only one living daughter, he had sold his farm and house to his nephew a dozen years ago, and he and Mammi had retired comfortably in the little house near the center of town. The Honeybee Sisters visited their grandparents every Saturday afternoon and one or two days during the week. Mammi and Dawdi weren't getting younger, and being their only grandchildren, Lily, Poppy, and Rose helped with the chores that proved increasingly difficult for them to manage.

Aunt B seldom came with them, claiming that she wanted her girls to have a good visit with Mammi and Dawdi without her getting in the way, but there was more to Aunt B's absence than that.

Poppy and Rose sat in the backseat of the buggy while Lily rode up front with Paul. He didn't have a particularly easy hand with the reins, and his posture remained stiff and uncomfortable while he drove. "Can you bring more honey on Monday? We're almost out."

Lily bloomed into a smile. "It's selling well yet?" That was *gute* news. Paul's family wouldn't be stuck with jars and jars of honey they couldn't sell.

"It's selling okay. My *mamm*'s raspberry preserves are selling better, but at least your honey isn't collecting dust on the shelves like your dandelion jelly is."

Every summer when other flowers started blooming, Aunt B would let the girls do one picking of dandelion blossoms for a batch of dandelion jelly. They sold a few jars at the market and gave the rest away as Christmas gifts. Lily loved dandelion jelly, but the tourists were a little suspicious of it.

"I'm glad to know our honey is doing well."

"We'll buy more, but we've probably sold most of what we're going to sell. We usually have to store several jars for the whole winter, and there's not a lot of space in our storage room."

Lily creased her brow. "*Ach.* I hope it's not too much trouble."

Paul glanced in her direction. "I'm doing it for you, Lily, and no other reason."

They pulled up in front of Mammi and Dawdi's house where Dawdi was taking a hoe to the flower bed. With his back to them and his hat on, they couldn't see his white hair and beard, but it wouldn't have been hard for a passerby to recognize that Dawdi was an old man. He stooped over his hoe as if it were the only thing keeping him from toppling to the ground.

Lily wished he would leave the yard work to her and her sisters. She feared he'd break a hip or cut off a finger in his stubborn independence. It must have been very hard to get old.

Dawdi looked up from his garden. "So, you've come to visit, have you?"

The screen door protested loudly as Mammi opened it. She stepped out onto the porch and let the screen crash back into place behind her. "Priscilla," she scolded. "You've got to take more care with your *kapp.* Your hair is blowing all over the place."

A few wisps of hair had broken free from Poppy's *kapp.* Poppy hated fussing with her hair in the mornings. Her impatience often resulted in unruly strands escaping the shelter of the *kapp.* Lily liked the way Poppy's untamed hair framed her face, but Mammi saw it as gross defiance of the *Ordnung.*

Poppy gave Mammi a properly repentant smile and tucked the errant hair behind her ears. That would have to do until she could get to a mirror and a comb.

At seventy-two years old, Mammi was nearly ten years younger than Dawdi, and the age contrast was significant. Although her hands were gnarled with crippling arthritis, Mammi's hair was still a beautiful light brown with only an occasional streak of gray. Except for the deep frown lines at her lips, her skin looked smooth and un-blemished, giving her the look of someone much younger.

She ambled down the stairs and hugged each of the sisters. She gave Rose a loud kiss on the cheek before pulling away to study her face. "Stand up straighter, Rosie. I've told you before, I can't abide slouch-ing."

Rose didn't really slouch. She simply tried to appear small so that as few people as pos-sible would take notice of her. While Mammi fussed with Poppy's hair, Lily re-assuringly squeezed Rose's hand. Rose responded with a resigned curl of her lips. They'd experienced Mammi's brusque manner thousands of times. Mammi couldn't help herself. Compliments were rare, and disapproval was as natural as breathing. It seemed she didn't know how to do anything but find fault.

Dawdi, with his stern looks and stiff

demeanor, was almost easier to bear than Mammi. As long as the sisters conducted themselves like proper Amish girls, Dawdi had no complaints.

Whenever she visited her grandparents, Lily always felt a little sad for Aunt B. Had she ever heard a word of sincere praise from her parents while growing up?

Still, Lily knew that Mammi's criticisms were clumsy attempts to show her affection. What better way to love your grandchildren to death than to push them to improve themselves? In Mammi's mind, she loved her granddaughters enough to want to change them for the better, and Dawdi loved them enough to care about their eternal salvation. He obviously felt he had to be vigilant.

Resting one hand on his hoe for support, Dawdi shook Paul's hand. "Your *dat* says you're going to build a house." Ever since Lily and Paul had gotten together in eighth grade, Dawdi had taken a keen interest in Paul's family. In his own way, he kept an eye out for his granddaughter.

"*Jah,*" Paul said. "I want it finished by next year."

Mammi smiled for the first time since they had arrived. She leaned close to Lily and whispered, "Don't let that one get away. His family makes *gute* money."

Lily curled her lips into a halfhearted smile. If she married Paul, it wouldn't be because he had money. She glanced doubtfully in his direction. Next year seemed too soon. When Paul finished his house, he'd put extra pressure on her to get married, but she was anything but sure she wanted to marry Paul. Dan Kanagy had planted too many doubts in her mind. "I don't care about money, Mammi."

Mammi eyed her as if she were a simpleton. "Of course not. But it doesn't hurt."

Though Aunt B rarely came with them for a visit, she always sent a jar of honey and something delicious from the oven. Lily handed Mammi a plastic zipper bag of granola.

"What's this?" Mammi asked.

"Granola with honey and wheat germ," Lily said. "It's wonderful-*gute* with milk. One of Aunt Bitsy's favorite recipes."

Mammi drew her brows together. "It's still warm. Elizabeth should know better than to put it in plastic before it cools. It will sweat."

"She made it right before we came," Lily said. "She thought you might like to eat it warm."

Mammi shrugged. "She should have let it cool first. Elizabeth never had the patience your *mamm* did with the baking. I told her, 'Mark my words. You'll never get a husband if you can't keep your cakes from falling.' And she hasn't."

"But she has, Mammi," Poppy interjected. "Aunt Bitsy's cakes hold up fine."

They followed Mammi as she marched into the house. "But she hasn't got herself a husband. And she certainly won't now, no matter how delicious her cakes are."

Mammi took the offensive granola to the kitchen while Lily and sisters sat down on the sofa in the small sitting room. Paul followed them and slid into the wooden chair closest to Lily. Dawdi hobbled in on his cane and shut the screen door behind him. After hooking his cane on the arm of his threadbare chair, he sat down and studied the girls as if trying to discover their hidden weaknesses and sins.

"Have you girls been good this week?" he said. "Does Elizabeth make sure you say your prayers and repent of your sins?"

"*Jah*, Dawdi," Lily said. Rose was too timid to do much more than nod at their *dawdi,* and Poppy didn't much like the questions. "We have tried to be humble and kind and turn the other cheek."

Paul chimed in as if he were already a grandson-in-law. "Lily is sometimes tempted by vanity, but I am helping her to see a better way."

Dawdi nodded thoughtfully. "The girls must watch themselves for any hint of vanity. Elizabeth indulged them with braces and peacock dresses. I never understood why the girls couldn't be like other good Amish and simply go without teeth."

She felt Poppy and Rose stiffen on either side of her. Lily glanced at Poppy's red and blotchy face, and she could see the anger threatening to boil over. It happened almost every time they came to visit. Poppy, Lily, and even Rose were forced to bite their tongues again and again when Dawdi made disparaging comments about Aunt B. Paul's condescending attitude didn't help matters today.

An unfamiliar annoyance simmered at the base of her throat. Usually when Paul started listing Lily's faults, she felt deep shame for being so wicked. But Dan didn't think she had anything to be ashamed of. He'd called her pretty. Was that so terrible? She'd grown tired of apologizing to Paul for simply existing.

Guilt wrapped an icy hand around her heart. She shouldn't think ill of Paul. He only wanted to help her. She kept forgetting that.

Ach! Paul was right. She was too vain and proud by half.

Mammi came from the kitchen carrying a tray filled with bowls of ice cream. She served one to each of them and then sat in her old rocker next to Dawdi.

Lily was grateful for the opportunity to change the subject. "We are sorry we haven't come around this week. We've been pulling the honey something wonderful."

Dawdi nodded. "You told us you wouldn't be by. Did it take long? The hives seem to have done well."

It was as close to a compliment as Dawdi would ever get.

"Not near as long, Dawdi." Poppy's lips twitched smugly, and she directed her next words at Paul. "Dan Kanagy helped us two whole days, and he built a clever honey extractor that made the work go twice as fast."

Paul turned three shades of green in succession. Stiffening as if someone had shoved an iron rod down his spine, he said, "I couldn't help. It's been busy at the market."

Poppy gave him a syrupy sweet smile. "*Ach,* Paul, we know how busy you are. You don't have to worry. If we need something, we ask Dan. He's never too busy to help."

In school, Poppy usually expressed her

displeasure with her fists, but Lily had never seen her deliver such a fantastic blow. Paul looked as if he'd been smacked upside the head with a hive tool.

Rose nodded eagerly. "We adore Dan. He takes very *gute* care of us," she said, in an unusual show of defiance.

Lily took no pleasure in Paul's discomfort, but she was grateful her sisters gave Dan the credit he deserved. Not only had he saved them hours of work, but he had made the long, hard days more fun than they had ever been. She smiled just thinking of him.

"Dan Kanagy?" Dawdi said. "Is them the Kanagys out on the county road?"

"*Jah,* Dawdi."

Dawdi thumbed his suspenders. "They're not in our district, but I hear tell they have a wonderful-*gute* dairy operation. I am glad there is someone who will do you a good turn. Elizabeth has always been stubborn about asking for help."

Paul swelled with indignation. "Dan Kanagy has a way of worming his way into people's good opinion, but don't forget how his family cheated mine out of that piece of land."

Dawdi turned his attention to Paul and narrowed his eyes. "That's an old argument.

You should forgive your brother his trespasses."

Lily smiled to herself. She and her *dawdi* actually saw eye to eye about something.

Paul squared his shoulders. "I have forgiven him, but I will never forget what happened. I won't let them cheat my family again."

Dawdi didn't back down. His eye could have seared a hole right through the straw hat in Paul's hand. "If you have truly forgiven, then you would forget. Search your heart. You're harboring bitterness there."

Paul didn't reply. He wouldn't argue with Dawdi, but he wouldn't admit that he might be wrong. His face turned from green to a dark shade of rose petal pink.

As justified as Lily felt, she'd rather not sit there and watch Paul squirm. "Dawdi, we need to ask your advice. Someone has been making mischief on our farm, and we don't know what to do about it."

"What kind of mischief?"

Lily met eyes with Poppy. They both knew they weren't to mention the barn incident. "Three weeks ago, someone tipped over one of our beehives. After that, they pulled our laundry off the line in the middle of the night, and yesterday, they sneaked into our barn and removed one of the wheels from our buggy."

Dawdi stroked his beard. "Have you any idea who it might be?"

"None at all," Poppy said. "Dan thinks it's *Englisch* teenagers playing pranks."

"That's what I said," Paul insisted, pouting as if another child had stolen his toy.

The lines on Dawdi's forehead bunched up as they always did when he stewed over a problem. "Years ago, there was a family in Cashton who was getting their propane stolen during the night. They put a watch at the tank, but the thief got smart and came around on Sundays when they weren't home. They thought of buying an expensive lock to secure the tank. Instead, their *dat* taped a simple note to the tank. It said, 'If you need our propane, take as much as you want. You are not stealing from us. We give it to you freely.' They didn't want the poor man to have more sins heaped upon his head. The thief never plagued them again. I hope he saw the error of his ways and came to sore repentance."

Lily thought on that for a minute. "Do you think we should write our own note?"

"Lord willing, it will prick someone's conscience," Dawdi said. "But if not, it might bring you a measure of peace. *Gotte*'s peace comes not by the world. As your friend Paul here has forgotten, Jesus said if a man takes your coat, give him your cloak also."

Beads of sweat appeared on Paul's forehead, and agitation rose off him like steam. "I haven't forgotten. I told you already I don't forget."

Dawdi regarded Paul with a critical gaze. "Look to the beam in your own eye before plucking your *bruder*'s mote."

With his face getting redder by the minute, Paul stood up, probably feeling the need to justify himself or divert Dawdi's attention. "There is a bigger problem, Solomon. I hate to say it, but I'm afraid your granddaughters have been led astray."

Led astray? Lily stole a look at Poppy. Poppy rolled her eyes.

Talk of sin and wickedness pricked Dawdi's interest more than anything else. "Who is leading my girls astray?"

Paul paced across the small room. "Bitsy is encouraging them to go against the *Ordnung.*"

Dawdi's face became a dark storm cloud. "What has she done?"

Lily was as curious as Dawdi and far more irritated.

Paul swept his hand in the direction of the sofa where Lily and her sisters sat. "All three of them wear *Englisch* jeans around the farm."

Englisch jeans? That was worse than a missing buggy wheel?

Lily's annoyance turned to indignation. She'd already explained the necessity of a bee suit. Had Paul not listened?

Poppy blew out air from between her lips and threw herself against the back of the sofa. Even Rose looked put out, and she never got annoyed.

Dawdi frowned, but he didn't erupt as Paul probably hoped he would. "Are you talking about the trousers they wear for beekeeping?"

Paul folded his arms across his chest and flashed a smug look in Poppy's direction. "*Jah.* It's unseemly and immodest."

Lily's chin nearly scraped the floor. What did Paul think he was doing, blatantly insulting her *schwesters* and Aunt B, not to mention straining Lily's patience something wonderful? He was obviously in an abominable mood.

When he got worked up like this, she could usually talk him down by meekly giving in to his wishes or apologizing for her unrighteousness. She felt too irked to do either. "Paul," she said, "I already explained —"

333

He looked at her as if she were a small child, too ignorant to understand. "Just because your *aendi* gives you permission does not mean it's right. She is a blind guide, leading you and your sisters into the ditch. Too many of *die youngie* follow worldly fashions." He turned to Dawdi. "Your granddaughters have been baptized. They shouldn't think of putting on men's clothing." Paul had the audacity to squat next to Lily and lay his hand over hers. She resisted the urge to snatch it away. "I'm sorry to have to resort to taking this to your *dawdi,* Lily, but he is the only one in your family who can see reason. Sometimes the men must put our foot down."

Lily came within inches from grabbing both her sisters' hands and storming out the door. Was it worth the extra hour it would take to walk home? It might be if she could be rid of Paul.

Dawdi looked as if he were carefully considering what Paul had told him. "I appreciate your concern for my granddaughters. They are already outsiders in the community because of their *aendi* Elizabeth. I have cautioned them time and again that they, of all people, must be strictly obedient to the *Ordnung.*"

Paul nodded so enthusiastically, his hair

slapped against his forehead. "As Lily's boyfriend, it is my duty to give the sisters correction when I see a need."

Dawdi bowed his head in resignation. "Heaven knows they don't get correction at home."

"Dawdi," Poppy protested, "please don't speak ill of Aunt Bitsy."

Poppy had enough courage to speak for the three of them, as she so often did at Dawdi's house. It was *gute* of Poppy to try, but there was no reason to bother. Defense of Aunt Bitsy fell on deaf ears.

With every bone in her body, Lily wanted to give Paul a good scolding, but she'd never hear the end of it if she embarrassed him in front of Dawdi and Mammi. Besides, her censure would only make him grumpier.

"I never speak ill of another man, Priscilla. I am only stating the truth," Dawdi said.

Paul looked exultant. *Ach,* how he loved to be right.

Dawdi settled back in his chair. "I have talked to the bishop about the beekeeper clothes. His nephew in Indiana keeps bees, and the girls can't wear dresses when they do it or they will be stung, not once but several times. Since Elizabeth and the girls seem to be coming along fine with their honey, the bishop has given permission."

In other words, since Aunt B had never asked for support from the church, they liked the honey business very much.

Dawdi eyed Paul. "Didn't Lily tell you she got the bishop's permission?"

"She did," Paul stammered. "I only wanted you to be aware of what goes on. The girls have no *fater* to be strict with them."

Was that the role of a *fater* — someone to be strict and unbending without a drop of mercy to temper his rules? Was that the kind of *fater* Paul would be? Lily didn't remember her own *dat* that way.

Dawdi's attention seemed to slide from Paul in an instant, and he turned to Mammi as if they were the only two people in the room. "I water my pillow every night with fears that Elizabeth will drag our girls to hell with her."

"He saw fit to take our Salome and then let the courts steal them from us," Mammi said. "*Gotte* will see that our girls are raised up right."

Dawdi gazed at his granddaughters. "You know you are always welcome to live with us. You are of age now to decide for yourselves, and we would give you a more godly home."

Lily sat with her arms folded and her lips pressed together. Dawdi often spoke of his fear for their souls. Mammi had never accepted the fact that Mamm and Dat had left their daughters to Aunt Bitsy in their will.

Lily could not share Mammi's distress. She thanked *Gotte* that she and her sisters had grown up with Aunt Bitsy instead of with their stern and unbending grandparents. Aunt Bitsy's home had been filled with patience and affection. She was fiercely loyal to her girls, and Lily and her sisters were fiercely loyal to Aunt B. She was their rock, and they wouldn't have traded her love for the world.

Poppy pressed her lips together in an amazing show of self-control. It was exhausting to sit and listen to insults being cast at the person Lily and her sisters loved most in the whole world, but defending Aunt B's character only made Dawdi more passionate about their salvation.

"She's colored her hair light blue," Paul said.

Mammi looked as if she were trying to keep her emotions in check. "I hear tell she's gotten a tattoo."

Could no one see what a wonderful-*gute* person Aunt Bitsy was? She'd raised three girls on her own, and they'd managed without relying on anyone's charity. All three girls had chosen baptism and could cook and sew and garden and do all the things a *gute* Amish *frau* was expected to do. Did that mean nothing to anyone?

Lily would have at least expected her own boyfriend to acknowledge Aunt Bitsy's accomplishments.

Poppy knew better, but she always felt she had to try. "Dawdi," she said, "Aunt Bitsy gave up her whole other life to raise us. She is your own daughter. Don't you even love her?"

Dawdi narrowed his eyes in resentment. "No parent loves a child more. If I didn't love her so much, I wouldn't be so fearful for her salvation. She rejected everything I taught her and stabbed me right in the heart." He shook a crooked finger in Poppy's direction. "You are too much like her, Priscilla."

"I have often told Lily that Poppy's stubborn streak will get her in hot water one day," Paul said, still determined to be important in the conversation.

Lily glared at Paul with all the harshness she could muster. Poppy's glare looked no less potent.

Rose, of all people, had the presence of

mind to take action before Poppy gave Paul a bloody nose. She stood, grabbed Lily's hand and Poppy's sleeve, and pulled them toward the kitchen. "What help do you need around the house before we go, Mammi?"

Mammi stood to follow them. "*Ach,* so many things. Can you do the floor?"

Paul cleared his throat. "I'm sure Poppy and Rose don't mind staying, but Lily is helping at the market today." He stood and smiled cheerfully as if he were unaware he had offended all three girls, including his bride-to-be. "Lily and I will be back to pick up the other girls in a couple of hours."

Even knowing how annoyed Paul would be, Lily couldn't abide the thought of spending another minute with him today. She pasted a smile on her face and made her voice as sweet as one-hundred-percent pure maple syrup. "Paul, I wouldn't dream of leaving my sisters to do all this work by themselves. You go on along, and we'll see you tomorrow at *gmay.*"

Paul studied Lily's face and obviously saw something he didn't like. His eyes tapered into slits, and his bottom lip protruded slightly from his face. He knew he had been dismissed.

Before he could protest, Mammi, oblivious to the brewing quarrel, started gathering up empty ice-cream bowls. "I would appreciate it if all three of you could stay. Poppy can help in the garden, Lily can mop floors, and Rose can bake bread for the fellowship supper after *gmay* tomorrow."

With the help of his cane, Dawdi stood as well. He patted Paul on the shoulder. "I could truly use Poppy's help in the garden. You can come back to fetch them at three o'clock."

Lily saw the tantrum brewing behind Paul's eyes, but she knew he wouldn't argue with Dawdi. "Okay then. I will do what I can without Lily's help at the market and come back in two hours."

"No need," Lily said, still with that syrupy, sticky sweetness to her voice. "It is a beautiful day. We will walk home."

"Of all the stuff, Lily," Paul said, trying to sound cheerful with a mouthful of bitterness. "It's the least I can do for my girlfriend."

"You're a *gute* man," Dawdi said.

Paul nodded, some of the tension falling from his face at Dawdi's praise. "I try to be nothing less for Lily."

Lily thought she should have felt something warm and gooey at Paul's declaration, but she felt nothing but an eagerness for him to be gone.

For the first time since eighth grade, she didn't believe him.

The thought was both shocking and liberating. She buried it deep.

CHAPTER TWENTY

"Oh, *sis yuscht,*" Poppy said under her breath as she turned and looked behind her. "He came after all."

Lily didn't even glance backward. Not fifteen minutes from home, and Paul had finally caught up to them in his buggy.

Lily and her sisters had decided that they would leave Mammi and Dawdi's half an hour early so they wouldn't be there when Paul came to pick them up. They hoped he'd be discouraged from following them. Lily had underestimated his determination. Or annoyance. She didn't know which had driven him to come so far out of his way.

With added determination, they kept walking even as Paul pulled his buggy beside them on the road. "Lily," he called out his window. "Lily, why didn't you wait for me?"

It surprised her that Paul actually sounded more hurt than irritated. Maybe he realized he crossed some sort of line at Mammi and Dawdi's.

Lily slackened her steps slightly. Her sisters quickly outpaced her.

Paul kept the buggy even with her. "Lily, look at me. Why won't you even look at me?"

She didn't stop even though she didn't believe he'd give up and head for home.

"Lily, don't you even care about my feelings?"

Lily huffed out a heavy breath. She'd have to give in. The silent treatment was no way to communicate with her boyfriend. She stopped walking and pinned Paul with an I-dare-you-to-make-me-madder glare.

Poppy and Rose turned in unison. "Lily, you don't have to explain anything," Poppy said. "Just ignore him and come home."

Lily shook her head. "You go ahead. I'll catch up."

Poppy's frown deepened. "Don't let him bully you."

"He can't help the way he is."

Still frowning, Poppy shrugged in surrender, hooked her arm around Rose's elbow, and kept walking.

Paul secured the reins and climbed out of the buggy. "What do you mean I can't help the way I am?" He placed his hands on his hips and stared in Poppy's direction. "I know Poppy doesn't like me. People often resist correction when they should embrace it."

Maybe she should have tried to explain things to Paul like she always did, tried to help him understand how much her unconventional family meant to her. She could usually talk him out of his foul mood if she worked hard enough and acted humble enough, but he had stretched her patience today until it had snapped like a rubber band. She wasn't in the mood to appease Paul. She wasn't even in the mood to talk to him.

Without a second glance, she turned on her heel and marched down the road, not even caring if Paul couldn't keep up with her.

"Lily, what are you doing? I had the decency to stop. You could at least have the decency to talk to me." The exasperation in his voice grew with every step.

She kept up her brisk pace. Paul wouldn't be able to stay up with her. He already breathed heavily.

He reached out and grabbed her elbow. "Of all the stuff, Lily, we can't talk if you run away."

Lily whirled around and gave Paul a

white-hot glare. She had always been the one to make peace. Today, come what may, she would give Paul a piece of her mind. "If you say one more word against Poppy or Aunt Bitsy or my beekeeping outfit, I will run home and lock you out of my house." She put extra determination in her voice. "And you know I can outrun you for sure and certain."

Paul raised his hands and took a step back. "Okay, okay. What are you so worked up about all of a sudden?"

Lily almost started walking again. Paul rarely admitted to having faults or being wrong in an argument, but this time, he knew plain as day why she was mad at him. "Why have you set yourself against Aunt Bitsy?"

Paul made a show of innocent surprise. "I am a Christian. I haven't set myself against anybody."

"You told Dawdi that she has led us astray."

Paul took the drastic measure of grabbing Lily's hand. She didn't pull away, mostly because he'd truly surprised her this time. He led her to a pasture fence that ran alongside the road and leaned against it. She kept her posture stiff, her hand in his the only indication that she wasn't made out of stone. "Lily, I can't believe you think I am against your aunt." He put his arm around her shoulders. He could have knocked her over with a feather. "My first concern has always been for you and only you. You have to admit that anyone would have a hard time believing that the bishop approved of the jeans. I had to make sure that your aunt Bitsy hadn't heard him wrong. Now that I know your *dawdi* also talked to the bishop, I can rest assured that you won't be shunned for breaking the *Ordnung*. Anxiety made me bold in speaking. I am sorry if you think I have anything against your aunt."

Lily pursed her lips. What he said made sense. He had always been concerned for her well-being, but did he understand how much she loved Aunt B? "She took us in, Paul. She didn't have to."

"And that was a very Christian thing to do." He pulled her more tightly to him. She didn't resist, but she didn't exactly give in either. "But we all know that your grandparents would have gladly raised you, and they would have been a more fitting choice for the daughters of a minister. Your *mammi* certainly wouldn't think of getting a tattoo on her neck."

She felt an emptiness at the pit of her

stomach as she slowly but forcefully slid out of Paul's grasp. "That's what I'm talking about, Paul. I don't appreciate your constant criticism."

"I'm trying to help you see that even though you love her, she has many faults. I don't want you to believe that the things she does are acceptable for a *gute frau.*"

Lily nibbled on her bottom lip. She wanted to be a *gute* wife, and Paul knew it. Which one of them was wrong? She hated how he always made her second-guess herself. "You can be concerned about me if you like, but I hope you'll leave my Aunt Bitsy out of it."

Paul sidled close again and took her hand. "You're right, Lily. My only concern is for you." He cleared his throat. "That's why I think we should get married in September, instead of waiting to finish the house."

Lily carefully swallowed the lump in her throat before it choked her. "We're not engaged," she whispered.

Paul drew his brows together. "I just asked, didn't I?"

"*Nae,* you didn't."

Irritation flashed across his features before he seemed to think better of it. His smile revealed the gap in his two front teeth that Lily had always thought was kind of cute. His grip on her hand nearly cut off her circulation as he tugged her closer. "Well, I'm asking now. Lily, will you marry me?"

Her heart rumbled in her chest like thunder from a looming thunderstorm. Is this what it felt like to be in love? "I . . . I don't know."

Clearly not the answer he expected. His brows inched closer together. "You don't know? Lily, we've been planning to marry ever since eighth grade."

Paul had just proposed to her, but she saw Dan's deep brown eyes in her imagination. *Does Paul ever try to make* you *happy? All I want is to see you happy,* he had said.

Questions and doubts irritated Paul to no end, but if they were going to be husband and wife, they would have to learn how to settle their differences. And like it or not, Paul would need to meet her halfway. She pulled her hand from his and folded her arms. "The truth is, Paul, you can't bring yourself to ask for forgiveness. Your proposal feels like a consolation prize for not giving me an apology for speaking badly of Aunt B."

He looked momentarily confused and permanently annoyed. "Of all the stuff, Lily. I already said I'm sorry."

"*Nae,* you didn't."

"Then I'm sorry," he snapped, taking off

his hat and running his fingers through his hair. "For what, I don't know, but I'm sorry."

It was probably not a *gute* time to insist on sincerity.

She thought about Dan and how giddy she felt when he looked at her. "Paul, do you think I'm pretty?"

His eyebrows had long since met in the middle and were forming a mountain range above his nose. "Shame on you for even asking. It's gross vanity, Lily, and I won't stand for it."

She felt as irritated with Paul as he seemed to be with her. "Dan Kanagy thinks I'm pretty." She regretted the words as soon as they left her mouth. Better to absorb the hurt than provoke Paul like this.

The mountain range got taller. "Dan Kanagy? Dan Kanagy?" Paul's voice rose in pitch until soon the dogs would be the only ones to hear him. "Dan Kanagy is feeding your vanity so you'll trust him. Have you forgotten all those cruel names he used to call you? Because I haven't." He spit them out of his mouth with more venom than Dan ever had. "Amtrak, Coke Bottle, Frog Eyes."

Lily didn't bat an eye. Since Wednesday, those names didn't hurt her anymore.

"Paul, do you love me?"

He practically slammed the hat back onto his head. "Now you're questioning my love? Don't you see what Dan Kanagy has done? He hates me, Lily. He's trying to break us up."

She'd never considered that, but it seemed a bit far-fetched. "You really think so?"

"What possible motive does Dan have to be nice to you but to get back at me?"

Maybe it was because Dan wanted to be her friend, that maybe he liked her a little. Her heart dropped to the ground. This is what Paul thought of her. He couldn't imagine another boy being interested. If she were honest with herself, she couldn't imagine another boy being interested either.

"I stuck by you when no one else did," Paul said. "I was your friend, the person you told all your secrets to. I didn't care if the other boys hated me. I did it because I love you. I've shown that I'm the only one who loves you."

He knew exactly what to say to make her doubt herself. Paul had sacrificed friendships and recesses for her. Was that love? She put a hand on Paul's arm before he broke a blood vessel in his neck. "Paul," she said, sufficiently humbled by her memories. "Everything is happening so fast. I don't mean to be difficult, but I'm confused. Since you and I became friends, I've never made a decision on my own. I don't trust my own judgment."

As Paul studied her face, his expression relaxed into something softer than the hard lines of frustration. "Then trust mine. This is right, Lily. You and I belong with each other. *Gotte* put us together eight years ago. Who are we to question His plan?"

Lily nodded doubtfully. Paul was so smart about these things. He knew his Bible well. She had always trusted his judgment and heeded his advice. What held her back this time?

Was this Dan Kanagy's doing? Had his flattery led her into temptation? He had certainly planted seeds of doubt.

She pressed her lips into a tight line. What had Dan done but make her feel important, as if he truly valued her opinion, truly valued her as a person? He didn't treat her like a nuisance, even when she disagreed with him, and he didn't act as if he thought everything he did was more important than anything she did. He helped with the bees, even though the hours at their farm took him away from his own chores.

Was it all to get back at Paul? Her hopeful heart wouldn't let her believe it. When he'd chased her to the willow tree, he hadn't been too proud to apologize, hadn't made her feel small or blamed her for misunderstanding him. He'd simply said he was sorry, with real remorse and real pain.

He had painted her barn doors an ugly shade of orange.

In the middle of the night.

Perhaps Dan had planted seeds, but it wasn't his fault that Lily felt as if she were being pulled and stretched like a piece of warm taffy. He'd simply shown her how a boy should treat a girl, and now she didn't want to have to settle for less.

And surely Paul could be more.

Paul narrowed his eyes. "Lily?"

"I need some time to think about it."

"But if you love me —" Paul sputtered.

"If you love me, you won't push me to make a decision."

His expression hovered between disgust and doubt, and he clamped his lips shut as if restraining himself from saying something he'd later regret.

It was a very *gute* sign. He could learn to be considerate of her feelings. "If we marry . . . I can't have you speaking against my aunt ever again."

"When we marry, you'll be out of your *aendi*'s house and living in mine. There won't be a need for me to watch to make sure she brings you up right."

"She and my sisters will still be a big part of my life."

He smiled vaguely, most likely in an attempt to reassure her. "We will make a decision we both feel satisfied with, for the good of our family."

"Okay," she said, not feeling all that reassured.

He patted her hand as if he could see the doubt lingering in the back of her mind. "As head of the household, I know you will trust my judgment and abide by my decisions. That's what it means to love someone better than yourself."

Confusion tied itself in a knot around her heart. Was that what it meant to truly love someone? In pledging her life to Paul, would she lose herself?

She still had so much to learn about love.

CHAPTER TWENTY-ONE

Paul dropped Lily off at the bridge like he usually did. "I don't want to get stung," he said. "And driving you all over town today has put me behind on my chores."

Lily climbed out of the buggy without complaint. She had enough to think about, and a short walk would help to clear her head. "Good-bye, Paul," she said. "Lord willing, I will see you at *gmay* tomorrow."

"And I hope you'll have an answer for me."

She sighed inwardly. Barring a vision or a miracle, she wouldn't be ready to give Paul an answer. He'd have to learn to be patient.

Poppy and Rose were only a few steps ahead of her. They turned when they heard Paul's buggy and waited for Lily to join them. They linked elbows, with Lily in the middle, and strolled the rest of the way to the house.

Rose glanced at Lily. "Is everything okay?"

Lily looked back and watched Paul's buggy drive out of sight. "I don't know. Paul is so sure of himself. My worries seem so silly after I talk to him."

Poppy grunted her disapproval. "I suppose he convinced you it was your fault."

"Poppy," Rose said. "That's not fair. You don't know what Paul said to her."

Nae, she didn't know, and after the scene at Dawdi's house, Lily wasn't about to tell them that Paul had proposed. Poppy might start trampling dandelions.

"He told me he was sorry," Lily said feebly. Even she knew he hadn't truly meant it.

Rose gave her a half smile. "That's something. See, Poppy? He apologized. He's sorry for saying all those things about Aunt Bitsy."

Poppy snorted. "I'll bet he is."

Lily's heart flipped all over itself when she saw Dan's open-air buggy parked in its usual spot. She hadn't dared hope she'd see him today.

"How nice," Rose said when she saw the buggy. The smile in her eyes lit up her entire face.

Even Poppy's mood brightened. "I'll win at Uno tonight for certain. He's too confident he can beat me."

Lily didn't say anything, but she felt so light, she could have floated into the house. Dan had a way of making every smile wider, every room brighter, every day better. It was turning out to be a *gute* day after all.

Dan tightened the bit in his drill and stifled a yawn. He'd crawled into bed way too late last night, and he felt it today. The full days spent with the Honeybees had pared down what time he had for his own chores at home, and he'd stayed up late last night to finish them. As the animal expert at their organic dairy, he saw to the health of the cattle. It wasn't something he could put off while he spent his days courting Lily.

He didn't mind the fatigue. He would have gladly missed several nights' sleep to spend every waking hour with Lily Christner. Three weeks ago, he wouldn't have thought he could be any more in love with her than he already was. Now he knew two things. He'd underestimated how far and wide his love could reach, and if she ended up choosing Paul Glick, it would hurt something wonderful.

Bitsy smirked in his direction. "Do you need a nap? I don't want you falling asleep and drilling a hole through your finger."

Dan chuckled. "*Nae.* I should be able to

manage."

Bitsy had seemed gloomy when Dan had arrived today with his supplies and his new idea for a mousetrap. She had told him that someone had pulled a wheel off their buggy in the middle of the night and that her girls had gone off with Paul Glick to visit their grandparents.

Of course, the girls' going off with Paul Glick probably didn't have anything to do with Bitsy's bad mood, but it sure took the wind out of Dan's sails.

Bitsy seemed to have perked up a bit since then. She only insulted, er, joked with him when she was in good humor. Her willingness to experiment with another mousetrap design seemed a good sign.

Dan glanced at her out of the corner of his eye as he wrote two *X*'s on either side of the five-gallon bucket. He'd never seen someone wear a *kapp* and earrings together. Bitsy wore, not one, but three earrings in each ear. The top earrings were sparkly white studs. Dan suspected they were real diamonds. The middle pair was tiny yellow sunflowers with ten petals each. Large turquoise circles, as big as canning lids, dangled from the bottom holes.

Amish women didn't usually wear lipstick — well, never wore lipstick — but Bitsy's lips were a dark shade of pink to match the subtle pink highlights in her formerly blue hair.

She looked colorful, to say the least.

Dan suspected the earrings and the lipstick and the hair all had something to do with Bitsy's bad mood. His *mamm* always wore her mint-green dress when she felt low and wanted to cheer herself up. Someone was doing some serious vandalism on Bitsy's farm. If earrings and lipstick helped Bitsy forget her troubles, who was he to judge?

He pressed his drill bit to the X and drilled a hole through the side of the bucket. The soda bottle mousetrap hadn't worked. The mouse had taken the cheese, tripped the mechanism, and escaped through the slit in the bottle, just as Bitsy had said it would.

Bitsy rolled the bucket over and Dan drilled a hole on the other side. This new mousetrap seemed even less likely to work than the first one, but the materials were cheap and Dan wanted to give it a try. At the very least, a failed mousetrap would mean Dan would have an excuse to come back another day.

The door opened, and the Honeybee Schwesters burst into the room like three brilliant rays of morning sunshine. Dan's gaze immediately flew to Lily's face. Her brilliant smile nearly blinded him. He wouldn't have thought it possible, but she grew prettier with every passing day. His lips curled automatically.

Although all three girls were smiling, Dan couldn't be sure they weren't trying to put on a brave face. Immediately tempering his grin, he made straight for Rose and laid his hands on her shoulders. "Bitsy told me about the buggy wheel. Are you okay?" He looked at Lily. "Is everybody okay?"

With Dan's hands still on her shoulders, Rose haltingly wrapped her arms around her waist. "It's just some teenagers playing pranks," she said, sounding as if she wanted to convince herself more than anyone else.

Dan certainly wasn't convinced. He squeezed Rose's shoulders reassuringly. "Don't you worry. I'm determined to find out who's making mischief. I'll keep an eye on things here, and I've asked my friends Luke and Josiah to watch for anything suspicious around town."

Rose nodded. "I'm sure it's teenagers playing tricks."

"I'm sure it is," Dan said. "But Luke, Josiah, and I are going to do everything we can to make them stop."

"Okay," Rose said.

"Do you know my friend Josiah Yoder?" Dan asked, glancing at Lily and giving her a secret wink. The unmistakable tenderness in her eyes made him feel light-headed. "He's a wonderful-*gute* farmer. Careful and responsible with his land. He's been working it on his own since his parents died."

Did a soft blush color Rose's cheeks? "*Jah*, I know Josiah. He seems very nice."

Bitsy tapped on the bucket with the palm of her hand. "Dan Kanagy, if you're going to start a job, you might as well finish it."

Dan grinned and returned to his bucket and drill. "Do you want to see our new mousetrap?" The girls gathered around the island. "We drilled two holes in the bucket." He threaded the wire through the holes in the can and then through the holes in the bucket and suspended the can over the bucket. "Then we spread peanut butter on the can." He held out his hand. "Bitsy, if you'll be so kind as to hand me the jar of peanut butter."

Bitsy looked at him sideways. "I'm not your lovely assistant, Dan. You can get your own peanut butter."

Poppy laughed and pulled the peanut butter out of the cupboard. "Here you go."

Dan grinned at her. "You can be my lovely assistant." He spread the peanut butter all around the can, then took a pitcher and filled the bucket about a third of the way full of water. "Supposedly, the mouse tries to eat the peanut butter on the can, the can spins, and the mouse falls into the water and drowns."

"Poor mouse," Rose said.

"You should feel sorry for the honey, Rose," Bitsy said. "The mice eat it without mercy."

"Luke Bontrager gave me the idea for this one." Dan winked at Lily a second time. "Poppy, do you know my friend Luke? He's a carpenter. Wonderful-*gute* with his hands."

Dan nearly laughed out loud at the look of surprised disgust on Poppy's face. Poppy and Luke were like oil and vinegar. They might go good together if someone shook them up a bit.

"Of course I know Luke Bontrager," Poppy said, as if she were talking about fresh horse manure. "He and his family are our nearest neighbors."

"And Poppy hates him," Rose said, burying a giggle in her hand.

Poppy folded her arms. "He's too big for his britches and thinks boys are better at everything. Just once I'd like to get him to agree to a footrace. I'd show him who's better."

"I'm glad he's your nearest neighbor," Dan said. "He can help keep an eye on things better than I can from four miles away."

Lily leaned her elbow on the counter. "Dawdi thinks we should leave our teenage pranksters a note."

Bitsy looked up from her wire cutters. "A note?"

"And tell them that we bear them no ill will and that they are welcome to ruin anything they want on our farm if it will make them feel better."

"How did your visit to the grandparents go?" Dan said, with a casual lilt to his voice. If he asked about the grandparents, no one would suspect how curious he was about Paul.

Poppy groaned, plopped into one of the kitchen chairs, and blew out a puff of air that vibrated her lips. "*Ach.* Between Mammi's criticism, Dawdi's lectures, and Paul's accusations, we had a wonderful-*gute* time."

Dan frowned. "I didn't mean to bring up a sore subject."

Lily joined Poppy at the table and slumped her shoulders as if she hadn't any energy left to fight. "We've gotten used to it."

Rose sat next to Lily. In unison, she and

Poppy each took hold of Lily's hands. Dan's heart sank. Something had happened at the Kiems' to upset Lily. He didn't like it.

Bitsy must have sensed the same thing. "Did Paul do something bad, little sister? Or was it my *dat*?" She looked up at the ceiling. "Lord, I know You felt You needed to give Dat a mouth, but did You have to give him such a sharp tongue, especially when my girls go to visit?"

Lily tried to treat it lightly, but Dan could see that something weighed heavily on her. "*Ach,* it was nothing really. Paul wanted to poke a wasp's nest, and Dawdi lent him a stick."

"He told Dawdi we were being led astray because you let us wear jeans for beekeeping," Poppy said.

Bitsy sat down at the table next to her girls. Dan stood at the counter, gripping his drill so tightly, his knuckles turned white. Half of him wished Paul Glick would keep his mouth shut. The other half secretly hoped Paul would never stop talking. Every time Paul said something, he wedged his foot more firmly into his mouth.

Bitsy sighed. "It wonders me why my *dat* wouldn't put Paul in his place. He knows the bishop approves."

"He did, Aunt Bitsy," Rose said. "Dawdi

told Paul that he had already talked to the bishop. He defended us."

A hint of a smile played at Bitsy's lips. "I would have liked to see the look on Paul's face."

Dan eyed Lily. She seemed more than a little distressed.

Bitsy cleared her throat. "I mean . . . I wouldn't have wanted to see it. I never enjoy witnessing someone else's humiliation."

Lily cracked a half smile. "I enjoyed it."

Rose's mouth fell open. "Lily!"

Lily lifted her chin. "Well, I was annoyed with him. He should never speak badly of the people I love."

Bitsy leaned an elbow on the table and propped her chin in her hand. Her dangly earrings leaned in with her. "Paul thinks I'm corrupting you, and your *dawdi* agreed."

Lily looked at her aunt, her eyes full of compassion, and gave a reluctant nod.

Bitsy didn't seem a bit offended. She glanced at each of the sisters and smirked. "It's about time someone noticed what a bad influence I am."

"Aunt Bitsy, don't say that," Rose protested.

Bitsy drummed her fingers on the table. "What's the use of working so hard to lead you girls astray if no one notices?"

Poppy and Lily joined Rose in protest. "That's not true," Lily said.

"You are the best substitute mother anyone could hope for," Poppy added.

Dan didn't know how, but he recognized real pain beneath Bitsy's good-natured teasing, and he felt like an intruder in a very personal family moment. "I should probably go now," he said, showing more dejection than he meant to.

Lily reached out a hand and motioned for him to join them at the table. "We don't mind if you know our family secrets, Dan. You're like a big brother to us."

Dan mentally smacked his palm to his forehead. The only thing worse than Lily considering Dan *just* a friend was her thinking of him as a big brother.

Luke would mock him mercilessly if he found out.

Dan would definitely have to do something about that. As soon as possible.

As reluctant as Dan was to be a big brother, he was also incredibly eager to know if Paul had redeemed himself at Sol Kiem's house. He slipped into the chair next to Poppy. If he couldn't sit by Lily, at least he could have a good view of her face.

Bitsy sat back and folded her arms. "I want you to know, Dan Kanagy, that I do the best I can for my girls."

"From what I've seen," Dan said, "nobody could do better."

Sorrow flashed in her eyes like distant lightning. "Except their *mater*. Nobody will ever be as good as Salome Kiem Christner."

"Your sister," Dan said.

"Older than me by fifteen months and wiser than me by many years." She slid an arm around Rose and pulled her close. "Growing up, I was like a popcorn kernel stuck in my *dat*'s tooth. I resisted correction, tested Dat's patience, and questioned every rule. By the time I reached ten, I'd been taken to the woodshed so many times, I could have found the place blindfolded."

Dan winced. His own *fater* had never once laid an angry hand on him.

"Salome was the leaven to Dat's anger and Mamm's disapproval. She would often stand between us and talk Dat into mercy instead of justice. She saved me many a sore backside. I loved Salome better than my own soul." Bitsy wiped some moisture from her eyes. It was the deepest emotion Dan had ever seen from her. "I would have done anything for her."

Tears shone in Lily's eyes, Rose sniffled quietly, and Poppy stared straight ahead as if willing herself not to cry. They had been old enough to know and love their *mater* before she died.

Dan wanted to reach out and take Lily's hand something wonderful. Instead, he made a fist and tried not to dwell on how good her skin would feel against his.

"I couldn't live under my *fater*'s roof once Salome was gone," Bitsy said. "When Salome married, I left home and the church. It's not that I didn't believe anymore, but I couldn't force myself to accept that my *dat*'s way of doing things was the way *Gotte* would have done them. Dat has never forgiven me for breaking his heart."

"You aren't responsible for Dawdi's heart, Aunt B," Lily said. "He drove you away because he wanted to control you instead of love you. I don't mean to speak ill of Mammi and Dawdi, but it would have been hard to grow up in a home with so little affection."

"*Jah,* it would have been," said Dan. "What other choice did you have?"

Lily's tender look radiated so much warmth, he could have toasted marshmallows by it.

Poppy smiled at Dan too. "I visit Mammi and Dawdi every week, but I would stay away if I didn't feel an obligation to my *mater*'s parents. Dawdi is hard and unforgiving. Mammi only criticizes. It's exhausting trying to keep from losing my temper."

"I'm glad you hold your tongue," Bitsy said. "I learned the hard way that no good can come of it."

Poppy shrugged. "It would make me feel better anyway."

Bitsy reached over and patted Poppy's hand. "My *dat* is sure I'm going to hell. Probably because he doesn't like the earrings."

"How could he not like the earrings?" Dan said, in mock amazement. "The sunflowers are my favorite."

This time, Rose, Poppy, and Lily all beamed at him. His heart did a flip.

Bitsy fingered the sunflowers in her ears. "A patient gave these to me because I did such a good job cleaning her teeth."

"A patient?"

"Aunt B worked as a dental hygienist before our parents died."

That explained her insistence about her girls' teeth. Dan rejoiced she'd been so particular. Lily's smile was about his favorite thing in the world.

Bitsy cocked an eyebrow in Dan's direction. "You thought you were so clever with your nicknames for Lily. I've heard teeth nicknames that would curdle your milk."

Dan frowned. How he regretted those horrid nicknames. He glanced at Lily, and she raised her eyebrows in a scold. She must have told him a dozen times that she had forgiven him. She went so far as to warn him to quit with the remorse or she'd throw his hat in the woodstove. If he hadn't felt so bad about it, her threat might have made him smile.

"Why did you decide to come back to the Amish?" Dan said.

Bitsy took one of the sunflower earrings out of her ear and twirled it in her finger. "Right after Rose was born, Aaron got thyroid cancer. They cured it, but that illness was enough to give us all a scare. Salome and Aaron wrote a will, leaving their girls to me because Salome didn't want our *dat* to raise her children. But Salome believed in the church with every bone in her body, and she was frantic that if her girls weren't baptized, they'd burn in hell. The sheer terror of it kept her up at night. She begged me to bring up the girls in the Amish faith if it ever came to that. I would have done anything for her, so I promised her that I would raise the girls Amish. I didn't promise they would stay Amish, but I promised I'd try. My *dat*'s mistake was thinking he could control my choices. I

369

haven't raised my girls that way."

"I'm glad they stayed Amish," Dan said, smiling at Lily so she had no doubt why he was glad.

Rose drew her eyebrows together. "You're glad we're Amish, aren't you, Aunt Bitsy?"

"Of course. Your *dawdi* is one kind of Amish, but you've seen for yourselves how many *gute* Christian people there are in our community. They are people worth knowing and loving. Being Amish makes you girls happy, and that's what I most want. I was unhappy growing up, but not because I grew up Amish. It was because I grew up in my *dat*'s home."

"Was this Aaron and Salome's farm?" Dan asked.

Bitsy shook her head. "After the cancer scare, I took out a life insurance policy in Salome's name. I knew Aaron would never buy insurance on himself. It's not the Amish way. But I wanted something for Salome if she lost her husband. I bought the farm with the insurance money. The bees and the orchards and the gardens support us."

"Most of our income comes from the hives. Paul's family buys all our honey," Lily said, as if the thought troubled her.

Poppy scrunched her lips to one side of her face. "If Paul had his way, we would tend to our hives in dresses and get stung to death before we could harvest our next batch."

Lily frowned, and her usually bright eyes glazed over as if she were deep in thought. "Paul was very sorry he made a fuss about the bee suits."

Bitsy narrowed her eyes. "Paul Glick would rather swallow a bee than apologize. Are you sure he was *very sorry*?"

"He cares for our family and is anxious for our well-being. He gives correction only because he cares so much. Just today he reminded me that I have been led away into vanity. I am grateful to him for his vigilance."

"Vanity?" Bitsy caught the word with resentment.

"Why would Paul accuse you of such a thing?" Rose said.

Lily glanced at Dan and quickly looked away. Her face glowed bright pink. "I told him that Dan thinks I'm pretty."

Dan's pulse beat double-time. He'd made an impression. This was a very, very *gute* thing. "I think you're beautiful," he said, so she knew where he stood.

Lily acted as if she hadn't heard him. Instead she lowered her eyes and stared faithfully at the table. "Paul said that Dan is only flattering me. And he's right. I took pleasure in Dan's compliments when I shouldn't have. It's pride, pure and simple."

Dan ground his teeth until they squealed like chalk against a blackboard. He thought every bone in his face might crack. Paul Glick could twist good principles beyond recognition.

"Paul's wrong," Poppy said.

Rose had difficulty believing anything but the best of people. "Why would he say that?"

Thank the Lord for Aendi Bitsy. "*Ach du lieva,* little sister," she said, so loudly that Farrah Fawcett lifted her head from her comfy bed on the window seat. "I'm tired of being told I'm wicked simply because *Gotte* made me pretty. It's okay to be pretty, Lily."

"It's not okay to be proud of it."

Bitsy growled. "You are the least vain person I know. You wear your glasses so Paul won't get mad at you. You walk with your head down, and you blush every time Dan gives you a compliment. Even though he makes a pest of himself, it's plain as day he has good taste."

Dan wanted to kiss that sadness right off Lily's face. Of course, he wanted to kiss her no matter what her expression, but that dejected look was especially heartbreaking.

If only he could convince her of a better way. If only he could convince her that he wasn't the big brother type.

"Paul doesn't think I'm pretty," she said.

"He does," Bitsy replied. "But you couldn't pry a compliment out of that boy's mouth with a crowbar."

"He doesn't want to tempt my vanity."

"Paul Glick should go jump in the lake," Poppy snapped.

Dan's sentiments exactly, but he would never say them out loud to anyone but Luke Bontrager.

"Poppy," Rose warned. "The Bible says —"

"I know what the Bible says, and I don't care."

Rose looked stricken with a dread disease. "You don't care?"

Poppy huffed out a breath and deflated slightly. "You know I didn't mean that, Rose."

Lily propped her elbows on the table and pressed her hands to her forehead. "He asked me to marry him," she said flatly.

It was as if the air had been sucked from the room. Everyone fell silent and stared at Lily, who pretended not to notice the reaction. She simply sat, quietly kneading her forehead as if trying to ward off a headache.

Bitsy was speechless. Rose looked as if she would burst into tears at any moment. Poppy might have been preparing to punch something.

Dan turned to ice. Cold, hard, aching dry ice.

The day he'd been dreading for years had finally come. If Lily so much as breathed another word, he thought he might crack into a million pieces.

"Congratulations," Rose murmured, as if saying that one word proved the hardest thing she'd ever done in her life.

Dan's gaze darted from Rose to Poppy to Bitsy, and his heart flipped over like a pancake. Lily's family didn't want her to marry Paul either.

He and Luke Bontrager weren't the only ones.

But it didn't matter what Dan wanted. Bitterness filled his mouth. Bile boiled in his throat. He'd lost her, and the pain was excruciating.

"Did you set a date?" Poppy might have been asking what day they'd scheduled her funeral.

"I told him I'd have to think about it," Lily said.

Dan drew in a great gulp of air like a condemned man who'd just been given a

374

stay of execution.

Lily wasn't engaged.

He still had time.

Rose tried valiantly to hold back a smile. Poppy turned her face from Lily and casually raised her hand to her mouth, hiding the fact that her lips also curled upward.

Bitsy looked to the ceiling. "*Gotte* moves in a mysterious way, His wonders to perform."

"What are you going to tell him?" Poppy asked.

Dan pressed his lips together as if his life depended on it. If he opened his mouth, he feared he'd get down on his knees and beg Lily not to make the biggest mistake of her life. Something told him that wouldn't be the best course of action at the moment.

But the temptation was sore.

"I don't know what I'll tell him," she said. "He wants me to give him an answer tomorrow after *gmay*."

"There's no rush," Bitsy said, looking at Dan as if she dared him to do something about it. "It never hurts to think on a problem for several weeks."

Lily seemed to perk up temporarily. "At least no rush to decide tomorrow. The buggy is missing a wheel. We don't have a way to get to church."

Dan's heart shrank to the size of a walnut. *Ach.* He'd done one too many good deeds today. "That's not entirely true," he murmured.

Bitsy slowly expelled the air from her lungs. "Dan brought his two friends over earlier, and they fixed the buggy."

He forced a weak smile. "My friends Luke and Josiah."

"Oh," Lily said, forcing her own smile. "Well, then."

Rose also feigned cheerfulness. It seemed no one was willing to say how they really felt. "*Denki,* Dan."

"*Jah,*" Poppy said. "*Denki.*"

Bitsy stood and strolled into the kitchen. "What's done is done. We'll have to make the best of it." She pulled a saucepan from the cupboard.

"Maybe we can miss *gmay* after all," Poppy said. "Aunt Bitsy could come down with the measles."

Lily frowned. "Paul is eager to make plans. To get on with our lives. He'll be disappointed if he has to wait."

Poppy jumped to her feet as if she couldn't bear to hear another word. "It won't hurt Paul to wait a month of Sundays."

Rose put an arm around Lily. "If he truly loves you, he'll want you to be sure."

Dan kept as quiet as a church mouse, with arguments and pleas and emotions swirling inside his head and desperation mounting in his heart. Lily couldn't say yes to Paul. She just couldn't.

He still had time.

He'd better use it wisely.

Glancing at the clock on the wall, he groaned inwardly. He'd already used it up. He stood reluctantly. "It's getting late. You've probably been wishing I'd leave for an hour now."

"But Lily made pie," Rose said. "Can't you stay for pie?"

Poppy looked at him like he was crazy. "Don't you want to stay for dinner?"

"More than anything." He smiled sadly at Lily. "But chores are piling up at home and I've got to get to them before the Sabbath."

Lily smiled at him with a hint of regret on her face. "Of course. You've sacrificed so much of your time for us already."

"I would never consider it a sacrifice." He stared at Lily for as long as he dared without making everyone in the room uncomfortable. He had to get to those chores. There was so little time and so much hay to make.

"Lily," Bitsy said, studying a recipe and only half paying attention to anything else. "Why don't you write that note your *dawdi* suggested, and Dan can help you hang it before he goes."

Lily glanced at Dan doubtfully. "Do you have time?"

The prospect of spending even a little more of the day with Lily sent his heart galloping. *"Jah."* He flexed his arm. "And I have the muscles for doing the heavy lifting."

Lily giggled in the first show of true happiness Dan had seen from her since she walked in the door. "It will be tape and a piece of paper."

"Even better."

She retrieved a thick felt pen and paper from the drawer and sat down once more at the table. "How does this sound? *If it makes you feel better, do what damage you must to our farm. We mean you no harm, and we have already forgiven you in our hearts.*"

Bitsy looked up from her recipe. "Can you cross out *we* and just put you girls' names? I have not forgiven them in my heart yet."

Lily looked up at the ceiling, as if considering Bitsy's request. "We'll pretend you've forgiven them. I don't want to mess up my note." She stood up. "Let's go find a *gute* place to hang this."

Dan waved cheerfully. "We could be gone for hours and hours."

Poppy handed Dan a roll of duct tape. "Don't get lost."

Dan nodded. "I promise to bring her safely home."

Dan and Lily stepped out on the porch and surveyed the area. "I think we should hang it on the barn door," Lily said. "They've struck there once. They're apt to do it again."

They strolled across the flagstones and past Dan's buggy. Lily held the note in place on the barn door while Dan tore four generous pieces of duct tape and attached the note by its corners.

They stood back to admire their work. "Good job, Dan," Lily said. "A tornado couldn't wrench that note off."

"I've always been *gute* with duct tape."

After a long pause, Lily sighed. "Well, then. I suppose I should help with dinner." She glanced tentatively toward the house as if she didn't really want to go in.

Someone as desperate as Dan didn't need any more encouragement than that. "Would you like to take a look around the farm with me first? I want to make sure everything looks secure before I go."

Her lips curled as if his suggestion were a pleasant surprise, and his heart started that galloping thing again.

"Shall we look at the orchard hives first?" he said.

Grinning, she inclined her head in the direction of the apple and cherry orchard. He walked beside her as she ambled around the barn and into the orchard. Little green apples the size of walnuts hung on the leafy branches. A wisp of a breeze danced through the trees, brushing past the leaves and rustling them gently.

"Lord willing, it will be a *gute* crop this year," Lily said.

A comfortable silence hung between them as they walked between rows of trees, Lily looking at the apples, Dan gazing at Lily. Every cell, every muscle and sinew in his body was aware of the beautiful, intelligent, amazing girl beside him.

She stopped walking, closed her eyes, and breathed in the fresh air. "I could very happily spend the rest of my days in the orchard."

"Taking time out for meals and church, of course."

She smiled wearily and started walking again. "Maybe I'm dreading *gmay* tomorrow and would rather be anywhere else."

His mouth felt as dry as dust. "Because of Paul?"

"*Jah.* He won't be happy, but I can't give

him an answer tomorrow. I won't say yes just to keep him from pouting."

To keep him from pouting.

That one phrase spoke volumes about Lily and Paul's relationship. Dan tried to steady his breathing. No use for Lily to see how angry he felt. "Paul will understand," he said, pushing the lie through his teeth. "It's the biggest decision of your life."

Lily's eyes were trained on the ripening fruit, and her toe grazed a rock causing her to stumble. He shot out his arm and grabbed her hand to steady her. "You okay?"

She nodded.

Now that he had hold of her, he never wanted to let go. So he didn't. He flashed a sheepish smile. She flashed him one right back.

And didn't pull away.

He thought he might faint.

They strolled hand in hand near the hives where the pleasant hum of thousands of bees greeted them. She hadn't stopped smiling, so he kept hold of her hand. He couldn't imagine heaven feeling more glorious.

"Our district doesn't have *gmay* tomorrow," he said. "Would you like me to come to yours? Just, I mean, just if you need a little extra courage."

She knit her brows together. "Seeing you would only irritate Paul. I hope that doesn't hurt your feelings."

"I know exactly how Paul feels about me."

She seemed to grasp his hand tighter as he led her out of the orchard and around behind the barn. "Paul can be difficult," she said. "But he was raised in a hard home, like Aunt B, and I know with time and encouragement he can change. He has a good heart. I've seen it. In school, he was the only boy who saw how badly I was hurting, how unsure I was of myself. He almost single-handedly pulled me through that last year of school, along with Rose and Poppy, of course."

It was another stinging reminder that if he lost Lily, it would be his fault and his fault alone. The thought sat heavy on his shoulders.

She guessed what he was thinking. "I will feel worse if you beat yourself up about it."

"I . . . I know." But that didn't make it any easier to breathe. "Do you feel you have to marry Paul because he was nice to you in school?"

"I owe him a great debt of gratitude."

"And marrying him pays that debt?"

Her lips twitched self-consciously as her gaze darted to his face. "It sounds quite drastic when you put it like that."

It *was* quite drastic, trading the rest of her life for a teenage memory — like selling her birthright for a mess of pottage.

Then again, Paul had been there to comfort Lily when Dan had not. He couldn't minimize Lily's gratitude. As much as it grated on him, Dan was grateful to Paul as well.

Still holding hands in broad daylight, they walked behind the honey house to the field of clover that had been cut last week and passed the hives that sat on the edge of the field. Every word, every step, every touch was sweet torture. How long could this wonderful, agonizing feeling go on?

"Paul says that *Gotte* brought us together, that we shouldn't question His plan."

Dan had resolved not to put pressure on Lily one way or the other, but there was something so unfair about Paul invoking *Gotte* to force Lily's hand. Who would dare argue with *Gotte*'s will? "I believe that *Gotte* has a plan, but it's not necessarily Paul's version."

She nodded thoughtfully. "*Jah.* You're right."

He wanted to cheer out loud.

After taking a good look at the field hives, they headed back toward the house. He really did have to get home.

"What do you think I should do about Paul?" Lily said as they walked to the house.

Forget Paul and choose me. Love me. Marry me. I will make you happier than you ever thought possible.

"You're smart," he finally said, though down to the marrow of his bones he ached to kneel down and beg her to marry him. "You know what will make you happy. I have faith that you'll make the right decision."

She smiled at him then, a true, straight-from-the-heart smile that made his knees weak. "*Denki* for saying that. I'm not really that smart, but I always feel better after talking to you."

He squeezed her hand. "I will always be here when you need to talk."

They walked up the porch steps. He had to leave no matter how badly he wanted to stay.

"*Denki* for helping me hang the sign," she said, finally letting go of his hand. He immediately felt as if an essential part of himself were missing. She turned and took a step toward the door.

He had restrained himself for a long time. At that moment, standing on Lily's porch, his self-control cracked. Then shattered.

"Lily, wait."

She turned back and eyed him expectantly. He curled his hand around her elbow and tugged her close to him. Very close. Slipping his arms around her waist, he pulled her even closer. She felt so soft, so very good in his embrace, like she belonged there. She caught her breath as, without pausing to consider, he brought his lips down on hers and kissed her with aching tenderness.

The breeze stilled, the birds fell silent. Nature itself seemed to wait.

Dan had never felt such deep contentment or such profound longing as he did in that one kiss in that blissfully perfect moment.

He pulled away, but his lips hovered mere inches from hers. Her eyes were half closed, and she wore a befuddled smile. "Lily," he whispered.

"Hmm?"

"I'm not your big brother."

Two hours later, Dan was helping his *dat* clean the milking machines when the three Honeybee Schwesters burst into the barn, smiling so wide, they could have stopped traffic with those nice white teeth.

"We've come to help you with your chores," Poppy said, leading the march.

Rose followed. "Because you always help us with ours."

Lily brought up the rear of the procession, holding a delectable-looking pie. "Snitz pie made with honey," she said, blushing slightly.

No doubt she was remembering that kiss.

But was she thinking of it with pleasure or disgust?

Dan bloomed into a smile. "You didn't have to come."

"We know," Poppy said. "But we want to help out our big brother."

Rose nodded. "You're like family to us."

Lily's eyes sparkled like stars in the sky. "I came to help out a friend. I don't even consider you a distant relative."

And with that he was forgiven. Or encouraged.

Or maybe both.

CHAPTER TWENTY-TWO

Lily fired up her smoker and pumped a generous amount of smoke into the top of the hive. They had placed twenty hives at Chidester's sunflower farm, five on the north end of the field and five in each of the other directions. Pulling honey from these hives was much more work because they had to transport the full supers back to the farm to extract the honey and then bring them back.

Mr. Chidester paid them a nice sum of money for pollinating services. Every drop of honey was a bonus. One more week of extracting honey, and the especially hard work would be over until autumn.

She and Poppy worked the five north hives while Aunt B and Rose worked the hives to the east. They worked ten hives in a day. They only had ten bee excluders, and extracting honey from ten supers was enough to keep them busy from sunup to sundown.

Lily blew another puff of smoke into the hive for good measure before she and Poppy each took two corners of the full super and lifted it to the ground. More smoke from both smokers. Poppy set the bee excluder in place, and they lifted the super back onto the hive. By tomorrow, the bees would be gone from the top super and they could take the honey without disturbing the colony.

Paul's proposal pressed on her, while thoughts of Dan and kissing and big brothers and marriage proposals crowded her brain like a pile of fat gumballs. Looking back, she could see that this — whatever it was between her and Dan — had been growing for a long time, until it had finally blossomed into something she couldn't understand and couldn't resist.

Dan liked her. The thought was as breathtaking as it was unbelievable. Why would someone as fun and attractive and perfect as Dan Kanagy take an interest in boring Lily Christner? The Amtrak girl. The girl who wore jeans. The girl with a tattooed aunt.

It didn't make sense.

Then she thought of Paul. He had made it very clear yesterday what he thought of her resistance, but he had also tried very hard to be understanding. What could she do? Paul wanted to marry her, but she truly didn't know if she wanted to marry him.

Dan's kiss had definitely muddied the waters.

Thinking about that heart-stopping, head-spinning kiss stole her breath. Her utter shock at being kissed by Dan Kanagy had soon given way to dizzy giddiness that lingered long after he'd gone home. She could think of nothing else all evening, especially when they traipsed to his dairy to help with his chores. She hadn't slept a wink Saturday night. She found it impossible to concentrate on the sermons at *gmay.* The memory of his lips against hers had even distracted her during her little talk with Paul at the fellowship supper.

She had no idea that a kiss could be so devastatingly amazing and so completely unnerving at the same time. And leave such a heavy weight on her shoulders.

It had been so easy to disregard Paul's feelings. She shouldn't have been kissing another boy on the very day that Paul had proposed. And she certainly shouldn't have enjoyed it.

She felt ecstatic and horrible thinking about that kiss.

Paul never had to find out.

389

She slumped her shoulders. She kept more secrets from Paul than she told him.

Her heart jumped to attention when Dan came tromping right out of the center of the sunflower patch. His face lit up when he saw her, and he changed direction toward the hives.

"Bitsy told me I'd find you over here," he said. "But a barbed-wire fence got in the way so I couldn't bring my buggy. I decided to take a shortcut. Do you need help?"

"Jah," Lily said, "but without a veil and gloves, they'll eat you alive."

She really liked that mischievous glint in his eye. "I've done enough research to know that honeybees do not eat people. Are you trying to scare me off?"

"I couldn't scare you off if I tried."

His gaze could have melted snow. "*Nae,* you couldn't."

Poppy laid her smoker on top of the next hive and took off her gloves and veil. "Here," she said, holding them out for Dan. "Much as I hate to admit it, you're stronger than I am. You can help Lily lift supers. I'll go see if I can help Bitsy and Rose."

"Without a veil?" Lily said.

Poppy started hiking around the perimeter of the field. "You need Dan's help, not mine."

390

Dan watched after her for a few moments before gifting Lily with a smile and donning the veil and gloves. "It took a lot for Poppy to admit that I'm stronger than she is. I hope she didn't strain herself."

"You can be sure she did."

Dan picked up the smoker. "What do you need me to do?"

Lily pried the lid from the next hive. "Blow some smoke into this super, then we'll lift it off the other supers and install the bee excluder. It won't take long. The real work starts tomorrow."

He winced. "I'll try to come help."

"You'll do no such thing. I know how busy you are at the dairy."

"Much as I love my *dat* and brothers," he said, "I'd rather be here with you."

Lily pretended not to catch his meaning. His sincerity was one more gumball to add to her already full jumble.

"I have some *gute* news," Dan said. "You told me last week that Paul pays you a dollar a pint for your honey. I was talking to a woman in Shawano who told me that the price of honey has gone up. She pays almost four dollars a pint wholesale."

"Four dollars?"

"She'd love to have a talk with you about buying some of your honey."

Lily knit her brows together as the doubts swirled in her head. It was always the same debate. Was she hurting her family with her indecision and ignorance? "I . . . I don't know. Paul pays me a little less because he takes on the risk of buying all our honey, whether it sells or not. He often has pints and pints left at the end of the season. He can't pay me more."

Dan's smile seemed to freeze in place. "I trust your judgment. I only thought I'd mention it in case you wanted to sell the surplus to someone else. You know, take some of the burden off Paul."

"Paul is my best friend. He doesn't see it as a burden," she said, even as she questioned herself.

He nodded. "Of course."

What about her family? Would they struggle to make ends meet without the extra money? "We've been blessed to have much honey this year. As long as they aren't purposefully tipped over by our trouble-maker, most of our hives should survive the winter, Lord willing."

"That reminds me. How did your little note work with our hoodlums?" Dan said. "Is it still on your barn door?"

Lily huffed out a breath. "The note was there yesterday morning, with eggs from our coop splattered all over it and the barn door."

He frowned in concern. "It was a *gute* idea anyway. At least I have a good excuse to paint the barn door again. Any other damage?"

"*Nae.* The chickens didn't even seem upset."

Dan shook his head. "I wish I knew what else to do."

"Me too. We're on tenterhooks wondering what he'll do next."

"Let's talk about something happier," Dan said, no doubt wanting to leave the subject as much as she did. He lowered a honey super to the ground. "Did you have a *gute* Sabbath?"

"*Jah.* After church we took some cookies to Mammi and Dawdi. Even Aunt B went in for a few minutes. Mammi made the expected comments about her pink hair, but Dawdi behaved himself. They even had a fairly pleasant conversation about tomatoes and rhubarb."

"What kind of cookies?"

"Honey with nutmeg," Lily said.

Dan bowed his head as if he were severely disappointed. "My favorite."

"Every kind is your favorite, and don't worry. We saved a whole plate for you." Lily put the bee excluder in place, and Dan hefted the super on top of it.

Dan gave the hive another smoke and leaned his elbow against it. "The truth is, I'm just making conversation because I am hoping you'll slip and tell me how it went yesterday with Paul."

Her heart beat faster. "You really shouldn't lean on the hive like that. I wouldn't want you or the supers to topple over."

He took three steps backward and studied her face. Trying to look through his veil and hers, he probably couldn't see much. "It's none of my business, is it? I'm sorry. I'll shut my mouth and never speak again."

"I don't really believe you'll never speak again."

His lips drooped. Didn't he know she was teasing? "I mean, I'll never ask about you and Paul again."

Did she want to tell him about their little encounter yesterday? Paul had not been at his best, and Dan didn't really understand Paul's personality quirks.

Still, Dan had faith in her. He didn't try to talk her into or out of anything. She wanted him to know what had happened with Paul yesterday, if for no other reason than she needed his assurance that she had done the right thing.

She gave him a playful smile. "I wouldn't want you to die of curiosity." Clumsily taking his gloved hand in her gloved hand, she pulled him several feet from the hives and took off her gloves and veil. He took his off as well, an unexpected look of tenderness in his eyes. What had she done to deserve that?

"You're smiling," he said doubtfully. "It must have gone well."

"It started out badly. I told him I couldn't give my answer yet. He accused me of not having faith in *Gotte*'s plan."

A muscle in Dan's jaw twitched. "What did you say to that?"

"I told him what you told me on Saturday, that I know *Gotte* has plans for me but they aren't necessarily the same plans Paul has."

Dan smiled with all the warmth of a summer day. "I'm glad I could help."

"He accused me of questioning his judgment. He reads his Bible every night, you know."

Dan reached out and took her hand. "I hope he didn't upset you."

She shook her head. Dan didn't need to know how truly upsetting it had been. "You would have been proud of me. I don't stand my ground often with Paul. He's very persuasive. But I told him if he loved me that he wouldn't be mad about it. I said maybe this was a test of his true love. I think he realized he can catch more bees with honey than with vinegar."

His jaw twitched again, but he didn't say anything.

"After we got home from Mammi and Dawdi's last night, Paul came over to play Scrabble. He hates Scrabble, so I know he's trying hard to be patient. I let him win."

"Did you?"

"It made him happy."

Dan stuck out his bottom lip and pretended to pout. "You never let me win."

"That's because no one would ever believe that you could beat me at Scrabble. The most impressive word I've ever seen you spell is three letters long. I'd be accused of cheating."

"That's not true. I got a triple word score for *farm* once. I can't believe you've forgotten my greatest Scrabble moment."

She raised her eyebrows. "I'm never letting you win. It would be the biggest embarrassment of my life."

Dan chuckled before gazing at her as if he were memorizing every line of her face. "*Denki* for telling me about Paul. I am proud of you for standing your ground. You have to make a decision you feel good about."

She placed the veil back on her head to hide her blush. "Knowing I have your confidence makes me braver."

He followed her lead and donned his veil and gloves. "We'd better get these excluders in place. Bitsy, Rose, and Poppy have probably finished and gone home by now."

"*Jah,* and you are probably needing to get home to the cows."

He nodded. "They don't appreciate what I sacrifice for them."

Lily giggled. "Rose is trying out a new honey lavender ice-cream recipe tonight. Would you like to come over after milking and eat some?" She felt only a momentary twinge of doubt. Should she have invited Paul?

Nae. Paul could come another night. He wasn't all that fond of ice cream.

"It wonders me if you'll let me turn the crank," Dan said.

"That's why I invited you."

His mouth fell open. "You only like me for my muscles."

"You're a very good crank turner."

"Okay. I will come. I want to see to the new mousetrap."

A laugh burst from Lily's lips. "Don't

bother."

He eyed her with amused curiosity. "Why not?"

"Aunt B checked it this morning. That mouse licked every bit of peanut butter from the can, but the bucket is empty."

Dan raised an eyebrow. "This is no ordinary mouse."

"I'd say not."

"I'm going to have to come up with a better solution. Or ask Luke." He winked at her from behind the veil. "Do you know my friend Luke Bontrager? He's a *gute* carpenter. He and Poppy might suit."

Lily grinned and nudged his shoulder with her gloved hand. "Don't even think about putting Luke and Poppy together. They'd fight like two cats with nothing but a pile of fur left when they were done."

"But it would be so fun to watch."

"Not if Luke still wants the use of his arms and legs later in life. You should leave that idea on the shelf where it belongs. Josiah and Rose might be a better fit."

Dan nodded thoughtfully. "Rose is afraid of actually having to talk to anybody. Josiah is afraid he'll scare her away with one uninvited hello. It could take years."

"Rose isn't afraid of you," Lily said.

"It's because she considers me a big

brother." He smiled and sent a giddy shiver up her spine. She knew exactly what he was thinking.

"Everyone is entitled to her own opinion," Lily said, putting her hands on her hips and studying Dan's tall frame and broad shoulders.

Dan was definitely not the big brother type.

Chapter Twenty-Three

Lily hurried up the sidewalk to Paul's front door. She was half an hour late already. Dan had been busy with a pile of chores at the dairy, and without his help, the honey had taken hours longer. She'd spent precious time changing her clothes so that she looked presentable for her dinner appointment, and Aunt B had driven her into town and dropped her off at Paul's house because she said a man in love should not be too lazy to drive his girl home. He might not be lazy, but Paul would probably be grumpy about it, just the same.

Lily felt an overpowering sense of dread as she knocked on the door. Paul had shown up at the house last night while Lily had been on a buggy ride with Dan. Dan had come last night after milking and invited everyone for a ride to the Shawano Lake overlook. Aunt Bitsy wanted to stay home and try out a new recipe, and Poppy and

400

Rose were too tired, so Lily and Dan had gone up to the lake by themselves.

When Paul had come by, instead of simply informing Paul that Lily had gone "out," Aunt B had given him all the incriminating details of how Dan had taken Lily for Yutzy's doughnuts and then to the lake. Didn't Aunt B know such news would give Paul an ulcer?

Paul had hand-delivered a note inviting Lily to dinner at his house *tonight,* which meant that his *mamm* and *dat* had closed the restaurant so the family could eat with Lily. She had a feeling Paul had enlisted his parents to put pressure on her to say yes to the marriage proposal. The thought of being attacked not only by Paul, but by his parents, made Lily want to throw up.

That didn't even begin to describe how sick she felt that Paul knew she'd been out with Dan the night before. What would he say?

Paul answered the door and quickly stepped onto the porch and closed the door behind him. "You're late," he whispered. "We've been sitting in there twiddling our thumbs for almost an hour."

"I'm sorry, Paul. We had to finish the last of the honey."

"Of all the stuff, Lily, it's always about the

honey. Sometimes I think you use the honey as an excuse for neglecting me."

"I'm sorry you had to wait." She was so tired of asking Paul's forgiveness. Wasn't he supposed to love her in spite of her flaws? At least he hadn't said anything about Dan. Dan wouldn't have been so easy to apologize for.

"I was hoping you'd make more of an effort to be here on time, knowing that we planned a dinner just for you."

"If you had talked to me instead of leaving a note, I could have told you that five o'clock was too early," she said, with more weariness than annoyance.

He frowned. "If you had been home instead of off to the lake with my sworn enemy, I would have had a chance to talk to you."

Sworn enemy? He *was* upset.

She should have known better than to even hint at an argument with Paul. He always got defensive. She'd given him no choice. Better to take the blame than to quarrel. "I'm truly sorry I'm late, Paul. If you're too upset to eat dinner with me, I can go home and we can do it another time. I'll come to the restaurant."

And pay for my own meal.

Anything to make him happy.

His mood seemed to shift as if he'd decided to let her win the argument, even though she hadn't put up much of a fight. "*Nae.* I want you to stay. Mamm made about eight things. We closed the restaurant." He placed his hand on the doorknob. "Where are your glasses?"

"Putting them on would have made me ten extra minutes late."

Paul sighed. "Okay. I guess it's okay. Dat might not even notice." He gave her a pleasant smile. "Tonight is your special night. Take as many helpings of everything as you want. My family wants you to have a *gute* time."

"Okay," she said, the sick feeling rising in her throat. Paul had always been so stingy with food. She'd only been to dinner at his house three other times, and he had always cautioned her to take food sparingly. He didn't want her to look like a pig in front of his parents.

Paul opened the door and motioned for her to go first. The heavenly smell of Martha's rolls greeted her. No matter how bad things got tonight, the rolls were sure to be as flaky and golden brown as ever.

Paul's *dat,* Raymond, sat on the sofa reading the paper, and his two younger brothers lounged on the chairs on either side of the sofa, looking as if they might starve to death at any moment. Paul's brother-in-law, Junior, was sprawled on his back in the middle of the floor taking a pre-dinner nap. Junior had married Paul's sister, Ada, last September, and they lived in the basement.

Raymond looked up from his paper. Lily steeled herself against his displeasure at her being tardy and spectacle-less, but he merely smiled stiffly. "Lily, welcome to our home. I hope you're hungry. Martha has made all your favorite foods tonight."

"I smell rolls," Lily said. "I could eat nothing but a whole plate full of rolls and be quite content."

"Hullo, Lily," Paul's brother, Perry, said. "We're glad you're here." Perry was a couple of years younger than Paul and probably fifty pounds heavier.

Peter James, Paul's other brother, jumped to his feet. "We're really hungry."

"Peter James," Raymond scolded. "Mind your manners. We don't care how late Lily is, we're very happy that she's here."

Peter James nodded dutifully. "*Jah,* Lily. We're happy you're here."

Lily's throat went dry. Raymond had never been so accommodating or Paul's brothers so friendly. They were going to try to charm her into saying yes to Paul. Would their goodwill disappear when she refused to give them an answer tonight?

She'd spent years being Paul's girlfriend, and while Paul was not always pleasant or even nice, their relationship felt familiar. There was a certain amount of comfort in always having someone to talk to, always having a friend willing to spend time with you, never having to take a risk or move away from the predictable routine.

Dan was a leap of faith. Was it foolhardy to jump?

"Cum," said Raymond, laying his paper on the sofa and standing up. "Let's eat before it gets any colder."

Raymond led the way into the kitchen where Martha poured lemonade into the glasses on the table and Ada, Paul's sister, put rolls into a basket. Ada was as thin as her brother Perry was plump. Her gaunt face made her look much older than her twenty-four years. Lily always thought Ada would be prettier if she smiled, but since Paul's *dat* didn't put much value on beauty, it was probably just as well she didn't.

White stoneware sat atop a lovely royal-blue tablecloth with matching blue napkins. Bowls of corn, candied carrots, and chow-chow sat on the table along with a lovely plate of herb-baked chicken. A long-stemmed, fluted glass of a layered gelatin dessert sat next to each plate. Martha had outdone herself.

Cloth napkins and candied carrots only served to heighten Lily's anxiety, but she didn't want to appear ungrateful. "Martha, this looks *wunderbarr*! I can't believe you went to all this work."

Martha smiled and finished pouring the lemonade. "It's all for you. We wanted to treat you to something special, didn't we, Ada?"

Ada looked as if she couldn't care less about whom dinner was for. "*Jah,* Mamm. We've been cooking all day."

Raymond pointed to a chair for Lily. "Paul says you've worked very hard on the honey this week."

"We extracted the last of it today," Lily said. "Until autumn."

Once they'd been seated, they bowed their heads for a silent blessing on the food. Lily nibbled on her bottom lip. She always felt a little out of sorts when she missed Aunt B's vocal blessing before silent grace.

After the prayer, Raymond filled Lily in on the market and the improvements he'd been making to attract more customers. Several tour buses stopped by the restaurant and market every month. Raymond was considering asking the bishop for permission to develop a Web site. That would surely attract more visitors.

"We'll need another *gute* cook in the family," Raymond said, gazing pointedly at Lily. "That's one thing your aunt Elizabeth has taught you girls well. Paul says your Bienenstich cake is delicious."

Lily nearly swallowed down the wrong pipe. They were already making plans for her to work at the restaurant? Maybe that was Raymond's strategy — talk as if a wedding were certain and make it so.

Despite the feast before her, Lily could barely eat. The food tasted delicious, but the family's attention centered squarely on her, as if they'd made a plan to corner her together and browbeat her into marrying Paul.

"What do you think of Paul's plan for a wedding this year?" Raymond said. "Ada and Junior can move into Junior's *dawdi* house so that you can have the basement to yourselves."

Ada did not look at all pleased with the prospect of being moved out of her home.

"What do you think, Lily?" Paul asked.

Lily looked up. The whole family stared at her as if a chicken were perched on her head.

She didn't think anything except that she would rather not speak. She didn't want to sound as if she were already planning on a wedding, but she didn't want to offend Paul's entire family either, especially when Paul's *mamm* had made rolls. Ignorance seemed her only refuge. "I . . . I don't know," she murmured.

"Of course you don't know," Raymond said reassuringly. "What does an inexperienced girl know about anything? Your *dawdi* and I have discussed the wedding in great detail. We both feel it is the right decision, a very *gute* match." He reached over Paul and patted Lily's hand. "A humble, godly girl knows when to heed the advice of those wiser than she."

Paul raised his eyebrows at her and gave her the I-told-you-so look he often wore.

"I am always eager to increase in wisdom," she finally said.

Raymond seemed pleased as punch with that answer. So did Paul. He launched into a recital of plans for the house.

After dinner, Lily, Ada, and Martha did the dishes while the men and boys relaxed in the living room. Though Lily tried ever so hard not to think of other boys while she was at her boyfriend's house, she couldn't help but compare Dan's eagerness to help in the kitchen to Paul's unwillingness to do "women's work." Of course, the difference was in how they had been raised. Lily couldn't help but think that Dan's *mamm* and *dat* had chosen the better path. A husband and wife should work together, with no one's labor more or less important than the other's.

Paul could learn. All he needed was a *gute* woman to show him the way.

After they'd finished the dishes, Martha, Ada, and Lily joined the men in the living room. Paul and his *dat* were engaged in a serious-looking conversation on the sofa, but they stopped abruptly when Lily walked into the room.

Raymond snatched a Bible from the end table and leafed through it. "Now," he said, "everyone sit down and let us study the word of *Gotte* together."

Martha sat on the sofa next to Raymond. Paul came to Lily, took her hand, and motioned for her to sit next to him on the floor at Raymond's feet.

Ach du lieva. She was going to get a lecture.

Ada and Junior sat on the sofa, and Peter James and Perry sat in the two chairs on either side where they had been when Lily had first come. She felt as if she were sitting in an arena surrounded by an angry crowd of onlookers. *Ach,* it was horrible.

Raymond opened to the Old Testament. "I thought you might like this one, Lily. *Happy is the man that findeth wisdom, and the man that getteth understanding.*"

Paul laughed nervously. "And woman too."

Lily was so uncomfortable, she almost couldn't breathe. Was there anything, anything at all she could do to get the family to stop staring at her? Raymond read scripture to her as if she were an errant youth in sore need of repentance. The embarrassment was stingingly acute. How could Paul do this to her?

She didn't even have to ask. He wanted her to marry him. He'd do whatever he thought he had to do.

It should have made her feel better to know he loved her so much.

She took a deep breath and tried to think humble thoughts even though she felt more humiliated than humble. Maybe *Gotte* wanted to teach her something through Paul's *dat.* Just because she felt uncomfortable and picked on didn't mean she didn't need to hear it. Paul often chastised her for questioning his wisdom. She still had so much to learn about being a meek disciple.

A godly *frau.*

"Poverty and shame shall be to him that re-fuseth instruction: but he that regardeth reproof shall be honored."

Would Dan ever put her through such torture to get what he wanted? Would he try to persuade her to do something she didn't want to do?

She caught her breath. *Didn't want to do?* Was that how she felt about marrying Paul, or was it just the aggravation of the moment?

Oblivious to her profound discomfort, Raymond read scripture after scripture that Lily supposed were meant to persuade her. They only made her grow increasingly distressed and bristle with resentment.

Ach, she was so proud yet.

"Gotte counseled us from the very beginning," Raymond said. *"Thy desire shall be to thy husband, and he shall rule over thee."*

Lily felt deep in her heart of hearts that a husband was not meant to "rule over" a wife the way Raymond ruled over Martha, but she did not know how to put that feeling into words or action. And she certainly wasn't about to debate scripture with a minister. She pasted a serene, even modest, look on her face and sincerely tried to be meek and teachable.

411

After half an hour, Raymond wound down. *"Favor is deceitful, and beauty is vain: but a woman that feareth the Lord, she shall be praised."*

Closing his Bible with a sense of finality, he eyed Lily as if he expected her to jump to her feet and accept Paul's marriage proposal immediately.

She pretended to be unaware of what they expected from her. Nodding at Paul, she got to her feet. "*Denki* for a *wunderbarr* dinner, Martha and Ada. I could eat your rolls every day of my life."

Raymond wasn't about to let her escape that easily. "I thought we could discuss the scriptures I just read."

"I'm sure I would never be able to tell a minister anything he doesn't already know about the Bible."

Raymond nodded. "That is true. Still, I would like to hear your thoughts."

"That is very kind of you," Lily said. "But I should be going. My sisters need help filling honey jars."

"I'll walk you out," Paul said.

"Ach," Lily said. "I forgot. I need you to take me home." She'd have to endure another half hour of Paul's persistent persuading.

Paul smashed his lips together until the

bottom one stuck out. "Where's your buggy?"

"Aunt B dropped me off."

"Why would she do that?" Paul said. "It's just as easy for you to bring the buggy."

"I suppose I can walk," Lily said. She glanced out the window into the half light of sunset. She'd make it a good part of the way home before it got dark. She should have brought a flashlight.

Maybe she could go to Dan's house and ask him to drive her home. He didn't live all that close to Paul, but he was closer than her farm by half.

Raymond thumped Paul on the shoulder. "Paul is always more than eager to drive his girl home, aren't you, Paul?"

Paul frowned. "They have all those bees."

Raymond forced an irritated smile. "A few bees shouldn't stand in the way of love."

Paul knit his brows together as if he'd never thought of that before. "Love. Okay." He took Lily's hand and pulled her toward the door. "Let's go before it gets too dark."

Paul hitched up the horse, and they were on their way in two shakes of a lamb's tail. Lily was almost glad to have a little time alone with Paul. If she could steer the conversation away from Dan Kanagy, they could have a frank discussion about the

413

honey. Dan had planted seeds of doubt in her mind, made her wonder if she shouldn't ask for more money. She'd never dared negotiate before. It wasn't seemly for an Amish girl to be pushy or greedy, and Paul valued humility and modesty above all else.

Still, she'd feel better if she tried. Paul might have no idea that honey could fetch such a price. He'd probably insist on paying her more once he found out. "It was a wonderful-*gute* dinner. Will you tell your *mamm denki* again for me?"

"I'm glad you liked it. We went to a lot of trouble."

"I'm sorry I was late."

Paul glanced in her direction. "What did you think of the scriptures? When my *dat* read from Proverbs tonight, I thought of you. *Her husband is known in the gates, when he sitteth among the elders of the land. She looketh well to the ways of her household, and eateth not the bread of idleness.* That's the kind of wife I hope you'll be someday."

"I hope so too." Lily squirmed. She hoped her husband wouldn't be disappointed in her, whoever he turned out to be. She hoped Paul wouldn't be disappointed in her when she asked about the honey. "Paul, I have a question about our honey."

Paul squinted into the dimming light

before turning on the battery-operated headlights. "Lily, don't worry. I know it's been a *gute* year for you. We'll buy it all."

"Well, you see . . . Dan says . . ."

Paul's lips immediately formed into a scowl.

Ach du lieva. How could she be so *deerich* as to mention Dan? She cleared her throat, which had suddenly turned as dry as a piece of burnt toast. "I mean . . . there is a grocery store in Shawano that pays four dollars a pint. Maybe I should sell them some of the extra you don't need."

Paul peered at her as if she'd gone crazy. "Four dollars? You must have heard wrong. Nobody's paying four dollars for honey."

"Oh. Okay. I'm sure you're right. But since there's such a surplus, you'd probably be grateful if I sold some of our extra honey elsewhere. Do you want me to call them?"

Paul seemed to expel all the air from his lungs. "How many times do I have to say it? We'll buy all your honey."

Her heart pounded against her rib cage, and her brain screamed at her to reconsider her next words. She didn't listen. "Then maybe you should pay me more for it." She sounded like a squeaky little mouse asking for mercy from a cat.

A look of annoyance stumbled across

Paul's face. "What do you want from me, Lily?"

"It wonders me if I should charge more for our honey."

Paul's face became an entire parade of emotions. Was he irritated or frantic? Aggravated or hurt? "I already told you. We're saving up for a new freezer, and Dat just bought an old racehorse for our other buggy. We can't afford to pay four dollars a pint. It isn't right for you to charge that much when we need the extra money."

"But if there's more honey than you can use, it wouldn't hurt to sell it to somebody else."

A deep furrow appeared between Paul's brows. "It boils down to loyalty, Lily. We buy your honey in lean years as well as in years of plenty. We've always been reliable. We expect you to be reliable in return. Where's the loyalty if you merely sell to the highest bidder every time? True friends stick with each other no matter what."

"I suppose that's true."

"You don't have a head for business, Lily," he said, patting her hand. "And I don't expect you to. A woman shouldn't concern herself with the details of buying and selling. If your *mammi* and *dawdi* had raised you instead of your aunt Bitsy, you wouldn't have been forced to worry about this in the first place."

Lily stiffened. "I wouldn't change the way I was raised."

"Well," he said, smiling as if he were so much wiser than she, "you don't know any different."

Paul spent the rest of the trip talking about his plans for the house, sure that she would love the layout and the great room with plenty of space for the *gmayna.* She didn't volunteer an opinion about house plans. He didn't ask.

It was half dark when he dropped her off at the lane, telling her he loved her but that he didn't want to fight the bees tonight or spare the time to drive her all the way to the house. She climbed out of the buggy, disquiet gnawing at the pit of her stomach.

She should feel good knowing that the honey question was settled. She might not know much about business, but she knew loyalty was more valuable than profit.

Thank goodness she had someone like Paul to remind her of what was important in life.

CHAPTER TWENTY-FOUR

Dan, Luke, and Josiah strolled around the makeshift stockyard looking at cattle before the auction.

Luke pointed to a Percheron horse that stood behind the temporary fence that corralled the stock. "How about that one, Josiah?"

"Nae," Josiah said. "I'm not buying today. I need another plow horse, but there's not one to tempt me today. I'll wait for the bigger auction in August."

"What about you, Dan?" Luke said. "Find anything you want to bid on?"

"Dat and I are selling two old heifers. We might buy a yearling if we find a *gute* one."

Josiah adjusted his hat to shade his eyes from the morning sun. "What are you bidding on, Luke?"

"Nothing. I came here to help Dan and look at the pretty girls."

Dan smirked in Luke's direction. "To help

me? Why do you think I need your help?"

"You're distracted. I'm here to make sure you don't get carried away and bid seven thousand for a heifer."

"Distracted? I'm not distracted."

Luke folded his arms. "Lily Christner still has a boyfriend. You're so distracted, you can't remember your own name."

Despondency washed over him like stinking, muddy swamp water. Lily Christner hadn't broken up with Paul despite all of Dan's efforts to the contrary. What was a boy in love supposed to do?

"She's still seeing Paul?" Josiah asked.

Luke kicked the dirt at his feet. "Let's not talk about Paul Glick. It leaves a bad taste in my mouth."

It left a bad taste in Dan's mouth too. Even if he washed his mouth out with soap three times, Paul Glick would still linger there.

He wouldn't be much help to his *dat* today. All he could think about was Lily. He'd shown up at the Honeybee Farm on Wednesday evening only to be told that Lily had gone to Paul's house for dinner. That news pretty much pushed him over the cliff and into the depths of despair. Was there even a chance that Lily would choose him over Paul? Maybe their bond would prove too strong for Dan to break, no matter how many books he bought or how many mousetraps he made. Thoughts of what he might have already lost tortured him until he couldn't breathe.

For the thousandth time, he told himself he should give up, but the mere thought of letting Lily go made him ache. As long as she wasn't married, Dan would keep fighting for her. He loved her. He had no other choice.

Josiah stared at Dan for a minute and forced a smile onto his face. "How about we get a pretzel? Food always makes me feel better."

"I'm not hungry," Dan said.

Luke shrugged and gave Josiah a sideways glance that Dan figured he wasn't meant to see. Luke and Josiah were probably ready to pull their hair out. Dan couldn't blame them. He couldn't have been much fun to be around today. "I want a pretzel," Luke said. "The Miller sisters are running the pretzel stand. They're both pretty."

Dan grinned in spite of his low mood. "You weren't kidding about being here for the girls, were you?"

Luke raised an eyebrow as they filed in line behind a dozen other people. "I'm getting old. I need to find a wife."

"We're only twenty-two," Josiah said.

"*Jah,*" Luke said. "My *mamm* thinks I'm lollygagging."

"What about Poppy Christner?" Dan said. "She's pretty."

Luke widened his eyes in horror. "I'd just as soon stay a bachelor."

Josiah nudged Dan in the arm. "Does Rose ever talk about me?"

Luke rolled his eyes. "You are pathetic, Joe. Pathetic."

Dan's heart stopped when the person in front of him in line turned around. Oh, *sis yuscht*! Was *Gotte* trying to torture him?

Paul Glick puckered his lips as if he'd just eaten a worm. "Dan Kanagy," he said, just in case Dan didn't know his own name.

Paul's two brothers, who were standing in line with Paul, turned and greeted him with matching sour expressions. Peter James was less meaty than Paul but still stocky and solid. His brother Perry was decidedly chubby.

What they lacked in height, they made up for in bulk. Dan, Luke, and Josiah, on the other hand, towered over the brothers like three stone pillars.

"*Gute maiya,* Paul," Josiah said. "It's a fine day for an auction, don't you think?"

Paul folded his arms across his chest and

glared at Dan. "You're trying to steal my girlfriend."

Gute maiya to you too.

Luke returned Paul's glare. He wasn't one to back down on anything.

Dan sort of nudged Luke back with his hand to calm him down a bit, then blew a puff of air from his mouth and shook his head in resignation. Paul didn't beat around the bush. Dan might as well be equally blunt. "I'm not trying to steal her, Paul. I'm trying to win her."

Paul's scowl could have been carved into his face. "A godly man wouldn't even consider courting another man's girlfriend."

Dan tried to appear calm even as he felt every muscle in his body pull tight. "Unless that godly man thinks the girlfriend would be happier with him."

Paul's face turned a sickly shade of dark purple. "Happier with the man who called her cruel names and made her miserable in school?"

He had to give Paul credit. He knew where to hit so it hurt the most. "Lily says she has forgiven me, and that's the end of it."

"You wish that was the end of it. I counseled Lily to forgive you, but she will never forget how your harsh words hurt her. You and your arrogant friends thought you were so funny."

A few people in line turned to see what all the fuss was about. Dan didn't want to make a scene or have a confrontation. He truly had nothing to say to Paul Glick, and anything Paul said to him would only make him angry. He who got angry with his brother was in danger of hellfire, and there weren't enough dirty dishes in Bienenstock to quell his irritation. It seemed better to walk away and get out of danger.

Luke looked like a coiled snake ready to strike. Dan grabbed his arm and pulled him backward, out of the line and away from Paul and his brothers.

Josiah followed, but only after giving Paul a pleasant smile and saying, "I hope you enjoy the auction." Dan nearly laughed out loud in spite of himself. Josiah was ever the peacemaker.

To Dan's surprise, Paul and his brothers left their place in the line and followed after Dan and his two friends. Were they looking for a fight? Even someone as abrasive as Paul wouldn't resort to blows. Except for Perry who hadn't been baptized yet, they had all taken a vow of nonviolence, and nobody, not even Luke, for all his bluster, would break that vow.

"I'm not done," Paul said.

Dan stretched to his full height and looked down at short and squatty Paul Glick. "I am."

"Lily is the only one you're hurting."

Dan nearly lost his composure. *He* was hurting Lily? Paul had done more to crush Lily's spirit than anything Dan could ever, would ever do.

Paul pointed to the buggies lined up on the road. "Let's go over there so we can talk privately. People are staring."

Dan nodded reluctantly. A conversation with Paul would do no good whatsoever and only tempt Dan to further anger. But it might be better to let Paul have his say and then be rid of him.

Paul motioned for his brothers to stay put. They leaned against one of the temporary fences and stared in Dan's direction. Luke and Josiah leaned against the same fence, Luke with a scowl pasted on his lips and Josiah with a doubtful, I'm-here-if-you-need-me half smile.

Dan found a nice spot between two buggies, out of the line of sight of most of the auction goers and with enough room so he wouldn't have to stand close to Paul. There was only so much a person could endure.

Paul lifted his chin as if daring Dan to

contradict him. "I want you to stop seeing Lily, for her own sake. She feels obligated to be nice to you, to show everybody that she's forgiven you for being so cruel. I understand it. Lily is a sweet girl. It's one of the reasons I love her."

Dan thought his teeth might crack.

"When you spend time on their farm and help them with their bees, you only upset her. She's confused because you're nice to her."

He felt immediately ashamed for it, but Dan couldn't resist a little dig. "I can understand that. A boy hasn't been nice to her in a long time."

Paul got close enough to bite Dan's nose off. "Don't try to justify yourself. I saved her from you."

An unexpected dose of humility slapped Dan upside the head. He lowered his gaze and his voice. "You did. I'm grateful for that."

Surprise flashed in Paul's eyes. He opened his mouth but nothing came out.

Dan stuffed his hands in his pockets. "I am glad Lily had a friend. But that doesn't mean you were the only one who liked her. I just didn't know how to show her."

Paul very nearly smiled. "I knew you liked her. Why do you think I took an interest in her in the first place? You got our property, but you didn't get the girl."

Dan drew his brows together. Paul and his family had convinced themselves that they had been cheated out of their property, and they despised Dan's family for it. "You . . . you used Lily to get back at me?" It was unthinkable. And made oh so much sense. He thought he might be sick.

Paul curled his lips into a sneer. "You can't bring yourself to believe that I might have befriended her out of the goodness of my heart."

"*Nae.* I can't."

"We stuck together because we had both been bullied by Dan Kanagy. We had a common enemy."

Dan flinched. Lily had once considered him an enemy. It made him even sicker.

"My *dat* had always encouraged me to find a homely girl to marry. They grow up more humble. More godly."

Dan balled his hands into fists. "Lily isn't homely."

"I've worked hard to keep her vanity in check, to mold her into the kind of wife I want. She was coming along well, until your flattery puffed her up and tempted her to be proud. You've done nothing but confuse her."

426

"I've only told her the truth," Dan said, his voice soft and threatening. How dare Paul talk about Lily that way? She had more goodness in her than Dan and Paul combined.

"I've warned her to beware of your flattery. You're a liar and a cheat, like your *dat.*"

Could he clench his jaw any tighter? Paul certainly had a way with words. Dan took a deep breath and started reciting poetry in his head.

Sticks and stones may break my bones . . .

He only had to repeat it in his head four times before he could speak with relative composure. "Is that everything you wanted to tell me? I'd like to go back to the auction."

Paul glared at him. "If you want what's best for Lily, you'll leave her alone. When she's with you, she forgets what she owes me."

"She doesn't owe you anything."

"I wouldn't expect you to understand virtues like loyalty and friendship," Paul said, practically spitting the words out of his mouth. He slid out from between the buggies and rejoined his brothers. They marched straight to the line at the pretzel stand.

Josiah and Luke kept vigil at the fence.

Josiah's gaze darted back and forth between Paul and Dan. Luke cleaned his fingernails with a pocketknife. His casual stance didn't fool Dan. He looked like a hornet's nest, poised to explode with one stiff poke.

Dan felt like a hornet's nest himself. For years Paul had been feeding Lily lies, not only about herself but about Dan and his family. Could he ever hope to counteract Paul's poison?

He took off his hat and scrubbed his fingers through his hair. Every muscle in his body ached at the thought of losing Lily. Every instinct told him he didn't have a chance. Paul had his hooks in her but good, and he wouldn't let go without a fight.

Dan wanted to cry. He wanted to overturn a few buggies in his path. He wanted to yell at the sky until somebody up there heard him.

He wanted Lily. He was strong enough to fight for her but smart enough to know he couldn't do it alone.

Dan squared his shoulders. If Paul wanted a fight, he'd get a fight.

What better person to help him than the woman who swung a mean meat cleaver and carried an unloaded shotgun?

Time to call on Aendi Bitsy.

CHAPTER TWENTY-FIVE

How appropriate that Bitsy would open the door with her trusty meat cleaver in her fist. Dan took a step back in case it slipped out of her hands and chopped off his foot.

"*Ach,* Dan. It's only you. *Cum reu,* but don't let any bees fly in with you."

It's only you? Who was she hoping to greet with that meat cleaver?

Dan tucked his bundle underneath his arm and pushed the door open wider. He gasped in amused surprise when he saw the new meat cleaver divot right in the center of the kitchen table. "Has the mouse been up on the furniture?"

Bitsy folded her arms with the cleaver still in her hand. It stood straight up like a stop sign. "Your mousetrap didn't work. I'm beginning to think you don't know anything, Dan Kanagy." She motioned toward the window seat with her shoulder where the cat lounged in padded luxury. "Farrah Fawcett better have lost her sense of smell or I'm about ready to turn her out of the house for neglecting her mouse duties."

As if summoned, that pesky mouse skittered from beneath the table and toward the storage room. Bitsy didn't even bother chasing it. She pitched that meat cleaver like a tomahawk in the mouse's direction. The mouse disappeared into the storage room unharmed. The cleaver landed with its pointy corner stuck an inch into the floor. Bitsy had a very *gute* aim. Still, Dan didn't like the idea of dodging meat cleavers every time he came over.

They really needed to get rid of that mouse while he still had toes and while Bitsy still had a wood floor.

Not to mention the fact that Farrah Fawcett's way of life was in jeopardy.

Bitsy pointed to her cat. "Farrah Fawcett, how could you not know he was hiding under the table this whole time? Don't look at me like that. I know you saw him."

Farrah Fawcett deigned to lift her head and peer at Bitsy as if she were the scullery maid. Bitsy narrowed her eyes. That cat was treading on dangerous ground.

Dan held up the shoe box he'd brought with him. "I think I finally discovered a mousetrap that will work."

Bitsy retrieved her cleaver from the floor. "I don't put much stock in your promises anymore, Dan Kanagy."

He laid the shoe box, tape, and scissors on the table along with the gift he had brought in a brown paper bag.

She immediately peeled back the brown paper and raised an eyebrow. "Everclear and a shoe box? Do you want to get drunk and then go dancing?"

Dan chuckled. "*Nae.* It's a gift. My book says that Everclear is *gute* for removing propolis from frames because it's not toxic."

"*Gute,* because I'll have you know that alcohol has never touched these lips before, and I'm not about to start now." She leaned in close to whisper, "I have done a little dancing in my day, but don't tell the girls. I don't want them to get any ideas."

He couldn't help but grin. "Of course not."

"What's the shoe box for?"

"It's for the new mousetrap," Dan said. "Very simple, and hopefully it will work."

Dan carried the mousetrap supplies to the counter while Bitsy shoved the bottle of Everclear underneath the sink behind the garbage can. "I'll take this to the honey house when the coast is clear," she said. "And *denki.* It's a thoughtful, innocent gift

431

that no respectable Amish woman would buy for herself."

Dan smiled. "All we need to do for this mousetrap is cut a trapdoor in the top so the mouse will fall through into the box. He won't be able to get out once he's in there."

He drew a square on the lid, and Bitsy cut it out with the scissors. She seemed to have forgotten about her meat cleaver. Now would be a *gute* time to act. "Bitsy," he said, cutting out a trapdoor from the sheet of cardstock he'd brought, "I need to tell you something."

She glanced at him out of the corner of her eye and frowned. "Did you trample my dandelions on the way in?"

"Paul Glick has convinced Lily to sell your honey to him for a dollar a pint when he knows it's worth four times that much. He's using his friendship to cheat you out of your profits. He makes Lily feel guilty and tells her he's doing her a favor." Dan put down the scissors and caught Bitsy's gaze. "He's not. And your family is suffering because of it."

"I see."

"There's a woman in Shawano who wants to buy all your honey for $4.00 a pint. She'll be here in a few minutes to talk to you about it. We can stop Paul from taking advantage of you."

Bitsy spread her hands and leaned them on the counter. "Why are you so concerned with the price we get for our honey?"

"Because Paul shouldn't be allowed to cheat you like that."

Bitsy looked at him as if she could read his mind. "Do you really want to help us? Or do you just want to get back at Paul for having first dibs on the girl you love?"

She knocked the wind right out of him. "How did you . . . what are you saying?"

She shook her head as if annoyed that she needed to explain herself. "I've got eyes. You've loved her since that first night you came to my door."

Dan didn't even try to deny it. He sighed and slumped his shoulders until they were almost scraping the floor. "A lot longer than that."

"No need to get dramatic. Boys have been in love with my girls before, you know."

"I don't doubt it."

"But you're different. Aside from the fact that you're not careful with dandelions, you're a *gute* boy who puts his love into action. I can get a lot of work done around here from a lovesick boy. It only stands to reason that you want to nudge Paul out of the way."

"I never set out to steal another boy's girlfriend, but Paul isn't right for her. You probably can't see it, but he doesn't treat her well."

"I see everything, Dan Kanagy, and don't you forget it." She pointed her finger in his direction. "No more kissing on my porch."

A shocked laugh escaped his lips. "You know about that?"

She curled her lips. "I do now."

His mouth fell open. She'd tricked a confession out of him.

She didn't, however, waste time dwelling on it. "Rose, Poppy, and I have all been worried sick about how Paul treats Lily. Contrary to what you think, we can all see it."

"If they marry, he'll crush her spirit."

"He'd very nearly done it until you came along." She taped the cardstock over the hole in the shoe box. "I asked *Gotte* every day to show me the way." She inclined her head in his direction. "I prayed you here."

Dan gazed at her doubtfully. "I've never been an answer to someone's prayer before."

"Don't get a big head about it."

"It only makes me anxious that I'll mess things up."

"My Lily took it wonderful hard when her parents died. She buried herself in her books so she wouldn't have to linger in the

434

pain. She has always been so sensitive, so easily wounded. She saw Paul as her champion during a difficult time in her life. She is very grateful to him."

Dan felt the familiar lump in his throat. "If it hadn't been for me . . ."

"You were a pill, Dan Kanagy."

"You have to believe I didn't mean for my teasing to hurt her."

Bitsy nodded. "It doesn't matter how it was meant, only how it was taken. Eight years ago, I saw Paul Glick as an answer to my prayers. At least Lily had a boy who paid attention to her."

The shame nearly choked him. "I know."

"Lily feels that she owes Paul a huge debt of gratitude. Her loyalty overshadows every decision she makes and motivates her to excuse every mean and selfish thing Paul does. At her lowest point, when she felt ugly and unlovable, Paul gave her a little attention."

She might as well have buried that meat cleaver in his chest.

Studying his face, Bitsy said, "What's done is done. You can't take it back."

"I might not be able to fix it either."

"Paul has shoved my Lily down so many times that she believes she doesn't deserve any better. And he's made her think he's wiser and more righteous than she is so she doesn't dare question him. We've done our best here at home to help her see herself the way she really is, but Paul's influence isn't easily undone."

Bitsy draped her arm over Dan's shoulder, and he thought maybe her eyes got a little misty. "And then you showed up. You don't even know how to make a good mousetrap, yet you've done more good for my girl in one short month than Rose, Poppy, or I have done in years of trying. And you're about to mess it up because you want revenge on Paul Glick."

"Not revenge. He's cheated you out of a lot of money over the years. I want to see you get the money you deserve."

"Sounds like revenge at Lily's expense."

"Nae," Dan said. "I would never do anything to hurt Lily."

Bitsy pinned him with a look that could have withered all her dandelions. "You told her you trust her to make the right decision about Paul. You told her you think she's smart."

"I do."

"Do you really? Because if you and I make this money decision for her, she'll know we don't truly have confidence in her ability to make the right choice. We'll crush her

436

confidence as sure as Paul ever did. Even if I go broke, she has to know that I trust her to do what is best for our family. If you invite that buyer over, all your professed faith will evaporate and your words will sound hollow and insincere. That's what she gets from Paul. She doesn't need it from you."

Dan ran his fingers through his hair. "I would never push her around or browbeat her into doing something she didn't want to do."

"But that's exactly what you're doing. You're letting your anger cloud your judgment. Paul manipulates Lily to get his way. He thinks it's his right as a man and her future husband. He justifies himself by telling her she's not smart enough or by making her believe he's more righteous. He convinces her that her opinions and desires are worthless, that *she* is worthless."

They heard the faint rumble of a car engine coming up the lane. Dan glanced at Bitsy. "There's the honey buyer."

"Get rid of her, or break Lily's heart."

Dan pressed his lips into a hard line and nodded. "I'll get rid of her."

"Do you want to take my shotgun?"

CHAPTER TWENTY-SIX

Lily followed the car up the lane in her buggy. They didn't often get *Englisch* visitors at the Honeybee Farm, especially this late in the day. The sun had already dipped halfway below the horizon.

"Who do you suppose that is?" Rose said, peering out the window and clutching the potted chrysanthemum Mammi had given her.

Poppy squinted against the car's bright red taillights. "It looks like somebody with really big hair."

The car stopped and parked behind the familiar open-air buggy that Lily had come to love seeing parked in her lane. Her pulse quickened at the mere thought of Dan Kanagy. He'd probably brought plans for a new mousetrap. Oh, that his designs would never work so he would have to come back again and again!

"Dan's here," Poppy said, as if it were the

best news they'd had all day.

Definitely the best news they'd had all day. The visit with Mammi and Dawdi had been taxing. Dawdi kept dropping hints that once Lily had married Paul, Poppy and Rose would move in with them. Lily and Poppy finally had to put their collective feet down to stop such talk. Even if Lily married Paul, there was no chance that Poppy and Rose would consider leaving Aunt B.

Rose fingered one of her tiny chrysanthemum petals. "It wonders me if Dan bought anything at the auction this morning. He said Josiah Yoder was going to help him pick out a heifer for the dairy."

Lily pulled the buggy beside the car and set the brake. Rose left her chrysanthemum on the seat as Lily and her sisters climbed out of the buggy, linked arms, and stood between the buggy and the car ready to greet the *Englisch* visitor.

A middle-aged woman with curly, brown hair and impossibly long fingernails gave them a toothy smile and jumped out of her car. "Is one of you girls Bitsy? Dan Kanagy asked me to come by and talk to you."

Lily smiled back. "Actually, we are her nieces. I'm Lily. This is Poppy and Rose. My aunt Bitsy is probably inside."

The woman shook hands with the three

of them. "I'm Carole Parker. I run a specialty market in Shawano. Dan says you have some honey you want to sell, and I'm ready to buy. The tourists love anything Amish, even honey."

Lily gazed at her in confusion. "Dan asked you to come by?"

"Yes. He called me this morning and wanted me to talk to your aunt Bitsy about honey. He says the market here in Bienenstock doesn't pay you near enough, and he thought Bitsy would want to know she has options."

"I'm in charge of selling our honey," Lily stuttered, finding it hard to breathe. She'd already told Dan that she would sell to Paul. Hadn't she explained herself well enough? Her heart sank. *Jah,* she had explained herself fine. He simply hadn't approved of her decision.

The front door opened, and Dan appeared on the porch. "Carole," he called, practically sprinting down the steps.

"Hi, Dan. It's nice to see you again."

Dan barely acknowledged her greeting as his eyes darted from Lily to Carole and back again. "Something's come up, and today is not a good day. Can I call you later?"

Carole put her hands on her hips and did a quick visual inspection of the house and garden. "All right. I suppose you know where to find me." She reached into her bright yellow handbag and pulled out a business card. "Do you like my bag? We sell these at the store. They're made by a local crafter. The tourists like local." She slipped the business card into Lily's hand. "Call me when you're ready to sell. Don't let those folks at the Amish market shortchange you. I'll buy every pint you've got." Carole climbed back into her car and spun the wheels before finding purchase on the gravel and backing down the lane.

A wave of nausea nearly knocked Lily over. She gazed after Carole, pretending to be very interested in the car inching its way off her property. Even though she didn't look, she could tell Dan was staring at her. Was he trying to find a way to soften his rebuke?

Guess what, Lily? You are too stupid to run your own honey business so I thought I'd step in and save you.

Poppy and Rose stiffened beside her. They were staring at her too, as if they'd suddenly figured out whom to blame for their money troubles.

Lily wanted to shrink into a little ball and blow away with the wind.

With her gaze squarely focused on Dan,

Poppy turned on like a switch. She grabbed Rose's elbow, pulled her along, and marched toward the house. "We'll go see what B is up to."

Just like that they disappeared, leaving Lily and Dan standing there all by themselves.

Dan slid his hands into his pockets. "It seemed like a good idea this morning," he said weakly.

Lily felt sick at heart. "You didn't think I'd be here."

His gaze intensified. "I was wrong to ask her to come. You're the one who makes the financial decisions."

"You went behind my back," she murmured, more to herself than anyone else. "Because I'm ruining the family finances."

"You are not ruining anything. I shouldn't have invited Carole over. I wasn't thinking straight."

Dan always talked a good story, but the truth was plainly written on his face. He thought he needed to save her and her family from her stupidity. All his talk of her being smart was just talk.

That knowledge hurt more than any name he'd ever called her. Dan, who'd claimed to have complete confidence in her, had gone straight to Aunt B. The shame nearly engulfed her. "I'm . . . I'm not as dumb as you think I am, Dan Kanagy. There are other things to consider besides profits." Lily said, feeling her power sinking even as she tried to sound forceful.

"I know, Lily. You're right. I'm sorry."

Even though Dan had backed down, Lily felt compelled to defend herself. "Paul is smart about these things. He gives us a lower price but takes on more risk by agreeing to buy all of my honey, no matter how much is left over at the end of the year. He loves me. He's willing to sacrifice profits so that we have a place to sell our honey no matter what."

Something flared hot behind Dan's eyes. He suddenly wasn't backing down anymore. "Have you ever had honey left over?"

His question took her confidence down a notch. She didn't know how much excess honey Glick's Market had at the end of each year. Paul always took care of those details. "Paul loves me," she said, her voice cracking like an eggshell. "He doesn't want me to have to worry about it."

"It's so kind of Paul to take care of you," Dan said, the bitterness evident in his voice. "You're barely scraping by on all that kindness."

"What makes you think we're barely scraping by? Oh, I remember. You don't think I'm smart enough to manage the finances."

"That's not what I mean." Dan took a deep breath and spoke as if he'd really rather not say anything. "Paul's been taking advantage of his relationship with you to get your honey for dirt cheap."

"Paul would never cheat me like that," she said.

Dan ran his fingers through his hair. "You're right. I didn't mean to make it sound like I think he's cheating you. But he's playing on your sympathies and your innocence to get a better price."

"My innocence?" Deep down, this is what he really thought of her. "You mean my stupidity. That's why you asked that woman all the way out here, because you think I can't manage my own money."

Dan pressed his lips together, as if her words tasted bitter in his mouth. "You're five million miles from stupid, Lily, but you have a trusting, compassionate nature. Paul was good to you in the past. You want to believe he has the best intentions."

Dan might think she was *deerich,* but things went deeper than the price of honey.

"It's not like that with Paul and me. What do you know of what we've been through together? Our first loyalty is to each other, always and forever." Her voice sounded harsh, even in her own ears.

He frowned. "Always and forever?"

She felt so angry and hurt, she half didn't know what she said. "There are ties of loyalty and friendship and love that you will never understand."

The fire in his eyes turned to cold, hard ice. He looked wounded and bewildered, as if she'd slapped him across the face. "I'll never understand loyalty and friendship?" He stumbled two steps backward. "Maybe you're right, Lily. Maybe I'll never understand how a sense of loyalty can blind someone to the faults of another person, or how friendship can be twisted into fear and submission. Is being obedient to Paul's wishes the same thing as love? Because that's not how I understand it."

His look of yearning almost made Lily lose her composure. "If you care for another person . . ."

"Love shouldn't diminish you for the sake of someone else. Love lifts and builds and rejoices. It never tries to control you or make you feel guilty. It's kind and patient and hopeful." He bowed his head. "If what you and Paul have together is real love, then you're right. I don't understand love, and I never will."

Lily felt empty and cold, like an abandoned barn in the dead of winter. This past month, Dan had been her friend, someone she felt almost safe with. She'd let down her guard even though Paul had warned her not to. It ached in the deepest part of her heart that Dan thought so little of her. In his mind, not only was she a failure at business but she was a failure at love. A failure at everything.

"You're holding on to the past because it's safe there," he said, "but Paul doesn't deserve you, and I'm dumbfounded you can't see it."

He was dumbfounded by her stupidity.

His words felt like so many shards of glass piercing her heart.

She closed her mouth tight like she always did when Paul was cross with her. Better not to make things worse by arguing or disagreeing. She didn't even know who she was anymore. Where did she belong? Could anybody love her just for herself?

Paul could.

He always stuck with her, no matter how many faults she had.

Paul's loyalty gave her courage to open her mouth. "I know what you think of me, Dan Kanagy. You've said plenty. I may have done everything all wrong, but I've only ever wanted to do what's right. I've tried hard to be the kind of girl a boy would be proud to take as a wife. Paul doesn't think I'm a disgrace. He's willing to take me with all my flaws and failures."

Dan scrubbed his fingers through his hair and growled like a bear. "I hate it when you put yourself down. Paul puts you down plenty all by himself."

"And you think I'm an idiot to stick with him."

"*Nae.* You are perfect, Lily." He sighed despondently. "Lily . . . you mean so much . . . I've messed it up." He closed his eyes. "I can't even say it right. Nothing is your fault. I lost my temper. I didn't call Carole because you can't handle your family's money. I did it to get back at Paul."

"He said you hate him."

"I don't hate him, but he has something that I want very much." His sad smile made her heart beat double time. "That's what breaking one of the commandments will get me. *Thou shalt not covet.* I let my anger and longing overrule my judgment. Paul and his family have been dragging my *dat*'s *gute* name through the mud for years because of a piece of land."

"And you want revenge?"

"Raymond Glick came to my *dat* and

447

asked him to buy the property because he was having some financial difficulties. My *dat* felt sorry for Raymond so paid the full asking price, even though the property was worth half that. We drained and seeded it, built a fence. We spent hours improving it so we could graze cattle there. Two years later Raymond wanted it back for less than we paid for it. My *dat* told him no, that we'd already put too much money into it. The Glicks haven't spoken to us for years. I suppose I've had a chip on my shoulder ever since Paul started calling my *dat* a cheat and a liar."

Lily took a deep breath. She didn't want to argue. "That's not the story I got from Paul."

He acted almost accepting of her distrust. "I know, and I can't blame you for believing his side of the story and not mine, especially when I hurt your feelings and he was nice to you."

Lily nodded slowly. Her heart felt as hard as lead.

Dan gently curled his hands around her upper arms. "I've made so many mistakes. Calling Carole was just the latest. I never meant to make you feel stupid or ashamed, and I'm sorry about what I said about Paul. He means a great deal to you, and I shouldn't have spoken badly of him."

She couldn't swallow. She couldn't breathe. He acted so humble, so gracious. So wonderful. And she didn't deserve his kindness. It was a wonder she could even speak. "Paul . . . and I have been through so much."

He nodded. "I know I'll never be able to make up for what I did to you eight years ago."

"I've already told you . . ."

"I know. You've forgiven me, but I also know the scars are deep, as is the bond you and Paul share. You've been trying to make me see that for a long time now." His lips curled into a weary and pitiful smile. "I'm not going to bother you anymore, Lily. It's pure torture being near you, knowing you're promised to another man. I don't want to make you feel bad or uncomfortable or even guilty, but I'll never forgive myself if I don't tell you. I love you, Lily and have for a very long time. I love you so much that my joints ache and my heart hurts with longing for you."

Lily met his gaze, and she suddenly felt light-headed. How could he love her? At the moment, she didn't even like herself.

"I'm sorry for so many things," he said. "But I'll never apologize for loving you."

He took two steps away from her and clamped his arms around his chest as if holding back an avalanche of emotions.

"Dan . . . I . . . I don't know what to say."

He smiled as if his heart might break. "Just say good-bye."

Without so much as another glance in her direction, he climbed into his buggy and tugged the reins. It took him a few passes back and forth to turn the horse and buggy in the right direction, but he was gone before Lily had drawn a breath.

Paul said turning the buggy was a chore. Dan had never seemed to mind. Paul had tried to keep her humble. Dan flattered her every chance he got.

Paul hated Scrabble.

Dan knew how to spell *farm*. It had been his only triple word score ever.

Out of loyalty to Paul, she held her tears until Dan disappeared in the gathering darkness.

Lily sat on the grass between her two sisters singing at the top of her lungs so the noise would drown out the ache in her heart. Why did she feel like this? If Paul was the one she had chosen, then forsaking all others should be easy as pie.

Paul sat next to Rose and scowled as if

he'd sucked on two lemons before the *sin-geon.* He seemed quite unhappy with the seating arrangements.

Lily tilted her head to meet his eye and gave him an encouraging nod. Rose and Poppy had been determined to stay by her side all night, as if they were stapled there, and nobody, not even an annoyed boyfriend, had been able to sway them. Poppy had told Lily that she wanted the sisters to stick together tonight for Rose's sake. The buggy wheel incident had made her extra skittish, and Poppy thought if the sisters could help make her more comfortable at the *singeon,* then the irritated boyfriend would just have to be understanding about it.

Lily didn't know why Poppy had been in such a snippy mood today. Lily hadn't told her family what had passed between her and Dan. She felt too ashamed, too angry to break the news that Dan wouldn't be coming around anymore. They'd be disappointed in her for driving their "big brother" away.

It was the off Sunday, so there had been no church this morning, but there was usually a singing in the evening for *die youngie.* The Wengerds had a big yard with lots of grass and the temperature hovered around seventy. Aunt Bitsy had even come with them. Dottie Wengerd had asked her to help with the eats, and Aunt B had made three different kinds of cake and two batches of cookies.

Despite their difference in hair color and preference for tattoos, Dottie Wengerd and Aunt B were dear friends. Dottie had eight children and a long scar down her arm, due to a farming accident years ago. She also hated to bake, so whenever she held an event at her house, Aunt B did most of the baking.

Lily glanced at Paul while they sang "God Make My Life a Little Light." It must have been hard to sing sticking his bottom lip out like that. Poor Paul. He was used to getting his way, and Poppy had put a wrench in all his plans.

She'd have to find a way to steal some time alone with him.

Lily sighed a deep, weary sigh. Spending time with Paul would make him happy, but it troubled her how little pleasure she took in the idea. Was she shallow, disloyal, or tired of Paul's moods? She couldn't make heads or tails of her feelings tonight. All she knew was that she'd rather stick with her sisters and let Paul fend for himself.

She certainly was a sorry excuse for a girlfriend.

Once the singing ended, the young people gravitated toward the table where Aunt B's cakes and lemonade awaited them. Poppy and Rose seemed to mirror Lily's every move, not letting her get ahead or fall behind as they marched to the eats table. It was almost as if they were protecting her the way Poppy and Lily usually protected Rose.

Paul tapped Lily on the shoulder. She turned around, as did her sisters, and smiled, as if she hadn't noticed him three feet away during the singing.

"Do you have some time to spare for your boyfriend?" he said, forcing a petulant smile.

"We have to help Aunt Bitsy clean up before we go home. You won't want to wait around that long," Poppy said, as if she were in charge of Lily's schedule.

Lily grabbed two pieces of cake and two plastic forks. "Come on, Paul. We'll go sit under that tree and eat some cake."

Poppy raised her eyebrows in a secret message of indignation. "Lily, we were going to stick together tonight, remember?"

"Get some cake and join us," Lily said.

Poppy seemed satisfied with that. Paul did not. He lifted his brows with his own secret message. "Lily, I want to talk to you privately."

She smiled sweetly. If she played dumb, he wouldn't get so mad. "You'd better talk fast then."

Paul marched across the grass as if he were trying to win a race. Lily scrambled to keep up with him. He'd taken her seriously about haste. "Come on, Lily. You're not even trying to go fast."

They sat at the base of the tree, and Paul set his plate on the grass. Talking to her was more important than cake? "I saw Dan at the auction yesterday. He practically admitted that he is trying to steal you to get back at me."

Lily knit her brows together. She didn't know what to believe anymore. "Did he?"

"You've got to beware of him, Lily. He's out to hurt you. He wants revenge."

"Revenge? For what?"

"Because I've hated him so much over the years, and he thinks I've ruined his good name."

"You don't have to worry about Dan. I don't think I'll be seeing much of him anymore." A knife seemed to slice right into her heart at that thought.

Several happy emotions traveled across Paul's face before he picked up his fork and took an impossibly large bite of cake. "Of course he won't come back," he said, forming the words around his mouthful of cake. He smiled wider than a cat who had eaten a mouse — except for a cat like Farrah Fawcett. Farrah Fawcett never smiled, and she certainly never ate mice. "I put him in his place but *gute* yesterday."

An ache throbbed between Lily's eyes. "You . . . you put him in his place?"

"I warned him that if he didn't leave you alone, he'd have to answer to me and my brothers. And maybe the bishop."

"You threatened him?"

Paul's eyes darted right and left before he grabbed Lily's hand and gave it a squeeze. "I did it for you, Lily. You should be grateful."

Grateful? She was devastated. How could Paul mistreat good, kind Dan Kanagy? She fell silent. Paul would get mad if she scolded him, but her heart ached for Dan all the same.

True to her word, Poppy, with Rose in tow, joined them under the tree, saving Lily from having to say another word. She wouldn't have been able to say anything polite if her life had depended on it.

Rose sat on Lily's right, while Poppy, bless her, squeezed herself between Lily and Paul. Lily scooted closer to Rose so Poppy wouldn't be forced to sit on Paul's lap.

Poppy pretended not to notice that Paul looked as if he were about to have a stroke.

"This is Aunt Bitsy's honey cake with the sour cream frosting," Poppy said, as if she hadn't just squeezed Paul out. "She made it yesterday."

Neither Paul nor Lily said anything in reply. Lily felt too upset by what Paul had told her. Paul was fuming that Poppy had usurped his seat.

Luke Bontrager, their nearest neighbor and one of Dan's best friends, strolled over to their tree. He squatted next to Rose, took off his hat, and scratched his head. "Paul, nice to see you again."

"Luke," Paul said, as if he'd rather not acknowledge Luke at all.

"I'm sorry to bother you, but your horse somehow got free and is eyeing the climbing roses on the north side of the barn."

"What?" Paul said, flinching to attention. "How did that happen?"

Luke gave Paul a look of wide-eyed innocence. "Dottie will have a heart attack if your horse eats her roses."

Paul growled and jumped to his feet. "I'll be right back." He hurried across the lawn and disappeared around the side of the house.

Luke grinned, leaned back on his hands,

and stretched his legs out in front of him. "We've got to talk fast. He probably won't be gone for more than half an hour."

Luke Bontrager was tall and broad with a carpenter's arms and dark, brooding eyes. A boy like him usually scared Rose to death, so Lily was quite surprised when Rose raised her eyebrows and accused him right to his face. "What did you do to Paul's horse, Luke Bontrager?"

Luke broadened that mischievous grin. "Animals are so unpredictable. One minute they're in the stall, the next minute they're trampling your petunias."

"But," Rose stuttered, "but that's not a very Christian thing to do."

Luke widened his eyes in guilty innocence. "I'm surprised at you, Rose. How can you judge me when you don't even know what I did or didn't do?"

Rose blushed and lowered her eyes, but Lily saw a smile playing at her lips.

"Besides," Luke said, "it's a harmless prank. The horse is fine, and he's not eating roses. I wouldn't want Dottie to have a heart attack."

"It's not very nice," Lily said, more curious than indignant, though she realized she should probably be mad that Luke had tricked her boyfriend.

"I know," Luke said, "but I really hate Paul Glick."

Poppy, who'd been trying not to even look at Luke, snapped her head around and bloomed into a beautiful smile. "You do?"

Lily eyed him doubtfully. "I don't think you should say that about my boyfriend."

"You shouldn't hate anyone," Rose said.

Luke huffed out a breath. "You're right. Josiah told me exactly the same thing. I suppose I don't hate Paul. I dislike him greatly."

Poppy, who'd once given Luke a bloody nose in school, now looked at if she wanted to give him a hug. The light shining in her eyes could have put the sun to shame. It was just as Lily suspected. Poppy didn't like Paul much either. If she weren't supposed to be trying to be indignant for Paul's sake, she would have grinned. Luke and Poppy had one thing in common.

And only one.

Luke leaned forward. "What I wanted to talk about is Dan."

"Dan?" Lily said, breathless just hearing his name.

"I don't know what happened between you two yesterday, but his *mamm* told me he went home, rearranged the cupboards, wiped down the kitchen walls, and refinished the wood floor."

"Is that bad?" Poppy asked.

Luke nodded. "He cleans when he's upset. He scrubs relentlessly when he's very upset."

Lily tried to keep a straight face. Was Dan upset because she liked Paul? Was he upset because she wouldn't sell her honey to Carole? Was he upset because he loved her?

Luke stood as quickly as he had sat down. "You should chew on what I said. I'd like to stay and talk, but Paul will be back any minute, and I'd rather not have to talk to him. Besides, I'm driving Dinah Eicher home. You know her, don't you, Poppy? Sweet, kind, gentle. Wouldn't dream of socking a boy in the mouth."

Poppy seemed to lose whatever goodwill she'd momentarily felt for Luke Bontrager. "Sounds like you're describing a horse."

Luke smirked and walked away without responding.

"That boy needs to learn some manners," Poppy said.

"Why is Dan so upset?" Rose asked.

Lily would have rather talked about anything else, but her sisters were looking at her as if she knew all the answers. She probably did. "He's mad at me. Or maybe I'm mad at him." She pressed her fingers into her forehead above her eyebrow. "*Ach,* I don't know."

Aunt B joined them under the tree with a plate of cookies in her hand. "I spied Luke Bontrager harassing you and thought I'd better come and chase him off. But he left before I had a chance to be rude." She plopped down on the ground like one of the *die youngie* and offered cookies to her nieces. Then she set the plate in the grass and leaned back on one hand. "What did he want?"

"He played a mean trick on Paul Glick," Rose said, squeezing Lily's hand as if trying to comfort her. Lily immediately felt guilty for not needing as much comfort as Rose wanted to give her.

"Paul is too big for his britches," Aunt B said. "And so is Luke Bontrager. That boy thinks the sun rises and sets with his permission."

"He told us that Dan is upset," Poppy said, looking pointedly at Lily. "Lily's mad at him."

Aunt B fingered the hole where one of her earrings usually went. "Because he invited that lady to our house?"

Lily nodded. There was much more to it than that, but Carole Parker seemed like a good starting point.

Bitsy looked into the sky. "Lord, are there

no smart boys You can spare for my girls?"

Lily's heart must have weighed a thousand pounds. "Maybe he's right, Aunt B. Maybe I'm ruining everything and our family will have to move in with Mammi and Dawdi because I am too weak to ask Paul for more money."

"You're not weak. Dan doesn't know how hard you've thought this through." Aunt B reached out and patted Lily's knee. "You have to be comfortable with the price *and* in your relationship with Paul. You're doing fine."

"Jah," Rose said. "We are all so proud of how smart you are. I would die of embarrassment if I had to talk about money with a man."

"We trust you to do what's best for the family," Poppy agreed, looking less convinced than either Rose or Aunt B. Or maybe Lily was imagining things. Poppy was probably still mulling over her encounter with Luke Bontrager.

Lily glanced around the yard, making sure no one with big ears lingered close. "He kissed me, you know."

Poppy pursed her lips. "Paul?"

"Dan."

Rose bloomed into a smile. "Really?"

"Oh, Lily!" Poppy said. "That's *wunder-*

461

barr. He's very handsome." She immediately lowered her eyes and her voice. "Unless, of course, you didn't think it was *wunderbarr.* Then I don't think it's *wunderbarr* either."

It had been more than *wunderbarr.* It had been better than summer picnics and Christmas morning and honey cake put together.

She felt her face get warm and turned to Aunt B. "Are you mad?"

Aunt B frowned. "Dan already told me, and I'm mad at him. Not you."

Lily's eyebrows nearly flew off her face. "He told you?"

"I tricked him into it, but that doesn't make it any better. You know I don't allow kissing."

"I know. I'm sorry."

Aunt B had that stern twinkle in her eye, as if she were keeping up appearances for the sake of her nieces. "I have my suspicions that you're not sorry at all."

Lily's blush got hotter. How did Aunt B know such things?

"Was it scary?" Rose asked.

"Did he ask if he could kiss you? I hate it when they ask," Poppy said.

Aunt Bitsy gave Poppy the evil eye. "What do you mean you hate it when they ask? How would you know?"

Poppy didn't look at all contrite for whatever knowledge she'd gained. "I don't know what you're talking about, B."

Aunt B looked heavenward again. "Deliver us from evil, Lord."

Sometimes the boldest things came from Rose's mouth. "Are you in love with Dan or Paul?"

Her family stared at her and seemed to hold their collective breath.

Lily deflated like a balloon. How could she explain herself? "Paul and I have been close for so long. We are tied together by friendship and gratitude."

"What about Dan?" Poppy said.

Lily deflated even more. "Paul and I have been practically inseparable since eighth grade. It seems unavoidable that we should marry."

"Unavoidable," Poppy murmured. "That sounds so romantic."

"Do I cast aside Paul and everything we've shared just because someone better-looking and more likable comes along? It seems so unfaithful."

Poppy opened her mouth to say something, glanced at Aunt B, and promptly closed it again.

"Paul says *Gotte* brought us together."

"*Ach,* Lily," Aunt B scolded. "You will

never find out what *Gotte* wants for your life by asking another person." She reached out and took Rose's hand to her left and Poppy's hand to her right. Rose and Poppy in turn grabbed Lily's hands. "My girls," Aunt B said, "you know I never take sides with boys, for any of you. Dan tramples dandelions and laughs about it, and he's a complete failure at mousetraps. Paul hates bees and makes you pay for your own meals at the restaurant."

"Nobody is perfect, I guess," Lily said.

Rose's lips curled encouragingly. "You just have to choose the one who's perfect for you."

"But you should never marry out of guilt or obligation," Poppy said.

Aunt B motioned for them to scoot closer into their circle. She reached out and pinched Lily's earlobes between her thumbs and index fingers. "Little sister, you don't owe Paul anything. You certainly don't owe him the rest of your life."

"But, Aunt B, you gave up your whole life out of gratitude to our *mamm,*" Lily said. "You felt like you owed her something for how she took care of you when you were children. Now you're stuck raising us when you'd rather be going to rock concerts and wearing high heels and dancing."

Aunt B scooted close enough to cup Lily's face in her hand. "I agreed to raise you girls because I fell in love the moment I laid eyes on you. I would have given up a lot more than Van Halen and *Baywatch.* You girls are my life, and don't you forget it."

Lily blinked back tears. Poppy and Rose did the same.

"Besides," Aunt B said, "if it weren't for you girls, I'd still be looking at people's tongues every day, and that's no way to spend your golden years."

A giggle tripped from Poppy's lips. "I'm glad we could help."

"Maybe I don't deserve better than Paul."

Aunt B frowned until her lips drooped below her chin. "You deserve the sun, the moon, and the stars, little sister, just like all of *Gotte*'s children do. He made us in His own image yet."

"What about Paul?"

"Paul deserves to reap what he sows." Aunt B cleared her throat. "Paul deserves happiness too, but not at the expense of your own."

Paul came charging at them with all the grace of a bull with a rump full of cockleburs. A smear of dirt ran down the side of his face, but other than that he seemed no worse for the wear. "Where is Luke Bontrager?" he demanded. "I had to ford a stream and chase my horse through two pastures."

Lily stood and handed Paul a cookie. "At least you found your horse."

Paul took a big bite. "I think he did that on purpose."

One corner of Poppy's mouth curled playfully, and she pointed toward the front of the house. "He's going to drive Dinah Eicher home. You can probably still catch him."

Paul glanced in the direction of the buggies lined along the roadway. "*Denki.* I will."

He tromped across the lawn. Lily had never seen him move so fast.

"I saw Luke drive away two minutes ago," Rose said.

Poppy looked genuinely disappointed. "Too bad. I would have liked to see Luke and Paul get into a shouting match."

It was hard to tell whom Poppy disliked more.

"Me too," said Aunt B.

It was hard to tell if Aunt B liked anybody.

CHAPTER TWENTY-SEVEN

As Lily had expected, Hannah and Mary Yutzy had a lot of friends. The lane in front of their house was lined with buggies and bicycles, and it seemed the sisters had invited the whole town to the quilting frolic. Lily, her sisters, and Aunt B walked around to the backyard where the Yutzys had set up five quilts under the trees, ready to quilt for the Labor Day auction. Everyone in Lily's family but Poppy loved to quilt. Poppy tolerated it. Aunt B had taught them how to sew and quilt when they were younger, but Poppy didn't enjoy it like the rest of them. She'd much rather be getting her hands dirty in the garden.

Treva Yutzy had four sisters and six daughters. They spent all winter piecing quilt tops together so they'd have several to sell at auction. The doughnut and produce stand provided a *gute* income. The quilts were to help the district pay medical expenses of their members.

Lily gazed at the sea of patchwork quilts set up in the yard. A magnificent blue-and-white Lone Star quilt sat in the center of the quilts. It had to be a king size. The other four quilts looked to be queen and smaller. Lily never tired of the way several different fabrics could be sewn together to create something so beautiful.

Hannah Yutzy ran toward them, enthusiastically waving her arm and smiling as wide as the river. "Lily! I'm so glad to see you." She pulled Lily, then Poppy, then Rose in for lung-crushing hugs. "The Honeybee Schwesters are the best quilters in Wisconsin," she said, giggling with sincere delight. She glanced behind her and lowered her voice. "I told the Miller sisters, Ruth Shetler, and my *aendi* Fern that they were the best quilters in Wisconsin too. I hope you don't mind that I gave you all first place."

"We are honored to share the award," Aunt B said.

Lily nodded with more enthusiasm than she felt. "We're happy to be able to help."

"Did you bring thimbles?" Hannah asked.

"*Jah.* And needles."

Hannah beamed as if they'd brought extra fingers. "*Gute.* Mamm is afraid we're going to run out." She made a sweeping motion

468

toward the five quilts. "Sit wherever you want. If you get bored with one, you can move to another. Like as not, we're going to be here all day."

Lily pretended to be excited, even though she had found it difficult mustering enthusiasm for much of anything for the last couple of days. It felt as if a black rain cloud hovered over her head and no matter how fast she moved, she couldn't get out from underneath it.

"*Cum,* Lily," Rose said, taking her hand and pulling her forward. "Let's go quilt the yellow one. It's bound to make us feel cheery."

Lily had always taken it upon herself to watch out for Rose, to be Rose's support when she needed a little extra courage. Today, Rose seemed to be watching out for Lily, trying to cheer her up even if there was no way to do it. Rose had a *gute* heart. It was nice of her to try to be the mother hen.

They strolled to the yellow-and-blue Log Cabin quilt and sat in a row of four on one side. Treva Yutzy glanced up from the needle she was threading. "It's the Honeybees," she said, laughing for the pure joy of it. She had the same sunny disposition as her giggly daughters, tempered with a dose of maturity. "It's been ages since I've seen any of you. Ages. I'm glad you could come. Any quilt that Bitsy Kiem works on will sell for double. You take the smallest stitches."

Aunt B brushed off Treva's praise. "Years of cleaning teeth. I work well in small spaces."

Treva laughed an infectious, throaty laugh that Lily found delightful. The Yutzys never held back their joy. "Well, then, thank the Lord for teeth cleaners."

"You look no worse the wear from your surgery," Aunt Bitsy said.

Treva squinted into the eye of the needle. "Only took me a day to feel better. But I let my girls wait on me for two weeks. It was good for them."

Aunt Bitsy pulled four needles and a pair of small scissors from her bag. "Hard work never killed nobody yet."

Treva finally managed to thread her needle. "We're doing a stitch in the ditch on this one."

Aunt B nodded. Experienced quilters didn't need any more instruction than that. Lily and her sisters each took a length of thread, threaded their needles, and started on their own squares.

Lily had always loved quilting because the steady, rhythmic motion of the needle through the fabric left her mind free to think about books and beehives. Today, she hated quilting because it left her mind free to think on things she'd rather not, like how long she could keep Paul dangling and how lonely she felt knowing that Dan loved her but had given her up because of Paul. Was Dan's absence just another message from *Gotte* that she should accept Paul's hand?

Paul said he didn't care that she wasn't smart, so how could she be expected to make heads or tails of anything?

Oh *sis yuscht.* Why hadn't she sat in between her sisters? Dan's *mamm,* Esther Kanagy, pulled a folding chair up to the quilt and sat down next to Lily. She had the same good-natured warmth in her expression that Dan always did, and Lily nearly choked on the emotion of seeing Dan in his *mamm*'s smile.

Esther acted as if nothing were amiss, although Lily sensed something deep and troubled behind her eyes. She smiled at Lily like they were best friends, as if her son hadn't wasted the better part of a month on the Honeybee Farm. "Lily, I haven't seen you since Mammi Erda's funeral. Dan says you pulled a wonderful-*gute* amount of honey in the last two weeks."

Lily thought her face might burst into

flames. "We . . . couldn't have done it without Dan," she stuttered.

"He worked as hard as we did," Poppy said, frowning at the knot she'd already created in her thread before even taking a stitch.

"And he made an extra extractor," Rose said, pushing her needle through the fabric with her thimble. "It saved us many hours."

A look of disquiet traveled across Esther's features. "He's clever like that, and so helpful. He woke up at three this morning and weeded my entire garden in the dark."

Lily tried to breathe normally as guilt and confusion pressed on her. Dan was doing yard work in the middle of the night, trying to work himself to death, according to Luke. She thought she might be sick.

Esther threaded a needle and started on the square next to Lily's. "On Saturday night after milking, he wiped out all my kitchen cupboards. He found my springform pan that had been missing for months. It inspired me to try making a cheesecake. Bitsy, have you got a *gute* recipe?"

Aunt B nodded. "Guaranteed to make you gain five pounds."

"Can I come over and get it from you?"

"I'll write it down for you today," Aunt B said. "I've got most of my favorite recipes memorized."

Aunt B was clever like that. Lily read books. Aunt B could memorize them. She raised her eyebrows. "Better yet, bring that springform pan to my house, and we'll make cheesecake together. That is, if you're not afraid of mice. Or bees. We have an abundance of both."

Esther laughed. "I'd love to come. Everything tastes better when Bitsy Kiem makes it. Just ask my Daniel. He never missed an opportunity to eat at your house." She glanced at Lily, and the laughter and happiness seemed to retreat from her face.

They stitched in uncomfortable silence for a few minutes — well, uncomfortable for Lily. She couldn't begin to guess how Esther felt. What had Dan told his *mamm* about them? About her? Was she resentful, indifferent, or relieved?

Lily watched Dan's *mamm* out of the corner of her eye. Esther's nimble fingers seemed to attack the quilt fabric. She worked just like Dan did, with intensity and single-minded purpose. Dan didn't have a lazy bone in his body. When he started a job, he finished it and didn't drag his feet no matter how tired he felt.

Lily adored that about him.

Her heart felt like a blacksmith's anvil.

Might as well admit it. She adored everything about him.

What would Paul say?

Esther leaned in and lowered her voice so that only Lily and Rose could hear. "I know it's a secret, but Dan says you and Paul are going to be married."

Lily pursed her lips together and shook her head. Why did that question make her stomach tilt and roll like a canoe in a windstorm?

Esther frowned, sat back, and became very interested in her thimble. "I'm sorry. It's none of my business. I'm always telling Dan it's none of his business, and now here I am, trying to make it my business."

Lily's voice came out barely above a whisper. "I'm not engaged to anybody. Paul and I are just friends."

What would Paul say if he'd heard her describe him that way?

Esther's lips twitched doubtfully. "I'll tell Dan. Maybe he'll stop with the window washing in the middle of the night."

Ach. Lily wished she were anywhere but here. Esther's presence was a painful reminder that she'd made a complete mess of things.

Mary Yutzy came out onto her back porch and waved in Lily's direction. "Lily!" she

474

called, loudly enough that everybody glanced up from their work to see what all the fuss was about. Mary had never been reserved.

When Lily smiled at her, Mary practically ran across the lawn to the Log Cabin quilt. Lily, along with her sisters, stood and sort of caught Mary in a hug so she wouldn't crash into the quilting frames. Mary embraced Lily then Rose and Poppy like long-lost relatives. "It's been ages, Poppy, just ages since I've seen you, but Lily comes by for doughnuts often. First she was with Paul Glick and then Dan Kanagy." She giggled. "It wonders me what boy she'll bring next."

Lily did her best to guide her sisters and Mary away from the quilts. Mary meant well, but no one needed to hear what she had to say about Lily's doughnut preferences.

"What about you, Mary?" Rose said, still in protect-Lily mode. "I hear tell you've been seen around town with Vernon Beiler."

Mary put her hand over her mouth to stifle a giggle, which was about as effective as Lily trying to hold back the river with her arm. "Vernon loves doughnuts."

"His *dat* has a nice wheelwright shop," Rose said.

Mary never stayed interested in one topic

for very long. She caught her breath as if she'd just remembered something and grabbed Lily's hand. "I want to show you what I found." She nodded to Rose and Poppy. "We'll be right back." Without waiting for Lily's agreement, she pulled her across the lawn, up the porch steps, and into the house.

Lily couldn't help but smile at Mary's enthusiasm. If only her own life could be so blissfully *wunderbarr.*

Mary pulled a jar of honey from the cupboard and handed it to Lily. It had the familiar Honeybee Sisters label on it. "Look at this," she said, as if she'd discovered a hundred-dollar bill in one of Aunt B's books.

"Jah," Lily said. "Honey from last season. I'm taking the new jars to Paul this week."

"*Nae,* silly," Mary said. She turned the jar in Lily's hand so Lily saw the unfamiliar label on the back. "I found this in a little store in Coloma when I visited my cousin last week. I kept telling everybody, 'I know the Honeybee Schwesters. I know them.' You're famous. It made me so excited, I just had to buy it."

Coloma? "It wonders me how our honey made it all the way to Coloma."

Mary raised her eyebrows. "You didn't

give it to them?"

"*Nae.* We sell our honey to Paul, and he sells it at the market."

"It's a mystery," Mary said, quite intrigued with the idea.

"*Jah.* I . . . don't understand."

Mary pointed to the small label on the back of the jar. "Here's their phone number. Why don't you ask them?"

"I'll call at the phone shack as soon as I get home."

Giggling was Mary's sincerest form of communication. "No need. James just got a cell phone, and he hides it in his underwear drawer. I don't mind fishing it out for you."

"Are you sure?" Lily said, hoping the answer was yes. Much as she hated the thought of Mary having to rifle through James's underwear, she might die of curiosity if she couldn't call that store immediately. Where had they come by a jar of Honeybee Sisters honey?

Mary was already halfway down the hall. "He can't take it to work," she called. "But he's on it constantly in the evenings. Dat keeps threatening to throw it in the creek."

Lily heard muffled noises as Mary searched for James's phone and a drawer slamming when she'd found it. Smiling as if she were the cleverest girl in Wisconsin, she came back into the kitchen and handed the phone to Lily. "James thinks it's safe with his underwear. He'll never know how often we steal it."

Lily quickly turned it on, her heart racing with an overpowering curiosity. Her hopes fizzled when she looked at the screen. "It has a password."

"*Ach,* we figured that out in two tries. It's Lily."

Lily tried not to let her eyes pop out of her head. "Me?"

Mary giggled again. "He has a crush on you, and he got his phone the day after you came to our doughnut stand with Paul. I guess you were fresh on his mind."

Lily didn't have time to dwell on how endearing James's password was. She typed it in and dialed the number on the label.

A man with a heavy Southern accent answered the phone. "Annie's Gifts."

Her tongue tripped all over itself. "Hello, I'm Lily Christner. Do you know me?" Was that all she had to say for herself? She mentally slapped her palm against her forehead.

A moment of silence on the other end. He was probably wondering if he should hang up on the strange young lady who obviously didn't have her wits about her. "Hold on," he said. She heard him turn his face from the receiver and yell, "Annie, do we know Lily Christner?"

Someone replied in the background. Another pause before he came back. "No, sweetie. We don't know you."

"I'm sorry. What I meant was, one of my friends bought some of my honey from your store last week."

"Some of your honey?"

"I am the Honeybee Sisters." Why was she so discombobulated all of a sudden? "I mean, I am one of the Honeybee Sisters, and my friend said you have some of our honey in your store."

She pulled the phone away from her ear as the man practically shouted. "The Honeybee Sisters! Well, of course we know who you are. The tourists love your honey. We can't keep it in stock. He brought us all he had not four months ago and we're completely out."

He? "Who brought you our honey?"

The man again turned from the phone. "Annie, what's the name of the Amish fellow who brings us the honey?"

Dread and confusion swirled about Lily like a dust devil as she waited. She knew who the Amish fellow was before the man even said it.

"He promised to bring us more next week," the man said. "His name is Paul Glick."

Paul Glick. Her boyfriend. The one who constantly reminded her what a burden it was to store all that surplus honey. A wave of nausea crashed into her. How long had Paul been lying to her?

"He's a real good salesman," said the man. "Not that your honey needs a salesman. It sells itself."

"How . . . how much is he asking for it?" It felt almost rude to mention money, but for her family, she had to be brave enough to ask the uncomfortable questions.

Again the man had to consult with someone else. "How much do we pay for that honey, Annie?" He paused. "$4.75. It flies off the shelves. We're eager to get that next batch." A woman in the background said something. "Annie says he just raised the price to $5.00 this morning with a promise to bring us double the pints."

$5.00? That was an outrageous profit added onto what he was paying Lily. She felt worse than ill. She could sense the sweat beading on her forehead, and a sick, shaky weakness compelled her to sit down at Mary's kitchen table.

Chewing on her fingernails, Mary sat next

to Lily at the table and eyed her with concern. Lily tried to smile. The best she could manage was a grimace.

She did her best to sound casually cheerful over the phone. The man on the other end need never know that she felt as if she were crumbling into tiny bits of ragged glass. "I'm so glad to know that people like our honey. What do you sell it for?"

"It goes for $8.50 a pint. The tourists love anything that says 'Amish' on it." The woman in the background said something else, and the man responded. "I'm glad you called, Lily Christner," he said. "We told Paul we wanted to meet the amazing Honeybee Sisters, and he said you kind of keep to yourselves, like most of the Amish do. Still, you're invited to come down anytime and see our store."

"Thank you," Lily said. "I appreciate the information."

"You have a good day, sweetie."

"You too." Lily pressed the screen to disconnect, placed James's phone on the table, and propped her head in her hand as an oppressive numbness set in. Was this friendship? Paul had always tried to protect her from the ruthless world of business. Is this what he was doing now? He had said a *gute* Amish *frau* shouldn't concern herself with such things as money and profits. Surely he had wanted to protect her.

Surely.

Surely he had lied to her because he loved her.

Or because he really needed a new freezer.

If Mary hadn't been sitting there, she would have burst into tears.

What had Paul done? And why had she let him do it?

CHAPTER TWENTY-EIGHT

Lily didn't like taking the buggy out alone at night, but Paul had asked her to come to the market at closing time on Tuesday, which was seven o'clock for the restaurant and market. Late by Amish standards, but the Glicks catered to many *Englischers* who kept the later hours.

Lily had spent more than twenty-four painful hours contemplating what Paul had done, and what, if anything, she should do about it. After reassuring Mary that she would be fine, she had pasted on a brave face at the quilting frolic yesterday and not said a word about honey to anyone. This morning she had read under her willow tree for almost two hours, but the time had done nothing to clear her head. She had been more confused and troubled and despondent than ever.

Paul had been right about at least one thing. She was an ignorant girl who couldn't

483

begin to handle the pressure and responsibility of caring for her family's finances or the family honey business. No wonder he felt a duty to protect her.

On the other hand, he had told her that nobody would buy her honey but him. It cut deep that he had lied to her. Even if he had lied to protect her, it didn't feel right. What else had he lied about? Could she trust anything he said anymore, even if his motives were unselfish? He was pocketing most of the profit that rightfully belonged to her family. Try as she might, she couldn't talk herself into believing that he had done it for her own good.

Paul had asked her to meet him at the store tonight so they could make final arrangements for honey delivery tomorrow. He always had a check ready for her as soon as she delivered the honey.

This afternoon she had finally decided that she wouldn't mention anything to Paul about the little store in Coloma that sold her honey for $8.50 a pint. Questions would only irritate him, and he'd accuse her of spying and sticking her nose into business that she was too naïve to understand. She'd rather not have a confrontation tonight — especially a confrontation that she knew she would lose.

She truly didn't understand all of Paul's business dealings, and she knew she'd only come across as ignorant and childish.

If she ever did find the courage to ask him, he'd probably laugh and say, *I thought you knew! I'm saving all that money as a surprise for when we get married.*

She would smile at his thoughtfulness. *Oh, Paul, I never should have doubted.*

The imaginary conversation gave her no comfort tonight. She tugged on the door handle of the market and found it locked. She must have been late. The Glicks locked their doors promptly at seven P.M., no matter what.

She cupped her hands around her eyes and peered into the store. The propane lanterns glowed brightly, and Paul was stocking one of the shelves at the back. He looked up when she tapped on the glass and smiled at her, not appearing the least bit annoyed at her tardiness. He didn't even act put out that he had to walk all the way to the front of the store to let her in.

He unlocked the door, she stepped inside, and he locked it behind her. "I'm almost done stocking. Mamm and Ada are in the restaurant cleaning up. Do you want to see our new display of clocks? I hung all of them myself."

"Of course," Lily said, encouraged and relieved by his good mood.

He took her to the far wall where a variety of clocks hung on the wall, clocks with clear faces so she could see the inner mechanisms, clocks with large gold pendulums and wooden cases, big and small alike. "Look at this one." He reached up and pushed a button on one of the clocks, and it chimed the tune to "Nearer, My God, to Thee."

"Mammi has a clock like that," Lily said.

"Too bad. I would have tried to sell her one." Paul picked up a rag and buffed the glass on one of the clocks, then leaned his elbow on the counter. "I have good news. Dat says I can give you $1.25 a pint for the honey."

Lily didn't change her expression even though her mouth felt as dry as sawdust. Twenty-five cents more, the increase he had passed on to that little store in Coloma. She cleared her throat and told herself that Paul's business dealings were for her own good. She almost made herself believe it. "I thought the price was set. What about your new freezer?"

"I told Dat that I love you more than a new freezer, and I know it would make you happy to get more money for your honey."

Paul loved her more than a new freezer. The declaration didn't make her heart flutter like it should have. All she felt was an oppressive weight that got heavier with every word from Paul's mouth. "*Denki,* Paul. That's very nice."

He seemed disappointed by her reaction. "It's more than nice, Lily. It's because I love you."

She tried her best to smile. Paul needed to see that she was bursting with gratitude. "It's *wunderbarr,* Paul. More than I could have ever dreamed of."

"*Ach,* Lily. You look so tired," he said, as if he felt truly sorry for her. "The honey is such a hardship. Next year we'll be married, and you'll never have to work the hives again."

"It won't matter if we're married. Aunt B and my sisters will still need me."

"You won't be helping," Paul said. "You'll be my wife."

"*Nae,* Paul. I'll always be there for my family."

He furrowed his brow. "You don't have to be difficult about it, Lily. We can cross that bridge when we come to it."

She didn't want to argue the point. She didn't want to argue about anything. A good *frau* was supposed to be submissive, meek, and humble. She wanted to be a good *frau.*

To her surprise, he wrapped an arm around her waist. She let out a surprised gasp. "Say you'll marry me," he whispered. "Right now. It would make my *mamm* so happy if we marched into the restaurant and announced our engagement. Mamm would give you all the leftover rolls."

Lily should have known he'd try to blind-side her. She probably deserved it. She'd kept him waiting for a long time.

If *Gotte* had put them together, why did a mountain of dread loom over her whenever she thought about marriage to Paul? Why did she feel giddy and light-headed whenever Dan was near? She loved his kindness and his enthusiasm, and how her heart bounced wildly around in her chest whenever he came over. She frowned to herself. Dan was exciting and unpredictable and attractive.

Paul was steady and comfortable. She never felt giddy around him.

Who seemed the better choice for a sensible, intelligent young woman?

Paul studied her face and scowled. He took his hand from around her waist and folded his arms across his chest. "You're thinking about Dan Kanagy."

"What makes you say that?"

"Because if it hadn't been for Dan, we'd be engaged by now. He's filled your head with vain notions, and he means none of what he says to you. He's only using your feelings to get revenge on me. He doesn't like you, and he never did. I was the one who wiped away the tears when he made you cry."

Lily didn't know what to believe anymore. "I know, Paul. I'm sorry. It's all so confusing."

Paul stuck out his bottom lip. "It should be plain as day that Dan doesn't love you and I do." He swiped his hand across his mouth. "I didn't want to have to tell you this, but we had a long talk at the auction. He called you ugly and lazy and stupid. I was so mad, my brothers had to hold me back from punching him, even though it would have gone against the *Ordnung.*"

Lily couldn't have been more shocked if Paul had slapped her across the face — not because she believed for a minute that Dan had said those things, but because Paul would be so cruel as to make up such a horrible story.

And he *had* made it up, no doubt. He had lied about the honey. What could hold him back from lying about Dan? In her heart, Lily knew Dan well enough to know that he would never say such things. She fell momentarily speechless. If she accused Paul of lying, he'd be mad. If she questioned his motives, he'd be livid.

She lowered her eyes and took a deep breath. She'd succeeded in putting Paul in a bad mood. Surely he wouldn't say such things if she hadn't irritated him in the first place. "How could Dan have been so mean?" she managed to choke out, because that's what she knew Paul wanted to hear.

"It's how he is. He never had a nice word to say about you behind your back."

She swallowed hard and took two steps backward. "I need to go, Paul. I will think on what you said."

"I want an answer, Lily."

"Tomorrow when I bring the honey," she squeaked, before she turned around and hurried for the door. They hadn't even talked about a check or a delivery time, but it didn't matter. She ached to get out of the Glick Family Amish Market and go home where it was safe and easy with no turmoil or contention. Paul would simmer down by tomorrow morning. Maybe they could even talk about the price of honey and the little store in Coloma.

"I'll be here tomorrow morning at eight," she said.

Just go. Give him a chance to calm down.

She nearly made it to the door. "Don't be late," he said. "I hate it when you're late."

"Okay."

"Before you come back tomorrow, repent of your vanity and remember Dan's wickedness."

Dan's wickedness? Dan was nosy and tenacious and impulsive, but he was not wicked. He helped with the honey. He made mousetraps. He sent her to the moon when he kissed her. He told her he loved her and then showed her in every deed.

Love lifts and builds and never tears someone down. Love is kind and patient.

She caught her breath as Dan's words seemed to pierce her soul. *If what you and Paul have together is real love, then you're right. I don't understand love, and I never will.*

Something snapped inside her, like a tree branch weighed down with wet snow. That same branch smacked her upside the head. *This is not love, Lily, and you've known it for a long time.*

She'd been too terrified by the truth to battle with the lies.

She couldn't let Paul talk about Dan that way. She couldn't let Paul abuse the person she loved the most in the whole world.

491

The person she loved most in the whole world.

The branch smacked her upside the head again. She had been so focused on loyalties and obligations that she had almost missed it. She loved Dan and she didn't love Paul. She didn't even like Paul. And she certainly didn't like herself when she was with him.

A spark of something hard as nails and determined grew inside her. She wouldn't stand up to Paul because Aunt Bitsy or Rose or Poppy or even Dan wanted her to. She had to stand up to Paul for herself, or she would bend until she broke. For her own sake, she would find the courage.

She turned around and looked Paul in the eye, trying to make herself taller by squaring her shoulders and raising her chin. "Paul," she said, her voice shaking. She didn't sound hard as nails. She didn't even sound as hard as pudding. Her heart beat so fast that she thought she might throw up, but she ignored the feeling. All that mattered was that she be strong enough to say what needed to be said. "Why would you tell me that I am ugly and stupid when you know it hurts me?"

Paul seemed surprised by her question. "I didn't say it. Dan did."

Her voice stopped quivering as Aunt

Bitsy's words played through her head. "A true friend would never want to hurt me like that."

"Dan said it, Lily. Go home and think about that."

"*Nae,* Paul. I can see it in your eyes. You're the one who wants to hurt me. You're lying to get what you want." She could see it more clearly with every passing minute. He wanted to break her heart into two pieces so that she had no choice but to give it to him.

Rage flared to life on Paul's face. "You're accusing me of lying?"

For some reason, his anger lent her courage. She wasn't cowering anymore. "I know you're lying. Dan would never say that."

"That's what you think."

"*Nae,* Paul. You lied about all our surplus honey being a burden to your family. How much money have you cheated me out of by taking advantage of my trusting heart? You're making quite a profit from that little gift shop in Coloma."

His face turned pale. "Lily, you don't know what you're talking about. The Coloma thing is business. You should leave the business decisions to me."

"Leaving the business decisions to you was my first mistake. Dan tried to warn me, but I trusted you. I didn't realize that you don't love me near as much as you love yourself."

She might as well have shoved him backward. "This is Dan's poison talking, not my sweet girl."

She nodded, almost sadly. "*Jah*. I have been a sweet girl, never questioning your decisions, absorbing the hurt and humiliation. You not only made me think that my opinions had no value, but that I shouldn't have opinions at all."

The truth of the last eight years came rushing at her. Paul had tried to crush her. And she had given him permission.

Paul frowned with every part of his face. "How can you say that, after all we have been through together? My only thought has been to help you be the *gute* wife I know you can be. And believe me, it hasn't been easy. Your aunt Bitsy is a bad influence."

Lily had heard enough of that talk to last her a lifetime. "I will not hear another bad word about Aendi Bitsy from you, ever. She is a better person than you will ever hope to be."

Paul refused to acknowledge that she'd even said anything. "The sooner you get away from your *aendi,* the better. And your sisters too. I've talked it over with your *dawdi.* When we marry, your sisters will go to live with Sarah and Sol, and Bitsy will be shunned and asked to leave the community. You will have no contact with her."

"Shunned?" Why would he tell her that? His anger must have made him incautious. Either that or he still believed that she would give in. She'd done it for so many years. Fear stabbed at her heart. Could Paul really arrange to have Aunt Bitsy shunned?

"As my wife, you will submit to my wishes. Bitsy will not come near our children."

Lily took a deep breath and gave Paul a fake smile. "What a relief."

"I knew you would come to see the wisdom in it."

"*Nae,* Paul. You misunderstand. It is a relief to know that I will never be your wife."

Paul scowled like Farrah Fawcett at a bowl of dry cat food. "*Nae,* Lily. You need me."

"You've made it perfectly clear over the years that I am not good enough to be your wife. You should start looking for someone better."

Little dots of perspiration appeared on Paul's upper lip. "You're not thinking straight. Dan has done this to you. Go home and consider —"

She'd never felt so strong, so in control of

her own life. "I don't need to consider anything. My answer is no, and it will still be no tomorrow and the next day. I won't marry you." She'd wasted so much time already.

"You don't want to marry me?" Paul said, his voice pitched high enough to crack the faces of every one of his precious clocks.

Nae, and she'd been trying to talk herself into it for years. "I don't want you to worry about the honey. I know it's been a burden to you. I will sell it to Carole in Shawano or call Coloma and see what they will give me for it."

His eyes grew bigger and rounder with each passing minute. "We had an agreement."

"You changed the agreement not ten minutes ago. It seems only fair that I be allowed to do the same. If you want my honey, you'll have to pay four dollars and seventy-five cents a pint for it."

Paul seemed to lose all sense of reason. His nostrils flared and a nasty scowl pulled at his mouth. "Do you understand what I sacrificed for you?"

"We've both sacrificed a great deal."

"I knew Dan liked you. I wanted to get back at him for cheating us out of our land. I befriended you even though I found you repulsive. Repulsive, Lily. But *Gotte* smiled on my sacrifice and made you beautiful. I knew I could mold you into the *gute frau* I wanted. I grew to love you, Lily. We were doing fine until Dan started puffing you up."

His words stung like a thousand yellow jackets. It seemed that even at the beginning, their friendship had been a sham. Paul's interest had been nothing more than petty revenge that turned into an attempt to groom her to be the perfect, controllable wife. Her eyes stung with tears, and she marveled that she had ever considered Dan Kanagy the mean one. Paul was showing her what unkindness really meant.

She studied Paul's face. How could someone live like that, letting anger and petty jealousies constantly eat away at his soul? She pitied him. She had never stood up to him, never contradicted him or questioned his authority before. She'd caught him off guard, and he had no idea what to do with all his hostile feelings.

"Good-bye, Paul," she said. "I wish you all the happiness in the world." Lord willing he would find himself an ugly wife.

Expelling the air from her lungs, she smothered that bitter thought and let it die. She truly hoped that the girl who married Paul would be stronger and braver than she had been.

"You'll be forced out, all of you," he said, spitting like a cat. "You and your aunt and sisters will be shunned until you come crawling home, begging me to take you back."

She had to get out of there. She refused to give him the satisfaction of seeing that his threat had hit its mark. Blinking rapidly to keep the tears at bay, she pushed hard on the door handle. It didn't budge, but her momentum took her face-first into the glass. Oh, *sis yuscht*! She'd forgotten it was locked.

Ouch.

Still scowling fiercely, Paul unlocked the door with a flick of his wrist. Lily ducked out of the market as fast as she could go before she burst into tears.

"Let that be a lesson to you," Paul yelled as she climbed into her buggy.

She heard the door lock once again, and she took a deep, cleansing breath in the solitude and blessed silence of her buggy.

Fear pumped like ice through her veins. Would Paul really try to have Aunt B shunned? Would he drive her out of the community? Had Lily unwittingly hurt her family by rejecting him?

Nae. He would have tried to have Aunt B

shunned whether she married him or not. It would be better not to be his wife if he tried.

How could she have been so blind to give so many years of her life to Paul? What must Dan think of her?

Her lungs ceased to work. She already knew what he thought.

Don't you think you deserve better, Amtrak? Is being obedient to Paul's wishes the same thing as love?

She finally admitted it to herself. She loved Dan to the depths of her soul, and she ached for him to love her back. But how could he ever love someone so pathetically weak?

The thought of losing Dan and the weight of the emotions of the last half hour finally crushed her. She tilted her head back and sobbed like the lost eighth grader she once had been.

CHAPTER TWENTY-NINE

It was nearly full dark outside when Lily pulled onto the lane. Last year, Bitsy had outfitted their buggy with battery-powered headlights and a heater. On late nights and dark times like this, Lily was grateful for the extra light.

She stumbled out of the buggy, opened the orange barn door, and led Queenie into the moist, pungent space. They had one horse, eight chickens, and no cows. The small barn was big enough for the buggy, the honey wagon, two horses, and hay to feed Queenie.

Lily found the flashlight hanging on a peg near the door and turned it on, then backed the buggy into the corner of the barn and unhitched Queenie with all the skill born of regular practice.

She yawned as exhaustion crept up on her. Her eyes stung and every muscle in her body ached, as if she'd spent the day pushing a boulder up a mountain.

Shining the flashlight to illuminate her way, she led Queenie into her stall. The stall door swung shut like a porch swing in a lazy breeze as Lily stroked Queenie's chestnut-brown muzzle and cooed soft words of thanks into Queenie's ear. Poppy had mucked out today, so the straw was fresh and the trough filled with water.

Now that she looked back, it seemed obvious that Aunt Bitsy and her sisters had been hoping for her to break things off with Paul for a very long time. Poppy had barely been civil to him, and Rose cowered behind Aunt B whenever Paul came over. Aunt B hadn't shown a preference for anyone, but she had insisted that Lily didn't owe Paul anything.

Little sister, you don't owe Paul anything. You certainly don't owe him the rest of your life.

They might be happy about the breakup, but would she upset them when she told them that Paul had threatened to have them shunned?

Lily's heart nearly hopped out of her chest when the door at the back of the barn opened and closed, and she saw a faint light shining in the space outside the stall. She almost called out before biting her lip doubtfully and holding her tongue. Was it one of her sisters? Why wouldn't they come in through the front doors? She heard the shuffling of heavy footsteps on the cement floor.

It didn't sound like Aunt Bitsy.

Was it Paul, come to ask for her forgiveness?

Something told her that Paul, for all his faults, wouldn't be so sneaky, and he certainly wouldn't ask for forgiveness. Besides, he didn't even know the barn had a back door.

Lily pressed herself against the far wall of the stall and turned off her flashlight as quietly as possible. She peered through the crack between the stall door and the wall, and what she saw curdled her blood.

By the light of a weak flashlight, she saw someone inch slowly toward her. He was short and stocky and wore a straw hat. Not Dan and definitely not Paul.

In panic, she clamped her eyes shut, hoping like a little child that if she couldn't see him, he wouldn't be able to see her. It wouldn't matter if she was invisible. He could probably hear her heart pounding wildly. Lily pressed her hand against her mouth to keep from crying out. Bile rose in her throat as those muffled footsteps came closer.

She didn't think he realized she was in the barn. Had he come to play another prank? Would he try to hurt Queenie? What if he turned on her? Her mind raced with a thousand horrible possibilities. She had to run away — now — but she couldn't get her legs to obey her. Paralyzed with fear, all she could do was hold her breath and listen to the steady thud of his feet as he came nearer.

The world seemed to stand still for one long, slow blink, and then the stall door creaked open. The man or boy shined the flashlight directly into her face. Letting the terror overcome her, she screamed with all her might as she pressed herself into the wall in hopes she would end up on the other side.

She startled him, and he dropped the flashlight into the straw. So, he hadn't known she was here. Before either of them got over their shock, Lily heard the barn door *swish* as if someone had thrown it open with a great deal of force. The barn flooded with light, and Lily heard the comforting hiss of a propane lantern and the even more comforting sound of Dan Kanagy's voice. "Lily! Are you in here?" He sounded as if he might choke on his panic.

She nearly fainted in relief. "I'm here,"

she called.

Lily couldn't see her, but she heard Aunt Bitsy clear as day. "Young man," she said in the threatening voice she saved for only the naughtiest of children. "I've got a shotgun, and I'm not afraid to use it."

The boy, who looked no older than Lily, left his flashlight and bolted toward the back door.

Lily heard Aunt B cock her shotgun as the boy hightailed it for the exit. "And don't come back unless you want buckshot for breakfast."

As soon as Lily heard the door at the back of the barn slam shut, her knees turned to jelly. She slid down the wall of Queenie's stall and came to rest on a thin pile of straw where she willed her heart to slow to a gallop. Hopefully, Queenie wouldn't get the jitters, because Lily didn't think she could move even if Queenie stepped on her. It was a *gute* thing the stall was so big. Queenie whinnied softly and eyed Lily curiously but didn't seem inclined to move.

Dan appeared at the door of the stall holding the lantern aloft, his eyes wild with fear. "Lily, are you all right?"

Afraid she might fall apart if she spoke, she simply nodded, making a valiant attempt at a smile and failing miserably.

Dan knelt on one knee and set the lamp at his feet. "Did he hurt you?"

She shook her head.

His breathing sounded more unsteady than hers. He reached out and pushed a tendril of hair from her face. A ribbon of warmth threaded its way down her spine. "Are you sure he didn't hurt you?"

Aunt Bitsy appeared at the open door of the stall with her elbow hooked under her shotgun and her face as grave as a funeral. "Are you okay, little sister?"

"I don't think he knew I was in the barn. He didn't hurt me," Lily said. She sounded like a mouse. "But he scared me to death."

"I hope I scared him to death," Aunt B said.

Dan nodded. "You did. I've stared into the wrong end of your shotgun before."

"But you wouldn't have shot him, would you, Aunt B?"

Aunt B waved her hand in Lily's direction. "*Nae*. I don't believe in guns."

Poppy and Rose appeared at the stall door, wide-eyed and pale. "What happened?" Poppy said. "One minute Aunt Bitsy was looking out the window and the next minute she grabbed her gun and ran outside."

Aunt B set the butt of her gun on the floor

and curled her fingers around the shooting end. "I heard the buggy drive up the lane and watched Lily take it into the barn. Then I thought I saw someone sneaking around behind the barn. I got a feeling it was our hoodlum. I was afraid he'd hurt my Lily, so I came running."

Rose gasped. "What happened?"

Saturated in concern, Dan didn't take his eyes from Lily's face. "He ran away when Bitsy came in with her gun."

Rose knelt beside Lily, her face pale, her hands trembling. "Did he hurt you?"

"*Nae,* but he gave me quite a fright."

Poppy let her gaze travel around the stall as if she were looking for clues to the intruder's identity. "What was he doing in our barn?"

Rose clapped her hand over her mouth. "Do you think he wanted to hurt Queenie?"

"I don't know," Lily said. "He wasn't expecting to see me."

"Did you see his face?" Poppy said. "Was it somebody we know?"

"I was too scared to think about trying to get a good look."

"Can you stand up?" Dan said. "We should probably get you into the house so Queenie doesn't trample you." He took hold of her hand and put his arm around her back.

Apparently, he was prepared to carry her all the way without a moment's hesitation. She thought she might melt like warm chocolate.

"I can walk," she said, with more confidence than she felt. Every muscle in her body quivered.

Dan stood and offered a hand. She took it, and he pulled her up, but she immediately grabbed on to his arm to keep her balance. He didn't seem to mind. In fact, he slid his arm around her waist and gripped her elbow with his other hand. "I won't let you fall," he said, giving her a look that did nothing to help the weak knees.

Bitsy handed her shotgun to Poppy and took Lily's other elbow. They ambled out of the barn with Lily, Dan, and Bitsy leading the way, and Poppy keeping a tight hold on both Rose and the gun. Rose looked almost as shaken up as Lily felt.

Dan opened the front door and helped Lily into one of the kitchen chairs. Then he went to the fridge and poured a glass of milk. "Here," he said, setting the milk on the table and sitting next to her. "This might help calm your nerves."

"Denki," Lily said. Could he be any more

wunderbarr? Could she be any less deserving? "But I think I am going to be okay. No harm done, for sure and certain."

"Then do you care if I . . ." He motioned to the glass.

She shook her head.

She watched as he finished off the milk in five swallows, took the empty glass to the fridge, and poured himself another glassful. "There isn't enough milk in Wisconsin to make *me* feel better," he said.

Aunt Bitsy pushed the fridge door shut and stood in front of it as if she were guarding the bank. "Don't drink it all, Dan Kanagy, or we'll have nothing for oatmeal in the morning." She shook her head. "Why did we ever feed you in the first place?"

Dan returned to Lily's side with his glass of milk. Only when he took another swig did she notice that his hands were shaking.

Rose sidled close to Aunt B. Aunt B clicked her tongue and squeezed Rose's hand. Poppy also went to Aunt B, put an arm around her, and raised an eyebrow at Dan. "I don't mean to sound rude, but what are you doing here?"

Dan lowered his eyes as his lips twitched downward. "I was in town when I saw Lily come out of Glick's Market. She seemed upset, and I wasn't comfortable with the thought of her driving all the way home in the dark. I jumped in my buggy and followed her." His lips twitched sheepishly. "Keeping my distance so I wouldn't frighten her."

Lily thought she might burst with gratitude. Dan didn't even know the meaning of *inconvenient,* while it seemed to be one of Paul's favorite words.

He cleared his throat. "I probably should have turned around once I saw you to the bridge, but I came all the way, just to be sure. I got to the end of the lane just as Bitsy stormed out of the house with her shotgun."

Bitsy propped her elbow on the island and rested her chin in her hand. "Even though you can be a pest, Dan Kanagy, I'm glad you came when you did. You scared that boy away."

"You don't need me when you have a shotgun," Dan insisted. "I was mostly useless."

"I would never call you useless, Dan Kanagy," Aunt Bitsy mumbled. Aunt Bitsy couldn't bring herself to give a compliment in full voice.

Still, Lily felt that compliment down to her bones. Dan was anything but useless, to her family and to her. He was fast becoming one of the most important people in her life. Could she muster the courage to tell him that? And would he reject her for all her past mistakes, the biggest one being Paul Glick? He certainly had every right to question her judgment.

"I'm glad I came," Dan said, "even if it's only so you know that I want to help any way I can. It wonders me if we should call the police."

The police? It wasn't the Amish way to involve the police in anything. Dan must really be worried.

"I don't want my girls in danger," Aunt B said. "I will think on that."

"My *dat* knows the county sheriff," Dan said. "Just say the word, and I will talk to him. In the meantime, I hate to be a pest, but I want to spend more time here." He gazed at Lily with those deep brown eyes that always made her a little breathless. "I know I promised to quit bothering you, but would you allow me to come tomorrow morning and help you load up the honey to take to Glick's Market? I know there's a lot of it, and I hate to think of you sisters loading all that honey by yourselves."

Lily's heart swelled as wide and as deep as Lake Michigan. How could she ever hope to deserve so much kindness? In a moment of pure joy and sheer insanity, she threw her arms around Dan's neck right where he sat, and laid a kiss smack on those uncertain lips.

She caught him completely off guard. He stiffened momentarily before standing up and pulling her with him, their lips still firmly attached. He wrapped his arms tentatively around her waist and tugged her closer. She felt dizzy as stars and fireworks and parades danced around in her head. Aunt B and her sisters stood not eight feet away, but all she wanted to do was savor the feel of Dan's arms around her and the sensation of his lips on hers. He felt so warm and alive, his heartbeat so strong and vital, as if he carried spring with him wherever he went.

They parted, both dazed and completely out of breath. The look of surprise on Dan's face was priceless. She probably could have knocked him over with a stiff puff of air.

Someone standing near the fridge cleared her throat. Lily and Dan slowly turned their heads in Aunt B's direction. Flanked by Rose and Poppy, she stood with her arms folded firmly across her chest and her mouth pressed into a line of indignation.

Dan took two steps backward, glancing at the shotgun in its usual place against the wall. His gaze traveled to Lily's face. "Fright has made you delirious," he said.

Giggling, Lily responded by putting her arms around his waist. He raised his hands as if Aunt B were pointing the shotgun at him. Rose and Poppy looked like their eyes might pop out of their heads. Aunt B narrowed her gaze, but Lily thought she might have caught a glint of amusement in her eyes.

"I have good news," Lily said, smiling so wide she thought her lips might break. "You might be surprised to hear that Paul is not paying us enough for our honey. I've decided to sell it to Carole Parker. And it's all thanks to Dan."

Rose beamed, Poppy gave a loud cheer, and Aunt B didn't change her expression. The honey price was secondary to the fact that her niece had her arms around a boy in plain sight in her own kitchen.

Dan risked Aunt B's wrath by sliding his arms around Lily and pulling her way too close. He gazed down at Lily, his expression overflowing with tenderness. "Are you sure it's what you want?"

She got on her tippy toes and wrapped her arms good and tight around his neck. "I finally figured out that Paul and I are a terrible match. It's over between us."

Dan caught his breath and his face lit up

like a brilliant sunrise. He immediately pulled her closer and kissed her thoroughly. Every cell in her body came to life as his lips touched hers.

In her distant consciousness, she heard loud and soft whispers and even louder footsteps. Aunt B made a muffled protest as it sounded as if her sisters were dragging her up the stairs.

Lily giggled with her lips still firmly pressed to Dan's. Aunt B was not one to go quietly.

Dan pulled away from her and smiled. "I think I'm growing on her."

"Like mold."

He chuckled. "If it weren't for mold, we'd never be able to make cheese." As if he couldn't bear to keep away, he kissed her again, with more tenderness than Lily could have imagined possible. She felt the strength of his heartbeat against hers.

So much love. So much happiness.

His lips were inches from hers when he whispered, "Marry me, Amtrak?"

Her heart thumped a wild rhythm. She finally understood the deep affection behind that word. *"Jah,"* she whispered back.

His eyes got moist, and his smile got sort of fuzzy. "I knew I'd have more of a chance if I asked while you were still delirious."

"I don't think I'll stop being delirious for the rest of my life."

Dan glanced over at the window seat, where Farrah Fawcett lounged like a princess. "Farrah Fawcett, is it all right with you if I marry Lily?"

Farrah Fawcett lifted her head and condescended to give them a curt meow before averting her eyes and pretending she didn't know them.

"I'll take that as a yes," he said. Once more he kissed her. It was glorious and achingly insufficient at the same time. From the warm thrumming of her pulse to the effervescent energy that traveled through her body, she might have been a bird about to take flight.

She suddenly understood why her aunt frowned on kissing. They'd have to stop soon or Aunt B would be waving that shotgun around with great energy yet.

There was so much more to tell Dan and her family. So much to apologize for. So much to rejoice in.

Aunt B would have to know about Paul's threat of shunning. It was the only thing that marred the perfection of Lily's happiness.

But all that could wait. Tonight, with Dan's arms around her and his love securely tucked inside her heart, it was enough.

With or without Farrah Fawcett's approval.

CHAPTER THIRTY

Lily, her sisters, and Aunt Bitsy surrounded the island and formed the popcorn into small balls with their butter-coated hands. They only made Rose's honey and vanilla popcorn balls on very special occasions, and today was most certainly an extra special occasion. This morning Dan had showed up with Carole, and Carole had brought her pickup truck to take every last pint of honey they had except for the fifteen gallons they kept for themselves for baking.

Carole had written out a big check, with a promise to buy more honey as soon as they extracted later in the fall.

That alone was cause for celebration, not to mention the little matter of Lily getting engaged to Dan last night. Poppy wanted to throw a party. They settled for popcorn balls and maybe Scrabble, if Dan didn't run away in horror at the very suggestion.

Plus a new mousetrap. Dan had promised

to bring a foolproof mousetrap when he came tonight.

Poppy finished forming a popcorn ball and placed it on the wax paper, grinning smugly at Lily. "Tell me again how red Paul's face got when you said you weren't going to marry him."

"Now, Priscilla," Aunt B scolded. "It isn't nice to dwell on another person's misfortunes."

"I feel sorry for him," Rose said. "To lose Lily must have been very painful." She shook her head. "But I'm not sorry enough to wish him back."

Lily smiled. Being free of the fear of Paul's disapproval made her giddy. She felt as if she'd finally crawled out of the hole she'd been living in for eight years. She wanted to lift her hands to the sky and shout.

They heard a firm knock, and Lily rushed to the door. Dan stood on her porch holding an apple box and looking so handsome Lily didn't know what to do with herself.

His smile was fast becoming her favorite sight in the world. "Hey, Amtrak," he said, sending a shiver of pleasure down her spine. "Is Bitsy here?"

"*Jah.* Inside."

"Too bad," he said in mock disappointment. "I was going to kiss you."

517

"I heard that," Aunt B said. "Don't even think about it."

Dan grinned and stepped over the threshold. "I wouldn't dream of kissing Lily in front of you, Bitsy. It's more fun behind your back."

Bitsy gave Dan the evil eye. "You can't pull one over on me. I see everything."

"I like your new tattoo," Dan said, setting his box on the table.

Today Aunt B sported a tiny green-and-yellow snake on her right forearm. It looked quite intimidating.

"Denki," Aunt Bitsy said. "Snakes eat mice, you know. I'm hoping for some good karma."

Lily had no idea what good karma was. Maybe she was another one of Aunt B's movie stars.

Rose gave Dan a sisterly peck on the cheek. "What did you bring us?"

Dan tapped on his box. "This is the last mousetrap you'll ever need," he said, winking at Lily.

Aunt Bitsy waved her hand dismissively. "Well, Dan Kanagy, I don't have much faith in you, but let's have a look."

He took the lid off the box, reached inside, and scooped out a . . . cat — the ugliest cat Lily had ever seen — a black-and-white cat with unruly fur and lopsided whiskers and one ear split right down the middle. Its right eye only opened halfway, and part of its tail was missing, as if it had seen a lot of street fights in its day. The half-open eye was yellow and the other eye was light green. A deep scar ran down one side of its mouth lifting its lip from its teeth permanently.

The cat scowled at the humans and hissed at Farrah Fawcett. Farrah Fawcett gave Dan a huffy sneer, jumped from her window seat, and ran, actually ran, from the room and up the stairs. Lily didn't know how this new cat would be with mice, but Farrah Fawcett seemed a little concerned.

Aunt B scowled in disgust. "Really, Dan Kanagy, really? Haven't we got enough stray cats around here?"

"Now, Bitsy," Dan said. "Roger Gordon, my farmer friend down the road, has had this cat since he was a kitten. Roger says he's a born hunter. He hasn't seen a mouse in his barn for years."

Bitsy lifted a suspicious eyebrow. "Then why is he willing to part with such a cat?"

"He has two other cats, and his grandchildren are terrified of this one. So I offered to take him. He'll have your place cleared of mice in a matter of weeks."

The cat sat in Dan's arms and glared at

his new family. He'd probably be able to rid them of squirrels, rabbits, and small raccoons as well.

Rose puckered her lips and spoke directly to the cat. "Oh, you're adorable, you poor little thing." She took him from Dan's arms and cuddled him like a baby. "Don't you worry. We'll take good care of you."

Aunt Bitsy wiped the butter from her hands. "Now, Rose, don't get attached. We're not keeping him."

"Of course we're keeping him," said Rose. "This poor kitty needs a place where he'll be loved."

"He won't be loved here," Aunt Bitsy insisted.

"Aunt Bitsy," Rose said, her eyes wide with childlike faith, "we can't give him back now. The grandkids don't like him. He needs a place where he'll feel acceptance." She scratched the sparse fur on the top of the cat's head. "Welcome to the family, kitty. We love you."

Aunt B's glare could have peeled the orange paint off the barn door. "Dan Kanagy, you have brought me nothing but a big, fat headache. I've a mind to get out my shotgun."

Dan smiled and backed away from Aunt B's wrath. "Now, Bitsy, remember that I am engaged to Lily, and she would be very sad if you murdered me."

Aunt B narrowed her eyes. "On a scale of one to ten, Lily, how sad would you be? It might be worth it."

Lily laughed. "Oh, Aunt B. Don't you think we could keep him for a few days to see if he'll catch our mouse?"

Aunt B sighed dramatically. "All right, he can stay. But he's going straight back to the Gordons if he proves as useless as Farrah Fawcett."

"He's never going back," insisted Rose.

Aunt B threw up her hands in surrender and looked heavenward to talk to *Gotte*. "You've brought the Apocalypse upon us."

Rose giggled, then snuggled the new cat against her chin. "What should we name him?"

"How about Dandelion?" Dan said. "You've got a lot of them around here."

Aunt Bitsy's upper lip twitched. "You should know, for as many as you've trampled."

"What about Charcoal?" Poppy said.

Aunt B propped her hands on her hips. "I'm the one who has to put up with this animal. I should be the one to name it."

Dan nodded. "Fair enough. What would you like to call him?"

Aunt B took the cat from Rose and met him face-to-face. "There's only one name for this cat. We're calling him Billy Idol."

Rose's Honey Lavender Ice Cream

Note from Rose: This is a yummy, different ice cream that Aunt Bitsy loves but Farrah Fawcett turns up her nose at, even when it's melted. If you like a stronger lavender taste, you can use up to 1/4 cup of dried lavender. I like just a hint.

Ingredients:

2 cups milk (2% or whole is fine)
1 cup heavy whipping cream
1/2 cup honey
1/2 Tbsp. dried lavender
4 egg yolks
1 Tbsp. vanilla

Bring the milk, cream, honey, and lavender to a gentle boil in a saucepan over medium-high heat. I add the lavender when I remove the milk mixture from the heat instead of boiling it with the other ingredients, but either way is fine.

Remove from the heat and let steep for ten to fifteen minutes. Strain out the lavender petals and let cool a bit.

In a separate bowl, beat the egg yolks, then gradually add some of the warm milk mixture, whisking as you pour. This helps warm the eggs slowly so they don't cook when you add them to the hot liquid.

Pour the warmed eggs back into the saucepan with the rest of the milk mixture. This mixture is now called custard because of the eggs. Cook over low heat, stirring constantly until the custard is thick enough to coat the back of a spoon (five to ten minutes).

Strain again into a bowl to make sure you got all the lavender pieces. Set the bowl of custard over a large bowl of ice water. Stir the custard until cool, then cover and refrigerate until thoroughly chilled (three hours or overnight).

Freeze in an ice-cream maker according to the manufacturer's instructions, and invite

Dan Kanagy over to do the crank turning. This ice cream is creamy and smooth and pleasantly soft. It doesn't freeze very hard because it uses honey instead of sugar.

The vanilla adds a lovely color, and the ice cream is a very pretty beige. The lavender doesn't add any color. I really like watching the little lavender pieces floating on top of the milk mixture, and the smell, while it cooks, is delightful.

AUNT BITSY'S
HONEY CURRY CHICKEN

Note from Bitsy: This recipe makes two chicken breasts. If you want more, you'll have to double it, and since you can read this recipe, I assume you know how to double everything for yourself. Don't over-cook or you'll end up with a pool of blackened honey at the bottom of your pan.

Ingredients:

1/4 cup melted butter (margarine might work too, but I hate margarine, so you're on your own)
1/4 cup prepared yellow mustard
1/2 teaspoon curry powder
1/2 cup honey
1/2 teaspoon salt

Mix all ingredients together and pour over two raw chicken breasts. Bake for one hour (or until chicken is cooked through) at 350 degrees. Serve over rice.

LILY'S BIENENSTICH CAKE (BEE STING CAKE)

Note from Lily: Aunt B thinks this cake is too much trouble to make, but it's so delicious and so perfect for special occasions that I think it's worth the effort. The cake is very dense and moist, but it's the cream filling and the almond topping that make this cake so *wunderbarr.* I think it's called Bee Sting Cake because it is so sweet that the bees want to eat it.

Cake

1 1/4 tsp. active dry yeast

3/4 cup whole milk, warmed just over room temperature with 1 Tbsp. honey added

4 Tbsp. unsalted butter, at room temperature

1/4 cup sugar

1 cup bread flour

1 cup all-purpose flour

3/4 tsp. table salt

2 large eggs, at room temperature

Honey-Almond Topping

9 Tbsp. unsalted butter
1/3 cup plus 3 Tbsp. granulated sugar
4 1/2 Tbsp. honey
3 Tbsp. heavy cream
1 1/2 cups (4 3/4 ounces) sliced almonds
3 pinches of sea salt

Pastry Cream Filling

1 cup whole milk
3 large egg yolks
1/4 cup granulated sugar
3 Tbsp. all-purpose flour
2 pinches sea salt
2 Tbsp. unsalted butter, softened
1 tsp. pure vanilla extract or 1/4 tsp. almond
   extract (I use almond)

To Make the Cake:

Combine the yeast and milk with honey and let sit for five minutes.

Cream the butter and sugar in a medium mixing bowl.

Add the yeast mixture to the butter mixture, and mix until combined.

Add bread flour, all-purpose flour, and salt. This is thick like dough, so if you are not Amish and you use electricity, you can mix this together in a stand mixer at low-medium speed for two to three minutes. If you are Amish, you've just got to use your muscles. (We often ask Poppy to do this part.)

Add eggs and mix.

Scrape down the sides of the bowl, cover with plastic wrap, and let rise in a warm place for sixty minutes until the dough is a little puffy. (It won't fully double.)

Butter a nine-inch round springform pan. Stir the batter a few times to deflate it slightly, then scrape it into the prepared pan and spread it until it fills the bottom.

Cover with plastic wrap (don't let the plastic sag and touch the dough) and let it rise for another thirty minutes.

Preheat oven to 350 degrees.

To Make the Honey-Almond Topping:
In a medium saucepan, stir butter, sugar, honey, cream, and salt over medium heat until butter is melted. Stirring frequently, bring to a simmer and let boil for three to five minutes, until the mixture goes from a yellowish color to a light beige.

Remove from heat and stir in the almonds.

Once the cake has finished its second rise — remember that it won't rise significantly — press the dough lightly to deflate it. Spoon the almond topping evenly over the top of the cake.

Bake cake for twenty to twenty-five minutes until the top is a lovely golden brown color and a toothpick inserted in the center comes out clean. Be sure to put a foil-lined cookie sheet under your springform pan in case the almond topping drips. This is very hard to get out of your oven when it's baked on. It puts Aunt B in a bad mood.

Transfer to a cooling rack and let it sit in the pan for ten minutes. After ten minutes, run a knife between the cake and the pan and remove the outer ring. Let cool completely.

To Make Pastry Cream:
Warm milk in a medium saucepan (not too warm or it will scald). Set aside.

Rinse saucepan with cool water and dry it. In the cool saucepan, whisk the egg yolks and sugar for one minute. Whisk in flour and salt until smooth. Drizzle in warm milk a spoonful at a time while whisking continuously. Once you add half of the milk, you can add the rest in a steady stream, whisking continuously. Return the saucepan to the stove and cook on medium-high heat until the mixture bubbles. Keep whisking (this is a *gute* job for Dan or some other boy who hangs around the house all the time), and simmer for one to two minutes.

Remove from heat and whisk in the butter and either the vanilla or almond extract. Cool the pastry cream completely — either in the fridge or over a bowl of ice water.

To Assemble the Cake:
Once both the cake and pastry cream are cooled, place the cake on a serving platter and cut it horizontally into two layers with a serrated knife. Spread pastry cream over bottom half of the cake. Place the top half of the cake on top of the pastry cream.

You can make the dough and pastry cream a day ahead and refrigerate it. It's quite a bit to do in one day.

HONEYBEE GRANOLA
Note from Poppy: We make this wonderful-*gute* granola at least once a month. Eat it

for breakfast with milk, or as a snack any-time. Aunt Bitsy likes it with raisins. I don't.

3 cups rolled oats
2 cups sweetened coconut
1/2 cup raw sunflower seeds
1/2 cup wheat germ
1 cup bran flakes
1 cup chopped nuts (walnuts, almonds, or pecans — I prefer pecans)
2 cups raisins (optional — I don't put raisins in, but Aunt Bitsy loves them)

Mix all the above together. To the dry mixture add:

1 cup honey
1/2 cup safflower oil (I use regular vegetable oil when I don't have safflower oil. The safflower oil is healthier. The vegetable oil is cheaper.)
2 tsp. vanilla

Preheat oven to 350 degrees.

Stir until well coated. Spread on large cookie sheet. Bake at 350 degrees for twenty minutes, turning occasionally with a spatula. Do not overcook.

Remove granola from the pan immediately

after taking it out of the oven. Store in plastic or glass container with a lid to keep it fresh. Does not need to be refrigerated. I usually double this. It is less likely to overcook, and it disappears as fast as I make it.

HONEY COOKIES

Note from Aunt Bitsy: I hear these cookies are good for when you have morning sickness. This may be an old wives' tale, but since I am not an old wife, I wouldn't know. The boys who come to bother us love these cookies. Warning: don't pass them out if you don't want the boys to come back. They're like stray cats.

Ingredients:

1 cup granulated sugar
1 cup shortening
1 cup honey
2 eggs
1 tsp. vanilla extract
1 tsp. baking soda
1 tsp. ground ginger
4 cups all-purpose flour

Preheat oven to 350 degrees.

In a saucepan over low heat, stir together

sugar, shortening, and honey until melted. Let cool.

Mix together eggs, vanilla, baking soda, and ginger. Gradually add to cooled honey mixture.

Slowly add four cups of flour to mixture. Stir until well blended. Drop by spoonfuls onto cookie sheet about 2 inches apart. Bake at 350 degrees until golden (about ten to eleven minutes). Do not overbake. They're better soft.

ABOUT THE AUTHOR

Jennifer Beckstrand is the bestselling author of *The Matchmakers of Huckleberry Hill* series and the *Forever After in Apple Lake* series, set in two Amish communities in beautiful Wisconsin. She has always been drawn to the strong faith and the enduring family ties of the Plain people and loves writing about the antics of Anna and Felty Helmuth. Jennifer has a degree in mathematics and a background in editing. She and her husband have been married for thirty years, and she has four daughters, two sons, and two adorable grandsons, whom she spoils rotten. Readers can visit her website at jenniferbeckstrand.com.